City of God

A Novel of

Passion and Wonder

in Old New York

BEVERLY SWERLING

SIMON & SCHUSTER PAPERBACKS

New York London Toronto Sydney

Simon & Schuster Paperbacks
A Division of Simon & Schuster, Inc.
1230 Avenue of the Americas
New York, NY 10020

First Simon & Schuster trade paperback edition September 2009

SIMON & SCHUSTER PAPERBACKS and colophon are registered trademarks
of Simon & Schuster, Inc.

For information about special discounts for bulk purchases, please contact Simon &
Schuster Special Sales at 1-866-506-1949 or business@simonandschuster.com.

The Simon & Schuster Speakers Bureau can bring authors to your live event. For
more information or to book an event contact the Simon & Schuster Speakers Bureau
at 1-866-248-3049 or visit our website at www.simonspeakers.com.

Designed by Jaime Putorti

Manufactured in the United States of America

10   9   8   7   6   5   4   3   2   1

The Library of Congress has cataloged the hardcover edition as follows:

Swerling, Beverly.
City of god : a novel of passion and wonder in Old New York / Beverly Swerling.
p. cm.
1. New York (N.Y.)—History—1775–1865—Fiction.   2. Manhattan
(New York, N.Y.)—Fiction.   I. Title.
PS3619.W47C63 2008
813'.6—dc22

ISBN 978-1-4165-4921-5
ISBN 978-1-4165-4922-2 (pbk)
ISBN 978-1-4165-9444-4 (ebook)

For Bill as always,
and for Michael, our forever darling boy. RIP.

PIED BEAUTY

Glory be to God for dappled things—
> *For skies of couple-colour as a brinded cow;*
> *For rose-moles all in stipple upon trout that swim;*
Fresh-firecoal chestnut-falls; finches' wings;
> *Landscape plotted and pieced—fold, fallow, and plough;*
> *And àll tràdes, their gear and tackle and trim.*

All things counter, original, spare, strange;
> *Whatever is fickle, freckled (who knows how?)*
> *With swift, slow; sweet, sour; adazzle, dim;*
He fathers-forth whose beauty is past change;
> *Praise him.*

—GERARD MANLEY HOPKINS (1844–1889)

Author's Note

THE DEVELOPMENT OF the theory and technology that in the 1840s led to the building of those breathtaking birds of paradise, the mighty clipper ships, is told as accurately as my research allowed, but in the matter of the timing of particular voyages and the exact dates when certain records were set, I have bent the truth to serve my need. The *Houqua* was launched in May of 1844, not 1843 as happens in this book. As for the *Hell Witch* of my tale, I made her up, and appropriated for her the accomplishments of a legendary ship called *Sea Witch*, who set out for Hong Kong in December of 1846. And while it's true that New York University was founded in 1831, the School of Medicine opened a decade later, not around the same time as I have it here.

How It Happened–

A Short History with No Quiz,

and No Penalty for Skipping Straight to the Story

SOMETIMES IT IS difficult to tease out history's threads; not so for this book. The spiritual currents that play a dominant role in this story were let loose in Europe in the early 1700s, in a phenomenon known as the Great Awakening. Reacting to the secularizing forces of the Enlightenment, which railed against organized churches and insisted that reason tells us all we need to know of life, there were those who protested that true religion did exist. Marked, they said, by reliance on the heart over the head, feeling over thinking, and the belief that biblical revelation is meant to be taken literally.

The Evangelical movement had been born, and its fervor swept it across the ocean. In 1730 the Scots-Irish Presbyterian minister William Tennent and his four clergyman sons began preaching in the colonies of Pennsylvania and New Jersey and established a seminary to train others who could bring sinners to Evangelical conversion. (Originally called Log College, that seminary is today Princeton University.) Before long the intensity of their conviction spread to the Congregationalists and Baptists of New England.

The fire of Evangelicalism burned brightly in the New World; then politics and war—first with the French and their Indian allies, next with the British—stole the oxygen from struggles of the spirit. The movement remained quiescent until the flint of the ideas that had fueled an unprecedented break with a king—the notions of individual freedom and every man's right to pursue happiness—met the spark of religion without hierarchical authority or complex theology and burst into new flames. What historians have since labeled the Second Great Awakening was nothing short of the rebirth of the Evangelical movement in the infant U.S.A.

In the years immediately after Independence, itinerant Methodist and Baptist preachers roamed the hardscrabble, largely churchless frontiers of Kentucky and Tennessee and sought out venues where they could address a crowd. Those gatherings became known as camp meetings. Dedicated to religious revival, frequently days long, they were occasions when prayer and witness were full of song and spirit and individual conversion in front of huge assemblies created a kind of public ecstasy. Adherents to this emotional and intensely personal form of religion shared an unshakable belief that they held the key to the perfection of society. Drink and crime, carnal excess, poverty and suffering, indeed all injustice and inequality could be eliminated by personal renunciation of sin, acceptance of Jesus Christ as Lord and Savior, and strict adherence to biblical teaching.

Such ardent American belief could not ignore the young nation's Sodom and Gomorrah. In the 1820s and 1830s revival meetings came to Broadway.

The response of entrenched mainstream Protestantism was to co-opt the new beliefs, and some Evangelical ideas soon found their way into sermons preached from Establishment pulpits.

At the same time New York's Catholics, long marginalized in a city where they had been a tiny minority, were seeing their nascent institutions—a few churches largely serving foreign diplomats and one rather grand edifice, St. Patrick's Cathedral, on the corner of Prince and Mott streets—overwhelmed by thousands of nominally Catholic, mostly Irish immigrants. Dirt poor, usually illiterate, and frequently in thrall to the twin evils of alcohol and violence—perceived as the only relief from daily struggle—they were crammed into an already notorious district known as the Five Points and turned it into a hellhole of indescribable misery.

The bishops summoned reinforcements. In the 1820s Catholic Sisters, religious women newly freed from the stricture of cloister, appeared for the first time on Manhattan streets. Black crows they were called. Jezebels. Satan's whores. They did not preach or hand out bibles, they did not cry out for temperance and abolition and women's rights and universal free education, the just causes espoused by the Evangelicals. They turned their back on a woman's highest calling, wife and mother, and instead made vows of poverty and chastity, swearing as well obedience to a foreign ruler, a pope many thought to be the Antichrist. Direct action—feed the hungry, clothe the naked—confronted the notion that true charity is to preach morality and Gospel salvation and allow American free market opportunity to meet economic needs. Only when epidemics of cholera and yellow fever turned the city into a charnel house and the Sisters went on exactly as before, did their fearless heroism win them a certain grudging respect and allow a truce of sorts to be established. It did not, however, put an end to the ongoing demonizing of popery and all its works.

As if this mix were not sufficiently combustible, another once minuscule group saw its numbers swelled by waves of immigrants come to satisfy the nation's insatiable hunger for workers. During the years 1835 to 1855 approximately one hundred and fifty thousand European Jews made their way across the Atlantic. Many settled in Baltimore, Cincinnati, and even San Francisco, but the large majority stayed in New York. Since 1654 when New York was New Amsterdam there had been one Jewish synagogue on the island of Manhattan, Shearith Israel, first located on Mill Street (now Stone Street), and in the time period of this book moved to Crosby Street. Shearith Israel followed the liturgical practice of the Sephardim, Jews who had lived in Spain and its colonies for the more than fifteen hundred years since their exile from the Holy Land. The new American congregants, mostly German Jews known as

Ashkenazim, wanted their prayer book and their liturgy to prevail. When Shearith Israel refused their demands, the Ashkenazim founded the new synagogue of B'nai Jeshurun, followed by Anshe Chesed, then dozens more. Meanwhile some among them were also hearing the siren song of change and renewal. The movement for Reform Judaism begun in Europe at the end of the 1700s came to New York in 1845 with the founding of Temple Emanu-El in the loft of a nondescript building on the corner of Grand and Clinton streets in what we now call the Lower East Side, soon followed by a move to a former Methodist church on Chrystie Street. (Thus began a progression up the island that culminated in 1927 with the building of Temple Emanu-El on Fifth Avenue and Sixty-fifth Street, today the largest Jewish house of worship in the world.)

On the island of Manhattan the bitter division that almost inevitably follows the inauguration of new ways was, like so much else, intensified by the city's dynamism, her lust for life, and the proximity of extremes. Introduce family feuds, heroes and villains, love and hate, and the still unchecked malignancy of human slavery, and the scene is set for this tale of miracles of medicine—painless surgery and antisepsis—and others that science cannot explain, though they are written in real flesh and real blood. Here, then, is a story of the city and its people in the run-up to what will be a devastating civil war, during a time when they meet a demanding and a jealous God.

City of God

THE TURNERS

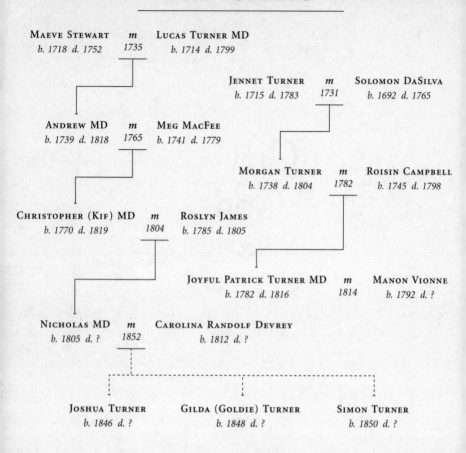

MAEVE STEWART *m* LUCAS TURNER MD
b. 1718 d. 1752 *1735* *b. 1714 d. 1799*

JENNET TURNER *m* SOLOMON DASILVA
b. 1715 d. 1783 *1731* *b. 1692 d. 1765*

ANDREW MD *m* MEG MACFEE
b. 1739 d. 1818 *1765* *b. 1741 d. 1779*

MORGAN TURNER *m* ROISIN CAMPBELL
b. 1738 d. 1804 *1782* *b. 1745 d. 1798*

CHRISTOPHER (KIF) MD *m* ROSLYN JAMES
b. 1770 d. 1819 *1804* *b. 1785 d. 1805*

JOYFUL PATRICK TURNER MD *m* MANON VIONNE
b. 1782 d. 1816 *1814* *b. 1792 d. ?*

NICHOLAS MD *m* CAROLINA RANDOLF DEVREY
b. 1805 d. ? *1852* *b. 1812 d. ?*

JOSHUA TURNER GILDA (GOLDIE) TURNER SIMON TURNER
b. 1846 d. ? *b. 1848 d. ?* *b. 1850 d. ?*

THE KLEINS

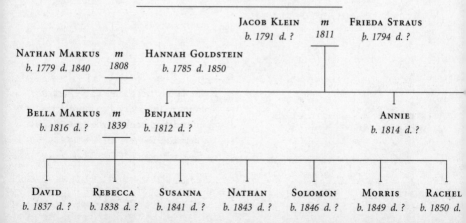

JACOB KLEIN *m* FRIEDA STRAUS
b. 1791 d. ? *1811* *b. 1794 d. ?*

NATHAN MARKUS *m* HANNAH GOLDSTEIN
b. 1779 d. 1840 *1808* *b. 1785 d. 1850*

BELLA MARKUS *m* BENJAMIN ANNIE
b. 1816 d. ? *1839* *b. 1812 d. ?* *b. 1814 d. ?*

DAVID REBECCA SUSANNA NATHAN SOLOMON MORRIS RACHEL
b. 1837 d. ? *b. 1838 d. ?* *b. 1841 d. ?* *b. 1843 d. ?* *b. 1846 d. ?* *b. 1849 d. ?* *b. 1850 d. ?*

THE DEVREYS

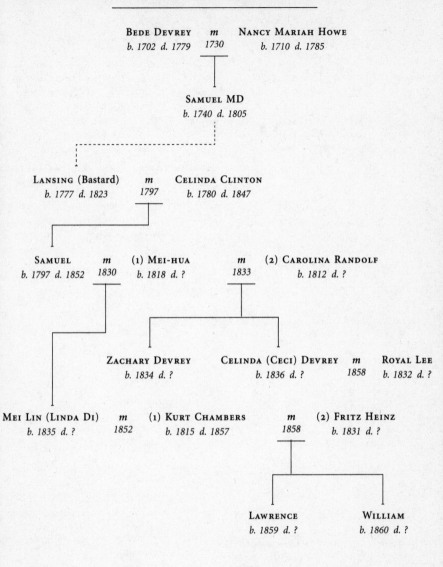

Bede Devrey *m* **Nancy Mariah Howe**
b. 1702 d. 1779   *1730*   b. 1710 d. 1785

Samuel MD
b. 1740 d. 1805

Lansing (Bastard) *m* **Celinda Clinton**
b. 1777 d. 1823   *1797*   b. 1780 d. 1847

Samuel *m* **(1) Mei-hua** *m* **(2) Carolina Randolf**
b. 1797 d. 1852   *1830*   b. 1818 d. ?   *1833*   b. 1812 d. ?

Zachary Devrey   **Celinda (Ceci) Devrey** *m* **Royal Lee**
b. 1834 d. ?   b. 1836 d. ?   *1858*   b. 1832 d. ?

Mei Lin (Linda Di) *m* **(1) Kurt Chambers** *m* **(2) Fritz Heinz**
b. 1835 d. ?   *1852*   b. 1815 d. 1857   *1858*   b. 1831 d. ?

Lawrence   **William**
b. 1859 d. ?   b. 1860 d. ?

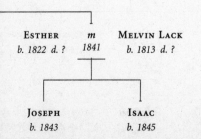

Esther *m* **Melvin Lack**
b. 1822 d. ?   *1841*   b. 1813 d. ?

Joseph   **Isaac**
b. 1843   b. 1845

*T*hese family trees show only characters
relevant to this story. For more detail
and information about earlier generations
of Turners and Devreys see *City of Dreams,*
Shadowbrook, and *City of Glory.*

Only children who survived infancy are shown.

Prologue

July 4, 1863,
The Temporary Field Hospital at Cemetery Ridge,
Gettysburg in Pennsylvania

"So you're here, Dr. Turner."

"I am here, Mr. Whitman. No, don't touch that."

Walter Whitman withdrew his hand from a table that held an array of scalpels and needles threaded with catgut. "I apologize. It looked as if you were ready for the next ligature."

"You have a good eye for surgery. I am." Turner leaned forward, procured the needle himself, and began carefully stitching the final flap of skin covering the soldier's elbow. There was no longer a forearm. "But I doubt, Mr. Whitman, that you washed your hands before you came to find me."

"Ah, yes. Your little . . . What do you call them?"

"Germs."

"Ah, yes. Germs."

The tent was pitched on a high ridge covered in silent dead, in one section of what had been the sprawling killing fields of a three-day battle engaging almost two hundred thousand fighting men. Inside the tent, among the living, it was hot and humid and stank of blood and feces and swiftly putrefying flesh. Bodies—most missing one or other appendage, all with some part of their person bandaged, some in blue uniforms, more in gray—were everywhere. A few lay on pallets; most lay on the ground. Two black-clad women moved among them.

"It hardly seems I could add anything more distasteful to this atmosphere," Whitman said.

"Indeed, in a general way you could not. But germs are particular, not general. Those ligatures were dipped in a solution of carbolic acid, a disinfectant. Your hands were not."

"The surgeons in Washington don't believe in your germs. They say you're a darned fool."

"Just as well," Turner said, "otherwise you'd probably be soliciting money on their behalf, not mine. Not so good for their patients, however. What have you brought me, Mr. Whitman?"

Whitman held out the small leather satchel in his left hand. "Soap. More of your carbolic acid. More of your sulfuric ether as well. Though it looks as though you've enough of that." He nodded towards the man on the table. No part of him twitched as Turner finished stitching his flesh.

"Wrong for once, Mr. Whitman. I used the last of my ether for this one."

"The Washington surgeons say chloroform and sulfuric ether are immoral. They say it's against the law of God to interfere with man's ability to feel pain."

Turner stopped stitching and raised his head. "Do they, now? And what do you say to that, Mr. Whitman? All these preachers telling us what to think, are they always right?" *Leaves of Grass* his book was called. Poems about people, bodies, sex. Biblically inspired the poet claimed, but his critics, many of them clergy, loudly disagreed. Even banned his book sometimes.

"Folks talk a lot about the law of God," Whitman said. "Doesn't mean they know much about it."

"Yes, that's my opinion as well." Turner again bent his head to his task. "As for the ether you brought me, I am enormously grateful. We've made an excellent job of killing vast numbers here in Pennsylvania these last few days, but I expect we are not done with maiming and murdering each other."

Back in Fredericksburg the year before, the first time Walt Whitman was ever in a field hospital, he watched men who called themselves doctors sawing screaming soldiers into pieces with nothing to deaden the pain at all—and no thought for Dr. Nicholas Turner's germs. He couldn't stand that there should be so much suffering and nothing he could do about it. It's why he took a government job, so he could be in Washington, closer to the war, and start visiting as many of the wounded as he could manage. And raise money to buy supplies for the doctors working on the battlefields. Most of that went to Dr. Turner these days. Turner's patients moaned as they came round, they didn't scream. And he treated them all, Yankees and Southerners alike. In the huge and lumbering Confederate retreat of the previous day, Lee had taken as many of his wounded with him as he could manage to cart away, but it was inevitable with a battle so enormous and so devastating that many were left behind. Turner's unconscious patient wore a gray uniform.

"There are some as give," Whitman said, "who wouldn't be pleased to think their contributions used to ease the enemy's pain."

"Then we will refrain from telling them." The surgeon looked up again, meeting the other man's gaze full on. "That's correct, isn't it, Mr. Whitman?"

"It's entirely correct, Dr. Turner."

Whitman figured Nicholas Turner was some fifteen years older than himself. Call it late fifties. He looked older still. Exhaustion had hollowed his cheeks and made dark circles around his gray eyes. Even his considerable height seemed diminished by the necessity to stoop beneath the low-slung canvas ceiling. His red hair was plastered to his scalp with sweat.

"Truth to tell, sir," he said, "I don't tell them exactly what the money's for either. Not about the carbolic or the ether." Help save the lives of our boys, Whitman told them, never said whose boys exactly. And as soon as he made his little speech about how their contributions would help the war, he switched to reading his poems. Even if they hated them, it was a distraction.

One of the black-clad women slipped out of the tent. Another arrived to replace her and came at once to stand beside Turner's operating table. "Are you finished, Doctor?"

"Yes. You can take him away now and . . ." Turner looked up, paused. "Oh . . . you are indeed a surprise. I didn't know . . . we should speak, my dear. I was—"

"You are busy. There is no need."

She sounded calm, Whitman thought, cool even. Turner on the other hand seemed unnerved. The woman wore one of those black bonnets that mostly shaded her face and like those he'd seen on the battlefield, a black frock. Black crows roaming among the dead, following behind the soldiers on burial detail, pecking at the earth and occasionally pulling up a prize, a body with some life left in it.

The other female in the tent came over, and the pair of them hoisted the soldier off the table and carried him away.

"Strange place for ladies," Whitman said.

"Perhaps. But more and more of them are nursing these days. Ever since that Nightingale woman over in England."

Whitman said he'd be going. Turner walked with him as far as the flap serving as the tent's door.

A carriage was parked a few feet away. Any number of gawkers and thrill-seekers had come by to observe the aftermath of carnage, but this was a brougham of the better sort, with all the windows tightly curtained, and a driver who sat up front staring straight ahead and keeping a loose grip on the reins.

While they watched, one of the curtains was pushed aside and a woman peered out. She looked as if she had stepped off one of the ceramic plates or vases or bowls that were so much a part of the China trade. Her black hair was upswept and threaded with ribbons and her face was painted and utterly unlike anything to be seen on Broadway or Fifth Avenue, much less on this blood-soaked battlefield.

"Sweet Christ," Turner murmured, "what is she thinking of coming here?" He turned as if to summon someone, but there was no need. One of the black-clad women—Whitman thought it to be the one Turner had spoken to and called his dear—pushed past them and climbed into the rig.

Her black dress was filthy and covered with blood and bits of flesh and bone. She had never, she thought, been quite so tired. Sitting, even for a moment, was a relief.

Outside, clusters of blue-clad soldiers were digging an endless succession of graves. How could they bury so many? Talk was of twenty, thirty, even fifty thousand dead. More gray uniforms than blue this time.

"This-place-red-hair *yi* is here. I saw him." That's how her mother had always referred to Nicholas Turner. This-place-red-hair *yi*, which was the Chinese word for "doctor." Mostly, however, he wasn't the one she talked about. "He said I would be princess," the older woman said. Her daughter knew who she meant and that it was not Dr. Turner.

"He said many things, Mamee. Most were not true."

They spoke in the formal Mandarin that was the daughter's first language until at the age of four she was released from the three rooms that had been her entire world and discovered that outside, on the streets of New York, people did not look as she looked or speak as she spoke.

"He lied almost always. This-place-red-hair *yi* sometimes also. That is correct," her mother agreed. "But here you will find truth. I wrote it for you to know." The book—rice paper pages bound in silk—was offered by a hand deformed by rheumatism, the joints swollen, the fingers bent into claws.

The daughter grasped her mother's wrist. "Have you been soaking your hands and feet every day the way I told you?" Her mother's feet had been bound at age three. She was forty-seven now and her feet were three inches in length. The beautiful and elaborate silk wrappings covered horned and calloused flesh and deeply ingrown nails, a source of constant pain. "The powder I gave you will help, Mamee, but you must use it regularly."

The older woman was called Mei-hua, plum blossom, a delicate and exquisite flower. Once it had suited her. "There is no reason. Nothing will change. I will not be young again."

The daughter's given name was Mei Lin, a Chinese phrase meaning beautiful grove. For a time she had taken another and then a third. None were what she was called today. "The soaking powder is to ease the pain, Mamee. Not to make you young."

Beyond the window of the carriage two of the women walking the battlefield pulled a body free of a stack of corpses and carried it towards the hospital tent. The daughter drew in a short, sharp breath. Dear God, they couldn't possibly find them all. The ones with a spark of life left in them but not the strength to crawl from beneath the piles of dead would be buried alive. "I must leave now, Mamee. I must return to my work."

Mei-hua leaned back against the red velvet upholstery and smoothed the silk of her long, slim skirt and her short jacket, both green silk shot with gold. Old, yes, but she looked better than her daughter. Ugly black bonnet. Ugly black dress. Ugly work to be picking and prying among the bloody dead. There was a rising stink about the place. About Mei Lin too if she stayed here. If those around you have fleas, soon you will itch. She had told her daughter that many times. Too late now to say words into deaf ears. "I am tired. Take me home."

"I will tell the driver, Mamee. I cannot go with you now. You know that."

"This-place-red-hair *yi* will not permit it?"

"He has nothing to do with it. I really must leave, Mamee."

"Very well. Go," Mei-hua said, waving a dismissive hand. "Tell the *yang gwei zih* to take me home."

The driver had been with Mei-hua for half a dozen years, but he was not Chinese and so was a *yang gwei zih,* a foreign devil. "I will tell him, Mamee."

The daughter leaned forward and kissed her mother's cheek, then she opened the door and climbed down to the world of dead bodies and suffering flesh. She paused just long enough to tuck Mei-hua's book beneath the short cape of the black habit of Mother Elizabeth Seton's Sisters of Charity. In moments it was safe and hidden. Just like her.

Except that Nicholas Turner still stood outside the hospital tent, watching both mother and daughter. And Nicholas Turner, the this-place-red-hair *yi*, knew everything.

1834—1835

Chapter One

MEI-HUA LAY CURLED next to him in the glow that followed love, her back against his chest, his arm around her waist, their breathing synchronized. Everything was perfect. Or so it seemed to Samuel Devrey.

After a time she moved just enough so one foot caressed his calf. The silken wrappings of her golden lily, the foot that had been first bound when she was three—excruciating pain inflicted and endured for him, indeed at his behest—were exquisitely erotic. Sam felt the sap rise in him yet again but he resisted. "There isn't time." He breathed the words into the jasmine scent of her hair.

His Mandarin could be understood, but it had been learned too late to be perfect. His tones were never exactly right. He spoke always the speech of the *yang gwei zih*, the foreign devil. Mei-hua would die a slow death before she would correct him. "My lord not need do much. Quick and easy. See."

She arched profoundly, one of those supple adjustments of her body that always astonished him, and her hips realigned so that he could take her effortlessly, in an act of possession as natural and undemanding as a whisper. It would have been against nature to refuse a generosity offered with such elegance. He moved the hand that had stroked her belly so it gripped her thigh, pressing her more closely to him. Both golden lilies were touching him now, wrapped around his legs. She was a silken splendid butterfly, tiny but exquisite, cocooned in his bulk. Her sigh of pleasure—more a vibration than a sound—thrilled him as if it were again the first time, three years earlier, when she was thirteen.

"You are astonishing," he said when he could speak.

She gently pulled away, then settled back against his body and pulled his hand back to her belly where it had been before. "What do you feel, lord?"

"Samuel," he corrected. "If I have to tell you again, I will spank you." Her smile was hidden from him, but he knew it was there. "For real this time." He attempted to sound severe. "You won't be able to sit for a week."

"I am sure I will deserve it. You are right in all things, lo—Samuel. But you cannot spank me now."

"Why not?"

"It maybe . . ." He heard the hesitation though she hurried to cover it. "Maybe disturb harmony. Your *tai-tai* never lose harmony. Never."

Repetition was the way the Chinese conveyed emphasis. *Tai-tai* meant not simply wife but senior wife, she to whom all other wives—if such there might be—owed allegiance. Devrey knew both things, but he seldom remembered to repeat a word he meant to strengthen. As for the rest, it wasn't practical.

He had married Mei-hua in the room beyond this one, in a ceremony he remembered as a bewildering shimmer of gongs and incense. Afterward she had been brought to this bed on its raised red satin platform hung about with quilted red velvet to perform her first duty as his wife, to sit absolutely still for hours and demonstrate her inner harmony. Meanwhile Devrey had been taken downstairs to eat and drink, and only occasionally remind himself that if he stepped out the door he would be not in this exotic Chinese world but on Cherry Street in New York, a few steps from the busy waterfront. Four hours later, when he had returned to the bedroom to claim what was his, Mei-hua was exactly as he'd left her. Except for her smile of joyous welcome.

"You could never be disharmonious," he said now.

His voice was steady, the words without any hint of anger or disapproval, but she could feel his fury in the heat of his skin and the coldness of his breath. "I try never displease you, lord." Not true. She had tried very hard. For many months now, as soon as he left her after lovemaking, she lay for long, boring hours with her feet above her head so his seed would find the son-making place deep inside. She had eaten only son-making food, though it was not always her favorite. Only the gods knew how hard she tried. And Ah Chee.

Mei-hua could not see the bedroom door from her present position, but she knew beyond doubt that her servant was near, probably listening. "I do nothing to displease my lord. Never. Never." Big lie, but never mind.

"Samuel," he corrected again, delivering at the same time one slap to her buttocks. Light enough to be playful but hard enough to sting.

Mei-hua stiffened and rolled away, clasping both hands below her waist as she did so. "Husband is correct. I deserve beating." She jumped off the bed, got the bamboo stick they used to close the red velvet curtains, and brought it to him, kneeling on the platform and leaning her head on her folded arms on the mattress. "I stay like this and husband beat back and shoulders until they bleed, only no part below waist. Then I will never—"

"I have never beaten you, Mei-hua. Why would I start now? Above or below the waist." He got up and put the stick back by the window, then drew her to her feet, kissing her face all the while, little soft kisses.

"Because husband is displeased with me."

"No, I am not. I understand you." The silk robe, the long *lung pao* he'd worn earlier, lay on a nearby chair, splendid green satin with dragons embroidered in silver thread. Samuel passed it by in favor of his western clothes, carefully hung in an elaborately carved wardrobe. He pulled on the tight black trousers and black boots and high-necked white shirt and tied his stock. "I must go."

"It is early. Useless old Ah Chee made soup you like, with duck and pumpkin."

"Perhaps tomorrow. You rest now." He picked up her pale yellow silk robe and draped it over her shoulders, lifting her back into the bed as he did so. "Sleep, Mei-hua. Stay beautiful for me."

The room beyond was as exotic and foreign as the bedroom, if not as sensuous. The furnishings—rosewood, ebony, ornaments of luminous porcelain and glowing brass—had all arrived from Canton when Mei-hua did, part of her dowry, along with the servant woman.

Ah Chee's skin was creased leather and her hair white, but she seemed to Samuel ageless. She stood by the front door, eyes cast down, hands folded, ready to usher him out. Hard to say if she knew he was leaving by the way he was dressed or if, as he suspected, she listened regularly to everything that happened in the bedroom. "My lord stay a little stay," she urged. "Maybe take some of this old woman's poor soup. Stay."

Samuel walked straight to her and slapped her hard across the face. She did not move, seemed barely even to flinch. He slapped her a second time. He knew she wouldn't react, but it calmed some of the rage in his belly. "When did *tai-tai* bleed last?" And when she didn't answer, "Tell me. If you lie, I swear I will cut out your tongue."

"In Last month, lord. Before start of Water Sheep year."

He did the calculation quickly. Last month was January, and this year, 1834, was Water Sheep. "When did she stop taking the special drink?" He bought the powder himself from a Mrs. Langton on Christopher Street. Guaranteed to prevent conception as long as a woman drank it dissolved in ale every morning before sunrise.

"Never, lord. Never. Never. Every day I wake up *tai-tai* and she drink." Ah Chee did not say that the girl hated the taste of ale with a rare passion, and spat it out almost as soon as the mixture touched her mouth. Anyway, the powder was probably useless. What did a *yang gwei zih* woman know of such things? Ah Chee, whose job it had been to look after this plum blossom since the day she was born, got make-no-baby powder from Hor Jick the apothecary—the closest thing to a proper doctor, a *yi*, in this place—and sprinkled it on the girl's food, and twice a day rubbed excellent lizard skin cream on Mei-hua's beautiful flat belly. Until, that is, she had judged the plum blossom to be ready and stopped sprinkling and rubbing. "Never, lord, never," she repeated. "*Tai-tai* drink every day."

"Still? Even after she missed two monthlies?"

"Yes, lord, yes. Drink. Drink."

"You are a lying old witch." He itched to slap her again but knew it would make no difference.

❦

Mei-hua, her ear pressed to the door, heard the latch click, signaling Samuel's departure. She ran from the bedroom in a whirl of yellow silk and flung herself at Ah Chee, fists flying, pounding out her rage. "You tell. You tell. Old woman say I do not bleed already two months. You tell."

Ah Chee stood calmly under the onslaught. Eventually Mei-hua's anger turned to misery, and she retreated to huddle, weeping, in the elaborately carved red-lacquered throne chair, usually reserved for her husband, under the scroll depicting Fu Xing, the god of happiness, whose benign smile did not alter whatever happened in this room.

For once the old woman did not rush to dry the girl's tears. "You think Lord Samuel stupid? Soon *tai-tai*'s flat little girl belly get big and round. Will the lord not see? Will he think *tai-tai* swallowed a melon?"

Such considerations were for the future. Mei-hua was concerned only with this terrible moment. "Now my lord will make you take me to the wretched Hor Jick devil *yi*, and he put filthy devil *yi* hands on me and make son jump out of belly and—"

"No, not happen. Not. No devil doctor Hor Taste Bad," Ah Chee said, using the nickname by which the apothecary was generally known.

Mei-hua stopped weeping and looked up. "Why you think this? Why?"

"Know definitely for sure. No Taste Bad. Absolutely." Ah Chee did not wait to answer more questions. Instead she went to the kitchen and returned with a bowl of hot soup. "*Tai-tai* open mouth. I feed son."

"Wait—"

Ah Chee did not wait. She spooned soup into the girl's open mouth. It was so hot that it scalded Mei-hua's throat, but she swallowed it quickly, turning her head aside so Ah Chee could not immediately force a second spoonful on her. "Wait, old woman. Wait. First tell why you are sure Lord Samuel not make you take *tai-tai* to Taste Bad devil *yi*."

"Because Taste Bad devil *yi* one of us, civilized person. Lord Samuel take *tai-tai* himself to white *yang gwei zih*. Make sure abortion done properly."

Mei-hua gasped in horror, and Ah Chee took the opportunity to spoon more hot soup down her throat.

Cherry Street ran parallel to the East River, two streets back from the docks, a little above the mercantile southern heart of the city. Though George Washington had lived briefly in a house on Cherry when he was president—Martha complained that the ceilings were too low for the feathers in the ladies' hats—the area was not the same. The wealthy had been fleeing the tumult of the lower town of late, deserting even their grand residences on Broadway and around Battery Park for the quiet of the numbered streets and avenues further up the island. These days, the grid adopted in 1809, a tight mesh of interlocking streets and avenues laid out across every inch of a Manhattan of hills and woods and streams, was closer to reality; it had been implemented from Tenth Street to Fourteenth and from First to Eighth avenues. The grid's virtue was that it allowed the greatest possible number of people to be housed on the island. It was a vision made inevitable because another had been realized.

Opened in 1827, the Erie Canal ran from Lake Erie in the west to the Hudson River in the east, establishing a direct water route to New York's magnificent harbor from the outer edge of the ever-expanding nation. There were twenty-four united states now, with Missouri the westernmost, and the far-flung territories of Michigan, Arkansas, and Florida bidding to join soon. The Erie Canal allowed the great city to open her mighty maw and swallow everything the industrious folk living so distant from the coast could produce, then spew it forth across the ocean. Such an increase of business was a racketing, riotous dream come true for the money men who had always ruled this town, but not one their wives wished to have clattering day and night outside their front doors. Uppertendom high society called themselves as they migrated north to the numbered streets above Bleecker. Cherry Street was no part of uppertendom's world.

A bitter wind blew off the river when Sam Devrey came into the street. Snow was coming down in earnest, and already the ragged roof line of the closely packed three- and four-story wooden houses was edged with a thick white border. The two buildings closest to the intersection of Cherry and Market Streets, numbers thirty-seven and thirty-nine, belonged to him personally, not to Devrey Shipping. Both were built of wood. Thirty-seven was three stories high, thirty-nine four, and each was three windows wide. Once private homes, they were now lodging houses like the others on the block, densely packed with laborers who paid fifty cents a week for whatever bit of floor they could claim. Devrey's lodgings were even more tightly packed than the others. His tenants were Chinese, willing to tolerate any degree of crowding to be with their own kind. Mostly they were sailors who had accidentally washed ashore, and mostly from one or another part of Canton, because that was the point on the globe where Asia touched the West. The single exception to the allocation of space was that Mei-hua and Ah Chee occupied the entire upper floor of the corner house, number thirty-nine, an area that would have housed at least twelve of the Chinese men.

None of Samuel's tenants questioned the arrangement, or in any way encroached on the young beauty most had never set eyes on, the supreme first lady *tai-tai*. As for Ah Chee, they nodded respectfully when she went past, and when sometimes she joined them for a game of cards and a drink of plum brandy, they were inclined to let her win. This despite the fact that except for those two, the tiny Chinese community was without females of any sort. It was but one of the hardships they bore. Another was their inability to look like everyone else in this place. That was not simply a matter of skin color or having almond-shape rather than round eyes. In China, since the coming of the Manchu in 1644, it was the law that every male must shave the front of his head and wear a queue, a long braid down his back. If he cut his queue a man could not return to die in what they called the Middle Kingdom, the land between heaven and earth. He would not be buried with his ancestors. In the matter of making a new life in America, Samuel's tenants considered themselves sojourners, those who had come to stay a little stay (so the expression in their language had it) and to return home. They found what work they could and sent as much money as possible back to relatives in China. In the matter of their attitude towards Devrey, he was a white man who spoke their language, a source of the temporary jobs on which they depended, and he could be counted on to provide rice when times were hard. In this place he need answer to no one.

"You leave now, lord?"

"Yes."

"Lord wait. I get horse."

The man was one of at least four called—in the Chinese fashion, family name first—Lee Yut. A good many were Lee Something else. Sixty-two tenants at this week's count, and pretty much all of them Lees or Hors or Bos, all from little villages where everyone was related and the second and third sons were sent to sea to be cooks and stewards to the officers of the ships in the China trade. Nicknames helped sort out the confusion. This particular Lee Yut was known as Leper Face because his skin was severely pitted by the pox, the scars so close together that in some places his flesh looked to have been eaten away.

Leper Face disappeared into the alley between the two buildings and returned a moment later with Devrey's mare. She snorted softly, pleased to see her master. Samuel patted her muzzle. Leper Face dropped to his knees and extended his clasped hands. Samuel took the leg-up and swung himself into the saddle. Horseback was not the most appealing manner of travel on a cold night like this one, but a private carriage would attract too much attention in these parts. There were a few of the new hansom cabs for hire in the city but no chance of finding one on Cherry Street. An omnibus, a large multiseat vehicle pulled by a team of six horses, ran a few streets to the west, but it was too public, and since it was used almost exclusively by the men of uppertendom traveling back and forth to their businesses, far too convivial.

Devrey adjusted his seat in the saddle, made a small sound in his throat, and the mare set out on the familiar northward journey. After a few seconds he turned and looked back. Leper Face had disappeared and Mei-hua's window was dark. Ah Chee was under strict instructions always to keep the curtains drawn after sunset, but once or twice he had seen a sliver of light and known Mei-hua was up there watching him, already—or so he fancied—counting the minutes until he returned.

Not tonight. All the windows were dark, and there were no gaslights in this neighborhood. Plenty to the south, of course, and recently as far up the town, to use the uppertendom expression, as his own front door on Fourteenth Street.

Chapter Two

MUCH OF FOURTEENTH Street was lined with red-brick houses. They'd been fashionable enough a few years back, but in New York nothing changed more quickly than fashion. Wilbur Randolf, who had made his money in tanning but owned a number of Fourteenth Street lots, had been one of the first to build with the newly desirable tawny-brown sandstone quarried in central New Jersey. In New York, where even speech was shortened so that business might proceed at a quicker pace, they were called simply brownstones. When Randolf's houses were finished, he arranged that the deed to the finest of them, number three East Fourteenth, on the corner of the somewhat improved Fifth Avenue (a rutted gully become a cobbled street beneath which flowed the now hidden stream known as Minetta Water) would on his death go to his only child, Carolina. Meanwhile it was hers to live in. The handsome gift marked the occasion of Carolina's marriage to Samuel Devrey.

"You're late, Samuel. I've been waiting for you." Carolina took his hat and gloves herself.

"Where's Dorothy?" They had only the one live-in servant unless you counted Barnabas, the boy who slept out back above the stable located in the communal mews. Other needs were met by day help. Still, his wife shouldn't have to attend her own front door.

"I sent her down to the kitchen to fetch a bit of supper for you as soon as I heard the mews gate."

"And how did you know it was me and not one of the neighbors?"

"I guessed. Besides, you haven't yet had the smith change your mare's left rear shoe. It has a loose ring. I told you so a week past."

"Barnabas checked. He said the shoe seemed tight enough to him."

"Well, Barnabas is wrong. It's loose. Please have it seen to, Samuel. I shall be sick with worry otherwise. Anyway, I don't know why you insist on riding horseback when we've a perfectly good buggy. I certainly don't need it these days." Carolina looked down at her belly, swollen with child.

He silenced her with a kiss on the cheek. "I like riding horseback, and I shall have the shoe looked at by the smith tomorrow or the next day. Promise."

"What of him, Samuel?" Carolina, placated by the promise and the kiss, drew his hand to her rounded middle. "No greeting for your son?"

"Or my daughter." He gave the bulge a dutiful pat. "You can't be expert in that as well as the sound made by properly shod horses."

"Oh, but I am. You shall have a son. A Devrey heir. Your mother came to see me today. She agrees. Says it's obvious since I bulge entirely in the front and not at all in the rear. She is insistent we name the boy Lansing. For your father."

"Insistent, is she? Well, I think she must be disappointed." Lansing Devrey had been known as Bastard all his life because his bachelor father never married his mother and the town never let him forget it. Didn't matter that he inherited one of the oldest shipping companies in the city and married a high-society Clinton. Bastard he was until the day he died.

If Mei-hua had a child, it too would be a bastard in the eyes of New York. Only the Chinese would recognize her as the first and senior wife and think it perfectly ordinary for him to acquire a second. That's what he'd been thinking standing next to Carolina in St. Paul's Church eleven months before, vowing before God that he would cleave only unto Wilbur Randolf's daughter. He was taking a second wife in the manner of any man in Asia. Besides, no Caucasian would recognize the marriage ceremony that took place on Cherry Street.

It was the arrival of children that complicated things.

Lavender water tonight, and the new white linen nightdress Carolina had made herself. It was open down the back, because the Irish midwife had suggested that now Mrs. Devrey was in her seventh month, if she had to give in to her husband, she must insist he approach her from the rear. "Sure, you'll not want him lying atop you and crushing the wee babe. That wouldn't be right, would it dearie?"

Carolina had turned aside so the midwife wouldn't see her blush and agreed it was not right. She also reminded herself that such a matter-of-fact approach to the business of conceiving and birthing was the reason she had insisted on having Maggie O'Brien attend her lying-in. Her mother-in-law had desperately wanted it to be Mrs. Carter, who was said to have recently delivered babies for an Astor as well as for Commodore Vanderbilt's eldest daughter. Carolina wouldn't give in. With no mother of her own since she was a tiny girl and a father she could always twist around her finger, she was accustomed to having her way, even when matched against as formidable an opponent as Celinda Clinton Devrey. Which was why she now had the frank and sensible Mrs. O'Brien advising her about the latest possible moment she could continue to accommodate her husband, as long as she offered him what the midwife called the backside way in.

But only for a week or two longer, even under Maggie O'Brien's forgiving regime. Before the end of March Carolina would start the eighth month of her pregnancy and must begin her confinement, which meant many weeks on either side of the birth when Samuel, like most men, would doubtless frequent a bordello. As far as men were concerned, that side of things was as it was and women were expected to turn a blind eye. Just as they must recognize their duty to submit in the marriage bed.

"You know what you must do, I expect," Carolina's father had said gruffly the day before her wedding, rising to the challenge of being the girl's only parent. "Leave everything to your husband and do exactly as you're bid. In all things, Carolina. However . . . odd they might seem." No one could say Wilbur Randolf didn't do his duty.

"I know, Papa."

"Yes, I expect you do." He'd turned aside, the matter done with and his obligation fulfilled. And the devil take all those folk who thought him a monster because he hadn't married a second time after the cholera of 1814 took his precious Penelope and left him with a broken heart and a two-year-old daughter. "I expect your Aunt Lucy has seen to it that you know such things. She's here often enough."

It would have been perfectly natural had Wilbur Randolf seen fit to marry his dead wife's widowed and childless sister. Everyone thought so, and Carolina had to agree it had a certain logic. Aunt Lucy was certainly fond of the idea; it was why she came around as frequently as she did. Though of course it was also her bounden duty to give her sister's motherless girl the benefit of female counsel.

Which, after a fashion, she did. Though nothing had turned out quite as Carolina anticipated in the matter of what Aunt Lucy called the expectations of the marriage bed, described as being best borne with fortitude, patience, and closed eyes. It must be dreadful, the girl thought. Why else would everyone be warning her in such mysterious terms? But perhaps they did not realize that she adored her dark and brawny husband or that she had decided to marry him the very first time she saw him, when the wind took his tall stovepipe hat on a blustery street corner and she, agile and quick-minded as always, had been the one to catch and return it. And they had both laughed heartily at the realization of how they had reversed a scene popular in every music hall in the town.

Dear lord, why hadn't she heard that hearty laugh more often since the wedding? And why was it that Samuel apparently had so few expectations of the marriage bed, despite the admonitions of her father and Aunt Lucy?

Lacking anyone with whom she would dare to discuss such questions, Carolina had devised an explanation of her own. Her husband worked so hard and such long hours that he spent most nights in a dead stupor. That's why he was always careful to remain on his side of the bed, and turned to her only very occasionally in a quick and explosive joining that however soon it was over at least gave her the rare freedom to wrap her arms around Samuel and whisper his name, hoping to convey some of the passion she had felt from that first wind-driven encounter. But soon she must face those eight, perhaps ten, weeks before the baby was born—and at least three months after—sequestered among women. Not even Samuel would be without female ease for such a length of time. He'd go to a bordello for certain and remind himself of whatever it was men found so attractive in such places. Else why were they permitted to exist, despite the railings of preachers and moral reformers alike?

She wouldn't think about it; it was far too distressing. She would have enough to deal with surviving her part of this affair.

Despite all the dreadful stories women whispered over their cups of tea in an afternoon "at home," to Carolina her confinement loomed as more trying than the actual birth. Thankfully, since she was in Mrs. O'Brien's care, her purgatory would be for the shortest possible time. The more fashionable midwives insisted the lying-in period must begin at the end of the fifth month. She had been granted an extra two months of normal life, or as normal as it could be with a great swollen belly preceding one everywhere one went. The time was nearing, however, when she would be required to spend most of every day abed or stretched out on a sofa, with the curtains drawn and windows closed tight. Only female visitors would be permitted, and only relatives at that.

Five long months of such restrictions. Dear lord, it would kill her.

No, it would not. She would endure. But thank heavens, as well as not confining her prospective mothers to their beds until the final eight weeks, Mrs. O'Brien said they need not sleep alone until then. "Though truth to tell, ma'am, once they're in the bed aside ye, it's for sure Adam will look for Eve. Big belly and all."

Would that it were so one more time before their separation began. So at least he would remember her. "Are you sleeping, Samuel?"

"I'm trying to."

"Stay awake a bit longer. Tell me about your day. What kept you so late?"

"Affairs of business, Carolina. They wouldn't interest you."

"Oh, but they would. Papa always told me about his business. I found it fascinating. I'm sure yours is as well."

"Shipping is a much more complex endeavor than leather goods." Wilbur Randolf had started as a maker of harnesses. These days he owned four tanneries, and some two dozen of the town's harness makers were part of the extensive business he had created. These skilled workers, each in his own tiny workshop, counted on Randolf to supply not only the raw materials of their trade but the orders for harnesses that kept food in the mouths of their families. It was a far steadier source of income than simply setting up shop and waiting for customers. They might grumble about giving away three-fourths of their earnings, but very few severed their relationship with Randolf Leather and set up on their own. At least half of those who did returned in a few months begging to be allowed to resume the former arrangement. Sometimes Wilbur took them back. Frequently he did not. An example, after all, had to be made.

From Sam's point of view, that Carolina was an only child who would inherit her father's estate—which for all practical purposes meant it would come to him as her husband—was one reason he'd decided to marry her. Or, as he thought of it, take her as a second wife. The other reason was that Carolina was a golden blonde and almost as tall as he. Her eyes were brown, while Mei-hua's were that remarkable blue-gray he'd seen in no other Chinese. Carolina being so different from Mei-hua would help him keep the two worlds apart, as distant in his mind as they were in reality. That had been the plan. The practice was not always reliable. He could feel the heat of her body pressing against his.

Samuel moved as far away as he could without falling out of the bed. "Sorry. I didn't mean to crowd you."

"You're not crowding me. I like nestling against you as if we were a pair of spoons in the drawer."

Mei-hua fit snugly against his midsection; it seemed he could encompass her completely simply by drawing his knees to his chest. Even when she was slender, Carolina's height made that impossible. Now with her big belly and her spreading hips . . .

"See," she whispered. "The gown opens from the back." He felt her draw it aside. "Mrs. O'Brien says it's quite safe this way for another little while."

"Are you telling me you discuss my most private life with that Irish midwife you insisted on engaging against all advice?" He didn't want to sound angry. Not in light of her condition. But . . . damned women. "Do you?"

"Not exactly, Samuel, but of course I—"

"Never mind, Carolina. I didn't mean to sound gruff. I understand you aren't entirely clearheaded these days." He rolled out of the bed as he spoke. "Anyway, it's high time I started sleeping in the room across the hall. It will be better for you, I'm sure. I'm sorry I did not suggest it earlier. I didn't mean to be so selfish."

Tell her about his business, she'd said. Sweet Christ, he was a Devrey, what would his business be but boats and seaports and trade?

Ships were bellied up to the eastern edge of Manhattan in a continuous line from South Street to well above Franklin. Barques and brigs and schooners and sloops stretched along the waterfront, their bowsprits overhanging Front Street, their masts aggressively thrusting towards the clouds. On any given day there were three hundred of them this side of the island and almost as many over on the Hudson side. Nearly half the goods exported from the entire country left from New York, and fully a third of everything the nation imported entered here. At any hour you could see pilot craft shepherding a newly arrived vessel to a mooring. Walk down the town far enough to look across the harbor to the open ocean, and fair to certain you'd see a spread of square sail against the horizon, royals and top gallants bellying in the wind, blazing white in the sun. Damn fine, Devrey thought. A rousing sight. But not likely to last. Not the way it was now.

Commercial craft were at war, with money and speed set to determine the outcome as sure as cannon balls did for the navy. The battle began eighteen years back in 1815 with Fulton's steamboat, but Cornelius Vanderbilt took the measure of that innovation better than Fulton had. The inventor died a man of modest means. Vanderbilt created a fortune based on his youthful mastery of the game of boat ramming that marked the early skirmishes between steam and sail. Now he was called commodore. Sweet Christ, would you believe it? Malicious mischief raised to a title. Commodore Vanderbilt was said to be worth half a million, and steam ruled the inland waterways and the coastal packets. There was even talk of steamboats that could carry enough coal to make the ocean crossing to Europe.

Steam was not the only enemy of traditional shipping. The second shot in the war had been fired by Jeremiah Thompson and his Black Ball Line. Thompson's sailing packets set out for England not when their holds were full and the weather fair but on an announced schedule. A few years back the first Black Ball vessel left the harbor in a snow squall, precisely as the clock of St. Paul's struck ten, carrying only a few passengers, some mail, and a bit of freight. She reached Liverpool twenty-five days later. Meanwhile a sister ship had set out for New York at exactly the same time. It took forty-nine days to make the westward journey, but men of business either side of the Atlantic fancied the notion of scheduled departures firmly adhered to and the idea caught on. Only the Black Ball's crews knew what brutalizing was required to make tars keep to those artificial schedules that disregarded wind and water. The line's flag was crimson with a black circle, but that's not why her ships were called blood ships.

Time and speed. Master them and you control commerce. Control commerce and you control the world. He was Samuel Devrey. That understanding was bred in his bone.

His twice great grandfather was Willem van Der Vries, son of a Dutch doctor, and Englishwoman Sally Turner, an apothecary, who murdered her Netherlander husband and hung his tarred body from the town gibbet. As for Willem, he recognized the rule of time and speed in the late 1600s, when he founded what became Devrey Shipping after its owner modified the name more appropriate to New Amsterdam than New York. Devrey's first ships were schooners engaged in the triangle trade, sailing from the American colonies south to the Caribbean, then east to the African coast and home again. Molasses to bibles to rum, that was the common explanation. It was a lie. The ships carried black gold—slaves. In those days the slave market at the foot of Wall Street was second in size only to that of Charleston in South Carolina, and had been the hub and heart of the slave trade here in the north. But though in this nation of twelve million, two million were still held as slaves, the practice was no longer legal in New York. Statewide Emancipation was declared in 1827.

No matter. Devrey ships had been off the Africa run for over a century. The nigras were docile enough stood up there on the block on Wall Street as long as the whipper was ready with his lash and the goods were properly shackled. But you had to take the irons off if you wanted any work out of them. You had to give your new property a place to sleep, and city life didn't offer space for the separate slave quarters of the southern plantations. So what was to keep those nigras housed under your roof from rising up to murder you in your bed? Two revolts, a few dead whites . . . After that, no amount of public burnings and rackings and hangings could restore New Yorkers' sense of ease, and bringing slaves direct from Africa was outlawed.

For a time they were replaced by seasoned slaves from the canebrakes of the Caribbean, already lash-trained to obedience. Eventually a flood of immigrants from the Old World came to meet the city's need for labor. As for the Devrey ships, these days they filled their holds with the made goods of England and France. And after Independence the bounty of the China trade.

Sweet Christ but didn't he know about that.

"Tea and silk and porcelains from the Orient. They'll make us rich again." So said Bastard Devrey after his foolhardy speculations with the moneymen of Wall Street nearly exhausted the Devrey fortune. That's why Bastard sent Samuel, his only son, to Canton, to learn the ways of doing business in Asia.

Fourteen years old Sam was in December of 1811 when he saw Canton for the first time. He should have been home in six months; instead the War of 1812 brought with it a British blockade, and he was marooned half a world away. He couldn't blame Bastard for that or for the fact that the war strangled the life out of American trade. Devrey ships were not the only ones left to rot in harbor.

But while most of the shippers hung on, Bastard Devrey pissed away Samuel's legacy. Mired in debt and drink, he lost everything to his despised cousin Joyful Turner and to Turner's partner, Jacob Astor, the richest man in New York. When Samuel returned from China in 1816 he was heir to nothing worth having. His mother was overseeing the building of a Broadway mansion that was gobbling the last of his father's resources, and Bastard was so steeped in Madeira he had little notion of what was happening.

Name Carolina's child after his feckless father? Not if Bastard's ghost came round rattling his chains and demanding the honor.

Nineteen years old when he finally got home, and only his wits to rely on, but Sam Devrey knew Canton by then. Spoke the language, knew the ways of the mighty ships cramming the treasures of Asia into their cavernous holds, knew the Pearl River trade. Knew the Hakka pirates, whose junks ruled the waterways surrounding the tiny offshore islands and controlled the receipt and distribution of the British shipments of wooden chests packed with balls of a new form of black gold. Opium.

"The Chinese call it *ya-p'ien*," he told Astor. "They smoke it, call it swallowing a cloud. Grabs them fast and won't let go. No way a man can do without swallowing clouds once he's developed a taste for it."

Opium was made from poppies, he'd explained. The best and the cheapest of it came from British-controlled India. No hope of getting any of that. But he'd heard of another source of supply, the Levant, and there was a web of distribution outside the grasp of the British. He knew how to tap into that.

"My partner in this Devrey shipping," Astor said softly. "Your cousin Joyful Turner . . ."

"I understand, sir. He will not approve." Spoken as knowingly as young Samuel Devrey could manage and with surprising calm, given that until a short time earlier he'd been worrying himself sick about the opposition of Joyful Turner. "I had word yesterday that my poor cousin is caught by the fever." Devrey had nodded toward the windows of Astor's Broadway mansion, tightly closed against the contagion of yellowing fever raging in the city. "He must not have been as cautious as you are, sir. They say one of Joyful's twin boys is abed with the selfsame affliction."

"As of this morning," Astor had said, "both boys."

He should have known John Jacob Astor would have the latest news.

"Then it seems to me"—Samuel had leaned forward and fixed Astor with a steady gaze—"you've a duty to make the decisions in my cousin's stead."

"A duty," Astor repeated. "*Ja.* Perhaps." And after a pause, "Your supply route, it is reliable?"

"Absolutely, Mr. Astor. I guarantee it." Why would it not be reliable? The money to be made in one exchange was frequently more than the smugglers had previously seen in a lifetime.

"And your guarantee, Mr. Samuel Devrey, it is worth something?"

"My bond, Mr. Astor," he replied, never letting himself look away from the older man, giving him the full brunt of that earnest stare.

"*Ja,* very well." Astor stood up and offered his hand. "Done, Mr. Devrey."

"Done, Mr. Astor."

Even so, they might not have gotten away with it. The emperor of China had recently outlawed trading opium for one thing. But corruption riddled Chinese governance, Chinese pirates were smarter than those charged with enforcing the law, and the British were not to be bested by a nation whose navy consisted of open boats propelled by oarsmen pulling to the beat of a drum. Moreover, Samuel's luck, what the Chinese called his joss, held. The yellowing fever took Joyful Turner's life as well as those of his two sons. Any loyalty Astor might have felt to his former partner was ended when he paid over a generous sum to Joyful's widow, who, it was said, consoled herself by nursing the poorest of the stinking poor in the hellhole of Five Points.

So Samuel Devrey need have no further concern for any opposition to opium that might have been voiced by Joyful Turner, much less for the longstanding enmity between the Turners and the Devreys. He was entirely on his own. It was up to him to get back what his foolish father had lost.

He'd been trying to do so from that day to this. Seventeen long years since he'd made his bargain with Astor and brought his first shipment of opium to China, and he'd still not achieved his goal. John Jacob Astor yet held the controlling position in Devrey Shipping, but the opium trade nonetheless changed Devrey's life forever. It took the young man back to the East, to the Hakka pirates on the Pearl River, and to Mei-hua.

She was three years old the first time he saw her, and he was twenty-two. She was sitting on her haunches at Ah Chee's feet on the deck of a sampan tied up to the one on which he was doing business with the man known as Di Short Neck. The river pirates roped their boats together to create equivalents of the mansions of wealthy men on the mainland, and the nursemaid and her charge were on the sampan that acted as the women's quarters. The servant's fingers deftly twisted the child's lustrous black hair into braids. The little girl looked up, straight over at him, and he saw those incredible sea-colored eyes. In that moment something to which he never gave a name was born in Samuel. "Your daughter?" he asked, careful to keep the wonder from his voice.

Short Neck looked across the deck to see what the *yang gwei zih* saw, then nodded. "I think so, yes. If she's the one I think she is, she's the youngest child of third wife, Mei Lin. She's called Mei-hua. At least I think that's her name."

"You do not value her?"

"Girls," the pirate said with a shrug. "You like little girls? I have a few more the same age. If you care to add an extra two chests of *ya-p'ien*, I will have two of them brought to you tonight. Four chests for three."

Devrey made his voice neutral, ignoring the fire that had been set alight inside him. "One only. And not now. I will claim her when she is bride age. But not one of the others. This one. This Mei-hua."

"Three chests of *ya-p'ien* if I am to lose her forever."

Samuel nodded agreement. He could easily make a paper accounting of the transaction and slip it past Wong Hai, the Canton-based company facilitator, the comprador, who had been with Devrey's for as long as Astor owned the controlling interest.

The child stood up just then and he saw her unbound feet. "She must have golden lilies," he said firmly. His first time had been here in China with the exquisitely tiny wife of a wealthy Hong merchant who had delighted in initiating a boy. There had been any number of Cantonese whores since then, always the smallest he could find. He'd tried a few times with white women, but their size, particularly their large feet, repulsed him.

"Of course. I will give the order for the binding to begin tonight." Short Neck looked at him without seeming to look, taking the foreign devil's measure and recognizing the need for power that was like a worm deep in the white man's belly, eating all else. "You can watch," he said softly. "And see that it is done for you. The way you wish."

The pirate, however, gave orders that the breaking of the instep arch with a heavy stone not be done until the *yang gwei zih* had left the sampans. He knew these foreign devil white men. They did not have the stomach for much that was real in life. They preferred only the illusions.

For Devrey there were many trips between the Levant and China after that, and a few times back to New York. But always he returned to Canton, to the Pearl River and the sampans of Di Short Neck to watch as Mei-hua grew. He became her friend and paid for tutors to come and teach her to read and to write, to draw and sing and play music on the zitherlike instrument called a *gu zheng*. He waited with ever increasing impatience while she acquired all the skills of a highborn lady. Waited for her to be thirteen. Bride age.

Later he realized he'd been on the river in July of 1823 on the precise day and at the hour when Bastard Devrey broke his neck in a drunken tumble off the half-built upper landing of the grand Broadway mansion he'd no money to finish. Bastard was long in the ground before Samuel heard he was dead. No matter. Samuel wouldn't have returned to do his father honor if he could have magicked himself back to New York on a broomstick.

But he had no choice when it was Jacob Astor who summoned him home to take over the New York end of the shipping that was but one of Astor's interests. A paltry interest some might say, given the size and the scope of the real estate and all the rest. Small and unimportant, like Samuel Devrey himself.

Let them talk. Astor did not own him. He was, for instance, entirely sure that Astor did not know about Mei-hua, brought to him two months after he returned to New York along with her dowry of furniture and clothing and the one-time wet nurse, Ah Chee. And while Astor probably did know of Samuel's investment in the Cherry Street lodging houses and even about their Chinese occupants, the man who was rumored to own most of Manhattan island was unlikely to be bothered by that. Much less, the fact that Wilbur Randolf's modest fortune would some day be in Samuel Devrey's control.

As for the rest, Samuel was prepared to bide his time.

Chapter Three

"HAVE YOU CONSIDERED my suggestion, Carolina?"

"What suggestion is that, Mrs. Devrey?"

"About the baby's name," Celinda said. "Calling him Lansing." Bastard had not turned out to be the sort of husband a woman wanted to memorialize, but it was important that Samuel and his wife recognized their duty. Not to the memory of Samuel's father. To her. "I can understand that you might be thinking of naming a boy Wilbur, but your dear papa is still alive. Surely the next wee one can be named for him. You don't look comfortable, Carolina," leaning forward over the sofa but not making any effort to alter things with her own hands. "Shall I summon Dorothy to adjust your pillows?"

Comfortable? With her mother-in-law paying two visits in as many days? And soon to be one of the very few people she was permitted to receive? "I'm fine, Mrs. Devrey. Though I thank you for paying me such mind."

Celinda Devrey held an embroidery hoop in her left hand and a needle in her right, but she hadn't taken a stitch in ten minutes. "Of course I'm mindful, my dear. It is my duty. Particularly since you have no mother of your own." One thing she had found to celebrate when Samuel announced his choice of bride. Because Carolina's mother was long dead, there was no other woman to contest the role of family matriarch. On the other hand, she'd known at once that being the indulged child of a wealthy widower had imbued the girl with more independence of spirit than was desirable in a daughter-in-law. Nonetheless, she would cope. Celinda had been coping since the first day she herself became a wife. Or put more accurately, the first night. A dreadful business at best, made worse by Bastard seldom actually managing to make a job of it—too drunk most of the time. No wonder they'd had only the one son. "Does your Mrs. O'Brien at last agree you must begin your lying-in?"

"Not quite yet, Mrs. Devrey. I believe I told you she says start of the eighth month. I calculate there are two weeks to go."

Celinda raised an eyebrow, remembered the embroidery and took a stitch, then held the hoop a bit away to admire the result. "Calculate," she said, as if it were an extraordinary notion. Then, before Carolina could start discussing the unpleasant details of what she would probably call, in the manner of young women these days, monthly visits from grandmother, "No matter. I'm sure Samuel is taking special care of you just now."

"Samuel is always most considerate."

"I'm pleased to hear it. I do know he works very long hours." At least that was the situation according to Barnabas, Samuel's stable boy, whom Celinda tipped handsomely whenever she left her little chaise and pony in his care. An encouragement to pass on household gossip. "Such a great responsibility," she said with a ladylike sigh, "managing all of Devrey Shipping. Samuel must be very tired much of the time."

"A very great responsibility indeed," Carolina agreed. And what had his mother done to protect Samuel's legacy so that today he would be owner of the company rather than simply its manager? Nothing. All New York knew Celinda Devrey's expensive tastes were as much to blame for the loss of the Devrey fortune as were Bastard's wastrel ways.

"Well," Celinda said. "I imagine these days you don't so much mind how frequently he is away from home."

"I always crave my husband's company, Mrs. Devrey." She could have bitten her tongue off the moment she spoke the words.

"Do you, Carolina? Quite natural, I'm sure, in one wed less than a year. But after the wee one comes, you'll be preoccupied. It won't matter so much."

"What won't matter?" God! Was there no end to her folly?

"The evenings Samuel is late home. The ways of men, my dear. We women must understand and seek to gently enlighten their baser nature with our sweet example." Stupid of the child to turn her head away as if she didn't want to hear. Her daughter-in-law, Celinda thought, must be made to see that her most important task was to allow nothing to disturb the household or change Wilbur Randolf's plan to leave the tannery business to Carolina and thus to Samuel. Celinda's husband had not provided for her old age; it was her son's responsibility to do so. "It is our cross to bear as women, dear Carolina. I wouldn't mention it—I'm sure you know your duty—except that with no mother of your own . . ."

By the time her mother-in-law left half an hour later, Carolina was finding it hard to breathe, much less quiet her beating heart. "Dorothy! Come here at once!" She shouted rather than ring the bell. A terrible breach of etiquette, but she could not control herself.

The servant appeared in the doorway almost instantly. "I was just seeing Mrs. Devrey out the door, ma'am."

"Where is Barnabas?"

"He helped Mrs. Devrey into her chaise, ma'am. Same as always. I expect now he's gone round the back and—"

"Yes, well I don't care where he actually is. Tell him I want him. I must talk to him about shoeing the riding mare. Bring him here."

"To the parlor, ma'am?"

"Yes, I can't—Oh, never mind. I shall go out back and talk to him there."

It was hard to lumber out to the mews in her condition and would probably cause a scandal if any of the neighbor men happened to see her now that it wasn't possible to disguise the bulge. But at least it meant Dorothy wouldn't hear her mistress questioning the stable boy about whether Mr. Samuel had that day ridden horseback to his business or taken the buggy. Once she knew that, Carolina would know whether her husband was to be late home, as he was most nights, or perhaps—as rarely happened—he might arrive back in time to take supper with her.

Market Street. Very too much bad name. Very too much tell you nothing. Ah Chee mumbled the complaints under her breath as she hobbled along on her seven-inch golden lilies.

Not really golden lilies at all. Must be she was an ugly baby from the first minute. So no one think she will maybe be a rich man's wife and don't do a good job and give her golden lilies that will fit inside a man's hand. Never mind. This *yang gwei zih* place had rock streets. Not smooth like the wood decks of sampans on the Pearl River or like sand streets on the shore. Three-inch golden lilies could easily break your neck in this foreign devil place.

Market Street. Very too much stupid name. Chicken Street. Rice Street. Street of green peas and cabbages. Those were names that could help a civilized person do her shopping. Never mind. She had anyway taught herself to say it. "Mar-ket-str-eet," she practiced.

Ah Chee's mouth made the sounds, but they had a foreign taste like all the lumps of words she had been storing up for so long. Since back on the Pearl River, since the day when she first bent the big toes of three-year-old Mei-hua toward the balls of the little girl's feet and tied the cotton wrappings that would keep them in place.

Not too very much tight that first time, though the plum blossom screamed and screamed as if worst thing had happened. It had not happened yet. Also not worst thing next night, when she made the wrappings tighter. Worst thing was when the heavy stone smashed down and broke the tiny bones so the girl's golden lilies would be straight, not arched.

First one foot, then the other. Smash. Smash. While Ah Chee cried and her plum blossom screamed.

Smash. Smash. Tears and screams. But not until the *yang gwei zih* had gone away. Dog turd pirate father of plum blossom told Ah Chee to wait. "*Yang gwei zih* want to watch," he said, "but not want to see."

That was one way *yang gwei zih* and civilized men were alike. Making sons with clouds and rain, very terrific good. Having sons almost as good. Getting born part? No men wanted to see that. Same thing with making golden lilies. Men cared only about the result, tiny little feet, swaying steps—make jade stalk get big and hard. Make clouds-and-rain-best-part of bed stuff be terrific good. How did it happen? *Mei won ti*, little sweet thing. No problem. Not for men.

So why was it that the first time she bound Mei-hua's feet there was a *yang gwei zih* watching from the other deck, thinking Ah Chee did not know he was there? Ah Chee knew.

Had to be that Di Short Neck, whom the women secretly called Short Stalk because his jade appendage was said to be as tiny as a courtesan's golden lilies, this dog turd pirate Di had promised the little girl to the Lord Samuel *yang gwei zih* as part of their business dealings. If so, Ah Chee needed to begin preparing to protect her tiny treasure. The first step was to acquire *yang gwei zih* words and never let on she knew them.

It was not so hard to learn such things on the sampans of the Pearl River, where foreign devil men of business were as thick as maggots on rotting meat. Even easier once the pair of them were shipped to New York with furniture and china and clothing. Enough for a grand mansion, though when they arrived Ah Chee discovered it was all to be crammed into three rooms on the top of what she right away thought was a not so special house, and got too much angry when she found out how many very terrific better houses there were in this place.

The Lord Samuel promised the plum blossom would be a princess in his faraway country. Why else learn music stuff and writing stuff and speaking like supreme first lady stuff? Super-special big important princess supreme lady *tai-tai.* Big lie. A princess would live in the best house, not three rooms on top of a not so good house with no garden and no wall. Never mind. Didn't matter as long as the plum blossom did not know. And how would she find out? A rich man's supreme lady *tai-tai* would never go outside in the Middle Kingdom. Same thing here, Ah Chee told Mei-hua. In reality, maybe yes, maybe no, Ah Chee wasn't sure. But only she went out most days to stupid name Market Street, and walked along the stalls, and did business as she would have done at home in the land between heaven and earth.

"Not good. Not fresh. More hard. More hard." And when at last a pumpkin was produced that had the right ring when she knocked on it, "How much?" And inevitably, "Too much. Too much. You think this old woman have so much money?" Followed by the half turn away from the stall and the pumpkin seller's agreement to lower the price by two pennies.

As always, Ah Chee counted out the agreed on price with care and put the coins she calculated she'd saved by clever bargaining in a separate purse.

The Lord Samuel gave Ah Chee three American dollars every week to buy food for herself and the *tai-tai.* By comparing what things cost here with what they would have cost at home she had carefully worked out that it was equivalent to half a string of copper cash. Half a string, to feed herself and one small female. The lord ate with his *tai-tai* only very occasionally, when, Ah Chee suspected, he longed for the tastes of the Middle Kingdom and was sickened by the slabs of meat and huge lumps of vegetables which according to Taste Bad and Leper Face and the rest it was customary to serve in this foreign devil place. For only that much food, half a string of copper cash? Who would spend so much on so little? Was she a wicked servant as well as an ignorant one that she could not get good value in any market, even this one full of foreign devils? No, she was not. She knew her duty was to protect the child who was as much hers as if she had squeezed her out between her own two legs. Her exquisite Mei-hua, given to the foreign lord, which was only a little better than being blinded or crippled and sent out to beg, as were the daughters of even some rich men in the Middle Kingdom. Never mind. That's how life was for women. Ah Chee did not expect things to be any easier here than they were there. Store up coins that you do not need now, because you will need them later.

The secret treasure purse was hidden below the quilted tunic she wore over a long narrow skirt of sturdy homespun slit on both sides to accommodate walking. Ah Chee pulled her hair into a bun and wore a conical straw hat tied firmly under her chin. It kept the rain and the snow away in winter and in summer protected her from the sun.

Plenty *yang gwei zih* this-place people looked at her and pointed and laughed. Sometimes little boys threw stones, bad stink things. Never mind. There was plenty of food to eat in this place. And even the house that was not terrific best house kept out the rain and wind and sun. Also, according to what the plum blossom told her, the Lord Samuel had a terrific big jade stalk that could go in very terrific deep. Make a son for supreme lady *tai-tai*, whatever he think.

The Lord Samuel had plans. Ah Chee knew that. Ah Chee also had plans. And very terrific best thing in this place was no mother-in-law to also have plans. She had burned twenty joss sticks in thanksgiving to Fu Xing, the god of happiness and good luck, when they arrived here and did not find a waiting mother-in-law.

But then she made Leper Face show her where Lord Samuel did his business and eventually found out he had taken a concubine, and that she lived in a very too much better house than the one where the lord kept Mei-hua and her Ah Chee.

Concubine not such a bad thing. Dog turd pirate Di Short Neck have plenty of concubines, even other wives. Her plum blossom was the Lord Samuel's supreme lady first wife *tai-tai*. But terrific hard to understand that he never bring yellow hair concubine to kowtow and serve the *tai-tai* to show she knew who was supreme lady. No respect for the *tai-tai* was very too bad business. Very important plum blossom have son to secure her position.

Ah Chee slapped her hand on the display of flounders at the front of the fishmonger's stall. "No good fish. Too small. You no have better fish? Bigger? More fresh?"

"Here now! Don't handle the merchandise if you're not intending to buy." The fishmonger sounded indignant, but he knew this peculiar old woman and what would please her. He pulled a basket of glistening and slithery mackerel from under the counter and grubbed through them until he found one he judged would suit his customer. The fish was alive and squirming in his hands—"God's truth, missus, how much fresher can it be?"—still he held it out for her to sniff. He'd grown accustomed to this ugly little creature's ways in the three years she'd been coming to his stall. These days he hardly noticed her yellow skin or her peculiar eyes. Couldn't help but stare at the stunted feet though.

Ah Chee, still intent on the fish, gave a reluctant nod. "Good enough for poor old woman like me. You take five pennies. I take your old stinking fish."

The fishmonger wrapped the squirming mackerel in a bit of paper and dropped it in the little woman's basket. "Six cents it is, and none of your arguments. That's the price and it ain't gonna change." He held out his hand and Ah Chee counted out the coins, mumbling under her breath all the while.

Six cents was a fair price, though she would never let him see she thought so. And the fish was magnificently fresh and fat. She would buy a bit of ham as well, then she could make the Land Sea Golden Wonder Soup that was the absolute terrific best thing for supreme lady with a child in her belly.

She hobbled quickly across the way to the stall of the pigman. "Small piece that meat," she said, pointing to a rosy pink ham. "Not much too fat bad stuff."

The man cut her a thin slice of the ham and they dickered over the price until she agreed to pay four pennies, then went to buy two big duck eggs. They were more expensive than they should have been, but still she was left with enough to tuck a few more coins into the special purse. Which, considering the Lord Samuel's plans and Ah Chee's plans, was bound to be terrific very much important.

Chapter Four

SINCE 1816 THE almshouse of the city of New York had occupied a red-brick complex on a sprawling tract of land stretching north-south from Twenty-second to Twenty-eighth streets, and east-west from the East River to Second Avenue. At least so said the signposts. To Dr. Nicholas Turner, just arrived from Rhode Island, the numbered streets and avenues seemed pretentious nonsense. The buildings were surrounded by woods and fields, and the populated part of the town ended at least half a mile to the south. But according to the driver of the hansom cab he'd taken from the pier, proposed streets and avenues were laid out and numbered and marked all the way up to the far end of Manhattan island, where One hundred and sixty-eighth Street could be found. City planning, they called it. Turner glanced around, trying to imagine these trees and hedgerows all disappeared, and buildings as far as the eye could see. Absurd.

The March wind off the river was bone-chilling, made worse because he hadn't been truly warm since the evening before, when he had boarded the coastal steam packet from Providence for the fourteen-hour journey. The miserly breakfast of black tea and stale biscuits he'd been offered before disembarking had not helped. Indeed, the whole notion of coming to New York seemed mad now that he was finally here.

All the same, here he was. Turner squared his particularly broad shoulders. He'd wanted a new challenge, a change from sleepy Providence, and it seemed that's what he'd got.

The word "Almshouse" was etched above the granite arch of the Twenty-sixth Street central entrance. The buildings on either side housed an orphanage, a workhouse for the destitute who were able to labor, and a poorhouse for those too old or too infirm to be put to any use. The hospital where he was to work was in the middle, dividing the poorhouse for men from that for women. It was supposed also to serve the sick of the city who could not pay for medical care, though probably few of them used it. Almshouses were the same the world over. Hospitals as well, for that matter. Given a choice, even the poorest of the poor preferred to die in whatever hovel they called home, where if nothing else they were spared regular visits from clergymen haranguing them about morals.

Enough stalling. Turner hefted his pair of valises—both heavy with more books than clothes—and strode beneath the arch into the place known everywhere simply by the single shudder-inducing word, Bellevue.

Abandon hope all ye who enter here.

"I apologize for not receiving you in my private residence, Dr. Turner. It's being refurbished at the moment. This office was the only place available."

"No apology required, Dr. Grant. This is after all where I am to be working."

"Here at the Almshouse Hospital. Yes, exactly. If you're quite sure . . ."

Grant let the words trail away and waited for him to say something. Nick knew what the other man expected. *I didn't realize how bad it would be. I'm afraid I must change my mind.* But that wasn't the case. Even in Providence they knew about Bellevue.

At first sight the hospital lived up to its reputation. Just to get this far he'd had to thread his way between pallets spread on the floor because the wards were full, and to dodge ambulatory patients who wandered around as if they had no notion where to go or what to do. Most patients wore little or no clothing and the pallets were without sheets or blankets. The stench of death and disease permeated even this quite decently appointed small office at the far end of the entrance hall.

It said "Director" on the door. That was the title of the man appointed to run the entire almshouse operation. By long tradition a doctor, he functioned as an administrator, and was empowered to hire a single Senior Medical Attendant to look after the hospital patients and oversee the work of one resident doctor and a few medical students. In practice they were those who could not manage to get themselves assigned to supervised work in the town's private hospital, New York Hospital on Broadway at Anthony Street. It was reputedly a decent place. In contrast to Bellevue, it was funded by private charity and served those known as the deserving poor, decent folk fallen on hard times. Worthy work, perhaps, but not for twenty-eight-year-old Nicholas Turner. A practicing physician for seven years, had seen the Bellevue position advertised in the *Evening Post,* known exactly what it was likely to be, and applied by mail and been hired—sight unseen—in a matter of days.

"I'm sure, Dr. Grant," he said.

"But a man such as yourself . . . You were in private practice in Providence, were you not?"

"I was." Then, when the other man's look of puzzled skepticism didn't alter, "Let me be quite frank, Dr. Grant. I don't think private practice suits me. I've never been particularly good at what I believe is called bedside manner. And as I wrote in my application, I have an interest in medical research. Surely here, with so many from such a wide variety of backgrounds, I shall see a good deal that is new to me."

"Oh, yes. A wide variety. Mostly the paupers are Irish, of course. I'm told we're getting some thirty thousand a year since England removed restrictions on their leaving, and they all seem to wind up in New York. But a goodly number of other nationalities are represented, bring all sorts of strange ailments with them. Taken all together, there are around two thousand inmates here at Bellevue."

"Inmates? I thought the prisoners had been separated from the almshouse a few years back when they opened the penitentiary up at Ossining."

The older man seemed suddenly to wake to the notion that he might lose this excellent prospect for his hospital. "They will be, Dr. Turner. Any day now, I assure you. There's yet another penitentiary being built on Blackwell's Island a bit up river from here. Finished soon, they tell us. The male prisoners we have here will all go there."

"The male prisoners? Then there are also women?"

"Some," Grant admitted. "Prostitutes mostly. The ministers have their way occasionally, and a great drive is made to pick up the more rowdy sorts. Working on the streets. You know."

Nick nodded. He did know. No need to leave Providence to see crabs and the French disease.

Grant was attuned to his reaction. "There are pickpockets as well. The women are quite good at that, I'm told. The Dubliners particularly."

"And they're imprisoned here at Bellevue?"

"Well, most are kept at the old bridewell next to City Hall, but we do get the overflow. Not for long, however. There's talk of yet another prison to be built. Center Street, I hear."

"It seems there is a never-ending need for prisons here in New York."

"The Irish, as I said. Dirt poor most of 'em. Roman Catholics. Refuse to work. Waiting for glory in the next life."

"Indeed. I would have thought"—Nick nodded towards the hall and the pallets on the floor—"the mere idea of this place would encourage better habits." In Providence newspapers were full of job notices that said no Catholics or Irish need apply. He had no doubt whatever it was the same in New York.

Grant was apparently not susceptible to irony. "I realize the conditions are not everything we would wish. Hippocratic oath, promise to heal. All that. But the budget the Common Council provides . . ." The director of Bellevue waved a hand as if the matter was not worth further discussion. "The hospital serves some two hundred of the inma . . . er . . . residents on any given day. As you say, you'll see it all here."

The office was warmed by a Franklin stove. It was almost too efficient; from being chilled to the bone Nick had gone to sweating. He was ready to get out of this small space, start moving about, see the rest of what awaited him. "Bellevue will suit me quite well, Dr. Grant. I'm quite sure."

The other man was still attempting to convince himself. "And there is the matter of your grandfather, Andrew Turner. One of my predecessors, wasn't he?"

Andrew Turner, who died in 1818, had taken on the job of director of Bellevue (then known as the City Hospital) before the Revolution and had continued for a decade after.

"Indeed," Nick said. "Also my three times great grandfather, Christopher Turner." In colonial times Christopher Turner had made his reputation for brilliant surgery at the first Almshouse Hospital, which stood where City Hall was now. Nick had been taken to see the spot when he was a lad on a visit to Grandfather Andrew.

"I'm aware," Grant said, "that you have a distinguished medical lineage, sir."

"I shall try to live up to it."

"Very well, you shall have a tour. Then I shall ask again if you're quite sure this post is for you."

"And I am quite certain I shall tell you again that it is." Nick had already given instructions that his house in Providence was to be sold.

Grant smiled and stood up. Nick did the same. He was at least a head taller than the man who would be his superior. And while Tobias Grant, though bald as a cue ball, cultivated a full beard, Nick Turner was clean shaven. He had the Turner family red hair, and it always seemed to him that a redhead with a beard looked like a pirate.

"You can leave your bags," Grant said. "Presuming your response remains that you will take us on, I'll have someone bring them to your rooms."

❦

The place was wretched beyond belief, filth and disarray and misery past any normal man's ability to imagine; in truth Nick had expected as much. He had not foreseen black magic.

The dispensary was in the basement, an evil-smelling dungeon hung about with ropes and pulleys and winches and lined with huge barrels and flagons and beakers, some bubbling atop coal stoves and others fitted with hoses that dripped strange fluids slowly into an assortment of pails. Along with all the chemical odors it stank of dead rodent, and there were mouse and rat droppings everywhere. Nick suspected Jeremiah Potter the chief apothecary might actually encourage the vermin. Eye of newt and toe of frog, that sort of thing.

Potter was wizened and old, with tufts of hair sprouting from both ears, and blind, or near enough as made no difference. A monocular was screwed in place in his left eye. The right was missing, and in its place he'd inserted a white ball painted with a fantastic and exaggerated black eyeball.

"Don't need to see. Been here forty years. Know where everything is," he'd told Nick the first time they met. "Do it all by touch and taste and feel."

"I'd be careful what I tasted if I were you," Nick said. "Now tell me what's available. I don't suppose you have a written list."

"Don't have time to write nothing down. Don't need to. Docs come down and tell me what the symptoms is and I give 'em what's needed. Never have no complaints. Anyway, report directly to the director, I do. Nothing to do with the Senior Medical Attendant. Jeremiah Potter, Chief Apothecary, runs his own department."

"Quite. I'm also told you charge me and the resident doctor and the medical students for whatever you prescribe."

"Course I do. How else am I going to pay for all what's needed down here?"

"From the hospital budget I imagine." He had ignored the apothecary's snort of derision. "Leaving myself out of it, how are the other doctors supposed to afford your"—he'd started to say rubbish, then decided there was no point in making Potter an enemy—"the medicaments you concoct. They can't afford it. I can't afford it." His salary was a hundred eighty a month augmented with room and board, though so far most of the food he'd been served was inedible. He'd taken to having his main meal of the day at a nearby farmhouse where a widow cooked for a few locals. The resident got a hundred, and the students—a changing roster of two or three from either the school of medicine at Columbia College or the one that was part of the new University of the City of New York—were supposed to pay ten dollars a week for the privilege of working on the Bellevue wards, three dollars of which had long been a perquisite of the Senior Medical Attendant, skimmed off before he turned the balance over. Nick had already informed the students that he would waive his bonus; they could pay only seven dollars a week as long as in return they promised conscientious execution of their duties. To further make the point he'd established a series of fines for lateness and other signs of slacking.

Jeremiah Potter was not concerned with any attempt to improve the quality of care at Bellevue. "Not my lookout how much money them student doctors has," he'd insisted on Nick's first visit. "They pays me and gets it back from the patients. That's how it's supposed to be done."

"Good Christ, man, the patients are paupers. If they were not, they wouldn't be here."

"Not my lookout," the old man repeated. And he'd walked away.

After five days at Bellevue, Nick intended this second encounter to end differently. "We need tincture of calomel on all the wards. Not as a purge." It was common practice to dose the constipated with mercurous chloride as calomel was scientifically known, but Nick had his doubts about the wisdom of that. "To treat flea bites and other skin lesions. I want four quarts at least delivered to my office every morning, including Sunday. It's a work of mercy. No preacher alive could object."

The apothecary closed shop on Sunday, saying he was busy with his devotions.

"I'll send up double the supply on Saturday," Potter said now. "Cost you three dollars a fortnight. Payable in advance."

"Tell the director what you're owed. It's a basic necessity of running the medical service. It should come out of general funds."

"You tell Grant whatever you like. I'll deliver your calomel just as you say, long as I'm paid in advance. Don't matter to me where the money comes from."

"But—"

"You are wasting your time arguing with him," a woman's voice said from somewhere over Nick's left shoulder. "He is a venal old devil who cares for nothing but his purse. Dr. Turner isn't it? The new senior attendant?"

Nick turned to the voice and found himself face to face with a lady, decently dressed and clearly respectable. She was the first such he'd seen in this place, where the only nurses—male and female—were a few unfortunates assigned from the prison wing. She carried a basket over her arm, covered with a clean white cloth. Clean cloths of any color were as rare in the almshouse as respectable women.

"You are correct, madam. Dr. Nicholas Turner," with a small bow. "And may I know who you are?"

"Mrs. Turner, as it happens." She shifted her attention to the apothecary, putting an assortment of walnut-sized half-cent coins and tiny half-dimes as well as two English shillings on the scarred wooden counter. "I will have a jar of tansy cream and a beaker of spring tonic." Then, turning back to Nick, "Mrs. Joyful Turner. My late husband was your second cousin once removed. At least that's as near as I can work it out. He had that same fiery red hair."

She was tall and slender, somewhere in her forties, Nick judged. Had to have been a beauty in her day, though now the hair that showed below her bonnet was more gray than gold and there were lines of tiredness and care creasing her face. "Joyful Turner. Yes, of course. My Grandfather Andrew spoke of him."

He remembered now. Grandfather had written of the tragedy when it happened. Cousin Joyful and his infant twin boys dead of the yellow fever in the epidemic of 1816. The old man had taken it hard, died himself two years later. And Nick's father, Andrew's son, the year after that in an influenza epidemic. Nick had been a lad of fourteen at the time, and since his mother had died bearing him and his father never remarried, he'd felt himself painfully bereft. What must it have been for this woman to lose husband and children together? "Cousin Manon," he said with a small bow.

"Cousin Nicholas." She smiled and he saw a flash of the old beauty. "A full beaker, you old rascal. I'll not be cheated." This directed at the apothecary who was siphoning a green and viscous liquid into a glass receptacle.

"But what are you doing here?" Nick asked.

"I come as often as I can to nurse the women. I was planning to visit the parturition ward today. Is that acceptable, Dr. Turner? No one has objected before, but of course if you—"

"No, no. Of course not. It's very good of you. And I take it," he nodded towards the coins the apothecary was just now sweeping from the counter into a canvas money bag, "you are paying for these supplies out of your own funds."

She shrugged. "I'm a widow, and childless. I do not need much. I'm happy to share what I have."

"What about this tincture of calomel you're wanting?" The apothecary was impatient with their talk. "Three dollars a fortnight, like I said. In advance."

"Yes, very well. Here's the first payment." Nick reached into his pocket and brought out two silver dollars, and a paper bill issued by the state of Rhode Island.

"Don't hold with paper money," the apothecary said.

"You'll take it and like it, old man. It's what I have."

The apothecary picked up the bill and held it close to his monocular. "Rhode Island, eh?"

"Yes. And backed by the same gold as backs the paper money of any state in the Union."

The bill and the two coins disappeared into the apothecary's canvas bag, and the two men spent another moment discussing the strength of the tincture Nick required. When Nick turned around, Manon was gone.

She was, however, waiting for him in the corridor beside the narrow and twisting stairs that led to the hospital wards above. "You can't go on simply buying medicine for every ward of the hospital out of your own pocket," she admonished.

"I believe that's what's known as the pot calling the kettle black."

"That's as may be. But I am here only two or three times each week, and I spend a few coppers on what might be useful for half a dozen patients on a given day. You are responsible for all of them every day. It's a different matter entirely."

"You're right, of course. I shall speak to the director."

She made a face. "You will have no joy of Dr. Grant. Don't waste your breath."

"The senior attendant before me . . ."

"Was as venal and greedy as Grant himself. To be allowed to continue here the students had to pay him an extra dollar a week beyond the customary three. And he spent his time in a lucrative private practice in the town and only came to Bellevue to collect what he could."

He'd wondered why his rooms, though a quite decent suite at the top of the building, had the air of not having been lived in for some time. "I see. What do you suggest I do, then? It all sounds rather hopeless."

"The only solution is to go over Grant's head to the Common Council. But you can't do so publicly. Grant would sack you at once. He has the power to do that."

"Then . . ."

"You have one possibility. I have considered it myself, but there is an old and bitter quarrel standing in the way."

"I'm afraid I don't understand."

"Samuel Devrey," Manon said. "He's a more distant cousin, but a cousin nonetheless. And he has a seat on the council."

"But if the Turner and Devrey family feud still counts for anything, and if you, a Turner by marriage, can't see him, why should I be—"

Manon shook her head. "I'm not referring to that ancient trouble. I don't even know what it was about. The unpleasantness between me and Sam Devrey is something entirely different."

After Joyful died and she heard about the opium (as inevitably she did), she'd gone to Mr. Astor to plead against the scheme, just as Joyful would have done. Her arguments counted for nothing. The profits were going to be enormous, Jacob Astor assured her. Young Sam Devrey had it all in hand, and Astor would see she had her fair share; he was, after all, an honorable man. She had, of course, refused any share in the money, and despite other interests they might have been said to have in common, she had not spoken to Astor or Sam Devrey again.

"What's between Cousin Samuel and myself doesn't involve you," Manon said. "But if anything is going to be done about Bellevue, it is the council that must do it. They can get rid of Tobias Grant for a start. See him, Cousin Nicholas. See Cousin Samuel. It's the only thing to do."

"Starting to snow," Sam Devrey said. "Middle of March and apparently winter's not yet done with us." Idle chatter to fill the awkward silence until this Dr. Nicholas Turner got around to saying what he'd come for.

The two men faced each other across a mahogany writing table in Sam's private office. The table was pristine and gleaming. The paperwork of Devrey Shipping was done in the hurly-burly of the outer room where half a dozen clerks stood behind tall desks. Even in here with the door closed there was a persistent hum from the activity outside.

"Not quite the end of winter yet," Nick agreed. He looked out the window; the snow seemed to have stopped. The ground floor of the Devrey counting house was a few feet above street level. Most buildings in New York were so constructed; the intent was to keep the smell of horse manure at a distance. It also meant that all Nick could see beyond the window were the tops of men's stovepipe hats bobbing along Little Dock Street. There were no bonnets among them. The press of commerce had driven the ladies from what the locals referred to as the down the town thick of things. It had driven away much else besides, Nick knew. Old two-story counting houses like this one were fast becoming obsolete. "I hear Devrey's is to have new premises, Cousin Samuel."

"We are, Dr. Turner." True, they were cousins, but most of the blood they shared was bad. Sam preferred not to acknowledge the relationship. "But somehow I don't think our new premises are what you've come to talk about." The new building would be five floors of white marble on prime land further up the town, Broadway and Canal Street. A temple raised to celebrate success, and Jacob Astor to get all the credit for it. The thought lodged in Sam's belly like a half-digested meal he could neither vomit up nor shit out. He kept his face and voice neutral, however. "You arrived from Providence, did you not, Doctor? A few weeks back?"

"Not quite two weeks, in fact." He was making a hash of this, Nick decided, and taking too long. Men of business were always in a hurry. Science, on the other hand, demanded patience and thoroughness. Since he'd decided that an appeal based on science would be better than one calling on human fellow feeling, it was up to him to bridge the gap. "I've been working at Bellevue since I came to New York."

"Ah yes, the almshouse hospital." Sam had presumed the visit would be about money. Now he knew what for.

"We are woefully underfunded, Cousin. Since you're a member of the Common Council I thought you might—"

"I'm afraid I have little influence over council business. Frankly, I doubt anyone has. Too many men with too many different agendas." Damned council nattered on about one thing or another at least twice a week. Sam didn't manage to attend more than one meeting in six, and those only because Jacob Astor insisted on it. It was he who had decided it was appropriate that the manager of Devrey's have a seat on the town's governing body; so, of course, it was arranged. But as far as Sam knew,

Jacob Astor had no interest in the Bellevue Almshouse. "Frankly, Dr. Turner, I believe we appropriate quite enough of the taxpayers' money to the care of sick and deranged paupers. I think it unlikely the council will entertain the idea of any increase."

"Then they are the most short-sighted men in this city, sir." Damn! Nothing would be served by losing his temper. "Cousin Samuel, allow me to explain. It's absolutely in the best interests of New York's taxpayers to—"

Sam raised a forestalling hand, snapped open his pocket watch, and laid it on the table between them. "Nearly four. I can give you five minutes more, Dr. Turner. Then you must excuse me. I have urgent matters of business."

His dinner more likely, and not to be disturbed by discussions of diseased paupers. "I take it that's five minutes exactly, Cousin Samuel. By your watch. To decide on who in this city of two hundred thousand should live and who should die."

"Actually, Dr. Turner, it is now four minutes and fifty seconds. And don't you think your characterization of the matter a bit extreme?"

"No, sir. I do not." Nicholas had conceived the plan in the few days since Manon Turner suggested he come here. Ask for money for something they would see as beneficial, then siphon some of it into the day-to-day care of the ill. "I'm suggesting we immediately inaugurate a program of scientific research at Bellevue. If we do so, we can learn ways to shorten the healing time for many diseases. Perhaps most. We can begin to understand the causes of the epidemics that so frequently lay waste to this city. Yellowing fever, typhus, the worst attacks of cholera . . ." Two summers earlier cholera had claimed almost four thousand lives. "If we understand these evils, I promise we can eventually cure them. Surely every taxpayer in the city would judge that an excellent use of his money."

Devrey's face remained impassive, but at least he was interested enough to ask a question. "How much money are we discussing, Dr. Turner?"

"Two thousand a year." Not very much in terms of the city budget the council oversaw.

"Two thousand a year, and we can cure diseases such as yellowing fever and typhus and cholera. That's your promise?"

"Not a promise. Nothing in science can be that certain. But I believe it to be a reasonable hope."

"I see. Well, for my part, Dr. Turner, I believe it to be totally unreasonable. Mankind has suffered these ills for all the years since Adam. Now you propose to cure them. With two thousand a year."

"I propose to study the methods by which they may be cured."

"At of all places the Almshouse Hospital."

"It's the perfect place to make a start, Cousin Samuel. I want to equip a laboratory and put a half-dozen promising medical students to doing anatomies under my close supervision. That's how—"

"Cutting up the bodies of the dead." Samuel snapped the watch closed. "It is a disgusting notion, Dr. Turner. Not to mention an illegal one. Not something the citizens of this city are likely to support, whatever you may think. Now, if you'll excuse me."

Over fifty years since the Doctors Mob Riot, when huge crowds took to the streets to protest grave robbing, but there was still a law saying only the bodies of hanged criminals could be dissected after death. Yet according to Manon, Sam Devrey had spent years in China. Surely that would broaden a man's mind. Instead his cousin sounded like every other man of business who could see no further than the bottom line of a ledger. "Sir, I promise you, in Europe men are already—"

"I must leave, Dr. Turner. And so must you." Sam stood up. So did Nick. They shared the same rangy height, Sam noted, but his hair was Devrey-black and his cousin's Turner-red. And no gray at Turner's temples, though his own were heavily salted. He was thirty-six, so Turner was—what? Sam wasn't sure, but some years younger certainly. "Good day to you, sir." Sam stood up and extended his hand.

Nick took it in a firm grip. "A final word if I may, Cousin." He didn't wait for permission. "If you're correct and the council won't appropriate the money, why don't you?"

"Me?"

"Yes. Well, not you personally. Devrey's. An act of philanthropy to mark your move to splendid new premises and celebrate the importance to New York's prosperity of this venerable company. It's an opportunity to associate Devrey Shipping with mankind's salvation." In the matter of flowery speech, that was the best he could do.

"You don't think small, Dr. Nicholas Turner. I'll grant you that." Sam started for the door. "But I think we'd best leave salvation to the preachers."

"No, we must not. At least not the kind of salvation that matters this side of the grave."

Sam's hat hung on a peg on the wall. In the new building his private room boasted a coat cupboard, and a fancy new window glazed with a single sheet of glass rather than a dozen small panes. He'd have a clear view as far as the harbor. He'd instructed them to build in a set of shelves as well, for the collection of jade ornaments he'd brought back from Canton and prized more highly than any other souvenirs, except, of course Mei-hua. "I'm afraid you overestimate my means, sir."

"A thousand a year, then. We could have a smaller facility and put three young men to work at—"

"Desecrating the bodies of the dead. We've already covered that, Dr. . . ." There was a slight hesitation, then, "Cousin Nicholas." Sam paused with his hand on the door. "Tell me one thing, if this is such an excellent plan, why hasn't it been put into effect at New York Hospital?"

"Because, as you point out, doing anatomies remains illegal. Besides, the bodies of the patients who die at New York Hospital are almost always claimed by relatives."

"While those who die in Bellevue have no relatives, at least none with sufficient money to give them a proper burial, and so are unclaimed."

"That is the usual circumstance," Nick admitted.

"However wretched their lives may be, Cousin Nicholas, does it not strike you as inhuman to deny them even the peace of a pauper's grave?"

Jesus God Almighty. The feral pigs roaming New York's streets lived better than the sick in the Almshouse Hospital, but Sam Devrey was worrying about what happened to their half-starved bodies after they were dead. "Progress always comes at some cost, Cousin Samuel. It is the nature of science to—"

Sam opened the door. The activity of the counting room assaulted them as a wall of sound. "Good day to you, Cousin Nicholas." His voice barely carried over the shouts of the clerks and captains and porters milling about. "I'm afraid we'll have no money to donate to worthy causes this year."

Chapter Five

SAM HAD CONSIDERED all the options for getting Mei-hua uptown and decided his one-horse buggy was the only possibility. The omnibus was far too public, and while a closed hansom cab might provide greater anonymity, it would mean one more person who knew where he'd taken her and of their association. The city's cabbies were noted for being hawk-eyed. If someone—Jacob Astor for instance—wanted to know something, he'd begin by questioning the cabbies.

The Devrey rig had a single seat covered in dark blue wool and a black leather canopy lined with red and blue stripes. The front was open, as were the sides; not much protection from the elements. Now, near to five P.M., there was a sharp chill in the air; it certainly didn't feel as if April would arrive in a few days. Mei-hua sat beside him and Ah Chee beside her. There wasn't another female to be seen until they reached Bleecker Street, and those who were out and about wore deep-brimmed bonnets and cloaks of black or blue or brown. Mei-hua's hair was pinned up with a jeweled ornament, and she wore a long green velvet shawl over a yellow silk skirt and jacket. Ah Chee wore her usual quilted homespun tunic and typical Chinese peasant's conical hat. Christ. In this place she looked more foreign and exotic than Mei-hua. Never mind. It would be dark soon. Besides, he couldn't have refused to bring Ah Chee; Mei-hua might die of terror without her. As it was she sat upright and stiff beside him. He could feel her trembling, but he was also aware of her glance darting everywhere, looking at everything.

Sam clucked softly to the horse and snapped the reins once or twice. Best get this done with and get Mei-hua home to a world she understood. But there was nothing to be done about the traffic. On Fourth Street they were trapped behind a large omnibus pulled by four great black horses, and hemmed in on one side by a wagon full of beer kegs and on the other by a fashionable carriage drawn by a pair of matched grays sporting tall red feathers in their headstalls.

Mei-hua nodded toward the grays and said something to Ah Chee. Sam didn't hear what it was because two newsboys were loudly hawking their wares as they threaded their way through the stalled vehicles. "Get the *Sun! Sun* here, only a penny!" "*Herald* for a copper," the other one shouted. "All the latest what's happenin'. A copper only."

The new presses were known to be able to print four thousand double impressions in an hour, and there were by count thirty-five penny papers being published in the city. They sent out men they called reporters to find stories. In fact, the exploits of the reporters were repeated with almost as much glee as the scandals and mayhem they uncovered. Sam fished a copper out of his vest pocket and signaled the lad who had just handed one of his papers through the window of the omnibus. "You there. I'll have a *Herald*."

Sam tucked the paper inside his coat. The omnibus suddenly clanged its bell and jerked forward. Sam's horse moved on without needing a command.

She called herself Mrs. Langton; Sam had never seen a Mr. Langton. He'd had to screw up his courage to come here the first time nearly a year ago. He'd seen the notice in the *Herald*. "Ladies requiring healthful assistance in disallowing a family beyond one's means" were encouraged to apply.

Sam had become a regular visitor to Mrs. Langton's rooms on Christopher Street, in what was still called Greenwich Village, though these days the streets were cobbled and the pavements flagged, and the village had been swallowed up by the expanding city. Mrs. Langton allowed him to collect a week's worth of the packets of powder very early each Monday morning before she received her regular clientele. Sam paid twice the going rate for the privilege of such privacy. That made him a specially favored customer, and meant there had been no difficulty arranging a discreet early evening appointment.

As promised, no one else was in her sitting room when they arrived. Sam carried a shivering Mei-hua in his arms, while Ah Chee tottered behind.

"This is the young woman I told you about. Do remember that she speaks no English and doesn't understand our ways. You must be particularly gentle, Mrs. Langton. Where do I bring her?"

Lilac Langton rushed to open a door behind a velvet curtain. "Right in here, Mr. Smith." Of course that wasn't his real name. Lilac had gone out of her way to find out about him after the first time he came. But Mr. Smith he'd told her to call him, so Mr. Smith he was. "You just put her on that treatment sofa over there and step outside and make yourself comfortable. Won't be long, I promise."

Ah Chee pushed in behind, chattering all the while. "My lord should take us home right away. Good way to do whatever he wants to do. Good way. Hor Taste Bad excellent for doing—"

"*Bi zue. Bi zue.*" Quiet, he told her. "If you had done what you were supposed to do, this wouldn't be necessary."

Ah Chee went on chattering as if he hadn't spoken. Sam ignored her and laid Mei-hua on the sofa. She was staring up at him, her eyes pleading. "*Bie dan xing,*" Sam murmured. Do not worry your heart. "Better this way for now, my love. You're too young. Later," he promised. "Later we'll have a son."

"Whatever he says, you talk nothing," Ah Chee had repeatedly warned her plum blossom. "I will complain, but you talk nothing. *Tai-tai* is dreadful bad liar. If you talk, my plan will spill out of your little rosebud mouth and everything will be spoiled. No talk. No talk."

It wasn't difficult for Mei-hua to do as Ah Chee instructed. She was truly terrified. The Lord Samuel and Ah Chee and the strange white woman however were all talking at once.

"You tell her I stay. Tell her. Tell her. Please, lord. *Tai-tai* will—"

"Stay. Stay. Understand. Understand, Ah Chee. Stop making tongue noise." He turned to Mrs. Langton. "The girl is from China. And very frightened. You must allow her old servant to remain with her. I will tell her to sit there and only hold the girl's hand. She won't interfere, I promise."

"No one else is allowed in the room, Mr. Smith. That's my rule. This is a delicate affair and I am very particular about—"

"Yes, of course. I know you are." Sam reached into the breast pocket of his swallowtail frock coat. Carolina had bought him the fine leather billfold the previous Christmas. Now that paper money was becoming so common, she'd said, it was sure to be of use to him. "Eighty dollars, Mrs. Langton. That's what we agreed, isn't it?"

"Yes, sir, that's correct." Her services were as cheap as ten for ordinary women, but for a gent like this one . . . She was a fool. She should have said ninety.

Sam counted out a thick wad of bills. "We'll make it a hundred, because I know you'll take special care. And you will allow the old woman to stay. Good New York currency," he added, when he held out the money.

Lilac took the wad without a word and slipped the bills into her pocket, then took his elbow and guided him to the door. "Very well, the servant may remain. You can wait outside, Mr. Smith. Now don't be alarmed, whatever you hear. I'm well thought of, you know. Ladies come to me because I know my trade and do it quickly. There you go, not to worry. Lilac Langton has everything in hand."

She'd been Francy Finders back in Spitalfields in London, then Francy Langton after she married poor Joe who had taken a fever and died during the crossing he'd so looked forward to, and picked God knows how many pockets to make possible. "New start in America, Francy," he'd promised her. Well, a newer start than she'd bargained for, that was sure. That's why she'd decided to take a new name, to sort of mark the occasion. So Lilac Langton it was who closed the door behind Mr. Samuel Devrey, who called himself Mr. Smith, and turned to look at the two women he'd brought her.

"Well now," she said, pulling on the homespun smock she wore over her frock for this sort of thing and moving purposefully across the room. "Sooner begun, sooner ended. That's what I always say. Let's get you in position, missy."

What Lilac called her treatment sofa was an upholstered couch with a curved back at one end and neither sides nor footboard. She moved to the bottom, intending to open the girl's legs, but the dress was tight all the way to the ankles. God's truth, what decent woman would wear a dress like that? She started to push it up, but the servant scurried to where Lilac stood, interrupting the process.

"How much? How much you only pretend take son?"

Lilac didn't understand a word. "Get out of my way, old woman, else I'll have to get Mr. Smith in here. Now go sit beside her. Hold her hand if you like." She gave Ah Chee a little shove to make her point. "Move yourself!" She'd managed to get the dress rolled up to the girl's hips by then. Not even a petticoat beneath it. God's truth.

"How much only do this?" Ah Chee pinched Mei-hua's thigh as hard as she could. Mei-hua screamed. Ah Chee pinched again. Mei-hua screamed again. "More loud. More loud," Ah Chee mumbled and pinched a third time, eliciting a shriek that was bound to be heard in the room beyond. With her other hand she withdrew the purse containing her secret treasure. "How much? How much?"

Lilac still couldn't understand a word the woman was saying, but the bulging purse required no explanation. "You're offering me money, is that it? To do what?"

"You make this. This." Ah Chee waved the hand that wasn't holding the purse in the vicinity of the plum blossom's beautiful privates. "No go inside. Only outside. Make this. This." She simulated the circular scraping motions of a proper baby clean-out. Easy to do since she'd seen the procedure dozens of times back on the women's sampans of the river pirate dog turd, who had caused all this trouble by not giving the girl to a proper civilized husband. "Like this. Like this." More hand gestures in the air between the girl's splayed thighs. "How much? How much?"

Lilac was beginning to understand the words as well as the gestures. "What will it cost, eh? To only pretend to do the job. Like this?" She repeated the gesture the old Chinee woman had made. "I can't do that, love. I've my reputation to look after. All I got's my good name, ducky. Now sit down."

Ah Chee didn't understand the words, but she didn't have to. They were bargaining now, eventually a price would be agreed upon. And this one time she honestly didn't care if she got the better of the transaction. "Say how much," she repeated, jiggling the purse so the coins inside could be heard.

Lilac's eyes narrowed and she drew her tongue across her lips. "How much you got?"

Ah Chee guessed the meaning of the words. She opened the purse and held it out.

Crikey. Chock full of coins, and not just coppers, neither. Lilac snatched at it. "I'll take that." After a moment's hesitation Ah Chee released her grip and let her have it. "I'll just play around a bit, not really scrape her out clean like I should. Enough so he'll think I've done my job." She jerked her head toward the outer room. "Get a few proper moans out of her. Maybe a touch of blood. But she'll probably go on and have a bouncing baby anyway. It happens sometimes. All right, clear off and let me get to it."

Ah Chee allowed herself to be shoved out of the way. With one hand the woman reached for one of her long needles and with the other she spread the plum blossom's privates.

Ah Chee flung herself at the woman. "Outside. Outside. Only outside. You take money and say—"

Lilac inserted the lady needle at the same moment the Chinese woman's shoulder made contact with her arm.

Mei-hua shrieked, a long extended note of agony.

Lilac yanked out the needle. There was no blood but there was a rush of fluid. "Stupid old fool," she snapped at Ah Chee. "You made me go in too far. Broke the sac I have. She's bound to miscarry now, and it's your fault, not mine." Never mind. The purse full of coins was deep in her pocket, and she had no intention of returning it. Lilac hurried to the sitting room door and flung it open. Samuel Devrey was standing just outside. Pouring sweat, as she'd known he would be. Damned men. Took whatever they wanted, then shivered and shook at the results. "She's done. Take her home and let her rest for a few days. Better if she stays abed for a time."

Sam strode across to the couch without answering. Ah Chee was busy rearranging Mei-hua's clothes. The girl was sobbing quietly. He gathered her up in his arms and carried her out of the room. Ah Chee hurried after them, but before she left she turned and gave Lilac a look of such malevolence the woman felt she'd been marked by the eye of Satan himself.

Mei-hua stopped sobbing soon after they left the abortionist, but by the time the buggy turned into Cherry Street she was moaning softly and hunched over in pain. They pulled up at number thirty-nine, Leper Face appeared and took the horse's reins. Sam jumped down, then turned and lifted Mei-hua out of the rig. He hurried into the building, leaving Leper Face to help Ah Chee descend and scurry after him. Damned old woman was mumbling but Sam paid no attention. This whole mess was her fault. If she hadn't allowed Mei-hua to stop taking the powders, as he was quite sure she had, it never would have happened. As soon as Mei-hua was well enough not to need her, he would beat Ah Chee to within an inch of her life.

He'd finally gotten Mei-hua inside her own apartment and Ah Chee still wouldn't leave him alone. "What is it, damn you?" She was tugging at his coat and speaking in such high-pitched hysterical tones he couldn't understand her words. "What? What?"

"Blood. Blood." Tears were running down Ah Chee's lined face. "Look. Look. Blood. Blood."

Sam laid Mei-hua on the bed. The back of both her green cloak and her yellow skirt were soaked in blood. "Mei-hua! Dear God!" She moaned louder and drew her knees up in shuddering agony. Her chest rose and fell rapidly and her face was drained of color.

"Look after her," Sam shouted at Ah Chee as he ran from the room. "I'll get help and be right back."

Sam delivered his card to a toothless old man who appeared to be a porter of sorts. Christ Almighty God, who'd have thought there could be any place that looked like this in New York. He'd heard stories about Bellevue, but the reality . . . "Take this to Dr. Turner and say I must see him at once. I'm his cousin. Urgent family business. Urgent, do you understand?"

"Aye, right enough."

The man disappeared. Sam stood staring straight ahead, trying not to see the human misery that surrounded him. The smell, however, could not be ignored. He fished out a handkerchief and pressed it to his nose. Someone tugged at his trouser leg and he looked down, expecting to see a child. It was a man with no legs, supporting his torso on a wheeled wooden platform. His hands were shackled to the contraption with just enough length of chain to allow him to push himself about. "I am a king sir," the man whispered. "Of a distant country. If you will take word of my imprisonment to my people, you will be handsomely rewarded."

"What? Yes, yes, of course. I'll go right now." Sam opened the door and stepped outside into the fresh air. He took a few deep breaths, but however welcome they were, he couldn't remain out here. Turner would think he'd left. He pushed the door open again just as his cousin was coming down the stairs.

"It is you," Nick said. "I thought it must be some sort of mistake when I was handed your card."

"No mistake." Sam kept his voice low. The legless man was trying again to get his attention, but Sam ignored him. "Look, I'm in desperate trouble and I don't know where else to turn. My buggy's just outside the gate. Will you come with me?"

"Trouble? But I—"

"You doctors take an oath, don't you? Can't refuse anyone who needs you."

"I don't need an oath to tell me my duty. But surely you have your own doctor to call on."

"There isn't time to explain. For the love of God, man. You can't refuse me."

Nick hesitated then said, "Wait right here. I'll get my bag."

When they were in Devrey's buggy and heading south, he asked, "Is it your wife?" Cousin Manon had shared the details of Devrey's domestic life. "I take it the midwife can't cope."

"It's not my wife. At least, not the way you mean."

Nick stared at him a moment, then looked away.

"No come in. No come in." Taste Bad stood at the door to Mei-hua's apartment, resisting Ah Chee's efforts to pull him inside. He had not wanted to come even this far; it had taken some time for Leper Face Lee to persuade him. "Do nothing for *tai-tai* unless Lord Samuel say. When the lord comes back, when his tongue say come in, Taste Bad come in."

"What kind of *yi* you are?" Ah Chee demanded. "Devil *yi*, just like they say. My lady sick, very too much *yin*. Needs *yi*. You come inside give her something make pain go away." Mei-hua had expelled the bloody clotted mass that would have been a son in screaming agony minutes after the Lord Samuel left. Ah Chee had thrown the thing on the kitchen fire. Tomorrow she would light a dozen joss sticks to purify the room for Zao Shen, the kitchen god, whose picture hung above the hearth. Right now there were more pressing duties. "You come inside," she insisted, tugging once more at Taste Bad's arm. "Give *tai-tai* something make more *yang*. Make *tai-tai* feel better."

Leper Face, standing a few feet behind them on the stairs, was the first to hear the street door open and shut. He leaned over the bannister, peering down to the hall. "Lord Samuel come. Bring someone."

Taste Bad yanked himself away from Ah Chee and turned and fled down the stairs, disappearing into a doorway on the floor below just as Sam and Nick came into sight. Leper Face bowed repeatedly as the two men rushed by him. "How is she?" Sam demanded, pushing past Ah Chee in the doorway.

"*Tai-tai* not good. Much pain."

Sam felt a rush of relief. She was still alive. "Then why in hell aren't you with her instead of standing out here? I saw Taste Bad leave. Did he give her anything?"

"No, No. Not without lord's permission."

Nick, who understood nothing of what was said, stood just inside the door taking in the colorful, exotic furnishing of the extraordinary room. There couldn't be another like it in all New York. "Where's my patient?"

"In here." Samuel led him to the bedroom. Mei-hua lay on her side in the bed. Her skirt and jacket had been removed and she wore a loose silk robe. Her knees were folded up to her chest. She hugged them, moaning softly and rocking back and forth. Sam put his hand on her forehead; it was hot and dry. Dear God, if anything happened to her . . . "I'm here, my love. I've brought you a proper doctor. He'll soon have you well." He straightened and turned to Nick. "You'll have seen this sort of thing before, I'm sure."

"An abortion gone bad? Yes, plenty of times." Nick took off his coat and began rolling up his sleeves. "Is there water here? And some soap?"

Sam shouted to Ah Chee to bring both. Nick stood waiting. "Aren't you going to examine her? I can leave if you . . ."

"Stay or go. Please yourself. I shall not examine the lady until I've washed my hands."

Sam started to protest, but Ah Chee arrived with the soap and a basin of water. Nick washed his hands carefully, then went to his patient. Mei-hua moaned in pain when he touched her, and Sam hastily backed out of the room.

❧

"She miscarried very recently," Nick said. "Not long before we arrived, I warrant, though I saw no sign of the fetus." He cast a quick look at the old servant woman, wondering if she'd performed the abortion, but he knew better than to ask. "I took care of the afterbirth, cleaned her up, and stopped the bleeding. There's every reason to believe she will be fine. Incidentally, the uterus seems intact. It frequently is not after these procedures, but in this case"—he shrugged—"she can probably have more children. If that's of any importance to you."

"Look, none of this is what it seems. I care deeply for Mei-hua. I was in China for years, you know, and—"

"It's no business of mine," Nick interrupted. "Though aborting a pregnancy is illegal now. You must know, since you sit on the council."

"Yes, I know."

"And?"

Sam shrugged.

"You won't be reporting the abortionist to the authorities, then?" Nick asked.

"I can't—" Samuel broke off and looked toward the bedroom. "And you . . . The law is fairly recent, you know. But she hadn't quickened. I'm sure of that. You need not—"

"No, I need not."

"Thank you." If Turner had stood on the legalities and demanded to know the abortionist's name, there would have been a scandal and hell to pay. It might even have made the papers. Carolina . . . Christ, what a mess. "Thank you very much."

"No need." Nick pulled on his coat and hefted his bag. "Go in and see her if you like. I'll find my own way uptown."

Chapter Six

THE BAMBOO ROD broke at the twelfth blow. It was only the third to land on Ah Chee's bent shoulders. She was an easy target, kneeling alone in the center of the room, accepting the punishment as her due, but Mei-hua had flailed at nearly everything else. The floor was littered with splintered china and shattered glass. Now, holding the stub of bamboo, she stopped cursing and broke into tears. "Promise. Promise. I fix. I fix. You said. Now my belly is empty and my son is dead. Useless old woman." She flung what was left of the rod across the room. It bounced off a large jade statue of Fu Xing the god of happiness and landed on the floor among the other remains of her rage.

Ah Chee, who had been expecting this tantrum for the three weeks since the plum blossom's son was taken from her belly, got to her feet and went to the kitchen, returning with a small corn husk broom and a big pail. "*Yang gwei zih yi*, doctor with hair the color of first-part-of-the-flow-blood say you will have another son. I heard him."

"He does not speak any civilized words. I tried and he did not understand me." Mei-hua sat in the lacquered throne chair and lifted her legs so that Ah Chee could sweep beneath them.

Ah Chee giggled. "Old useless woman speaks the *yang gwei zih* words." She shook her head over the broken bits of a particularly pretty lapis lazuli vase and dumped them into the pail.

It was one of the things Mei-hua had puzzled about all the while she lay abed recovering. "I saw you give devil woman money, but words too. Why did she take your money and stab my son to death anyway? Why?"

"Who knows why foreign devil woman does things? I have burned twenty joss sticks that she may have boils in twenty places. All over her privates." Every time she lit incense on behalf of the plum blossom's healing, she added a stick for vengeance.

Mei-hua looked thoughtful. "You can really understand the foreign devil words?"

"Only some of them," Ah Chee admitted. "Always when I go to the market, I practice. Learn to say more. Sometimes easier to say than to hear."

Mei-hua nodded. When she still lived on the sampan of her father, she had been tutored in English. It had proved impossible to learn. Sometimes she could make her tongue form the strange sounds, but she could almost never make her ears hear them; always they were noise without meaning. No matter, the Lord Samuel had said. It is not important. You are my princess, whether or not you learn the words of my kingdom. No matter. No matter. But it did matter. Only now was she learning how much. "I should go to the market with you," she said. "Learn to speak foreign devil language."

Ah Chee nodded toward the plum blossom's three-inch golden lilies. "How you walk on these rock streets? Besides, *tai-tai* does not go to market."

"Rock streets." That was another of the things she had been thinking of in these three weeks of misery. "When Lord Samuel took us to that place. The houses we saw all nicer than this house. Why *tai-tai* not in best house? Lord Samuel gives you half a string of copper cash every week to buy food. Very rich man. Why *tai-tai* not have best house in city?"

Ah Chee's heart fell into her belly, just as it used to do when the plum blossom was a child and demanded to know if she was to be sent away from the sampans of her father and everything familiar to her, as the other women said she would be. How to answer? Ah Chee's own mother had told her that when she did not tell the truth her tongue got shorter. Enough lies and she would have no tongue at all and be silent forever. Maybe go, maybe stay, she had told the girl back then. Who knows anything for sure? "You think any house more beautiful inside than this one? Have pretty things. Now you break them all. Stupid girl. Stupid." She swept up the last of the mess and dumped it in the bucket, then picked it up and started to go.

"Wait. You are not speaking true words, old woman. I am not a child to tell maybe this, maybe that. Now I am *tai-tai*. Why I am not in most beautiful house in this New York place? Why?"

Ah Chee shook her head and grumbled something under her breath. In the kitchen she dumped the pail of shards into an even bigger pail of rubbish. When that was full, she would pull it as far as the front hall and the man they called Empty Buckets would come and take it away. In the big house far away in the part of the city the foreign devils called up the town—even further than the house of the devil woman whose privates must now be so full of boils she could neither sit nor stand—would there be civilized people to do such things as take away full buckets of rubbish? People who would understand who was the plum blossom *tai-tai* and how much respect she deserved? Probably not. That must be why the *tai-tai* was here and the giant size yellow hair concubine was in a far up the town house. One made of stone not wood, with a tree in front whose waving branches kept away evil spirits, so the *feng shui* would be perfect and evil devil woman not break her promise and steal the child out of her belly. Very bad if concubine have son before *tai-tai*. Very bad.

Ah Chee gazed up at the picture of the kitchen god and reached for a joss stick. Then, on second thought, two more.

"Thank you for meeting me here," Sam said.

"No trouble at all." The boat yard was on Thirty-fourth Street and the East River. Nick could look downstream a short way and see the Bellevue dock. According to Cousin Manon, in the summer of '32, when the cholera was raging and the streets were thick with the smoke of bonfires burning everything the sick had touched, victims were ferried upriver and simply dumped in a heap on that dock. New York Hospital flatly refused to admit cholera patients. Bellevue took in two thousand, warding them in tents pitched on the shoreline. The dead house sometimes held as many as forty bodies at a time because no one was available to bury them.

It was May, and spring was in full bud and blossom. If this summer of '34 was to bring another feverish misery, Nick knew, it would soon be upon them. Maybe he should be thinking of a secondary off-loading place. "Is this yard new?" he asked, looking around.

"Sort of. It belongs to Danny Parker. He and his father and grandfather before him have looked after Devrey ships for eighty years. Their big yard is south of here on Montgomery Street. This up-the-island location is an extension."

A few cows grazed peacefully in a nearby pasture, otherwise the landscape was empty. "Thirty-fourth Street's pretty isolated," Nick said. "Seems a fine place for a shipyard."

"Yes," Sam agreed, "and the river's deep here. Parker plans to put the ways just there in that cove."

"To build steamships, I imagine."

"Maybe," Sam said softly. "Maybe not. We'll see."

"I came down from Providence on a Black Ball steam packet," Nick said. "Bellowed black smoke all the way and did the entire journey in fourteen hours. Under sail it used to take twenty-six in a stiff breeze. More if you weren't lucky with the wind."

"Do you have any idea how much coal that required?" Devrey asked. "Or how many men to keep stoking the boilers? I know everyone says the future is in steam, but I'm not so sure. In theory, if you could raise enough canvas, clean, sweet wind would beat coal any day of the week."

Nick shrugged. Sam Devrey hadn't asked him up here to talk about shipping. "Possibly. More your line of country than mine."

"That's not why we're here. I expect you know that."

"It occurred to me."

"Mei-hua—her name means plum blossom—is doing remarkably well. No ill effects at all that I can see."

"I'm glad to hear it."

Both men stared out at the empty river. It seemed to Nick that he was the more uncomfortable, as if he were the one who had been caught letting his appetites disorder his life. "Look here, Cousin Samuel, I'm not in the judgement business. It's none of my affair what you do."

"But I involved you," Sam said. "And Mei-hua is under my protection. She understands nothing of our ways, of life here in America."

"She has nothing to fear from me."

"I didn't for a moment think she had." That was not entirely true. It was one of the reasons he'd asked Turner to meet him here. If the man said something to the wrong person, the scandal could be ruinous. "I was in China for many years. I learned to appreciate their customs, how they do things."

The way Nick heard it from Cousin Manon, what Sam learned was how much opium Devrey Shipping could smuggle into China and how fast, and that ever since, he had been Astor's creature. "Yes, I understand."

"No, I don't think you do. In China—in all of Asia in fact—few men have only one wife."

"Good God. Are you implying . . ." One saw and heard a great deal in the practice of medicine, but a confession of bigamy was novel in his experience.

"As far as Mei-hua knows," Sam said, "she is married to me. Of course it's not a Christian marriage. But—"

"And she knows you have an American wife?"

"No," Sam said. "She does not. And Mrs. Devrey does not know about Mei-hua."

"Yet you're telling me the whole story."

"As much of it as I think you need to know, Cousin Nicholas."

"Which makes me wonder why you believe I need to know any of it."

"So you will understand the need to be discreet. Why else?"

"I'm not sure, since being discreet is part of the practice of medicine."

A man wearing a carpenter's apron walked past them, tipped his cap, and went as far as the inlet where the ways were to be built. After a minute they could hear the sound of his hammer.

"Conditions seem quite terrible at your Bellevue," Sam remarked. "I was appalled at what I saw."

If anything the place was worse now that warmer weather had arrived. To make more room on the wards, the insane, still in their shackles and straitjackets, were transferred to outdoor cages at sunup. They were supposed to be brought inside to sleep, but they seldom were. Nick had an almighty row with Grant about it. That didn't change anything. "I told you how bad things were when I came to see you the first time, Cousin Samuel. It's why I want the council to look into the matter. Tobias Grant is stealing from the poor and the indigent, not to mention the New York taxpayers."

"Look, I'm in your debt and I know it. But I have very little influence on the council. And if what you say is true, increasing the hospital's budget would just mean more for Grant to skim."

"He serves at the council's pleasure. They can be rid of him whenever they like."

"And give the job to you, perhaps?"

"I wouldn't take Grant's job if anyone were daft enough to offer it to me. I'm no administrator. And contrary to what you seem to think, I'm not ambitious. I'm interested in medical research, Cousin Samuel."

"So you say. Look, Tobias Grant has powerful friends on the council. He couldn't get away with his activities otherwise. It's far more likely you'd be the one to go if questions about his practices were raised."

Nick shrugged. "I'm a decent enough doctor. I'll always find work."

"You're better than decent on my evidence. I wasn't threatening you, Cousin. Simply telling you how the land lies." Sam reached into the breast pocket of his coat. "This is for the hospital, but I've made it out to you. Do with it what you will."

Sam held out a check, but Nick didn't take it. "All you owe me is the fee for a night visit to a sickbed. That's a dollar here in New York, I'm told. In any case, it's waived."

"Don't be pigheaded, man, take the money. I'm in your debt. A few weeks ago you were keen to have me finance a laboratory for the hospital. This isn't anywhere near the two thousand you wanted, but it's a start. And as you say, the hospital is in dire need."

Nick hesitated a moment more, than took the check. It was, as Devrey had said, made out to him; three hundred dollars drawn on what appeared to be Sam Devrey's personal account. "That's extremely generous."

"As much as I can afford just now," Sam said. "There may be more in the future."

"Look, I'm not . . . I told you, your personal circumstances are no concern of mine."

"I know you're not an extortionist, Cousin Nicholas. I'm simply grateful."

"Then on behalf of the Bellevue patients, thank you."

"Not at all. Now I have two questions. About medicine."

"Happy to answer if I can."

"First, that business of washing your hands the other night. What was that all about?"

"Germs," Nick said. "Minute beasties. There's a theory that they cause the spread of disease by being transferred from the sick to the healthy. A Dutchman named Antoni van Leeuwenhoek first identified them nearly two hundred years ago. Most medical men don't agree, say the germs are spontaneously generated by the disease itself. Happens I subscribe to the former theory. So I try to wash my hands before touching a patient."

"Soap and water flushes away these invisible germs, does it?"

"Mostly. What's the second question?"

Sam turned so he was once more staring at the river. "These pills and powders that are supposed to stop a woman conceiving a child. Are they any good?"

"On the evidence," Nick said quietly, "it doesn't seem that they are."

"On the evidence, not much good at all," Sam agreed. "Is there nothing to be done then? If it's not the right moment for a child, I mean."

"If the sperm doesn't have an opportunity to fertilize the woman's ovum," Nick began, "then—" He broke off, seeing the look of total puzzlement on the other man's face. "Look, it's the union of the male seed, the sperm, carried in the semen, with one of the ova—" He tried again. "The eggs, man. The woman's eggs and the man's seed. That's how babies happen."

"The woman's . . . But I thought . . ." Sam felt himself coloring and was the more embarrassed for that. "I know about the womb, of course. Still . . ."

"No reason you would know about the new findings. Chap over in St. Petersburg published his research a few years ago. It seems that women produce eggs. Just like chickens."

"Chicken eggs!"

"No, of course not. That's an entirely different system of reproduction. I was simply trying to give you a familiar example. According to Professor von Baer, women have eggs as well." Nick noted his cousin's grimace but plowed on. "Tiny, microscopic actually, and not capable of becoming a child unless the male seed, the sperm, carried in the semen, is—"

"You've been to St. Petersburg?"

Nick sighed. "Never."

"Then how do you know about this von whats-his-name? Is he a medical doctor?"

"A professor of zoology. His results have been published in many languages. I've read about them."

"Zoology? I begin to think, Cousin Nicholas, that you are entirely mad."

"Trust me, Cousin Samuel, it's quite straightforward. If the semen does not reach the ovum, and the fertilized egg does not then become implanted in the uterus, or the womb as you call it, there can be no pregnancy."

"Good God, man. If one has to live like a monk—"

"That's not what I'm suggesting. It's only at the end of the act of love that fertilization can take place."

"Yes, I see. Foolish of me, I suppose. I just never thought . . ."

Nick wanted to laugh. Instead he nodded and tried to look grave.

Coitus interruptus. The Greeks and the Romans had known of its effectiveness thousands of years ago. Now Sam Devrey did as well.

"All right, madam," Maggie O'Brien said. "Time to start pushing."

Past time, by God. Carolina had been in agony since the previous midnight, and it was now nearly dinner time the following day.

It was her mother-in-law who had shown the most interest in the procedure during those long hours of misery. Her Aunt Lucy had spent the night sitting in a corner, tatting and sighing and occasionally wiping away a sympathetic tear each time the midwife said, "Not yet, madam. Do you a real disservice I would if I let you push now." Until just a few moments before, when she'd murmured to Celinda Devrey, who was leaning over her shoulder, using a lorgnette and peering carefully between her daughter-in-law's legs, "Here we go, two thumbs wide. That's what we've been waiting for. Now, madam. Push! Push!"

Carolina pushed. And for all that she'd promised herself she would be brave, screamed. As long and as hard as she could. It did seem to help some.

Lucy finally dropped her tatting and went to stand by the top of the bed, giving her niece her two hands to hold and encouraging Carolina to squeeze as hard as she liked. "There you go, dearest. There you go."

"Now wait for the next cramp, madam," Mrs. O'Brien said. "The wee one's almost here. I can see it." If this were a normal birth, she'd say she could see the top of the babe's head, but what she was looking at was the foot of one leg and the knee of the other. The left leg was bent behind the right, and the child was being born wrong way round. She'd known that to be the case for the past three hours. She had tried turning it. Sometimes a clever midwife with good technique—and Maggie O'Brien prided herself on her technique—could do that if the woman's hips were very wide and the babe truly tiny. It wasn't often possible at a first birth, and certainly not this time. The girl was really quite slim and the babe a goodly size. "Once more now, madam. Push!"

The pain was fearsome; Carolina had never felt the like. She squeezed Aunt Lucy's hands as hard as she could and bore down. "Oh! Oh dear!"

Both the babe's legs free and out now, the left not permanently bent as the midwife had first feared. And it was a boy. Sure and couldn't she see his little willie plain as you like. The mother-in-law made a cooing sound behind her. Wanted a boy apparently. Didn't they all. Particularly this sort with so much to pass on.

"Push, madam. We're almost there. Push as hard as you can."

"It's a boy, my dear!" Celinda Devrey burst out. "You've made a bit of a muddle of it and he's coming feet first, but you're producing a son and heir for Samuel. Now do push harder and get the job done."

Lucy Philmore née James drew in a quick breath. Babies born the wrong way round were the curse of the James women. She'd had only one pregnancy before her husband died, and that babe had suffocated before she could push his head out. And wasn't that precisely how poor dear Penelope had died, birthing this girl who now lay here under the same malediction? When Carolina married, Wilbur wanted to give the girl the bed that had been his and his dead wife's. Utter folly, Lucy told him. *My sister died in that bed. Do you want that to happen to Carolina?* Of course he had not and had a new bed made for the newlyweds. Solid mahogany with four posts, each topped with a winged cherub. It did not seem to have helped much. "The shoulders," Lucy whispered in Celinda Devrey's direction. "Are the shoulders out yet?"

"Just coming," Celinda said, leaning further forward and peering more closely at the bloody carry-on in the bed. No point in being squeamish, not now when her grandson was appearing. But imagine Samuel insisting that the midwife wash her hands before she could go upstairs and attend Carolina. How utterly silly. If her son had any idea just what a messy sort of event this was . . . If any man had, for that matter. Ah well, it probably wouldn't put them off their pleasure even so. "Push, Carolina! Push!"

The midwife shot her a sharp look. "I'll say when, if you don't mind, madam." She'd been busy trying to adjust things so the girl would push out one shoulder at a time, and her practiced hands could feel the onset of each contraction. The time to push was when nature was lending a helping hand. The girl was shrieking pretty steadily now. She'd been marvelous, no doubt about it, but a point came for them all when it just seemed that a ripping good holler was the only way to get through the thing. She didn't hold with all this nonsense of keep 'em silent so the men downstairs won't worry. Why shouldn't they bloody worry? All their doing, after all. "Now, madam. One good push will do it. Now!"

Carolina used all her breath to push as hard as she might and for as long as she could. Then she drew in one more and let it loose in a fearsome yell.

"It's the head coming now," Celinda reported eagerly. "Little Lansing's shoulders are free and clear and only his head to go!" She was quite breathless with excitement. Samuel would be beside himself with pride. She would be well ensconced as little Lansing's only living grandmother. It was really too perfect. If only Carolina would get it done and over with.

Maggie O'Brien had no time for either the woman gawping over her shoulder or the one at the top of the bed. The little lad's shoulders were out now and the cord looked to be in the right position, not wrapped around the neck, thanks be to Holy Mary and all the Saints. But the head—the midwife could do nothing about that but pull and encourage. Here it was, the final contraction probably. And depending on how long it took, they would get either a dead baby or a live one. "Now, madam. Summon all your strength for one final push. That's it! That's it exactly! Well done, madam. Here he is!"

Dorothy had earlier been sent downstairs to prepare dinner for Mr. Devrey and his father-in-law, but the men barely touched their food, wincing visibly each time Carolina's shrieks shattered the peace of the dining room. Then came silence.

Both men looked at the ceiling, as if they might be able to see what was happening above their heads. After a time Wilbur Randolf gave up the pretense of eating his mutton chop and went to the sideboard, poured himself a full snifter of brandy, and knocked it back as if it were water. "Get you something, Sam? Trying business this."

Sam shook his head. He was too queasy for drink. What did that quiet overhead portend? What if Carolina were to lose this child? Or if it were deformed or otherwise defective? Would it be his fault? His punishment for Mei-hua? No, of course not. He'd spent too long in Asia. He was a Christian. Well, if he was anything. The Christian God was supposed to be just. Fair enough. Carolina hadn't done anything wrong. But there was no accounting for good and bad joss; he'd seen enough of that to know.

"Congratulations, Samuel dear." Celinda threw open the doors to the dining room. "You have a healthy son."

Randolf held the brandy snifter in a white-knuckled grip. "My daughter? How is Carolina?"

"She's fine as well."

"Can I see her?"

"Yes, she's ready now. Come along, both of you." Samuel still hadn't said a word. He was staring straight ahead as if he'd been struck dumb. "Come along, dear boy," his mother repeated. "Come and see our precious little Lansing."

"No," Sam said.

"What do you mean no? Surely you want to see—"

"Yes, of course I want to see my son. I mean he's not to be called Lansing."

Wilbur Randolf made a sound that implied satisfaction.

"Carolina and I talked it over," Sam said. "His name will be Zachary." He pushed past his mother and took the stairs two at a time. A healthy son. The best possible joss, by God. His duty done and over with, and Carolina bound to be entirely occupied now that she was a mother. Excellent joss.

Manon was coming down the hall when Nick spotted her. "There you are, Cousin Manon. I've been looking for you."

"Here I am, Cousin Nicholas."

As usual, she had a basket over her arm and she wore her plain, black-ribboned bonnet and dark gray cloak.

"You've not been on the wards yet, I take it," Nick said.

"Not yet? Is there someone you want me to look for?"

"Yes, there is. A little girl called Bridget."

"They are a great many little girls called Bridget in this place," Manon said. "What is her complaint?"

Nick hesitated. "She has two broken wrists," he said finally. "And has suppurating wounds on her back and shoulders."

"You mean she's been tied up and beaten to within an inch of her life, do you not? Repeatedly."

"That's what I mean, yes."

"I take it she comes from our own Bellevue orphanage, that Christian refuge of the abandoned child."

He nodded, too miserable to speak, as if it were his fault.

In the normal way of things Nick probably would have known nothing about this particular Bridget, but young Monty Chance—the resident doctor working under him—had shown himself quite conscientious. He had asked for Nick's help setting the delicate wrist bones. "Don't want to mess it up, sir. I take her for five or six. How will she live the rest of her life if her hands are useless?"

How indeed? They had done the best they could, but the girl was never going to have a normal amount of flexibility in those hands; presuming, of course, that the wounds on her back didn't go black with poison and kill her before disabled hands became something to contend with.

He could not simply let it go by.

The warden of the orphanage was at dinner in his private apartments when Nick found him. Indeed, the enticing smell of cooked meat permeated the place, though by all accounts the children were fed on porridge and watery soup. So, it was said, they wouldn't have expectations beyond their station when they went out in the world. "You are a bloody disgrace, sir," Nick announced, "and a fool with it."

The warden had a napkin tucked under his chin and a forkful of meat dripping with gravy halfway to his mouth. He didn't bother to reply until he'd closed his lips around the morsel. Then, opening his mouth and exhibiting half-chewed food, he said, "Hare. My wife does a mighty fine jugged hare. Dr. Turner, isn't it? Been planning to come along and introduce meself. Been busy." He swallowed his meat with an audible gulp, then pointed to a chair. "Sit yourself down, sir."

"No, I won't sit down. Not with you. And your charges have introduced you well enough for me to know as much as I want about you."

The warden pushed his plate aside, produced a gold toothpick, and began working on the bits of meat stuck between his protruding front teeth. That combined with his fat cheeks and short, wide nose gave him the look of a pig. "I do my duty, sir. I'm charged with training up these misbegotten unwanteds with enough docility in 'em so's they can go into service with decent New York families and give no trouble. Never have no complaints from them as gets a serving maid or a stable boy from my orphanage, Dr. Turner. They knows their place, my orphans do."

The nature of the fractures meant that the little girl had to have been hung by her hands while she was whipped. God alone knew how long she'd been left without treatment after. According to Monty Chance, the weals made by the lash were already full of pus when she arrived at the hospital. Nick grabbed a long-handled serving fork from the table and leaned forward, pressing the two prongs against the warden's fat neck. "Listen to me, you pitiful excuse for a man. If I see one more child who's been abused by your barbaric notions of duty, I'll take a lash to you myself."

The warden pushed the fork away with one hand and tipped his chair back so it was leaning against the wall. "Will you now, Dr. Turner? I don't think so. Just as I don't think you're likely to stab me with that there fork. You're a gentleman, you are. Your kind needs my kind to do what needs to be done in that sort o' matter. Frankly Clement's me name. Clement as a summer's day. Long as you don't get me dander up. That's what I tell all the wee ones soon as they come here. But if you do . . . well, even a summer day can turn to lightning and thunder, Dr. Turner. And if I can't be getting the best out of 'em here, there's always the Refuge."

That was the ultimate threat, over west on the Bloomingdale Road. Leg irons and solitary confinement for those adjudicated delinquent children. But Nick was not treating the miscreant eight-year-olds of the House of Refuge. "One more abused child," he repeated, spitting the words through clenched teeth, "and I'll have your job. I swear it."

"We'll see, Dr. Turner. We'll see." Clement let the chair fall forward with a thud and stood up. He was considerably shorter than Nick but at least twice as wide. "You're new here and you don't know how things are, so I'll not be taking this bit o' bother to Dr. Grant. All that pleased with you he is so far, Dr. Turner. All that pleased to have found a respected doctor from a long line o' respected doctors to take over at our hospital. Gives him good standing with the council, that does. But my line o' work here at the orphanage, that earns brass. Pay good money the gentry do for servants trained up at my orphanage. Very good money indeed."

And most of it going into Tobias Grant's pocket.

Nick had left without another word, but two days later he was still seething. "A Christian refuge," he said, repeating Manon's words. "I can't think that anyone with any sense would call it that."

"Oh, but that's exactly what most of the town does call it. We have a succession of preachers here, Cousin Nicholas. Most from among the New Order Evangelicals, as they're now known. New breeds of mostly Presbyterians, with some Methodists and Baptists as well. What they have in common is that they find the Episcopalians and Lutherans too mealy-mouthed for their liking. But whatever side of the theological argument they take, all are upstanding Protestants. Because, of course, the council doesn't want to encourage the Irish in their superstitious Catholic ways. The preachers bring the good news of the Gospel to the orphanage at least twice a week, even sing a hymn or two. They do not, of course, bother to ask if the children are fed and warm."

"Are we complicit, Cousin Manon? Does having anything to do with this place make us part of what happens here?"

She reached up and patted his shoulder. "Oh my, Cousin Nicholas. You have had some sort of troubling encounter I take it." She looked over at what was supposed to be the infants' ward, though females of all ages were shoved together wherever there was space. "Was it Frankly Clement or perhaps his equally odious wife who put you in this mood?"

"I've never met her, but he's a barbarian. And by not denouncing him we—

"We help to mitigate his excesses, Cousin Nicholas. At least that's what I believe. It's why I continue to come here. Were you looking for me to talk about Frankly Clement?"

"No, not really. I've been given three hundred dollars. It would buy blankets, at least enough for the women's wing. Maybe some sheets as well. Or I could get some covering for those damned cages so if it rains the lunatics aren't . . ." He let the words trail away. "God Almighty, it all seems like such a drop of relief in an ocean of misery."

"Indeed," Manon agreed. "There is no point in fooling ourselves that whatever we do is anything more."

"Which then? Blankets or covers for the cages?"

"Or? Come, Cousin Nicholas, I think you have an alternative in mind. Otherwise you would not be speaking to me about it, merely making a judgment based on practicality."

"You are a wise woman."

"I've been force-fed wisdom, Cousin. Our bad decisions are frequently the most effective teacher."

The birthday of her twins had come round the week before. They would have been seventeen. If Manon had done what she was advised to do and taken herself and her babies over to Long Island to get away from the pestilence and allowed someone else to nurse Joyful, already down with the disease, perhaps her babies would have lived. If, if, if.

She'd marked her sons' birthday by a visit to their grave in the yard of the old French Church on Pine Street, put two small nosegays of pansies by the single headstone, just as she always did, and left a third bunch of flowers a short distance away for her beloved Joyful. He had never been a member of the French Church, but Papa had persuaded the rector to allow Joyful to lie near his sons. Now Papa was in the ground as well. Each time she visited the graveyard she looked at the plot waiting for her, and not with sorrow.

"So, Cousin Nicholas, what do you have in mind?"

"A laboratory," Nick said, the words coming out in a rush now that he'd decided to speak them. "Where we can investigate the causes of illness. Forgive me, Cousin Manon, but we're only sopping up the blood after it has started to flow. Research can—"

"You're talking about dissection."

"Other studies as well, but yes, anatomies are part of my plan." He saw no point in equivocating.

Manon smiled. "I doubt our poor lunatics are likely to notice if they are beset by sun or rain in their cages. It's the nature of lunacy, is it not? Fortunate in a way. As for the blankets, if you buy them, Cousin Nicholas, they will soon be ruined or stolen, because there is no proper organizing authority in this place, and as long as Tobias Grant rules, you will not be allowed to establish any. Use the gift to start your laboratory. Not even a villain like Tobias Grant can steal knowledge."

Chapter Seven

"ALL RIGHT, DOROTHY." Carolina took a good grip on the bedpost. "I'm going to take the deepest breath possible and you pull the laces as tight as ever you can."

Carolina didn't have a lady's maid. It was up to Dorothy to put her knee in the small of madam's back and apply all her strength to closing the corset.

"There, I think that's got it, ma'am. If the dress don't fit now, it never will."

"Oh, it will fit, Dorothy. I am determined that it shall."

The frock was made of bronze-colored silk taffeta—a lovely autumn color the dressmaker had said—with a fashionable off-the-shoulder neck framed by a wide collar, gloriously huge puffed sleeves, and a sweep of skirt worn over four petticoats. No one had seen it, not even Samuel. It was her first new frock since Zachary's birth four months before. Carolina twirled before the mirror, frankly enchanted by her appearance. "I don't look old and plump and past my age of charm, do I, Dorothy?"

"Not a bit of it, ma'am. The color's unusual, but it suits you. If I may say."

"Oh, you may. You may." All that width above and below made her waist appear positively tiny, just as the dressmaker promised. If anything, she looked slimmer than she had before the birth of her son.

"Will you wear your pearls, ma'am? Look right lovely with it they will."

The long strand of matched pearls had belonged to her mother. Papa had given them to her on her wedding day. "Not now, Dorothy. A twenty-inch strand of pearls is too dressy for an afternoon do." But she would put them on as soon as she returned, and she wouldn't take off the frock until Samuel arrived home, whatever hour that turned out to be. Then perhaps he . . . Carolina glanced at the bed then looked quickly away. Surely now that she was past her confinement, a nocturnal visit would be in order.

"Shall I tell Barnabas to bring the buggy round, ma'am?"

"Yes, thank you, Dorothy. Right away. I'll just pop up to the nursery and say goodbye to little Zachary and Nurse." She would be away three or four hours, the longest she'd been separated from her son since his birth. She knew it was silly, but she was already feeling pangs of loneliness and misgiving. That wouldn't do. Nurse was entirely capable and trustworthy. Besides, it was in a good cause. She wasn't leaving Zac for frivolous nonsense, Carolina reminded herself. This was for charity.

There were those who denounced assistance to what they called the undeserving poor. Prosperous and portly men, former New Englanders, who joined those Presbyterian congregations where New Order Evangelicals dominated. Indiscriminate charity, they said, encourages ignorance, idleness, intemperance, extravagance, imprudent marriages, and defective child-rearing practices. Giving aid to women with children incites them to become pregnant yet again in the hope of getting still more aid, they said. Not to mention that such burdens drive up taxes.

In a city as bustling and unruly as New York, where the needs of the have-nots seemed both endless and impossible ever to be fully met, the idea that it might be possible without guilt to relieve oneself of the burden of care proved particularly attractive. In recent years a great many genteel ladies had stopped their participation in such things as the Society for the Relief of Poor Widows with Small Children. Charity, the respectable ladies said in agreement with their husbands, should consist solely of exhortations to sobriety, cleanliness, frugality, and doing for oneself in place of hand-outs. Otherwise there was Bellevue.

A small but influential minority—mostly but not entirely female— did not share that view. Manon Turner had sought them out. If she were a man she'd have convened this meeting of some thirty like-minded people in one of the city's many new and very pleasant hotels, but that was not an option for a woman. What Manon's invitations called an afternoon Tea and Reception was held in the spacious downstairs parlor of her house on Wall Street. There, before allowing even a sip of the promised tea, she spent twenty minutes telling her guests of her proposed Society for Aid to Poor Families. Mostly it was a recitation of the reality of conditions at Bellevue. Then she introduced Nick. "No long speech is needed, Cousin Nicholas," she'd promised when she inveigled him into attending. "Just tell them I'm not lying about how things are. And say that if we can keep the poor from needing to abandon what homes they have, however humble, we will be wise as well as merciful."

"And will you tell them why things are as they are at Bellevue?"

"Certainly not. I shall say only that the conditions are a result of overcrowding."

"But—"

"If Tobias Grant ever believes I am his enemy, I shall be enjoined from ever coming near Bellevue. And he will see to it that my society never gets to be more than the notion of a slightly addled old woman."

"You're not old."

Old enough. Forty-two her next birthday. "Though I confess I don't feel so. Nor am I addled. But if Dr. Grant did not have powerful allies, he wouldn't be allowed to do what he does. We must choose our battles, Cousin Nicholas."

She was right, so now he was at the gathering on Wall Street, doing exactly what Manon had asked him to do. "In closing I can only say that I attest to everything Mrs. Turner has told you. And I commend her and all of you for your foresighted wisdom, as well as your great kindness and charity. The Society for Aid to Poor Families will make an enormous difference to our city and to Bellevue, I'm sure."

There was polite applause; Manon expected no more. It wasn't fashionable to show public enthusiasm unless you were in a theater or a music hall. As for all the ladies busy studying Nicholas from behind their fans—particularly the half-dozen or so with unmarried daughters—she'd expected that as well.

Nicholas sat down, and Manon took his place. "Thank you all for coming. Please be sure to see our secretary, Miss Adelaide Bellingham, before you leave." She nodded in the direction of a middle-aged woman sitting at a table near the door. Bit of a lump of dough Addie was. Wearing sturdy brown kersey and laced-up shoes, in contrast to the birds of plumage who filled the parlor. Perhaps, Manon thought, she'd made a mistake by including her. Never mind, Addie was ready to inscribe the names and subscriptions of the society's new members, a necessary task. "First do please have some refreshments," Manon said. "I look forward to a private word with each of you before you go. And thank you again for joining us, Dr. Turner."

Nick nodded an acknowledgment and stood up. Off the leash at last. He'd spied the ravishing golden-haired creature the moment she arrived and now he headed straight for her. Any number of women interrupted his progress, each pressing a visiting card upon him, some mentioning a charming daughter who hadn't managed to be here. He promised to call on them all. "How very kind of you. I shall look forward to it," he kept repeating, mindful to be seen putting the card carefully in his breast pocket. "Now, if you'll excuse me . . ."

By the time he got to the young woman with the golden curls, she was nearly finished with a small glass of punch. "Isn't it extraordinary to think Devrey Shipping actually began in these very rooms, Dr. Turner?"

"Did it? I didn't know that." Damn. Silk gloves. No way to tell if she wore a wedding band. Manon would know, of course.

"Yes, it did. Willem van Der Vries built this house in 1700. His counting rooms were here on the ground floor, and he and his family lived upstairs. A very Dutch way of doing business. Though earlier, as soon as we became New York rather than New Amsterdam, old Willem had changed his name to Devrey."

"You are a historian, I see. I am mightily impressed." Her smile was enchanting, and the unusual color of her frock brought out gold flecks in her brown eyes.

"Oh, not really a historian, Dr. Turner. But I do know ..." She stopped speaking when Manon joined them.

"I see you've met Cousin Carolina, Cousin Nicholas. I meant to introduce you, but obviously I'm too late."

"Cousin Carolina? I didn't know." He'd suspected as soon as she mentioned Devrey Shipping.

"Indeed," the golden princess said and held out her hand. "I'm Carolina Devrey. Samuel's wife."

He managed to take her hand and bow over it, he even mumbled something appropriate, but his heart was pounding as if he'd run a mile at high speed. Hard to say which he felt more, disappointment or astonishment. Sam Devrey had a wife like this, yet he was maintaining that extraordinary second household on Cherry Street. Damn, he'd been hanging onto Carolina Devrey's hand far too long. Nick let go.

Carolina looked at him with almost as much intensity as he had looked at her. Manon broke the silence. "I heard you telling Cousin Nicholas about the old Devrey counting rooms. They shall soon be resurrected."

"Surely not," Carolina protested. "Devrey's are to have wonderful new quarters on Canal Street. My husband has told me all about them."

"Yes, of course. I only meant that since this is one of the last private homes on Wall Street, I've decided to sell. My attorney tells me we've a decent offer from a firm that deals in the importing of tea. I've no doubt that in good New York fashion they will tear down this old brick pile and put up a brand-new counting house in its place."

"But where shall you live?" Carolina asked.

"Oh, I'll find somewhere. A widow on her own doesn't need a large establishment. Perhaps I'll take rooms in some lodging house and share them with Addie over there."

Carolina glanced in the direction of the woman by the door. "But Cousin Manon. She's not—"

"Not our sort?" Manon laughed. "You're right, of course." She'd found Adelaide Bellingham among the able-bodied poor in Bellevue nearly a year before. An orphan and never married, she had lost her job as a seamstress when she broke her leg in a fall. All downhill from there. Until Manon took her in, and since Addie could read and write as well as sew, managed to keep her busy. "She's a good sort, nonetheless," she added. "What do you think, Cousin Nicholas? Shall I share lodgings with Miss Bellingham?" And what would they say, it crossed her mind to wonder, if she mentioned the one remarkable thing tucked away in the baggage she would be bringing with her to whatever ordinary rooms she managed to find once this romantic old pile of bricks was sold? No time for that now. Cousin Nicholas was still staring at Carolina as if she were Venus rising from the waves. Best make sure he was clear about the situation. "How is your new son, Cousin Carolina?"

"Zachary's quite wonderful. You must call round and meet him, Cousin Manon. Come for tea. Just you and I." Both women smiled at the acknowledgment that it was best if Manon came when Samuel was not at home. "You can tell me more about your plans for the new society. Now I must go."

"Don't forget to leave your name with Miss Bellingham," Manon cautioned.

Carolina promised she would and that she was delighted to have met Nicholas, who must also come and visit the Devrey household sometime soon. "Don't let that old Turner and Devrey feud keep you away," she said. "I have no idea what it was about, and I'm sure my husband doesn't either." Nick made the correct sort of response, and, in a flurry of her fashionably wide skirts, Carolina was gone.

"You're not to leave until everyone else has, Cousin Nicholas," Manon instructed him. "I want you to accompany me on a brief visit. And stop looking like a deserted puppy dog. I agree that Carolina's lovely, but never fear, there's a goodly supply of lovely young New York ladies. And only one happens to be married to Sam Devrey."

No, Nick thought, that was precisely the problem. There were two.

"Well," Manon demanded, after a brisk twenty-minute walk had brought them to Prince Street, "what do you think?"

"I'd absolutely no idea the place was here. It's remarkable." Nick removed his tall hat so he could tip his head back and examine the double-width, three-story red-brick building. A small sign announced the place as St. Patrick's Orphan Asylum. According to Manon, it had been built by something called the Roman Catholic Diocese of New York. "Preachers who do more than harangue the poor about reforming their profligate ways," Nick said. "What a novel idea."

"Not preachers," Manon said. "Women. The Sisters of Charity. They live here together and look after the children themselves."

"Good heavens. What do their husbands think?"

"They have no husbands. They take vows of poverty and chastity, and promise to be obedient to the bishop rather than a husband."

"And to the pope in Rome," Nick said with a sigh. He abhorred the prejudice that weighed like a boot on the necks of the immigrant poor, but they did seem to bring some of it on themselves with their odd notions about religion. "That doesn't seem a very American idea. And does this bishop treat them all as his wives?"

"You have been listening to spiteful talk, Cousin Nicholas. One might even call it bigotry."

"Now look here—"

"I'm sorry. I didn't mean to accuse you. These women obey the pope and the bishop in spiritual matters. Nothing else. Now come inside and meet Mother Louise. Then tell me if you think it likely the Sisters of Charity are the sort of women you imply they may be."

"Yes, I will if you wish, but . . . Cousin Manon, are you a Catholic?"

"Heavens no! I merely admire what these women have accomplished with good will and determination."

Like black crows they were, wearing black bonnets with a floppy ruffle and black dresses with a short cape and a high neck and long sleeves. Nick was confronted with a pair of them sitting primly on straight-backed chairs. The younger said nothing, only fingered the string of wooden beads hanging at her waist. The talkative one, whom Manon had introduced as Mother Louise, had a long, sharp nose, exactly like a crow's beak. And apparently she read minds. "You are thinking how odd we look, Dr. Turner, and how unfashionable. Mother Seton was in Italy when her husband died, and she adopted the style of dress of widows there. And we after her."

"No, really, I wasn't thinking anything of the sort."

Her chuckle was rich and warm. "It doesn't matter, we're quite accustomed to being oddities. We're the first in this city, you see. In Mother Seton's day there were a few nuns representing various congregations in other states and many in Europe, but in New York, in 1804, there were none. If that were not the case she might have joined a congregation, rather than starting a new one."

He listened out of politeness at first, but it was a fascinating story, and he soon found himself intrigued. Elizabeth Bayley she'd been. Born in 1774. Then Mrs. William Seton. When she was twenty-nine, while they were traveling in Italy, her husband died and left her with five small children. A year later, when she and her children returned to New York, Elizabeth Seton had converted to the Catholic faith. "Both the Bayleys and the Setons completely ostracized her, but she was not deterred," Mother Louise said. "And she burned to do something for the poor."

"Before her conversion Mrs. Seton founded the Society for the Relief of Poor Widows," Manon interrupted. "I've always thought it was her going over to Rome that caused New York society to withdraw its support from such charities."

"Protestants look at these things differently," Mother Louise said, smiling. "I should know. I was one for thirty years."

The week before, at Bellevue, Nick had seen a minister go into the stone building that housed the stepping wheel. Sixteen men—prisoners mostly, though a few of the able-bodied poor were pressed into service when they were needed to make up the numbers—walking a flight of turning steps that drove a mill to grind grain; eight minutes on, eight minutes off, by the bell, sixteen hours out of every twenty-four. A preacher went daily to read to the men from the Bible. Of all the stories told about Bellevue by rich and poor, none were more fearsome than tales of the Stepping House.

"Did you become a Catholic, Mother Louise, so you could join these Sisters of Charity?"

"Quite the other way round, Dr. Turner. I joined Mother Seton and her Sisters for the same reason I became a Catholic. For the love of Our Lord and Savior Jesus Christ. Now would you like to see something of our work here?"

However unusual these black-clad women might be, the orphans were the biggest surprise of the visit. They looked well fed and clean; some were even apple-cheeked and rosy. Everything in the place was clean, come to that. No dark corners or droppings of vermin here. Indeed, no sloth or idleness was permitted. The children marched to and from their various tasks—including, he was told, lessons in reading and writing and numbers—in perfect drill formation. And everything he was seeing was repeated next door in the home for half-orphans also established by the Catholic Diocese and staffed by the Sisters of Charity. Because among the poor in New York, Mother Louise said, losing one parent was every bit as devastating as losing both.

"Your Mother Louise seems a formidable lady," Nick told Manon when they left. "I shouldn't like to be in her bad books."

"No fear of that, not with you promising to come if she'd need of a doctor."

"Well, when she said there was no physician they could regularly call on. . . . You know, I don't understand that. Surely there must be some Catholic doctor who—"

"There are some, yes. But the Sisters are not entirely uncontroversial even among those who share their religion. New York's Catholic doctors belong to the class that does not believe in separating itself from Protestants in every particular. And it has been at loggerheads with both the previous Bishop Connolly and the current Bishop Dubois, both of whom do."

"Want to separate the Catholics, you mean?"

"From what they see as Protestant heresy, yes. The bishops are not great defenders of American notions of democracy and republicanism. Which, whatever their other faults may be, are worthy ideas much trumpeted by the Evangelicals."

"You know a great deal of politics, my dear Cousin Manon. Not to mention this religion to which you say you do not belong."

"Politics? I'm a woman, dear Cousin Nicholas. What has politics to do with me?" Long ago, when Joyful was alive, he had been deeply involved in the city's political fortunes. But Joyful was dead, and she had been left with only one extraordinary vestige of that involvement.

"Manon?" Nick touched her arm. "Penny for your thoughts? You seem to have gone quite far away."

"My thoughts are not worth a penny," Manon said briskly. A king's ransom more like, but she had no intention of saying that. "And if you want to know about religion, you've only to read *The Truth Teller* for the Catholic point of view, or *The Protestant* for that side. You can decide for yourself which tells more lies. As for these nuns, after the plague of cholera in '32 the whole city thought them heroines because they were the only ones unafraid to nurse the sick of whatever religion. But in ordinary times the Sisters serve mostly the Irish rabble who live in Five Points, if living it can be called. I've not met any doctors down there."

"You go to Five Points often, I hear. To nurse that Irish rabble."

"When I can," Manon said with a dismissive shrug. "Though to be fair, Five Points offers misery in a variety of nationalities. And there are the Negroes, of course."

Nick fully expected Manon to be an abolitionist, at least in her heart of hearts. He had leanings that way himself. Nonetheless, he knew it was a dangerous thing to be in New York. Slavery might have been outlawed in this state five years past, but the plantation owners mostly shipped their tobacco and cotton to Europe from New York City, just like the rest of the country. Putting them all out of business would be no favor for this town. "In Five Points," Nick said, "are the blacks mostly runaway slaves?"

"Not entirely. Free Negroes as well. These days most of them can't get work either."

"You're doing a good thing," Nick said, touching her arm.

She put her hand over his, grateful for the gesture. Sometimes, when she was bone-tired, she could not help but wonder. After an exhausting six or seven hours in those hulking tenements crammed with so much wretchedness, were the poor any better off? And did she feel any less the pain of guilt? Young men her twins would be, if she had not put Joyful first and thus lost all three. She had tried to speak about it. Once to the rector of the French Church—who didn't understand one word, and told her she must learn to accept God's will. Another time to Mother Louise. *It doesn't matter, my dear. No matter how grievous an error of judgement, Christ makes all things new. All you need do is say you're sorry, that you will try to do better, and that you love. Love meets every need.* For a nun, perhaps. For Catholics.

"You're well matched," Nick said. "You and Mother Louise."

"No," Manon replied. "No, we are not well matched at all."

When she was a child on the sampans of Di Short-Neck, Mei-hua had heard the women speak of the clouds and the rain, that moment when a man exploded with greatest sexual pleasure. She had never heard any talk about using a silk cloth to catch the rain part.

That's what the Lord Samuel did these days. He spread a silk cloth on her belly, and when he reached that moment of ecstasy, he withdrew from her and deposited his seed on the silk cloth. Later it was up to her to dispose of it. "And always supreme lady *tai-tai* must be on bottom and he on top. Why? Why?" she asked Ah Chee. "In past days not the same. Before you took my son from my belly the Lord Samuel liked me to sometimes—"

"This old woman did not take son. This old woman tried—"

"Yes. Yes. I know." Secretly she blamed the this-place-red-hair *yi* who had come to take care of her after they left the place of the devil woman. He knew very important special medicine Taste Bad did not know. That's what her lord said. So how come this-place *yi* didn't put the son back in her belly? Never mind. She had other things to think about now. "Why Lord Samuel does this thing?"

"Better than you take make-no-baby powder. More sure."

Mei-hua's eyes grew round with wonder. "Yes. Yes. No think. No think. Stupid supreme lady *tai-tai*. Stupid." She smacked her forehead with her hand, as if she would waken the cleverness that had gone to sleep.

Ah Chee could not comment. Her lips were now closed tight around the hollow stick of bamboo she was using to blow air between the flesh and the skin of the fat duck she'd brought home from the market. She had carefully sewn up the openings at the neck and the tail end of the bird, so after a few moments of determined puffing, the duck looked like a round ball. Ah Chee pinched closed the little hole she'd made to insert the bamboo stick, then she opened her mouth and let the stick fall to the floor while she sewed up the hole before too much of the air could escape. After it was cooked, the crispy, dark mahogany skin would be served separately from the succulent flesh. Very special delicious way to cook duck. Only for special very much important feasts.

Ah Chee had learned to prepare the dish by watching a man who said he had made it for the emperor in the Forbidden City. The man had found his way to the sampans of the Pearl River when his need to swallow clouds made him an unreliable chef and the emperor decreed that the ends of all his fingers be cut off and he be turned out of the royal court. Never mind. Even with bad-to-look-at ugly short fingers, the one-time chef made the most happy in your mouth food anyone on the sampans had ever tasted.

Ah Chee's duck would be served to the Lord Samuel in three days time, at *Chongjiu,* the ninth day of the ninth month, Double Nine Feast. Very necessary to eat good food and drink chrysanthemum tea to drive away evil. Also, Lord Samuel said this double nine was his birthday. The Lord Samuel was very much too young to celebrate his birthday. Birthdays were for old people. But the plum blossom said the lord told her this double nine was the eleventh day of November in this place, and that was his birthday. Better to make a celebration here than let the yellow hair concubine get ahead of the plum blossom supreme lady *tai-tai.*

Mei-hua was not thinking about the coming celebrations. She had picked up the hollow stick of bamboo and was staring at it with great concentration.

"What? What?" Ah Chee demanded. "I need that thing. It came with us all the way from the Middle Kingdom so this old woman could—"

Mei-hua ignored her and put the piece of bamboo in her mouth, first blowing air out, then drawing it in. After a moment she leaned over a bowl in which rice was soaking and sucked up some of the water, then she covered the hole with her finger and turned to another bowl and took her finger away and watched while the water dripped out. "So. So," she whispered. "Like that."

Ah Chee's eyes narrowed and she too drew in a long breath. She understood, and she was both afraid and very too much damn happy. The plum blossom's scheme might work. Who could say about such things? Maybe if they burned much incense to god of happiness Fu Xing and if Ah Chee made the girl eat the strong-son soup every day . . . Never mind. "Bad idea," she said, looking at Zao Shen, the kitchen god, so he would be sure to hear and understand that Ah Chee had not given her approval to the scheme. In case it went wrong. "Very bad. Very bad. If belly gets round like this," she gestured to the inflated duck, "how does *tai-tai* explain to the Lord Samuel?"

Mei-hua considered for some moments. "I will tell my lord that gods arrange such things. I will say gods are stronger than silk cloths. And that if he does not allow his son to be born, all gods, especially Chuan Yin, will be very angry and his business will not prosper."

Ah Chee shrugged, showing her disdain for this appeal to the power of the goddess of fertility and compassion.

Mei-hua, who knew exactly what the old woman was thinking, stamped her tiny silk-wrapped foot. "My Lord very clever businessman. How you think he got so rich if not? How? You think it is clever business to make gods angry?"

"The Lord Samuel does not believe in the gods of the Middle Kingdom."

"Then why is there a beautiful statue of Chuan Yin above the big bed. Why? Why?"

"Chuan Yin watches bed because supreme lady *tai-tai* put her there."

True, the Lord Samuel burned much incense on the day of his wedding to the plum blossom, but only because it was the custom and everyone was watching. Ever since, not a single grain. Ah Chee would bet twenty strings of copper cash there were no altars in the house of the yellow haired concubine. "You do this thing, Lord Samuel take you back to devil woman with devil needles. Make baby come out of your belly a second time." Her new secret treasure purse was filling again, but it had much less in it than before. "No can." With a sideways glance at Zao Shen.

"Yes can," Mei-hua insisted. "Yes can. I will think of a way."

Ah Chee did not argue. Instead she busied herself tying a string around the neck of the blown-up duck so she could hang it from a hook in the ceiling. Over the next two days she would fan the duck whenever she passed. When she was ready to cook it, the fat would be gone and the skin as dry as paper. Very important duck hang before cooking, short fingers cook man had explained.

When the duck was hung exactly as Ah Chee wished, she turned around to speak to Mei-hua, but the plum blossom was no longer in the kitchen. Neither was the hollow bamboo rod. Ah Chee thought of going after her to continue the argument, then decided against it. Instead she lit a joss stick and carried it to the picture of the kitchen god. He had heard everything they said. If it turned out badly, come the New Year his wife would carry tales of their stupidity to the Jade Emperor in heaven. Not good.

Incense maybe not enough. Ah Chee found a small pale green china dish decorated with a picture of a swallow in flight, put three drops of honey on it, and carried it to the wooden table that served as Zao Shen's altar. Sticky things to close up his ears and his mouth.

Chapter Eight

"I HAVE HEARD about this place, Dr. Turner. I thought it time I came to see for myself."

Tobias Grant was obviously winded by his climb up the four flights of stairs. Nick gave him a few moments to catch his breath and look around. No point in hiding anything and he hadn't tried. It was inevitable that sooner or later the director would confront him concerning the activities of his small laboratory. Nick had, in a manner of speaking, been looking forward to this visit.

"Have a seat over there by the window, Dr. Grant. And forgive me, but this won't wait. I like to make them decent for burial. A fresh cadaver . . . rigor sets in quickly and makes it harder to get the job done. Bloody cold in here besides. Doesn't help." There was a small stove in one corner of the room, but it wasn't adequate to fend off the invasive November chill.

He was sewing up the belly of a woman who less than an hour earlier had died in terrible agony, holding her stomach and retching vicious brown bile. "Liver possibly," he said, continuing with his task, "but I think it more likely the gall bladder." He'd extracted both organs, the gall bladder still connected to the liver by the biliary tract. The bloody mass lay in a chipped china basin on a small table beside the chair he'd offered Grant. "Looks a bit like the jellied pudding they serve in the dining hall here," Nick said cheerfully. "Not quite set. Give the liver a poke if you like, but don't touch the gall bladder, please. Liable to burst. I've a mind to examine the contents *in situ*."

Grant looked up, his complexion a sickly green. Nick pretended not to notice. "See all those stiff, thickened spots on the liver? They're the wrong color. A sure sign of cirrhosis. The whole thing should be soft and squishy like the healthy dark red bits. Comes from that cheap gin the Five Points rabble call mother's ruin. Drink's the Irish curse, of course, but while it's the obvious culprit, I don't think it's her liver that killed poor Maggie O'Houlihan."

Grant at last found his voice. "I did not come up here for an exposition of medicine, Dr. Turner. Though of course I admire your inquiring mind." He nodded towards the shelf of books and pamphlets in one corner of the room. "What"—the director looked once more at the oozing mess in the basin—"In God's name, sir, what do you intend to do with it?"

"Not cook it up for the patients' supper, if that's what you're thinking." The stitching of Maggie O'Houlihan's belly was complete. Nick clipped the length of catgut and put down the needle. Not an elegant job, but that was hardly the point. He covered the body with a sheet, turned to the basin of water he had someone put here every day, and retrieved the bar of soap he kept on the shelf next to it. "I am going to examine that liver and gall bladder, Dr. Grant." His ablutions finished, he reached for the linen towel.

"Dr. Turner, it appears to me that Mrs. O'Houlihan's liver has already had a great deal of your attention."

"Yes, but I don't yet know everything it has to tell me. I shall cut a series of thin sections of the organ—from the parts that look normal and those that do not—and compare them. Using that miraculous invention over there."

He nodded towards the long counter that held most of his kit, including the bulky and complex piece of equipment that took up most of the space. "It's a compound microscope. The latest thing. Lenses in the eyepiece as well as the part underneath that's called the objective."

The microscope had cost ninety of the three hundred dollars that Sam Devrey donated. Much of the remainder had gone on scalpels and needles and catgut and probes. Plus a few more books of course. The ones in here were only part of his collection, his private rooms were crammed with them. He'd put a little of the money by to pay an assistant, one of the students most likely, but he'd been holding off on making the offer until after this meeting, which he'd known must occur. Manon had advised Nick to confront Grant immediately, but he'd decided against it. *I shall let the director come to me, Cousin Manon. My turf for the encounter, not his.* So far so good.

In spite of himself Grant was obviously fascinated.

"What do you expect to see, Dr. Turner?"

"For one thing, the differences in the tissues. For another, why that gall bladder is pale and yellow when it should be bright green. My guess is that the gall bladder stopped processing the bile as it should and tipped it all into the poor creature's stomach. Ate her gut away. Just look at the biliary tract. Even with the naked eye you can see—"

The director of Bellevue stood up and extended a forestalling hand. "Enough. Tell me instead, Dr. Turner, if, when you have the answers to all your questions, the unfortunate Mrs. O'Houlihan will be restored to life."

Nick leaned back on the long counter, slouching a bit so that he and his superior were eye to eye. "The question every short-sighted skeptic asks, Dr. Grant. I expected more of you."

"And I of you, Dr. Turner. Surely you are aware that anatomies are illegal unless performed on the bodies of hanged villains."

"A law that can be enforced only if the anatomies are discovered, Dr. Grant. In this case, unlikely. For one thing, no one will come to claim the body of poor dead Maggie O'Houlihan. For another, I'm up here on the fourth floor, where there are only my private apartments. And I'm not about to wave body parts out the window." That's how the riot of 1788 got started. Some damn fool of a medical student waved a severed arm at a small boy peering in the window and told him it was his mother's. In fact the boy's mother had died a few days earlier. Pretty soon all of lower Manhattan was full of screaming protesters.

"Much of Bellevue knows about this laboratory of yours, Dr. Turner. How can they not? You don't cart the cadavers up here by yourself, do you? Or clean up after you're done."

"Indeed I do not, Dr. Grant. But I don't think much of Bellevue gives a tinker's cuss for what I do up here in my aerie. They've plenty of other things to occupy their minds."

"Perhaps, Dr. Turner. Perhaps not. Both the orphanage warden and the chief apothecary have mentioned the matter to me. You put all our work in peril, sir. If anyone should—"

Nick hooted. "That's what Frankly Clement and Jeremiah Potter are worried about, is it? Our work, as you call it, being imperiled? By whom, Dr. Grant? The poor and misbegotten who find themselves here? The prisoners? The orphans? Who would listen to them? The objects of our ministrations have no voice, sir. So who in holy hell will speak out about illegal anatomies at Bellevue, when doing so might attract attention to the rest of the self-serving, greedy, stinking misery that abounds in this place? All of which occurs, I might add, on your watch."

Grant took a moment before he replied. "Dr. Turner," he said finally, "since you think so little of this facility and my administration of it, and since I have it on good authority that you do not avail yourself of the financial opportunities your work affords, can you tell me why you remain as Senior Medical Attendant of the hospital here at Bellevue? No don't bother. I will tell you. You stay because of all this." He waved an arm to indicate the laboratory. "This is what you care about. Bellevue meets your needs exactly as it meets mine. Or those of the warden of the orphanage or the chief apothecary. We all have our passions and our price, Dr. Turner. Even you."

"I don't deny that."

"Very well. Then allow me to make myself clear. I will turn a blind eye to your activities in this small and if I may say makeshift facility, Dr. Turner. And you will do me the favor of discontinuing public discussions of what you judge to be the unfortunate state of affairs at Bellevue. That mutual silence will suit us both, sir."

"And if I do not?"

"Then I shall, of course, terminate your employment here. That, as I'm sure you know, is entirely in my authority."

"An authority granted you by the Common Council."

"Indeed, Dr. Turner, and something unlikely to change. You may have a cousin who sits on the council, but I have many good friends there. I take pride in friendship, sir, and I make it my business to reward loyalty."

"You're saying this dreadful Dr. Grant knows about the kinship between you and my husband?" Carolina had sent for tea as soon as Samuel's cousin arrived—unannounced and uninvited—at her front door. She gripped her cup and leaned forward. "How is that possible?"

She was close enough for Nick to smell the floral scent she wore. It was nothing he could put a name to, but delicious. He'd told himself he wouldn't find her so damnably attractive now he knew she was married. Unfortunately that was not true. "The Turner and Devrey families were among the earliest settlers of New York," he said. "I imagine a great many people know the connection between them." He put down his cup, and she immediately reached for the teapot. "No more, thank you." He set his spoon slantwise across the rim, the signal that he was done.

"Only one cup? You do not like our blend, Dr. Turner?"

"On the contrary. I've seldom tasted a more delicious brew. Or, dare I say, one more beautifully served." Her deep blue cotton frock was simpler than the sumptuous gown she had worn to Manon's reception, and her hair was pulled back in a tumble of curls with a few ringlets escaping around her face. She was enchanting.

"Apparently you do dare, Dr. Turner."

"What?"

Carolina laughed. "To tell me that my tea is delicious and beautifully served. You dare to flatter."

"But it's not flattery. I—"

She laughed again. "I am teasing you, Dr. Turner. Are you quite sure you will have no more tea?"

"Quite sure. And please . . . We're cousins by marriage. Can't I be Cousin Nicholas? Or even Cousin Nick?"

"That will please me. And I am Cousin Carolina."

He could think of nothing further to say. The envelope he'd brought lay on the table between them. He glanced at it; Carolina did as well.

"I can't say when my husband will return home. He works very late many evenings. It is of course a great responsibility to have charge of a large fleet of sailing ships. As a man with a responsible post of your own, I'm sure you understand that, Dr.—Cousin Nick."

"Yes, of course." He felt a tingle of pleasure that she'd chosen the familiar form of his name. "As you say, working late goes along with responsibility." Undoubtedly she was sincere. It wasn't possible she knew anything about Sam Devrey's arrangements on Cherry Street.

"As do I, Cousin Nick. Understand, I mean." He must not think she was criticizing Samuel. But today was November 11, Samuel's birthday. Carolina had gone to the butcher herself and selected a joint of beef that promised to be tender as well as succulent. Even now it was turning on the spit before the fire below stairs in the kitchen. Surely her husband would come home to dine on his birthday.

"It doesn't matter," Nick said. "There's no need for Cousin Samuel to read this now. It's only a contingency plan, as I said."

"I see. Your letter is to be used in case Dr. Grant denounces you to the council?"

"Yes. I've set forth an explanation of the conditions at Bellevue as of this date, what I said to Dr. Grant, and his reply. If the council becomes involved, I'd appreciate Cousin Samuel—or someone—producing this document."

"I can't speak for my husband, of course, but if that does happen . . ." She left the rest in the air.

"I was wondering," he said, "would you be good enough to date and seal the letter? After you've read it, of course."

"I have no need to read it, Cousin Nick." Carolina got up and went to a small chest over by the window. "But I do have a question."

"Ask away."

"If the conditions at Bellevue are as dreadful as you and Cousin Manon say they are, why go to all this trouble to protect yourself?" She had returned to where he sat, carrying a slant-topped wooden correspondence box. "Surely you could find other employment. Why do you remain in such a terrible place, Cousin Nick?"

He hesitated. "There's a noble explanation," he said finally, "and one that's perhaps not quite so high-minded."

"Which one is true?"

"Both, after a fashion. If I left now, I'd feel as if I'd deserted people in dire need, and I know that whoever Grant put in my place would likely be chosen precisely because he would care only for the opportunity for profit the appointment offers."

"That, I take it is the high-minded reason." She was busying herself meanwhile with a stick of sealing wax and a small candle.

"Does it sound absurdly pompous?"

"No, it does not." She had one of the new lucifers, a small wooden stick tipped with chemicals that flared into flame as soon as she rubbed it on a strip of pumice. Her nose wrinkled at the smell of the burning sulfide, but the candle was instantly alight. In seconds she was able to drip a blob of pale lilac wax over the fold, then, while it was yet warm, press into it the mark of her engraved wedding band. "There," she said. "Properly sealed. And I shall write the date. Will that do, Cousin Nick?"

"Admirably."

The ring had been her mother's. It had pleased Papa for her to wear the same one as the woman he had cherished. Carolina often thought that if her mother had lived, she might have a more clear idea of how things were supposed to be between a man and the wife he loved. Perhaps her expectations were unreasonable. "And now will you tell me the other reason, Cousin Nick?"

"Because I'm free to do medical research. No one cares about what happens at the Almshouse Hospital. Despite all the preachers in and out of the place, I'm free to do as I please without churchly restriction. That wouldn't happen at New York Hospital, and in private practice . . . Well, I'd hardly see the range of illness one encounters at Bellevue." Or have much in the way of access to corpses, but he didn't say that.

"I see. And your research is important?"

"Vital. If we know the causes of disease, we may someday come to know the cure. Fevers, injuries, even such things as infant deformities."

"Really, Cousin Nick? You honestly think we may someday be able to prevent diseases, even deformities as you say, from occurring?"

"You think I'm mad." So had her husband when Nick first broached the topic of the benefits of research, but he wouldn't say that either.

"Well, no. It just seems so . . . fanciful, I think that's the word."

"Cousin Carolina, you like modern things, don't you? You lit the candle with a lucifer, and the coal in that scuttle over there is Pennsylvania anthracite, which makes less smoke and dust."

"Yes," Carolina agreed. "But what has that to do with—"

"Only that there are innovations in medicine too. In the past we could only react to illness after it appeared. These days it's possible to do more, or at least we can try. There's a theory, for instance, about illness coming from entities called germs, which can only be seen with a microscope. If that's correct, then the simple act of washing one's hands can make an enormous difference between health and sickness. I have a microscope and I examine . . . diseased things." He smiled at her. "You must think me ghoulish."

"No, I do not. In fact, I am quite"—she searched for a word—"quite taken with your enthusiasm," she finished. "Now about this letter. Shall I mark my initials after the date?"

"Yes, if you don't mind."

Dipping a quill into her inkpot, she wrote the letters C. R. D. above the wax seal, then picked up the letter and blew on it to dry the ink. "I'm just the right person to do it, aren't I? A respectable married lady of whom no one takes the least bit of notice. The perfect witness."

"I take notice," he said softly. "Most particularly of the fact that you're very kind."

"Not at all." She spoke quickly and decisively so there was no chance he would see that his words had brought her to the edge of tears. "I am merely practical. I do not have Cousin Manon's single-mindedness, Cousin Nick. And I'm far too weak-stomached to care for the destitute with my own hands. But I cannot think it right that some should have so much and others be in such terrible straits. And if you could find ways to prevent disease and cure the sick . . . The rich become ill as well as the poor, I've noted." She put the sealed and dated letter in the box, closing the lid with a small and decisive thump. "Your document will be quite safe here, I promise, in the event you should ever need it."

"Thank you." He stood up. There was no excuse to stay longer. "I'll be going. And once again, I'm very grateful."

Later, when she'd closed the door behind him, she remembered the story her mother-in-law had told about Samuel insisting that the midwife wash her hands before she climbed the stairs to attend to Carolina when she was birthing. Where would Samuel have gotten such an idea if not from Nick Turner? So the two must have met. Odd that neither man had mentioned such a meeting to her.

The entire *Chongjiu* banquet had been delicious, but the duck was remarkable. Samuel had never tasted the like anywhere in China, much less New York. Ah Chee had beamed at his pleasure even while she kept insisting it was terrible food and unworthy of the occasion. Wily old fox. She'd poison him if she dared, and they both knew it. But she could surely cook and she was devoted to Mei-hua.

His thoughts were interrupted when he turned his key in the lock of three East Fourteenth Street and the door did not open.

The residence with which Wilbur Randolf had dowered his daughter was fitted with the best of everything suitable for a dwelling of its class, including a door with a knocker of solid brass and the latest version of Jeremiah Chubb's detector lock, which could be opened only by a key made to match the tumblers. Samuel had one such key and Carolina the other. He tried his key again. This time the door opened immediately, meaning that when he tried it the first time, despite the lateness of the hour, it had not been locked.

The front hall was dark, but Sam saw a faint glow from the drawing room. "Carolina."

She was sitting in an upright chair beside the door, wearing a nightdress and a satin negligee. A single lit candle was on the table beside her. The drawing room fire had long since gone out, and the November chill was as noticeable here as it had been outside.

"What's the matter? Are you ill? The door wasn't locked. I thought—"

"I've been sitting right here since ten in the evening, Samuel. I saw no reason to lock the door."

"But why aren't you in bed?"

"I chose to wait for you. Since, among other things, it's your birthday. At least it was." The clock on the mantel had chimed midnight some time ago.

"How good of you to remember. I didn't—"

"Of course I remembered, Samuel. I'm your wife. Though I more and more doubt that you think of me as such."

"What do you mean? Of course I think of you as my wife. Look, I'm sorry about this evening. I should have sent word that I'd be delayed." He could still smell the faint odor of a roast of beef. She must have organized a celebration meal. A large joint, no doubt, with potatoes and probably boiled cabbage. All of which would require being cut at the table by the diner. He was never quite sure he wouldn't gag. "It didn't occur to me, Carolina. What can I do except apologize?"

"Nothing, Samuel. I can't do anything either. I've tried. Repeatedly. But nothing I do or say seems to make you happy. So I also apologize."

She stood up, lifting the candle as she did so. In its light he could see that her cheeks were streaked with tears. "Carolina, I'm genuinely sorry. I wish I could make you happier."

"But you do make me happy, Samuel. Clearly the problem is that I do not make you happy."

"Why should you say such a thing? You're a dutiful wife and you've given me a strong son and—"

"Would you not like more children, Samuel? A daughter perhaps? Another boy to be a companion to Zachary?"

"Yes, of course I would. Why do you ask?"

"Why? Samuel, you have not visited my bed, much less shared it, since I was confined for Zac's birth. What am I to think, except that I do not please you and you do not wish for me to bear you any more children."

"That's absurd!"

"Is it? Unless you come to my bed, how are we to get more children, Samuel? Will I conceive of the Holy Spirit, like Mary in the Bible?"

"Carolina, that's blasphemous." His tone was icy. "And entirely unworthy of you. Not to mention unbecoming of a lady."

She reached past him and pushed shut the drawing room door. Then she blew out the candle.

"Carolina, what are you doing? It's very late and I've a busy day tomorrow. I'm going to bed. We can discuss this further some other—"

"It's past time for discussion, Samuel." She walked to the front window and spread wide the velvet curtains. The street was gaslit, and there was the glow of a full moon. "In fact it's entirely past time for words of any sort." She turned to him and let the negligee fall from her shoulders, then reached down and pulled the nightdress over her head. "Am I so totally unpleasing to you, Samuel?"

"When you make such a lascivious display of yourself, yes." Her belly was flat and unmarked. He didn't know that could be the case after childbirth. One of the things he had most dreaded about allowing Mei-hua to conceive was that her exquisite little body would be marked. Carolina's breasts had changed, however. They were fuller and the nipples more pronounced. He did not know if she herself gave the baby suck or if she had found a wet nurse. Such things were outside his domain. "Put on your wrapper," he said. "Go upstairs."

"No." She took a step closer and tilted her head to look directly at him. "Not unless you agree to sleep beside me."

"You are shameless."

"I am, but it is desperation that has made me so. I want a normal marriage, Samuel, and a husband who—"

He did not know he was going to slap her until he did it. The sound of his hand striking her cheek reached him before he felt his palm tingle from the blow. She did not move. He slapped her again. And a third time. Then, entirely without expectation, he desired her. He had made love to Mei-hua not two hours before. What he wanted to do to Carolina was something entirely different. And, he realized, he was capable of doing it.

He intended to force her back onto the sofa, but they wound up on the floor, missing even the comfort of the Turkey carpet. He heard the sound of her body thumping against the bare wood each time he thrust. No careful withdrawal before he spilled his seed this time. With joss she'd be pregnant again.

It was over in seconds. He rolled off her and got up, adjusted the buttons of his trousers, and went out to the hall, shutting the drawing room door behind him. Closing out the sound of her sobs.

Chapter Nine

NOT MUCH COULD be done in a shipyard in the dead of winter, even one as well placed as Parker's on Montgomery Street, with its East River ways in spitting distance of the harbor. In late January the river was hard frozen, the tide running dark and deep below nearly two inches of ice. Even on clear days the weak winter sun wasn't enough to warm a half-laid keel to the point where the shipwrights could work without fear of splintering the wood. Mornings and afternoons Danny Parker kept the most skilled of his craftsmen—the ones he dare not lay off lest his rivals snag them—busy in the sheds, carving trunks into masts and thick planks into rudders, or in the chandlery, where strands of hemp were woven into sheets as thick as a man's wrist and twice as flexible, and canvas was stretched and stitched and formed into the mainsails and jibs and topgallants and royals that would someday catch the wind and pump speed not just into a ship but into the hearts of all who saw her.

Evenings were for sitting close to the stove and nursing a glass of rum, and spreading the plans of a ship yet to be built on a nearby table. Or maybe one already built that might serve as an inspiration for something better.

"The full set," Sam Devrey said. "The *Ann McKim* exactly as she was made."

Danny Parker whistled softly through his teeth. "I heard those plans were under guard down there in Maryland. How did you get them?"

Devrey shrugged. "Doesn't matter. They're authentic, that's all you need to know."

Parker took another swallow of his rum and leaned closer to the drawings. Much of what they showed he already knew. The *Ann McKim* was the talk of every port in the nation. Her bow was less bluff than anything afloat, and she had a low freeboard, a narrow V-shaped hull, and three masts rather than the two of the Baltimore clippers that were her forerunners. Not to mention live oak frames and a hull sheathed in copper and deck fittings of the finest mahogany and the best brass. The result was not just the fastest ship afloat able to make the China run but the most beautiful. Christ, what wouldn't he give to build a ship like that here at Parker's? His right arm maybe. "Does Mr. Astor know you've got—"

"Mr. Astor need not be troubled by these conversations. I've told you that before."

"Aye, you have, Mr. Devrey. But if you'll excuse me saying so, the money required to build a ship like this . . ."

"Never fear, when the proper time comes, I will put the funds in your hands." Lately he'd been thinking he might be able to raise some money by borrowing against his collection of jade. It was hard to imagine putting his treasures at risk, but if it were necessary . . . No need to face that now. They needed to solve the design problems first.

"Ship like you're after would cost a fair bit to build," Danny said again.

Parker had no real reason not to trust Sam Devrey. He just didn't. Old man Astor was a right bastard, of that he was certain. And he didn't blame Devrey for wanting to have a ship or two of his own in the fleet, maybe even set up a rival firm. All the same, he needed to protect himself. "Say we came to an agreement and I did build her, would you be able to guarantee further commissions?" Astor would drop him quick as he sneezed if he found out that Parker's had built a rival ship for Sam Devrey. And Devrey Shipping was his largest and most important customer.

"You mistake my meaning, Danny. I've no intention of building a sister ship of the *Ann McKim*."

"But she's the fastest thing there is on the China run and—"

"Fast, yes. But too damned narrow, and only four hundred ninety-four tons burthen. She can carry only half as much as a full-bodied ship of the same size. It is not enough to be fast, Danny, I need a ship that will be profitable."

"Then I don't suppose we'll be needing these." The shipwright rolled up the plans as he spoke. "However much you had to pay to get them."

"Keep them, Danny. Study them. I've made a copy and I shall do the same. Let us see what is to be learned from Mr. McKim's exquisite folly." The Baltimore trader who commissioned the ship had named her for his wife and put her face on the figurehead. When his ship was built, Sam had already decided, he would call her the *Mei-hua*. He'd tell Carolina he was naming the vessel for a mythical Chinese princess. Though the way things were between them now, she might not ask. He wasn't proud of what he'd done on his birthday, but he wasn't sorry either. She was far less demanding and more docile. Probably not pregnant, though. He suspected she'd have told him if she were. Bad joss. "Think on the *Ann McKim*, Danny. Long and narrow gives you speed but not enough lading. How can we have both?"

According to Ah Chee, it was Wood Monkey year. Some of the men said Wood Rooster, others Fire Dog. Lee Leper Face insisted it would be Water Sheep year in a few days. Bo One Ear—who was the closest thing on Cherry Street to a proper astrologer from the Middle Kingdom and who posed as an expert in *feng shui*—was certain only that this new year, celebrated always on the second new moon after the shortest sun day, would arrive in ten days' time.

Mei-hua was insistent that they celebrate the correct new year.

"No mistake. No mistake," she said, stamping her tiny foot. "Very important."

Ah Chee had been attentive. She knew the plum blossom had bled in Chrysanthemum month and Good month and Closed-up-Virgin month. But there had been no evidence of blood in Last month. Now it was First month, and though the bamboo straw had not yet reappeared in her kitchen, so conceivably Mei-hua thought it might still be required in the bedroom, Ah Chee understood the urgency of the question. "Too long away from Middle Kingdom," she muttered. "Don't know up or down anymore."

She would ask those for whom this was their home place.

"For the love of God, woman," the pigman repeated for the third time, "it's February, 1835. What else could it be after 1834? Where have you been all this time?"

Ah Chee shook her fist at him, almost weeping with frustration. "What year? What year?"

"1835," he bellowed at the top of his voice. "Just like I keep telling you. The fourth of February, 1835!"

At home in her kitchen it took all Ah Chee's good sense to keep from lighting ten incense sticks to make sure the pigman would come down with plague. He provided her with very special excellent ham and pork at a not too terrible price. One joss stick only. Ask that maybe he would be constipated for a week. "No shit," she murmured as the first tendrils of scented smoke rose toward the benign face of Zao Shen. "Seven days no shit." On the twenty-third day of Last month she had made special sweet moon cakes in the kitchen god's honor. Best-tasting moon cakes ever, with sweet bean paste inside and honey on the top. Had to be Zao Shen would listen to her request, he might even get carried away. "No very too much no shit," she murmured before she knelt in a deep and respectful kowtow. "One week only. Good pigman most of the time."

Mei-hua had been napping before Ah Chee returned from the market. Indeed, she was taking many naps these days. That was another reason to hope, though neither woman had yet spoken aloud the possibility. Now the plum blossom appeared at the door of the kitchen. "What are you asking of Zao Shen?"

"Not your business." If the pigman suspected the real reason he was suffering, his reciprocal curses must not fall on Mei-hua. "You think only good thoughts about every people."

Mei-hua shrugged. "What did you find out? Is it Water Sheep or Wood Monkey?" She was hoping for Wood Rooster—pride and willingness to fight were fine attributes for a son—so she did not mention that one. In case Zao Shen might choose to spite her.

"Very stupid peoples in this place. Pigman keep shouting numbers at me. 1835. He say 1835. Wouldn't tell what year."

Fortunately, the next day a new man arrived on Cherry Street. He was called Bo Fat Cheeks, and he'd been a cook's helper on a Devrey merchantman until he broke his leg. One of the men from downstairs took his place on the ship's return journey to Canton, while Fat Cheeks was installed in his place in the Lord Samuel's lodging house. This Bo had been away from home less than a year, and he was astonished there could be doubt in anyone's mind. It would soon become Wood Monkey year.

Ah Chee was only somewhat gratified to have been right all along. Wood Monkey was a better girl year. Chattering. Jumps around a lot. Small. But if *tai-tai* had a small son, better than no son at all. Ah Chee made plans for the new year feast. They were immeasurably improved by the fact that Fat Cheeks had brought with him a sack of mung beans and quickly understood that he must give a large share to the household of the supreme lady *tai-tai* upstairs. So Ah Chee would have proper long, white bean sprouts, not the short, stubby brown things that were all she had managed to achieve by sprouting the beans she could buy in this place. She would save most of the mung beans to make sprouts for strong son soup and use only a few for the feast to welcome Wood Monkey year. A girl year wasn't worth more.

"Carolina, who is that peculiar creature?"

"What creature, Aunt Lucy?" Carolina did not look up from her sewing.

"Over there on the park bench." Lucy stood by the window, gazing through the lace curtains rather than pushing them aside.

The park—really only a small square of grass and two trees and three benches, grudgingly installed by the speculators because it was easier to sell family houses when such amenities were present—was where Nurse took little Zachary on these April afternoons. Carolina immediately sprang to her feet and rushed to stand beside her aunt. A tiny woman was seated on a bench next to the one where Carolina's baby-nurse and her son were enjoying the spring sunshine. The woman was so short her feet didn't reach the ground but stuck straight out in front of her, and she wore the oddest imaginable conical straw bonnet. "Oh her," Carolina said. "Very peculiar, I agree. But harmless, I'm sure."

"How can you be sure, my dear? These days the papers are full of the most dreadful goings-on. All these horrid immigrants and their fighting and this talk of laboring people forming associations and going on . . . What do they call it?"

"On strike. And they're called unions, not associations," Carolina said, her gaze still firmly fixed on the park across the road.

"Yes, that's it. Such times. Perhaps that creature over the way has something to do with these unions. You should notify the constable of the ward, my dear. Or even the High Constable."

"The High Constable has more important things to be concerned with."

"Well, yes, I suppose. But the neighborhood has a marshal, I'm sure."

"It is not necessary to do anything, Aunt Lucy. Look, they're coming back now." Nurse had risen from the bench and started for home. She pushed little Zac's pram right past the strange woman. "Harmless, as I said." Carolina turned away, unwilling to let her aunt observe her too closely when she added, "I suspect she may have something to do with Samuel."

"With your husband? However do you mean?"

"The shipping business deals with foreigners every day, Aunt Lucy. All the Devrey ships go to foreign ports. I expect that strange little woman is from one of them. Canton perhaps."

"But why is she sitting over there watching this house? Carolina, I think you must—"

"I must do nothing, Aunt." The nurse had reached the front door with her charge, and Carolina rushed to open it herself. "Give Zachary to his Aunt Lucy, Nurse."

Cooing over the baby provided an adequate distraction. Even someone as flighty as Lucy might otherwise suspect that Carolina had seen the little woman before. God help her if her mother-in-law had been visiting. There was no question in Carolina's mind that Celinda Devrey would have marched across the road and confronted the creature. And if that were to happen, if Carolina had actually to think about what these visits meant, of what was happening to her and to her marriage and by inference to her son, she had no idea what she would do.

Sometimes she could convince herself that terrible night five months ago had not happened. Particularly since there were no consequences. What had she been thinking? How could she have made such a wanton display of herself? No wonder her husband treated her as he did. Once, on the evening before her ninth birthday, she had sneaked downstairs after her bedtime, intending to peek into the parlor and see if Papa had laid out an array of presents as he did every year. Her papa was indeed in the parlor. Lying on the floor on top of Peg, the fat little housemaid. Bouncing up and down with such force poor Peg's head was thumping on the carpet.

If she was treated like a housemaid, it could not be Samuel's fault. It must be hers.

Samuel was her husband, the father of her child. If she blamed him for the coldness between them, where would she be? She was somehow an unnatural wife and quite probably an unfit mother. She must deserve to be treated exactly as Samuel treated her. Otherwise why would he do so?

Sitting on the bench, watching the house of the yellow hair concubine, even seeing her when she opened the door to let in the baby boy and the servant who looked after him, Ah Chee calculated it to be *shen* hour. Once she had heard the lord explain to Mei-hua about time in this place. Hours here, he said, were only half as long as hours in the Middle Kingdom and without names. Ah Chee could never understand about such a ridiculous way of telling time, but she did not have to. She had only to look up at the sky and see that the sun had traveled about half the way from being right overhead to disappearing altogether. So, because this was Peach Blossom month, she knew it was *shen* hour. And in this place, just as in Middle Kingdom, *shen* would be followed by *you*. This time of year it was dark by the end of *you* and the start of *xu*. Long way to go home to Cherry Street. If she did not start now, Ah Chee was not sure she could find her way.

Three times before she had made this long march, following the big carriages pulled by many horses. "Om-nee-bus." She had attempted to get on an om-nee-bus a long time ago, before she knew what it was called, when she first tried to come and see where Lord Samuel went when he left his *tai-tai*. A man inside the big om-nee-bus wore a jacket with shiny button things and a funny cap. Told her she must pay money to ride. So Ah Chee got off. Walked along the road and watched. As long as the big carriages kept going by her, she was in the right place. But now it would be dark soon. Could be no om-nee-bus go up road or down road when it was dark. Could be that if the plum blossom was alone when it got dark she would forget it was very too much necessary she lie still and make a strong son. Almost four months now since she had bled, and every Peach Blossom morning so far she retched green *yin* juice from her stomach. So son definitely coming.

Wait here too much. Know only bad things she knew before. Yellow hair had a big fine house, bigger than the whole house on Cherry Street. And yellow hair didn't share her house with many men. Only servants. Yellow hair also had a son. The first time she saw him Ah Chee had convinced herself the baby was a girl, but today she saw a for-sure-boy baby in push thing with wheels. For-sure-son of yellow hair and Lord Samuel. As for the only thing she wanted to see, that did not appear. She had waited and waited, but the lord had not come. Leper Face and Taste Bad and the others said he made business in a new very too much big house on Canal Street. She had passed Canal Street on her long trudges up and down the rock streets of this place. Many too much big new houses. Ah Chee had no idea which one was the business place of Lord Samuel and no intention of trusting one of the men to take her there. They would whisper about it to the lord, and he would for sure guess what Ah Chee knew. It was no good to know things if other people knew you knew before you told them. Very much too late to stay here now. Ah Chee got off the bench and began hobbling south in the direction of Cherry Street.

She heard the sound of a small rig and a horse behind her, but she'd heard many of those during the course of her long wait. Too much trouble turn around and look. Be wrong one more time.

"*Nì gan she me?*" a voice demanded. What are you doing here?

Ah Chee's smile was so wide it showed all the empty places where teeth had been before she got old. Jade Emperor was at last satisfied with her. Make Lord Samuel come to yellow hair house while Ah Chee still here. She made the smile go away before she turned. "*Zhang san li shih,* come to this place," she said. "Why not this old woman?" The world and his wife came to Fourteenth Street and Fifth Avenue. Why not Ah Chee?

Sam had reined in the buggy as soon as he saw her. Now he leaned forward and stretched out his arm. "Get in. I'll give you a hand up."

Ah Chee allowed herself to be hauled into the buggy, though the thought of the last time she rode beside the Lord Samuel, when the devil woman stole Mei-hua's son as well as Ah Chee's money, made her shudder.

Sam looked over at his house. There was no indication that he had been seen, but even if he had, he could not go inside and leave Ah Chee to her own devices. "How did you know to come here looking for me?"

"This old woman did not come looking for the lord. This old woman—"

Sam flicked the whip over the horse's back and the buggy started forward. Another flick of the whip and the horse broke into a trot.

The buggy's metal wheels struck sparks from the cobbles and the whole rig shook. Ah Chee gripped the edge of the seat with both hands. "Where you go so fast with this old woman?"

"Into the woods," Sam shouted over the rattling. "Where I can beat you and no one will hear your screams." There was construction as far north as Twenty-fifth Street, but there were still stretches of the old Manhattan wilderness to be found near Fourteenth Street. When he pulled up the buggy was hidden beneath a stand of willows showing the first traces of April green. "Now you will tell me how you got here and why. Otherwise I will beat you to death with this horse whip and leave your body for the dogs to eat."

They both knew it was an idle threat, just as they both knew Ah Chee had come here for the very purpose of telling him something. Sam, however, was not quite sure why she hadn't simply made an opportunity to speak to him back on Cherry Street. He'd wager any amount that she had walked the two miles from there to here. It must have hurt like the very devil. The only reason she would put herself through such an ordeal had to be to let him know she could. Or, more precisely, that she knew where to find him. Still more to the point, that she knew about Carolina and his son. So what did Ah Chee really want?

Sam jumped down from the buggy, went around to the other side and yanked the old servant down as well. She made a great show of cowering. He brought the horse whip down on her shoulder. Not too hard, just enough to give her the opportunity to say what she'd come to say not because that's what she'd intended to do right along but because he'd beaten the truth out of her. A dog barked in the distance, and Sam said, "He is waiting for his dinner. Now talk, or he will get it immediately." He accompanied this speech with much flailing of the horsewhip. He had not spent all those years in China without learning about face.

Ah Chee put up her hands as if to protect herself from the onslaught, though the whip was striking everywhere but her. She allowed this to go on for a few moments before whispering, "Supreme lady *tai-tai* does not bleed since First month."

Sam wasn't sure he'd heard her. He stopped the charade of whipping Ah Chee and stood very still. *"Zai suo yi bien,"* he commanded. Again say it. "Right now. *Zai suo yi bien.*"

"Tai-tai does not bleed any month since First month. Pretty soon her belly get round. In Osmanthus month she give lord strong son."

Sam allowed the whip to fall from his hand. There was no wind, but he felt chilled. A baby due in September. *"Bu ke nen."* Not possible. "I have taken steps. *Tai-tai* cannot be expecting a child."

"Ke nen." Possible. "Son of the Lord Samuel comes in Osmanthus month. *Ke nen.*" The look on the Lord Samuel's face was what Ah Chee had feared most, why she could not simply let Mei-hua tell the news herself and plead to be allowed to give birth to their son. Ah Chee knew what the Lord Samuel was thinking. "No other man go near plum blossom's privates," she said. "No other. Never since first time the Lord saw her. On the sampan of Di Short Neck. Never. Never."

"Bu ke nen," Sam repeated. There could be no pregnancy if the seed did not reach the womb. That's what Nick Turner said. *"Jue duay bu ke nen."* Absolutely not possible.

"Ke nen. Ke nen." Possible. Possible. "Look." Ah Chee reached below her tunic and produced the hollow bamboo rod that had reappeared in her kitchen as soon as the second month of no blood passed and Mei-hua was sure. "Look. Supreme *tai-tai* use this. Suck up seed from silk cloth and put it deep inside pleasure place. Like this. Like this." Ah Chee put the bamboo rod in her mouth and made loud sucking sounds, then clapped her finger over the hole and waved the thing in the direction of her crotch.

It took him a moment to understand, and then he was more furious than astonished. "Who did this? You?"

"This old woman not do no thing. Not this thing, not no other thing. Plum blossom *tai-tai* do thing herself. Because if she not give her lord strong son she will weep so many tears she will die."

"But she's too young. There's plenty of time. I don't want—"

"*Tai-tai* want. She want much. Much. This time you let son grow inside her. Have son from real *tai-tai*, not ugly too big yellow hair."

Samuel spun around and walked away. Mei-hua really was pregnant. Indeed, if Ah Chee was to be believed, she had taken extraordinary steps to become so. The child was his. But the rest of it. . . . Ah Chee not only knew where to find him she knew who Carolina was and she knew they had a son. "Bad joss," he whispered, then chided himself for having become as superstitious as the most ignorant coolie. All the same, he could feel it in his bones. The whole thing was all very bad joss.

Carolina was standing by the window in her bedroom when Samuel drove the buggy back past the house and continued south on Fifth Avenue. The peculiar little woman was still sitting beside him with her feet sticking straight out, just as she had been after he pulled her into the rig nearly twenty minutes earlier.

Now, Carolina guessed, he would drive her back where she came from. For a wild moment she toyed with the notion of running downstairs and out the back, of throwing her old sidesaddle on the riding mare and taking off after the buggy.

And maybe pigs would fly.

Where would Barnabas the stable boy be when she set out on this adventure? Watching her, of course. And he would run and report the whole extraordinary business to Celinda Devrey. And what would that harridan do with the information? No way to know, except that it would not be to the advantage of Carolina.

And when Samuel took the wizened little creature to wherever he was bringing her, they would speak Chinese. She had once heard him mouth those extraordinary sounds he claimed were words when a man came to the door bringing him a note about some emergency on the docks. *There are any number of Chinese dialects, Carolina. That man speaks the Cantonese of Toishan to his familiars, Mandarin to me. Yes, of course I learned the language when I was there.*

She held the lace curtain back and peered up the avenue until the buggy could no longer be seen. Pigs did not fly, and she could not take the chance of following Samuel, because what she learned would probably be worse than her suspicions and doubts, and her actions would likely have terrible and unpredictable consequences. Like the night she waited up for him and forced that terrible and shaming confrontation. She had acted like a strumpet, a street whore, and Samuel had responded by meting out exactly the treatment such behavior deserved.

There was no way to avoid seeing her reflection in the glass above her dressing table. She looked, Carolina thought, old and tired and worn out. No wonder her husband had so little use for her and so little love.

Chapter Ten

IT WASN'T AS if Lilac Langton had been a churchgoer back home in London, and heaven knows Joe Langton weren't the sort to spend his Sundays listening to any sort of preaching. Nursing his sore head from Saturday's boozing more like. But they was married proper in a Methodist chapel the way her ma wanted, and Lilac always remembered how good that made her feel. She was a wife in the sight of God. Poor Joe. She had a duty to his memory. There had to be a heaven, didn't there, for Joe to be in it?

The other reason she put on her best bonnet and her newest frock and her gorgeous new cloak with the genuine rabbit fur collar and tucked her gloved hands into the matching muff (just enough early October chill in the late afternoon air so that didn't look out of place) was all the fuss everyone was making about Charles Finney's preaching. The papers were full of how ordinary folk were flocking to hear him and be saved for certain sure. More fuss than ever since a couple of years back, when some rich men bought the old Chatham Street Theater and turned it into a church where Mr. Finney could hold his revival meetings three days every week, as well as a regular church service on Sunday.

It was the Wednesday afternoon meeting Lilac had decided to attend. Quite a distance down the town from Christopher Street to Chatham Street, but Lilac knew her way. She'd been once before when it had been a theater. Went to see that minstrel fellow who blacked his face with burnt cork and pretended he was an old nigra. Jim Crow he called himself. Quite amusing, she recalled, but to be honest, she was with a gentleman friend on that occasion, and she was a bit tiddly by the time they got to the theater. And thinking about what she might expect later in the evening and whether she would or she wouldn't. Ah, nice gent he'd been, but that must have been the Bowery Theater. She didn't remember anything as big as this.

What was now officially known as the Second Free Presbyterian Church—unlike every denomination in New York except the Methodists, Finney's churches charged no pew rents—had been built in 1825 as a splendid and elaborate theater that could seat 2,500. The entrance was through a set of triple doors fronted with eight tall pillars, then up a double stairway to a great balcony with row after row of seats, all looking down at a ground-level pit filled with yet more seats.

The gilt had been painted white and the interior shorn as much as possible of theatrical frippery. What had been the stage was now an austere altar, backed with an enormous and utterly plain wooden cross. "Whereon Our Blessed Lord Jesus Christ died to save sinners," Finney intoned in a voice that was somehow both sweet as honey and compelling as a trumpet blast. "Where he waits for those who choose the salvation he offers."

Lilac's gaze never left the preacher's face. She'd come early enough to get a seat in the very front row of the balcony, right next to the stairway down to the pit. And near the aisle leading to what they called the Anxious Bench, where Mr. Finney invited those whose souls were troubled by sin, who knew they had done evil in God's sight, to come and sit and be prayed over by him and by the congregation. Then, if you thought and prayed hard enough and so did everyone else, you would choose Jesus as your personal savior. After which, sure as anything, you would have enough faith to go to heaven when you died. But what if you didn't?

Mr. Finney seemed to have heard her thoughts. "And what of sinners who do not choose Jesus, who do not respond to this call? I tell you what the Gospel tells us. It was better for them had they never been born. Hellfire awaits them, burning and torment. Not just for a time, my brothers and sisters. For eternity! Can you imagine what that means? I admit that I cannot. Burning and torment forever and ever. And all because you do not choose Jesus, the loving and good Jesus who prays to the Heavenly Father to forgive our sins. Your sins, my brothers and sisters. Yours! Yours!"

God help her. All those babies. But if she didn't do something for the women, they'd be after shoving lord knows what up their twats. What about Joe? How sick he was, and she left him anyway, because it was so terrible hot down in the bowels of the ship.

"Your sins, sisters and brothers! Weighing down your soul with black misery!"

It wasn't like she could do anything for him, burning up with fever the way he was. When she came back she brought a wet cloth, except by the time she returned poor Joe was dead. And far as she knew, Joe never declared Jesus Christ to be his personal savior.

"Jesus is the only way to heaven, my brothers and sisters! So if you think you might be ready, and if you are hoping to be ready, even though you do not yet feel the light of faith in your soul, come and sit on the Anxious Bench and we will pray over you and you will be saved. You, madam, will be saved and happy in heaven with Jesus forever. Tell us your name, dear sister, that we may pray for the light of faith to enter your soul."

"Lilac Langton." She didn't realize until she said the words aloud that she had walked down those steps and along that aisle and was sitting on the Anxious Bench with Mr. Charles Finney himself standing over her, bending down from his great height, with his piercing blue eyes looking directly into hers. God Almighty! How could she begin getting saved with a lie? "Least wise it's Lilac now. Used to be Francy."

"Lilac suits you, sister. A sweet flower. And you, sister"—moving on to the woman sitting beside her—"what is your name?"

"Adelaide Bellingham, Mr. Finney, sir, and I'm guilty of terrible sins. I been aiding and abetting them as encourages the poor in their profligate ways, and my soul is black with guilt."

"Now, gentlemen, a small demonstration. Cup your hand around one ear. Like this." Nick performed the action even as he explained it. The three medical students who were watching him did the same. "Do you see how that channels the sound of my voice?"

The students nodded in unison like marionettes whose strings were being pulled. Christ. Had he been so Godawful ignorant at their stage of medical experience? Probably. "Now, as doctors, when do you most need to hear as clearly as possible?" Silence. "Come, gentlemen. Your professors have surely discussed with you the art of auscultation. You put your ear to a patient's chest and listen to . . . to what, Dr. Klein?"

"The heartbeat, sir."

"Excellent." Klein, one of the student assistants, was of the Hebrew race, from Germany originally. Spoke English quite well, but had the dark and swarthy looks of most Jews. Sinister some people said. Nick had known too few of them to have an opinion about that, but this one certainly had a quick mind, though when he asked, "What else can you hear with auscultation, gentlemen?" even the clever Klein appeared stumped. "Good God, gentlemen, the lungs. If we can hear clearly enough, it's possible to tell if the lungs are clear or filled with filth. Like those blackened things I showed you in the laboratory the other day."

The man in the bed around which Nick had assembled his young assistants, an Irishman named Patrick Heffernen, grew wide-eyed with terror. "You'll not be after taking me up to the laboratory for slicing and dicing, Dr. Turner? I'll not be dying, will I?"

"Of course you will, Patrick, but not this afternoon." The man had broken his leg in the stepping house, and Nick was not entirely sure he hadn't stepped into the gears of the turning wheel on purpose. "I told you I was having the students listen to your chest for practice. Ah, here's Dr. Chance."

Monty Chance appeared at the bedside carrying a wooden box stamped "Portugal" on one side and "Port Wine" on the other. It looked the right size for about four bottles.

"Don't get your hopes up, gentlemen. Dr. Chance has not brought us a libation. He has instead procured the latest invention designed to serve medical science, made for us in one of our own Bellevue workshops exactly to my specifications. Show them what you have, Dr. Chance."

"Yes, sir." Chance knelt down, put the box on the floor, and lifted the lid. Inside were hollow black tubes, shiny and stiff, each about twelve inches long and three inches in diameter. He handed the first to Nick, then one to each of the three students. The fifth was for himself.

"What are they made of, sir?" Klein didn't wait for an answer before holding one up to his ear.

"Newspaper," Nick said. He leaned towards the young student, pitching his voice straight at the cylinder. "Layers of newspaper held together with pitch, then finished off with a few coats of shellac. They'll last a good long while if you take care of them. Chap in France who came up with the idea is calling them stethoscopes."

"In France, sir? You have been there?"

The same question Sam Devrey had asked about reproductive theory. Nick sighed. "No, Mr. Klein, but in medicine we write about what we discover, so other doctors can read and learn and medical knowledge can spread. Now tell me what you think. Can you hear me better through the stethoscope than without it?"

"Enormously better, sir. It's amazing. And so . . . forgive me, sir, so simple." It sounded like "zo zimple." A carryover from his mother tongue, Nick supposed.

"Indeed. Now watch." Nick bent over Patrick Heffernan's bed and put one end of the cylinder to the man's chest while holding the other end tight to his ear. The heartbeat, steady and strong, was many times amplified. After a moment he raised his head. "You'll definitely not be among the dying today, Patrick. Now gentlemen, one after another. And for your information, this is what a healthy heart sounds like. Be sure you move the stethoscope to allow you to distinguish the sounds of the two separate chambers." He had dissected a pair of hearts for them the previous month, one a three-year-old child's, the other that of an old woman. The old woman's was normal in all respects, the child's flabby and one side collapsed. Expect the unexpected when you do an anatomy he'd told them. He might have added that it was not the only thing unexpected in the practice of modern medicine.

"Soap, Dr. Turner? Ordinary soap?"

"Ordinary soap, Sister Mary, as long as you use plenty of it. Wash your hands with soap and water between treating your patients. It will work wonders, I promise. Particularly with an outbreak such as this." Nick dismissed the last of the six young orphans who had been presented to him, all with the same itchy and ugly red rash, mostly on their legs, though one or two had it on their arms as well.

Sister Mary did not follow her young charge out of the small room the nuns provided for these consultations. "With the greatest respect, Dr. Turner, my hands are clean. As clean as this. Always." She held them out. Red and roughened, but the nails pared and no trace of grime anywhere.

"What concerns me, Sister, cannot be seen with the naked eye."

He had taken to visiting St. Patrick's Orphan Asylum once a week, usually in the late afternoon, when he could most easily get away from Bellevue. Sister Mary was the Infirmarian, as she was called among the Sisters of Charity, so he saw more of her than of Mother Louise or any of the others. Notwithstanding the evidence of hard physical labor, the hands she had presented for his inspection were long-fingered and elegant. Like much else about her, they made it obvious that in another place and had she made other choices, Sister Mary would be mistress of a grand household. Even wearing the black habit of the Sisters of Charity, it was easy to see that she was a patrician beauty, and educated with it.

"It occurred to me, Doctor . . ."

"Yes, Sister Mary. Do go on."

She folded the reddened hands beneath the short black cape she wore over her black dress. "The children are not ill, sir. They do not feel sick and they have neither fever nor loss of appetite. Except for the itching, they appear to enjoy their play time and do their chores and their lessons with the same will as usual. How then can this eruption on their skin be a medical matter?" He had to struggle to hear her, and Sister Mary did not look directly at him in her usual fashion but stared at a spot on the floor.

"And you make of this—what?"

"Perhaps"—she was now barely whispering—"it is a manifestation of something I should be discussing not with a doctor but with a priest."

"Sister Mary . . ." Nick hesitated. But she was intelligent. And devoted to her duty. "I assure you that you're wrong. Illness is not merely what we can see. It's not just based on the symptoms the patient reports and the patterns we build up of those symptoms. The best medicine requires an understanding of what happens inside our bodies and what we can learn when peering through a microscope."

"The study of anatomy," she said.

She was looking straight at him now. Nick was quite sure they were both thinking the same thing. The word anatomy hung in the air between them. "Yes," he said, making no effort to avoid her gaze. If he backed off now, he would simply confirm her worst suspicions. He suspected the Catholic Church, along with all the rest of the clerical establishment, to be virulent in its condemnation of what it would see as showing disrespect for the dead.

Sister Mary seemed to make a conscious decision to avoid the perilous topic. She drew a deep and audible breath. "We seem to have strayed from the subject, Dr. Turner. You believe then that despite their having no symptoms except for this prickly rash, the children are diseased?"

"In a manner of speaking. This irritation may come from some sickened internal organ, but I can't say that for sure, and frankly I doubt it. What I'm quite convinced of, because of previous observation, is that they are passing it to each other through ordinary contact. Or that you, in all innocence may have passed it from one to the rest."

"Me!"

"You, Sister. That's why I want you to wash your hands between putting soothing lotion on one and then another. You told me you were using calomel."

"Yes. It's the usual recommendation, is it not?"

"It is. Exactly the right thing. But if you touch the rash on one child and then touch another who is not infected, you transfer the germs."

She had grown quite pale. "It is . . . almost unthinkable."

He'd been afraid she would say diabolical. And mean exactly that and go screaming to the priest she'd considered consulting earlier, which would probably get him tossed out on his ear and forbidden to return. A pity if that happened, he quite enjoyed coming to St. Patrick's Orphan Asylum. "It is a problem easily remedied," he promised, as cheerfully as he could. "Ordinary soap, Sister Mary."

There was a sharp rap on the door, and it opened before either Nick or Sister Mary could say a word. One of the older girls stepped in and bobbed a quick curtsy.

"'Scuse me, Sister Mary, he's wanted. Right away."

"Dr. Turner, Elizabeth. Not he. And wanted by whom?"

"A man, Sister. At the door. Mother Louise sent me. Said to tell him—I mean Dr. Turner. Mother said I was to say his cousin needed to see Dr. Turner at once. On an urgent family matter."

Chapter Eleven

THE SAME TINY and beautiful and exotic creature Nick had treated when she was in danger of bleeding to death from a botched abortion was on the floor, huddled in a corner beside the elaborate bed draped in red. There was not enough light for him to see anything very clearly, but he had no doubt about the distended abdomen visible beneath a covering of silk shawls and wrappings. This time, despite his instructions to Sam Devrey about *coitus interruptus,* she had carried a pregnancy to term. And her moans made it apparent she was in labor. "How long has she been like this?"

Sam turned to Ah Chee. "How long exactly? Since the first pain."

Ah Chee could not take her eyes from the big this-place-red-hair *yi.* Very too much confusion in her head. Should she weep for her plum blossom or thank Chuan Yin for a miracle? Red-hair *yi* stopped blood last time. Unless he do that little supreme lady *tai-tai* already dead. But very terrible joss for there to be men in the room when the baby came. That's what she told the lord when he arrived while the birthing was still going on. But the plum blossom screamed and screamed, and the Lord Samuel stayed outside the bedroom for *shen* hour and *you* and *xu.* Then couldn't wait anymore and went into the bedroom to see how it was with his supreme lady *tai-tai*. Then run and bring this-place-red-hair *yi*.

"How long?" Sam demanded again. "How long, Ah Chee? What time did the pains start?"

Ah Chee chose the truth simply because it was easier. "Since maybe two-*ke* of *zi* hour."

"Dear God." Sam turned back to his cousin. "Since just before midnight yesterday. Almost twenty-four hours." Saying the words made him feel quite ill. Carolina had labored ten, perhaps twelve hours delivering Zachary. And Carolina was a robust American girl, while Mei-hua . . . What would he do if he lost her? What would there be of beauty or satisfaction in his world?

Ah Chee meanwhile had disappeared and quickly returned with the basin of water and bar of soap he'd demanded last time he was here. Nick began rolling up his sleeves. "I've heard of longer labor. I take it no midwife has been with her?"

Sam shook his head. "Just Ah Chee here. I didn't think . . . As I told you before, the Chinese have their own way of—" Mei-hua's shriek cut him off. He started towards her but shrank back. "Do something, Turner. I beg you. She can't—"

"Get out. Take the old woman with you. No, wait, tell her to bring more candles. Or a lantern if there is one. I need more light." The room was dim, only a few candles making long black shadows on the walls. "And where's that peculiar smell coming from?"

As soon as Mei-hua screamed Ah Chee had rushed to the altar of Chan Yin. "Incense," Sam said. He didn't explain further, just grabbed Ah Chee and pulled her from the room.

Nick did not have much experience of birthing. Of late a number of doctors had become active in the business, but not he. Women had been doing quite well with midwifery for God knew how long. He could see little point in the medical profession becoming involved, except in cases like this when clearly the mother was entirely too tiny to cope. Kneeling on the floor beside her, it occurred to him that this might be an argument against the mixing of the races. The infant was crowning, but the girl's pelvis was far too narrow and the baby's head apparently too big.

The flesh either side of the vulva was torn and bloody, and every minute or so Nick could see the top of the baby's head covered in matted black hair. Instinctively the girl was pushing with all her might whenever that happened, but she simply wasn't strong enough, especially now after so much time and effort.

Nick thought of lifting her into the bed, but she seemed to be taking support from the wall behind her and the pile of cushions either side. Best leave her where she was, but he couldn't simply let her go on suffering like this. There was Cesarean birth, of course. The literature was full of tales of attempts to cut the child from the mother's body. Almost without exception, the mother died. Whether to condemn this young woman to death in favor of her babe was not his decision to make. He'd ask Sam Devrey if he must, but it wasn't a question he looked forward to posing or an operation he felt confident would save either of them. Might be too late for the baby even now. He'd heard talk that long and difficult births like this often resulted in a child dead of strangulation.

Very well. What else?

He could crush the child's head with his bare hands, or with the pair of retracting forceps that were in the black bag he'd taken from Bellevue when he left to visit St. Patrick's.

There was another piercing scream. The baby's head was crowning again. This time he actually got a look at the top inch, perhaps two inches, of the skull. Next time that happened, he could get a grip with the forceps. It was an awful thought, but the mother was his patient. Nick took the auscultation tube from his bag and pressed one end to her chest; the girl's heart was racing at a pace that could surely not be sustained much longer. When he pressed the tube into the distended flesh of her lower abdomen, he could hear another heartbeat, also very rapid, but he seemed to remember reading somewhere that was normal. And the one thing he now knew for sure was that the baby was alive. His job was to keep them both that way. He'd read about an English family who in the sixteen hundreds made a profession of rescuing difficult births with the use of a secret tool that turned out to be a sort of forceps. It was worth a try.

He was fishing for the forceps at the bottom of his bag when suddenly there was more light. The old woman had returned and was holding a lantern over his head. "Thank you," he murmured, then went back to rummaging in his bag. There they were. Forged for him at a blacksmith's shop back in Providence. There were lighter and more delicate such instruments available, but he'd never practiced enough surgery to make him feel the expense justified. Too late to wish for such an improved tool now. He drew the heavy black forceps out of the bag and heard the sound of a quick gasp behind him.

"Not do. Not this thing." Ah Chee shouted the words into his ear. "Not do. Very bad. Do other thing."

The only words Nick could make out were "not" and "bad." "She's going to die." He nodded at Mei-hua. "Your mistress cannot continue to labor with this child."

Holding the lantern with one hand, Ah Chee grabbed at the forceps. "Not do. Not do."

Nick was quite sure she understood exactly his intention, but the decision was not hers to make. "Get your master," he said. "Get him in here." He put the forceps back in the bag. "I will do nothing until he comes. Go on!" He gestured toward the door of the room. "Leave the lantern and go get him."

Ah Chee hesitated a second then put down the lantern and hobbled away.

He could see the girl's tiny silk-wrapped feet as well. Even smaller than the serving woman's. What could you expect from a race who deformed their women in such a manner? He bent over and listened to her heart again. Faster than before, though he'd not have thought it possible. And another contraction starting.

Mei-hua screamed. The baby's head showed itself as she leaned forward, supporting herself on her elbows and straining to push out her child. Nick pressed down on her belly. For a moment he thought that might have helped just enough, but the head receded, the contraction passed, and she fell back gasping for air, sobbing and pouring sweat.

"These things. These things." The old woman was back, and she was holding out a pair of long sticks and what looked like a slightly smaller version of a butcher's cleaver. Jesus God Almighty. Was she suggesting those tools to crush the skull so he could draw out the child? Or that he hack the girl apart and get the child that way. "Where's your master. I told you to—"

"Right here." Devrey was standing in the doorway. "How . . . how is she?"

"Not good. There's a decision to be made, and you must make it."

Ah Chee was not entirely sure what the two men were talking about, but she was very sure what must be done for the plum blossom. She had been preparing to do it when the Lord Samuel arrived back with the this-place-red-hair *yi*. She had seen it done by proper birthing women on the sampans of Di Short Neck.

"Cut. Cut," she told red-hair *yi*. "Cut. Make little bit more room. Then pull."

Nick stared at her for a moment. "What are those wooden things?" He cut Devrey off while the man was telling him exactly what he'd expected to hear: that he should do anything necessary to save the life of the mother, the woman Samuel called Mei-hua. "The sticks, what are they for?"

"They're called *xingsheng*," Samuel said. "Chopsticks. They're for eating. Picking things up. But in God's name what's that to do with—"

"Picking things up or pulling them towards you," Nick murmured. After cutting to make a bit more room. It bloody hell should work. It was certainly worth trying. "Get out," he ordered Devrey, looking for the small scalpel he always carried in his bag. "Here," he ordered Ah Chee, "bring that lantern closer. Now lift it so I can see."

Ah Chee appreciated the advantage of the tiny little knife thing over the cleaver, and lantern was a word she knew. She held it high. The plum blossom's privates were on full display, which was very much too bad, but nothing to be done about it now. Maybe later the Lord Samuel would have to kill the this-place-red-hair *yi* because he had looked at the privates of the supreme lady *tai-tai*, not turned his back and pointed to a doll and told Ah Chee what to do, the way a proper Middle Kingdom *yi* would do.

Mei-hua was in the midst of a full contraction. Nick doubted she felt the additional pain of his quick cut of the thin skin between the vulva and the anus. Excellent. He'd enlarged the vaginal opening by a good inch. And here was the child's head yet again.

Nick dropped the scalpel and felt the sticks instantly in his hand.

"Now pull. Now pull," Ah Chee said.

Nick concentrated on inserting the slim, rounded wooden sticks into either side of the vagina between the baby's skull and the mother's flesh. He pressed them against the sides of the child's head and drew the infant towards him. And the mother, bless her pluck, was pushing again, with more strength than he might have imagined she could summon at the end of such a long ordeal.

Samuel was sitting on the red lacquer throne, facing the bedroom. He heard the silence that followed Mei-hua's last shriek of agony. He thought he heard Ah Chee and Nick Turner speaking. Nick Turner could not speak Chinese, so Ah Chee must speak some English. That was a fact he should consider more carefully, but he could not do so now when only one thing mattered.

He heard the first cries of an infant.

Nothing from Mei-hua.

He could not make himself move. The door to the bedroom opened, and Ah Chee appeared with a swaddled bundle in her arms. "Girl baby. Very much too bad. But supreme lady *tai-tai* be fine this-place-red-hair *yi* say. Have son next time."

"Never." Sam experienced the exquisite intensity of the rush of relief as if it were something liquid, a tide starting at his feet and moving up to his head. He made no move to look at the daughter Ah Chee held out for his inspection. "Never. Never. No next time. If there is, I will kill you. I swear it, old woman. If you allow her to become with child again, I will kill you. And," he added, knowing it would be the ultimate convincer, "I will put Mei-hua aside and go and live only with the yellow hair concubine."

Ah Chee did not hesitate. "Never. Never," she agreed. "It will be exactly as the lord wishes."

Manon had no doubt the girl was dying. In the years since she had taken up visiting the sick, she had stood beside any number of people approaching the end. There was a look about them, frequently a sound. Eileen O'Connor, not yet fourteen the other women on the ward said, had both.

Moments later the wheezing, struggling breaths so typical of the consumptive were silent, and her chest no longer moved. Manon listened carefully and heard only the soft murmuring of old Mrs. Kelly telling her beads at the far end of the room. Usually this place echoed with all kinds of moaning and sometimes wailing and caterwauling and cursing. The women were if anything more contentious than the men, but fifteen minutes earlier the entire ward had become as silent as a church. It was that unnatural and respectful quiet that had drawn Manon when she was hurrying past on her way home.

Only the soft clacking of the wooden beads now, and the girl dead. Manon brushed her eyes closed and pressed the slack jaw upward. Not a pretty youngster.

The murmured prayers continued. " . . . full of grace . . . Holy Mary, mother of God . . ."

The cackling of superstitious harpies, the ministers said, when they caught the Irish women mumbling these incantations. It seemed as if all of mighty New York City was terrified of the floods of Catholic immigrants, while at the same time it craved their labor. A few months before, the New York Protestant Association had held a public meeting to debate the proposition, "Is Popery Compatible with Civil Liberty?" Such ministerial nonsense.

None of those worthy gentlemen were around at this hour. Let the women tell their beads if they wanted. It had grown dark while Eileen O'Connor was going about her dying. Not enough light now even to see the patients lying on pallets on the floor because the beds were full. Nothing in their bellies since midafternoon, when they'd been given what passed for dinner at Bellevue. The ministers, meanwhile, were home with a glass of ale and an ample supper of bread and cheese, and they would sleep on feather mattresses, secure in the knowledge that they were the elect.

" . . . pray for us sinners, now and at the hour of our death, Amen."

Finally the prayers finished, but the unnatural silence remained, as if the ward were holding its collective breath. Until finally another voice called out, "Is she gone yet? Is the little saint gone to God, bless her soul?"

"She has," Manon said.

"Right, then I'll be having her bed." The speaker was struggling to get up from the floor.

"You will not! It's me Eileen said as could have it. Promised she did!"

"She did nothing o' the sort. Sure and didn't the little saint say as—"

Manon saw the struggle as a ferocious dance of scrawny shadows on the floor at the far end of the ward. "Be quiet!" Her authority was born of her service. "Hush, all of you. Go back to your prayers. I'll get her ready for burying, then we'll arrange who moves up." The O'Connor girl had been in a proper bed in a choice corner of the room, near a window. "You can draw straws to see who gets the bed."

The pair involved in the scuffle quieted. A woman approached the bed carrying a basin and a sponge. "Sure and I'll do it, Mrs. Turner."

"No, Bridey. I shall. Leave the water and go back to your bed."

"Remember what she said, Bridey," a voice called from the shadows. "Sure and isn't it exactly what the little saint predicted?"

Bridey set down the basin and disappeared into the shadows.

Manon had no notion what the prediction might have been. The wards were rife with conspiracies and intrigues she knew it best to ignore. That said, she had no real idea why she hadn't stepped aside and let Bridey prepare the body for burial, just as she didn't know why she felt compelled to remain beside Eileen O'Connor's bed while she died. The girl was an ordinary consumptive as far as Manon knew, one of the thousands of Irish who arrived and swarmed over the city, poor and ill and frequently dead before their time, beyond the reach of the tiny handful of priests and the town's few Catholic churches.

There was no gaslight in the wards of Bellevue, and candles were in short supply. The women hoarded their little wax stubs as if they were gold, and they often served as items of barter for still more urgent necessities. Still, as the dark encroached, at least half a dozen of the patients lit whatever bit of candle they had. All at once the ward was full of flickering shadows.

Manon rolled back the blanket that had covered Eileen O'Connor's wasted body. That she had such a luxury long after she was able to fight to preserve it was a mark of the esteem of the others.

Dear God.

There was a gaping wound in the palm of the girl's hand. As if someone had driven a nail right through it. Why had no one ever bandaged it?

There was no sign of pus. Only blood, dark black-red and obviously fresh, as if the wound had opened minutes before. But she had been standing here for almost half an hour.

Dear God.

The shadows cast by the flames of the candles became longer and more erratic as the dark deepened beyond the windows. No one spoke. Manon had not heard the ward this silent for this long in all the years she had been coming here.

"Look at t' other hand, Mrs. Turner. Eileen said as—"

"Shut your fracking gob! Told us not to say nothin' didn't she? Never."

Manon ignored the bickering and leaned across the corpse. The other hand was wounded in exactly the same fashion. She touched the blood: slick and warm. Not a figment of her imagination.

What in heaven's name . . . She felt dizzy and leaned against the wall to steady herself. Of its own accord, it seemed, the blanket she had thrown back slipped to the floor, revealing Eileen O'Connor's feet crossed at the ankles. She must have been in that position when she died. The nails were much in need of paring, and two of the toes were clubbed, probably since birth.

In the middle of the girl's two feet was another bloody wound, as if a spike or a nail had been driven through both at the same time.

Lord Jesus Christ have mercy. Do not take my mind. It is all I have that is of any value. Please do not take my mind.

She could not remain in this place. "Bridey. Are you still there?"

"Yes, Mrs. Turner. Right here."

"Then you must finish preparing the body for burial. It is late and I must go."

"Just as you say, Mrs. Turner."

Manon started to step away but paused for one more look at Eileen O'Connor's hands.

They were painfully thin, every vein and bone showing, an indication of a long illness as well as the near-starvation diet of abject poverty. She leaned forward, looking closely. They were unmarked. There was not even a trace of a scar.

After ten and the full harvest moon risen by the time Nick approached the Bellevue gate. Closed at this hour, naturally. He had walked from the new horse-drawn street railway that ran up and down Fourth Avenue on tracks set atop cinder blocks—the only transport he could find at the late hour when he left Sam Devrey's peculiar second household on Cherry Street—and he was anxious for his bed. He tugged firmly on the bell hanging beside the locked gate. No one came. He rang again. This time the night porter appeared and let him in. He had taken only a few steps across the shadowy grounds when he heard a voice.

"Cousin Nicholas."

"Cousin Manon! What are you doing here at this hour?"

"I am not sure." She had been sitting on a bench well back in the shadows of the trees since she left the women's ward. She had very little idea why or why she had chosen to stand up and approach Nicholas as soon as she saw him striding up the path.

"My dear Manon, are you ill?"

She shook her head. "No. I am not ill." She had determined that some time since. She was not ill. And despite her worst fears, she was not mad.

There was dried blood on the first two fingers of her right hand. It had not been there before she approached the bed of Eileen O'Connor, and she had tended no open wound while she waited for the girl to die. Except of course for the brief moment when she touched the holes in the girl's palms.

She could see the dark red streaks clearly in the moonlight. Some extraordinary medical manifestation perhaps. A matter of science, as her husband or indeed his much younger and so clever cousin might have said.

Manon could not imagine discussing the phenomenon with Nicholas Turner. Superstitious Irish nonsense, he was bound to say. You have been in a hospital. You could have touched blood in any number of places. "I am tired, Cousin Nicholas. I was overcome as I was leaving and had to sit down."

"Yes, well, I'm not surprised with all you do. Let me—"

He was opening his bag. Manon put out her clean hand to stop him. "I'm not ill, Nicholas. Truly. Only fatigued. You're late back, aren't you?"

"Yes. I had gone to the orphanage to see Sister Mary's charges." He could not tell her more. It would be a violation of his oath as well as his promise of confidence to Sam Devrey. But someone had told Devrey where to find him. "Did Cousin Samuel come here looking for me?"

She nodded. "I didn't speak with him directly, but one of the porters had Cousin Samuel's card and was making noises about something urgent. I told him to suggest St. Patrick's Orphan Asylum. I hope that was not against your wishes."

"Not at all. You did quite the right thing." She would not ask more and he would not tell. "Come," he said, "let's see about getting you home."

He insisted she must take a hansom, though they had to walk some way west to find one. Over her protests Nick slipped some coins into the cabby's hand and started to tell him her destination, then realized he did not know. "Are you already moved from Wall Street, Cousin Manon?"

"I am, Cousin Nicholas. The wreckers have turned the old place to dust. I'm living in lodgings at number six Vandam Street with Miss Bellingham. You might remember meeting her at the reception for my Society for Aid to Poor Families."

"How do you mean guilty?" Lilac was feeling quite lighthearted. Not only had Mr. Finney assured her she was now reborn in the spirit and her sins of no account since she had accepted Jesus, she was surrounded by brightness and gaiety. Beyond the large plateglass windows of the Crystal Pavilion at Niblo's Pleasure Garden on Broadway there were red and green colored lanterns strung everywhere, and tonight a full harvest moon added to the gaiety of the scene. And since in the interest of frugality she and her new friend, Miss Addie Bellingham, had walked up the town from Mr. Finney's church, she had been quite prepared to buy a ten-cent ticket of entrance for the Garden, as well as indulge in a two-penny glass of sweet and fizzy apple cider and not one but two four-penny slices of iced pound cake. Imagine Miss Bellingham looking so gloomy in the face of so many delights. "All our guilt is washed away in the spirit. That's what Mr. Finney said."

"Well, yes, but he said we had to change our ways. Now that we've been reborn."

"Oh, we must, Miss Bellingham, we clearly must. But I'm sure Mr. Finney wasn't advising anything too drastic. I mean, there's the virtue of prudence, as they call it. Are you going to eat that cake?"

Miss Bellingham had ordered only a single slice of pound cake with pink ratafia icing, and it sat ignored on her plate. "No, I don't think so. I'll take it home for her, though. Eats like a bird."

"Who does?" Lilac watched while her companion folded the untouched cake into a handkerchief and put it in her bag.

"Lady I live with." Then with sudden ferocity, "I'm not a servant, mind. It's nothing like that."

"Don't get so excited. I never thought you were a servant." Miss Bellingham was a frump in dark and ill-becoming clothes. Serving girls made it their business to wear bright and gay clothes when not in uniform. "Is she a relative then?" The pastry had now disappeared into the tightly closed drawstring bag hanging from Adelaide Bellingham's wrist.

"Not exactly. A friend. Least, I thought she was, but . . ."

"But what?" A good story might be every bit as satisfactory as a third piece of ratafia iced pound cake.

"But she's the one who—" Miss Bellingham was suddenly choked with tears. She reached into her bag for a handkerchief, then remembered. "Oh dear, the cake."

"Here, take this." Lilac offered her own handkerchief. Nice and clean it was with a proper tatted edge. Many of the women who came to her Christopher Street rooms were of a better class, and Lilac had a good eye for how they did things. "Go on, take it. And stop crying. This lady can't be much of a friend if she makes you weep like that."

"Oh but she is. I mean she was. After my poor dear mother died. I had no one, you see. Then I fell and broke my leg and—" Addie broke off. She couldn't tell about losing her job as a seamstress's assistant and finishing up in the workhouse when she couldn't pay her rent. It was too humiliating. "Mrs. Turner's been a good friend to me ever since. Except—"

"Except what? Let's have another sweet cider, shall we? My treat." Lilac raised her hand and summoned one of the white-aproned waiters and gave him her order. Then, when he had left, "Now, dear Miss Bellingham, as you were saying . . ."

"I was having a difficult patch. You understand."

"Yes, of course I do. Happens to all of us sometimes."

"Then Mrs. Turner came along and was ever so helpful."

The harpies in the workhouse had fair to killed her. Robbed her of what little she possessed and would probably have had the skin off her bones in the bargain if Mrs. Turner hadn't seen how it was and invited her into her home. Gave her sewing to do at first. Then made her secretary of her new society at a dollar a week plus room and board. Not so nice now that the big house on Wall Street had been sold and they were in lodgings, but still a good deal better than the Bellevue workhouse. Only how could she go on working for Mrs. Turner's society, now that she had learned from Mr. Finney (this October Wednesday was the sixth of his revival meetings she had attended, though the first when she'd actually found the courage to sit on the Anxious Bench) that the poor were as they were because of their immoral carrying-on and lack of frugality? If they only declared Jesus Christ their personal savior and heeded the words of the Bible and began living moral lives, they would find the strength to better themselves.

It all seemed quite clear to her, but how could she explain it to Mrs. Langton, who had been on the Anxious Bench beside her, but was it seemed not in the least unsettled by the conversion they had both undergone.

"Black with sin I am," Miss Bellingham said with another burst of tears. "My soul is black with sin."

Chapter Twelve

"THINK OF THE patient," Dr. Turner was always telling them. "Be aware of the science of your treatment but remember that the point of the whole enterprise is the person you are treating. And above all, do no harm."

Benjamin Klein—a student at the brand-new medical school of the only slightly less new University of the City of New York and an assistant at, (*Hashem* permit he should survive in such a place), Bellevue Hospital—understood what Dr. Turner meant. Actions have consequences. Sometimes enormously far-reaching. For instance, here he was sitting on the narrow wooden bench of the Ashkenazic synagogue called B'nai Jeshurun, not in the town's other synagogue, the Sephardic Shearith Israel.

Because, as Benjamin knew, most of the original Jewish population of New York were descended from Jews expelled from the sun-kissed lands of Spain and Portugal. They were known as Sephardim, while those from Germany, Galicia, and Poland were known as Ashkenazim. And over the centuries the two groups had developed a few differences in the manner of prayer and observance.

Then, around 1825, the Ashkenazim became the majority of the
Jews of New York—never a large number according to Papa, who was
a silversmith but studied such things. Some six hundred families out of
nearly two hundred fifty thousand people in the city. The Ashkenazim
wanted the synagogue rites to be those with which they were familiar,
but the elders of Shearith Israel refused to change from the Sephardic
prayer book. So the Ashkenazim left.

The breakaways banded together and bought what had been the
First Colored Presbyterian Church, run by a free-born black man from
Delaware named Samuel Cornish who had gotten himself into all sorts
of trouble about abolition and such controversial ideas, so he sold his
building to those he called with exaggerated politeness Hebrews as if
calling them Jews might insult them.

It was a good building, brick, built to last. Even more important, it
was on Elm Street, near where these days a lot of Jewish families like
Benjamin's own—not rich enough to live over on the west side of the
town or poor enough, *Hashem* help them, to have to live on Centre
Street or Pearl Street or White Street, where they were practically in
the dreaded Five Points—could walk to services on the Sabbath, when
riding was forbidden. Near enough so Papa could drag him here for
this Thursday *shachris*, the daily morning service. Because, Papa said,
Ben was required to complete a *minyan*, the quorum of ten Jewish men
necessary for a prayer service. And that was a *mitzvah*, a commandment
to righteousness, that even a not-so-observant Jew like Ben Klein could
not ignore. Never mind that Dr. Turner expected him at Bellevue early
this morning and had said they had something special to discuss.

Nothing to worry about, Papa insisted. Even though the Thursday
shachris was one of the two long weekday services when in addition to
the ordinary daily prayers a portion of the holy *Torah* was read, it would
take only an hour or so. Dr. Turner, Papa said, was no doubt a very good
man since Benjy thought so highly of him, but he was a *goy*. He did not
have the same obligations.

The shachris was almost over. Rabbi Schiff had reached the point
in the proceedings where he cradled the scroll in his arms, came down

from the *bimah*, the platform, and paraded around the room, so the men could all for a moment see up close the *Torah,* this most precious gift of *Hashem*. Ben and the others rose to their feet in respect, and as a sign of devotion when the sacred scroll passed, touched it with the fringe of their *talaysim*, their prayer shawls. All the while continuing to *daven*, chant their prayers while they rocked back and forth, as their ancestors had done since the days when the tribes of Israel first entered the land of milk and honey. At least that's what the rabbis, the learned teachers, all said.

Fine. Everything was fine. The sun was just coming through the windows on the right side of the synagogue. This time of year, November, that meant not yet quarter past eight. If he got to the hospital by nine, he would still be on the early side. Dr. Turner would not feel that his student had ignored his request.

Rabbi Schiff finished his circuit, placed the sacred text on the lectern, and since there was no cantor to do it, chanted the name of the first man who was to come forward and read the holy words. "Benjamin *ben* Jacob *ben* Abraham." Papa had to elbow Ben in the ribs before he realized the *aliyah*, the honor to be called, was his.

"It is called the stigmata," Mother Louise said. "A replication of the wounds the crucifixion made in the hands and feet of our Blessed Lord."

"Then you have heard of such a thing?" Manon found some solace in that.

"Oh yes. There are stories. It has been noted among the saints, the holy men and women who are meant to serve as examples to us. St. Francis, I believe, had the stigmata. It is said that St. Clare tended his wounds."

"Her name was Eileen O'Connor. The others called her the little saint. They are not given to speaking kindly about each other, and no sooner was she dead than they were squabbling over who would have her bed. But in her last moments they told their beads aloud with what sounded like true devotion. Out of respect, I thought."

"Yes, I know what you mean. Real goodness is compelling even to the least noble spirit."

The calmness of Mother Louise, her placid acceptance of the extraordinary tale, gave Manon courage. "There's something else. I hesitate to say, but . . ." She was twisting her handkerchief into knots, acting like a guilty schoolgirl. Ridiculous. Equally so that it had taken every bit of courage she could summon to come and tell this story. As if, once she told it, she would have passed to the other side of an enormous chasm, one she found utterly terrifying but felt compelled to cross nonetheless. "Moments later, when I looked again at her hands and her feet . . ."

"Yes, my dear Mrs. Turner. Do go on."

"The wounds were gone."

"I see. And that disturbed you most of all, did it?"

"Yes. It made it seem as if I had imagined the entire incident. But I don't believe I did. At least at the time I did not think so. Because I had bloodstains on these two fingers." She held out the index and middle finger of her right hand. "They're gone now, of course."

"Of course. But you saw them. And knew that you had not imagined the stigmata."

"I did then. Now sometimes I think . . . I suspect, Mother Louise, that . . ." She could not speak the words in her normal tone. Her voice dropped to a whisper. "I suspect I am losing my mind."

"What nonsense!" It was the first time the nun seemed agitated. "If you cannot believe the evidence of your own eyes, Mrs. Turner, what are you to believe?"

"I don't know. And if I did see these . . . stigmata, what does it mean? Who was Eileen O'Connor that such a thing should happen to her?"

"Ah yes, an interesting speculation. A poor Irish girl, utterly ignorant in all probability, dies of consumption and is buried in a pauper's grave, and the world goes on exactly as if she had never lived. Except that some of the women in the Almshouse Hospital, and you, my dear Mrs. Turner, are privileged to see that she was somehow very close to God and marked by Him with special favor. The question is not who was Eileen O'Connor, who I suspect needs nothing from us, not even our poor prayers, to have entered into glory. Why, we must ask, was her secret revealed to you? It is a special responsibility, is it not?"

"Oh no! Don't say that, Mother Louise. You must not." Another burden when she was already so unsure what to do about the one she had carried alone since Joyful's death. "I'm only one person, a woman, I cannot be expected to decide about every— About such things."

The nun smiled. "I'm not sure I know exactly what you mean, but you need not carry any burden alone. None of us need do so. Apparently you have been made privy to a great, and if I may say, a highly personal and private, mystery. Your duty now is simply to pray about it and hold yourself open to hear the voice of the Spirit when it speaks. I shall pray with you, dear Mrs. Turner. We shall storm heaven together."

"Dr. Klein, a word if I may."

Ben was just hurrying down the steps of the synagogue, about to wave goodbye to his father and head over towards Broadway, where he could get an omnibus that would take him up the town to Twenty-second Street. He'd have to walk—even run—the rest of the way, but he was sure he could get to the hospital by quarter past nine. Except that a well-dressed gentleman of some considerable years was blocking his way forward. "I can't stop now. I'm sorry, sir. I'm already late and—"

"This is Mr. Samson Simson, Benjy. He is an important man." Papa's voice came from just behind Ben's left shoulder, speaking right into his ear, as if he didn't wish to be overheard by the other men leaving the service. "Mr. Simson wants to talk to you for a moment."

Ben knew exactly who Samson Simson was. Every Jew in New York knew who he was. The Simson family had been here since the city was New Amsterdam, and Samson Simson was New York's first Jewish attorney. As a young man Samson Simson had been admitted to study law at Columbia under no less a personage than Aaron Burr, who—however far he'd fallen since that dreadful duel and however quietly he lived now with, it was said, a wife who was a former prostitute—had been the third vice president of the United States. Without that first step taken by Mr. Samson Simson, would he, Benjamin Klein, have been allowed to study medicine at the University of the City of New York? Probably not.

Both his father and Mr. Simson wore grave expressions and both were watching him intently. It was apparent that Papa knew Mr. Simson would be here. That's why he'd insisted that Ben attend this particular *shachris*, and probably why he was given the honor of the first *aliyah*. Papa wanted to soften him up. Though he had no idea why or for what.

"Mr. Simson has been waiting for some time, Benjy. He wants to talk to you."

Samson Simson was an elder of Shearith Israel, one of those wealthy Jews who had been here so much longer than the Kleins and their mostly German neighbors. Mr. Simson had not come to B'nai Jeshurun to pray. He had not attended the morning service at the synagogue of the Ashkenazim. He had waited out here in the cold to see Benjamin Klein. But why? If Samson Simson wanted medical advice, it wouldn't be from him.

Jacob Klein's small smithy and fine goods shop was also on Elm Street, three doors down from B'nai Jeshurun. He had been gently propelling his son and Mr. Simson in that direction since they began speaking. It did not surprise Ben to see his father produce the key to the shop door, open it wide, and step aside for Mr. Simson to precede him. "After you, sir. Come, Benjy."

"Papa, Dr. Turner is waiting—"

The bell on the door jangled as Papa closed it behind them. "It is November, Benjy. Sensible people do not stand in the street and talk in the cold."

"But I can't stay and talk. I told Dr. Turner I—"

"I promise I will not keep you long, young Dr. Klein," Mr. Simson said. "And this concerns Dr. Turner as well. In a manner of speaking."

"It does?" Ben didn't bother saying that he was not yet entitled to be called "doctor." A small moral lapse only. "My Dr. Turner at Bellevue?"

"Indirectly, yes. Because he is, I believe, a cousin by marriage to the widow of Dr. Joyful Turner."

"I don't—Ah, yes. Mrs. Manon Turner. I've heard her and Dr. Turner address each other as cousin."

"Exactly. I knew Mrs. Turner's husband for a time. We had business together a few years before he died in the yellowing fever epidemic of 1816. Their two children died at the same time. A tragedy."

"Terrible. But Dr. Nicholas Turner says that if we pay enough attention to science we can someday find out the cause of the worst diseases that plague us and learn to cure them. Yellowing fever, cholera, even the deadly croup. The other day he showed us—" Ben broke off. He had been about to describe the diseased bronchial tubes and trachea of a little girl who died of the croup. All the students knew they were not supposed to discuss the anatomies. "Dr. Turner is a wonderful man of science," Ben finished, not quite looking Mr. Simson in the eye. "Wonderful. A man worthy of great respect."

"I'm sure, Dr.—May I call you Ben?"

"Yes, please, sir. Of course. But I really have to go. I promised Dr. Turner."

In the corner of the shop, where it could be seen by anyone who came through the door, was a tall clock, the workings of which had come from Switzerland, while the face and case were trimmed with intricate and very beautiful silver fretwork done by Jacob Klein. Papa's clock kept excellent time, and now the silver hands pointed to twenty minutes before nine. If he left this very minute he couldn't possibly be at the hospital before nine thirty. Dr. Turner would choose one of the other assistants to talk to about whatever it was he had wanted to discuss with Ben. "Papa, I—"

"I apologize for making you late, young man," Simson said before Ben's father could speak. "And I appreciate your concern about punctuality. It is an admirable trait. My carriage is waiting just around the corner, and my driver will take you directly to Bellevue as soon as we are done here. Will that make it easier?"

"Yes, of course. That's very kind. But what do you want with me?"

"What I want, Ben, is simply that you watch the Widow Turner as closely as you are able. And report to me anything she does that is in the least suspicious."

Ben knew he was staring and that his mouth was open. After a few seconds he found his voice. "Suspicious in what way? She helps the women patients. At least she tries to. What can I possibly report to you?"

Simson carried a walking stick with a beautiful gold fox head. The old man planted the stick on the polished wooden floor of Papa's smithy, put both his hands on the head of the cane, and leaned towards Ben. "I believe, indeed I know, that Manon Vionne, the lady who was then Joyful Turner's fiancée and became his wife, is aware of certain elements of my dealings with her deceased husband. It is a matter of grave urgency, Ben. And it involves as well Mr. Jacob Astor."

"Old Mr. Astor?"

"Yes. The man himself. We were allies at the time of which I speak. Our interests have since diverged, but some old business remains unfinished. The Widow Turner is central to that business. I tried to speak with her directly recently and I was . . . I believe the word is rebuffed. Further, I had the impression that she is not as stable as she once was. If she begins acting in any way—I suppose the word is odd—I wish to know about it at once."

"But I don't know her. I only see her at the hospital sometimes. How will I know if she is acting odd, as you put it?"

"I am not sure, young man. But when I came to your father's shop a few days ago to commission a *kiddush* cup for a nephew who is about to be married, I learned in passing that the son of the admired smith, Jacob Klein"—with a formal nod in Papa's direction—"was studying medicine and was at present an assistant at Bellevue. Considering how much time the Widow Turner is known to spend there, it seemed to me a fortunate opportunity. We Jews are a very small group here in New York, Ben. We are privileged to be in this place, here in these United States. I have long thought so. We must be ever alert to our responsibilities to our nation as well as to our people."

She was wearing a green velvet frock with a silky sheen and full sleeves ruffled below the elbow. They emphasized that expressive way Carolina

Devrey had of using her hands. The mannerism was one of many that absolutely charmed Nick. It's why he had found a dozen different excuses to call since the day more than a year ago when he'd come to ask her to help him guard his future by witnessing his notes about Tobias Grant and the situation at the hospital.

She had always seemed pleased to see him.

That welcoming look in her eyes and the warmth of her smile were what encouraged him to return. He had not, however, visited her in the two months since he'd delivered Mei-hua's baby. Sam Devrey's daughter. He didn't know how he could face Carolina when he possessed such guilty knowledge.

This Wednesday evening, unable to stay away, he'd found yet another reason and given in to his impulse.

"Cousin Nick! I'm delighted to see you. It's been ages. That's fine, Dorothy, you may leave us." When the maid had gone, she closed the double doors of the front parlor against the December chill that pervaded the front hall. "It's far too late for tea, I'm afraid."

"After eight, I know. I apologize for the hour. I couldn't get away any earlier."

"You are welcome at any time. I've been waiting for Samuel. I expect he'll be home any minute now. You must join us for a late supper. Meanwhile I insist we celebrate with a glass of my raspberry brandy. I steeped the fruit myself last summer."

"I should like that." He watched while she poured brandy into a pair of snifters. It seemed to him that everything she did was marked with a special grace. "I've been meaning to stop by for ages, but it's been so busy at the hospital that—"

"I understand. Your good health, Cousin Nick."

"And yours, Cousin Carolina." They each had a long sip of raspberry brandy and settled in two chairs on either side of the lively coal fire. "I've brought you something." He produced a small parcel wrapped in green paper and tied with a red ribbon. "Because it's so close to Christmas."

"How very kind. I'm afraid I don't have anything for—"

"Oh, it's not for you. I wouldn't presume." Nick felt himself flush like a bumbling schoolboy. No woman had so unnerved him since he was fourteen. "What I'm trying so awkwardly to say is that it's a present for young Zachary. How is he?"

"Wonderful. Nineteen months and blooming. Asleep now, of course. You must come of an afternoon so you can see him." She was opening the package while she spoke. "A book. How charming."

"I know Zac can't read yet, of course. But I'm well known to the bookseller and he tells me this is newly translated from the Danish and just available here."

"Hans Christian Andersen. *Fairy Tales Told for Children*," she read, turning the small paper-bound volume this way and that to study it more carefully. "It looks quite delightful. I'm sure Zac will love it. I've been reading him a few verses of *A Visit from St. Nicholas* every night before he goes to bed for a week now. I think he's getting the idea that something wonderful's afoot." Twice when Samuel was home before Zachary's bedtime she'd tried to interest him in joining in the ritual. He always claimed to be too tired or too busy.

"No child could fail to notice that." Nick nodded towards the tall fir tree standing between the pair of windows fronting on the street. It was hung with ornaments of every sort, and small candles were fixed to the tips of many of the branches. "I thought you'd have a Christmas tree. I'm told they're becoming immensely popular."

"Is that why you thought I'd have one? Because I'm a slave to the latest fashion?"

"Not in the least. Because I always associate you with whatever is pretty and gay."

She couldn't answer for a moment. Pretty and gay. When she was a girl, before she married, those had frequently been words applied to her. Had she changed so dramatically in three years? In her own eyes perhaps. Certainly in Samuel's. "You flatter me, Cousin Nick, and I adore it. We have not yet lit the candles on the tree. Closer to the holiday perhaps."

"Do be careful. If the branches are very dry—"

"Yes, I know." She nodded towards the *New York Herald,* folded beside her chair. "I was reading about yesterday's blaze just before you came. The paper says thirteen buildings and two shops were destroyed. The city must have more watchtowers and watchmen."

"The wooden towers are useless. They burn along with everything else and only contribute to a false sense of security. What the city must have is a decent supply of water. Does the *Herald* tell you they nearly pumped the fire cisterns dry last night? Or that a number of the firemen were brought to Bellevue overcome with exhaustion and hardly able to breathe for all the smoke they'd inhaled?"

"The paper mentioned the cisterns. But I read nothing about the poor firemen. Were you able to help them?"

Nick shrugged. "Not a great deal, I'm afraid. Rest's what they need. And a better supply of water so it need not take so long to put the fires out."

"Papa says the same. He was going on at Samuel about it only the other week. Because Sam's on the council. Papa says there's an inexhaustible supply of fresh water in the Croton River up in Westchester County. If the council would simply vote the funds to build a decent aqueduct, Papa and a number of the other businessmen in the city would undertake to—"

"To enrich themselves by having a long and speculative go at building something that's an engineering nightmare and will cost a fortune. Don't worry, we've already approved a commission to study the matter, which is about all the council ever does. Good evening, Cousin Nicholas. I'm surprised to find you here."

"Good evening to you, Cousin Samuel. I came to bring a present for young Zachary, and your charming wife was kind enough to offer me refreshment. Now I must be going."

"The moment I arrive? Indeed you must not. What will that cause me to think?"

It was meant to be humor, Carolina knew, but the two men were circling each other . . . they were like a pair of strange dogs unsure whether to bark or wag their tail. She'd never kept Nick's visits a secret from Samuel. That had been Aunt Lucy's advice years ago: never give a husband any cause to suspect you are deceiving him. Her husband seemed entirely indifferent to the possibility, but now . . . how funny! Samuel, who apparently had so little interest in her, was jealous. He must be. What else could explain the way he was looking at Nick? And at her.

"I shall sample your raspberry brandy, Carolina," Sam said. "So I may drink Cousin Nicholas's—"

"'Scuse me, but you've got to come." Dorothy had thrown open both parlor doors and was almost shouting. "All of you, you've got to come and see this."

"See what?" Sam demanded.

"The sky, sir. It's turned bright red. Armageddon, like the preacher's been warning us about. I think it must be."

Chapter Thirteen

Bitter cold and a shuddering wind getting up, but men and women alike stood silent and stunned outside their front doors on Fourteenth Street, heads thrown back, staring at the sky to the south, streaked with fiery red and splotched with great billows of black smoke. Soon the eerie silence was broken by the sound of distant bells. Nick thought he could distinguish the full-throated clanging of the great bell in the cupola atop City Hall. That was the designated fire bell, since the wooden watchtowers had proved themselves nothing but more tinder for the flames.

The clamor came rapidly closer as nearby church belfries took up the alarm, indicating the need for the more northerly of the city's engine companies to rally down the town. "Jesus God Almighty," Nick heard one of the men murmur. "Must be a big one. So soon again."

"I'll be needed at the hospital," Nick said. "I'd best be going." But he made no move to go back inside and claim his greatcoat and hat and gloves.

As usual the servants knew more than their masters and knew it more quickly. Two stable boys pelted up Fifth Avenue, riding one behind the other on a single lathered horse and shouting at the top of their lungs words that the wind snatched away and blew into nonsense. Barnabas, just come from the mews behind number three, ran to grab the horse's bridle and slow her enough so he could hear their news, then brought it back to his employer. "Started at Morse's warehouse on Pearl and Exchange. There's a dozen buildings as is already burning. Number One Company was there right at the first, but they couldn't hold it. Spreading fast it is. Perishing fast."

Sam grabbed the stable boy's shoulder. "They can't hold it?"

"No, sir, Mr. Devrey. According to them two"—tossing his head to indicate the pair who had brought the news—"it's moving up the town."

Of course, because that was the direction of the wind. Cherry Street was in the fire's path. Sam turned without a word and ran to the stable. Moments later they heard the sound of hooves on the packed snow, and Sam raced by them and down Fifth Avenue, leaning forward over the mare's head, whipping her flank to summon every bit of speed.

"He has no coat," Carolina said. "He'll freeze."

She sounded, Nick thought, like a small child. "He'll be fine." He tried to put his arm around her. "And you have no wraps either. Come inside, Cousin Carolina, you must—"

She turned away. "Barnabas, get the buggy ready. Quickly!" She had clearly made a decision.

"It's ready now, ma'am, sort of. Mr. Devrey drove it home, and I ain't yet unhitched the—"

"Bring it round. Hurry."

She turned and started for the house and Nick followed her. "Carolina, where are you going?"

"I'm going after my husband. Please excuse me."

She'd dreamed of following Samuel, seeing where he went all those hours when other men were home with their families and he was not with her. She'd never dared to do it. But now she had the best opportunity she would ever have, and God forgive her for sparing no worry for the victims of the fire, she would not let it go by. "The buggy,

Barnabas!" she called out, reminding him of his task, but the boy had already disappeared in the direction of the stable.

Carolina ran into the front hall, calling for Dorothy to bring her a wrap and pulling on her warmest bonnet—dark purple felt, with a woolen tie wide enough to give some protection to her neck and ears—and gloves lined with rabbit fur.

"Where are you going?" Nick repeated. "It's not safe, Carolina. A woman alone. You can't."

"I must." Dorothy brought a black cloak also lined with fur. Carolina wrapped it around her shoulders, heading for the door before she'd managed all the fastenings and grabbing her fur muff and Samuel's greatcoat from a tall cupboard in the hall. "My husband might need me," she said. "I must go."

Nick hauled his own coat from the cupboard and snatched his hat and gloves from the table beside the door. "I'm coming with you."

"I assure you that's entirely unnecessary. I can drive the buggy perfectly well."

"No doubt. But I'm still coming with you."

He handed her up into the seat of the rig and jumped in beside her before she had a chance to drive away. "Come, don't be foolish. Give me the reins. And put that damned greatcoat over your knees." Barnabas had apparently brought the buggy round in the same condition in which Samuel had brought it home. It was not equipped for a lady and there were no blankets that he could see.

"There's really no cause, Cousin Nick. You said you would be needed at the hospital, and I'm quite—"

"Need is relative, Carolina. The looters will be out in full force. A woman alone. It's out of the question." He clucked the horse into movement and headed south down Fifth Avenue in the direction Sam Devrey had taken. "Do you want to tell me where you wish to go?"

"I have told you. I'm following my husband. I believe he will need me. He will certainly need this coat."

"Very well." A fire engine caught them up and passed them, its bell clanging wildly and twelve men pulling the wagon in a demonstration of the bloody-mindedness that still refused to use horses, much less wagons fitted with the steam-driven pumping apparatus now in use all over London. An all-volunteer corps of firefighters demonstrating their manliness, and the entire city cheering them on, wagering on one company over another, in the face of something such as this. Sheer madness.

He waited until the men pulling the wagon and chanting the ditties that kept them trotting in unison had gotten far enough ahead for Carolina to hear him, then asked again, "Where do you think we'll find your husband?" If she said Cherry Street, well and good. The responsibility would not be his. If she did not know about the place, he would not be the one to tell her.

"I'm not entirely sure," Carolina admitted, straining forward as if she might catch sight of Samuel, though his head start and the differing speed of a riding horse and a buggy made it extremely unlikely. The clang of fire-wagon bells from the east and the west indicated still more companies heading down the island to join in battling the blaze. The windows of every house they passed were lighted, and there were any number of men about, both on foot and on horseback. She saw no other women, but Carolina did not allow herself to dwell on that, or on the likelihood that a great many of the men she saw were ruffians rather than gentlemen.

They drew level with Washington Square. Carolina avoided looking at the houses on the north side. Papa's house was number sixteen. He'd moved there two years earlier, and her girlhood home in no longer fashionable Bowling Green was now a boardinghouse. She knew what Papa would say if he saw her heading into the fire district. The buggy had slowed to a crawl. "Please Nick, we must hurry."

"Hurry to where?"

She allowed herself one glance at her father's house, where windows were lit on all four floors. He was likely to be out in the street among the throng. The rig wasn't particularly distinctive; still, he might recognize it. "Devrey's new premises on Canal Street," she said with conviction. "That has to be where he's gone."

Nick made a noncommittal sound. "Very well. Devrey's on Canal Street." He urged the horse forward until they were finally clear enough of the crush to trot through the park and into the confusing warren of streets beyond. They were on the edge of the old village of Greenwich, which wealthy local landowners had insisted not be forced into compliance with the grid. Nick took a moment to get his bearings, then tugged on the reins and turned the horse's head west.

At Canal Street on the corner of Broadway the smoke was thick enough to choke, and the glow of the fire was reflected in dancing shadows on the marble facade of Devrey Shipping's brand-new and resplendent five stories.

The buggy pulled up beside Devrey's impressive front door. All around was motion and shouting and what seemed to be a chaotic back and forth of men and animals and still more fire wagons, some with the names of Brooklyn companies on their side.

"There does not seem to be anyone there," she said, looking up at Devrey's windows, illuminated only by the gaslights of the street. "If Samuel were—" She broke off, overcome by a fit of coughing.

"It's the smoke," Nick said, holding out his handkerchief. She shook her head and withdrew one of her own from the interior of her muff.

"We can't stay here, Cousin Carolina." As he spoke, a wagon pulled by a pair of men and piled high with an assortment of goods—probably looted, Nick thought—passed so close beside the buggy that the horse neighed loudly and tossed his head in fractious discontent. Nick had to tug hard on the reins to steady him. "You can see Devrey's is dark and entirely closed. Samuel's not here. We can't stay, Carolina. Let me take you home."

"Cherry Street," she said.

His heart sank. "What did you say?"

"My husband owns two lodging houses on Cherry Street. It is further down the town and closer to the fire. No doubt those are the properties he has gone to check upon. I must go to Cherry Street."

"No. You can't." God help him, what would he say if she asked why not?

"I must." She reached to take the reins from his hands. Nick pulled them away from her. The horse sensed the uncertainty about who was in charge and pawed the cobbles, acting as if he might break and run at any moment. Carolina hesitated a moment more, then gathered Sam's coat into her arms and started to climb down from the buggy.

"Where are you going? You can't—"

"I must go to Cherry Street. If you won't take me, I will walk."

Nick could neither force Carolina to return home nor allow her to be alone in the increasing tumult. "Sit down." Nick bit out the words. "And hang on. This is not going to be an easy journey."

Close enough now to hear the roar and crackle of the flames, and the night a thing of sparks and smoke, with the sky a red-and-black dome above their heads. Yet still so bitterly cold. And narrow Cherry Street a frozen corridor of rutted snow and ice down which howled a ferocious gale.

"I believe the two houses on the corner are Samuel's." Carolina had to bend close and shout the words against the wind.

"Yes, I know." A damn fool thing to say, but she was too preoccupied to ask him how he knew. In any event he could move the buggy no closer to Sam Devrey's property. Lodgers from the houses lining both sides of the street had come outside despite the fierce weather. Some were fully dressed, others wrapped in blankets they had apparently snatched from their beds when the alarms sounded, all shouting and shoving and pushing. He saw one likely thief slip into a house ignored by the presumed occupants who had literally turned their backs on whatever of value they'd left behind. More important, he sensed the throng developing that strange composite being that identified a mob. "Carolina, we can never find Samuel in this crush."

She did not hear him, or if she did, she chose not to answer. Before Nick could stop her, she had climbed out of the buggy and was thrusting her way through the crowd, headed for the houses on the corner.

"Carolina!" Nick shouted. "Carolina!" She paid him no mind. He jumped down after her, dropping the reins and leaving the buggy where it was since he had no hope of getting anywhere near a hitching post. Damn the rig. If he must choose between protecting the woman or the horse and buggy, there was no debate. "Carolina!"

She was well ahead of him now. But her height meant that every few seconds he caught sight of her purple bonnet as she forced her way through the crowd. "Carolina!"

The Chinese, some fifty-odd of them, were huddled together on the street in front of their lodgings. Sam noted a number of the nearby whites staring at the queues and quilted jackets of the foreigners, as if until this moment they had not realized quite how many of these alien beings lived among them. Mei-hua leaned against him, and he kept a sheltering arm around her. If the whites grew ugly, he would just pick her up and force his way into the alley to the right. It was too narrow to allow any large number to follow, and it debouched cleanly on the street behind. He'd head north after that, away from the fire.

Ah Chee was beside them, holding the child Sam knew was called Mei Lin, though he seldom thought of her by any name. The infant was asleep in the old woman's arms, oblivious to all the excitement. Mei-hua reached out and adjusted the silk shawl in which the tiny bundle was swaddled. Both women were also wrapped in silk, as was he. He'd arrived coatless, and Mei-hua had poured plum wine into him and insisted he put a thick red satin *lung p'ao* on over his western clothes. He was grateful for the robe now. It was killingly cold, damned well hurt to breathe. Had to be a bloody great obstacle in the way of properly fighting the fire, however many companies showed up. A short time back a few of the neighbors had gotten the idea of hooking up the hose that was kept beside the Cherry Street hydrant. A waste of time and effort as it turned out. The hempen hose was thick with ice, and when they managed to thaw it out enough to uncoil it, they discovered that the water in the cistern that fed the hydrant had frozen solid.

Good God. He could have sworn he'd heard someone shouting "Carolina."

Surely that was not possible.

Carolina knew only that Samuel let rooms in the Cherry Street houses to sailors seeking a place to stay between voyages. It always sounded a sensible business investment. She had never thought much about what sorts of sailors they might be, but the moment she recognized the Asian features and dress of some members of the crowd, she knew the entire story. Or thought she did.

Oh. Oh dear.

The little woman who sometimes watched Carolina's house from across the street was in the crowd. Carolina could see only her head, but she at once recognized the oddly shaped straw bonnet. Another woman stood beside her, her black hair wound into a tall coiffure twisted with colored ribbons. Behind her stood a tall man wearing an odd foreign robe. He appeared to be embracing her and . . . a swirl of smoke blotted out the vision.

Carolina struggled to see, but her eyes stung and teared, and she was being shoved in the opposite direction from where she wanted to go. She tried to push back and felt someone tugging at Sam's greatcoat. "No. You can't have it. Let go." Seconds later the pressure was eased as whoever had thought to steal the garment gave up. Carolina clutched the coat and her muff ever tighter and struggled to get closer to her husband's houses. Possibly one of the sailors spoke something other than that peculiar gibberish Samuel said was the Chinese language. English must be needed on the Devrey ships. She could ask if anyone had seen Samuel, if they knew where he was. She felt an arm encircle her.

"Please let me get you out of this terrible place," Nick said. "It's a dreadful night, Carolina. You'll never find—"

"Yes," she said. "Yes. I will. I have." She was speaking more to herself than to Nicholas Turner. The smoke had cleared for the moment, blown away in a sustained gust of bone-chilling wind, and though there were no street lights on Cherry Street, the glow of the leaping flames reflected in the sky allowed Carolina Devrey to see her husband standing directly ahead.

Nick had kept hold of her, and they were both being shoved forward through the throng, close enough so Carolina had a clear view of Samuel. He wore a bright crimson robe and had his arms wrapped around the woman with the ribbons in her hair. At this distance it was possible to see as well that her face was painted in an exotic and foreign fashion.

Carolina did not know if the girl was beautiful or even pretty. She was too strange for such terms to apply. But she knew that the woman beside her, wizened and ugly in an ugly conical bonnet, was staring, as if she, Carolina Devrey, might be some threat to whatever it was the old woman held clasped in her arms.

A baby.

It was a baby. And Samuel was standing with them. Protecting them. Claiming ownership of all three.

She might have fainted but for the press of the crowd and Nick's firm grip.

"Let's go," she heard him say. "There's nothing to be gained by your being here. Let me take you home."

Carolina felt him tugging her away from the tableau of Samuel with his . . . his what? His mistress? And her servant. And her child.

His child.

Nick was still trying to pull her away but she resisted, and the crowd seemed to take her part. The endless jostling served to thrust her nearer to Samuel and the family he preferred to her and his son.

She was close enough to touch him now, and Samuel was staring back at her, seemingly as shocked as she.

It was Carolina who found her voice first. "Good evening," she said. "I brought you this." She held out the greatcoat. "I'm afraid it may have been torn in all this crush."

Sam spoke over her head. "I cannot imagine what you thought you would gain by bringing her here, Turner."

"I did no such thing. She was determined to come. I simply—" A roar of wind and more frantic pealing of nearby bells drowned out the rest of his words.

"Get her out of here," Sam said. "Can you do that? Will you?"

"Yes."

Carolina heard their words but did not register their meaning. "I brought your coat, Samuel," she said again. "It is such a dreadfully cold night. You will surely need your coat." She thrust it towards him. Someone took it out of her hands, a little man with a horribly pock-marked face. She had not the strength to keep him from taking it, and Samuel had not moved. "You must have your coat, Samuel. Whatever that is you're wearing, it cannot be warm enough for a night like this. Tell that man he must give you your coat."

"Turner, for God's sake, man. If she means anything to you at all . . ."

The Asian men, Nick realized, might be short and slight, but they did not lack for strength. They had formed a tight ring around himself, Devrey, and the women. It gave him enough space to pick Carolina up. He felt her body go limp in his grip and knew she'd fainted. Just as well probably. He heard Devrey say something in Chinese, and the men formed a V-shaped wedge that forced a path through the crowd and allowed him to carry Carolina back to the buggy. It had already been stripped of fringe and cushions and the carrying chest that had been strapped to the rear, but miraculously the wheels were still attached. And the horse yet stood between the traces, though the bit and bridle and reins had all disappeared.

"*Eh. Deng yi deng,*" one of the men said. Nick had no idea what the words meant, but he understood the gesture. He was to wait.

Carolina was starting to regain consciousness. Nick lifted her into the buggy and got in beside her, letting her body lean against his. Minutes later the pock-marked man appeared with the necessary tack. He and one of the others hitched the horse back to the wagon and handed Nick the reins. He heard Carolina murmuring questions as she came out of her faint, but the noise of the fire and the crowd was getting louder and he couldn't make out what she was saying.

How in hell was he to turn the damned buggy around so they could get out of here? They were entirely hemmed in. Then he felt the rig rise just enough to free the wheels from the rutted road. Half a dozen of the men were carrying it backwards, north up Cherry Street. He had only to maintain a hold on the reins and encourage the horse to keep backing up. It was the weight of Sam Devrey's orders, the power of his command, that had produced their unusual exit from—what? Hell for the woman now crying softly beside him, her face pressed against his arm. Paradise for Devrey apparently. Must be, since he was willing to risk so much to keep it.

And for the city of New York, at least so it seemed, death by fire.

The bitter weather was as vicious an enemy as the flames. What water was left in the cisterns had frozen solid. A dozen engine companies rushed to the East River and used their axes to cut holes in the thick ice, but the water they gained with so much effort turned at once to slush and then to ice in the hoses, and resisted the pounding feet of cadres of firemen jumping up and down on the hoses to melt ice back into the water they so desperately needed. The weak streams they did manage to aim at the inferno blew back in their faces. Fifteen hundred firemen—a number that had grown by less than three hundred in the past decade, though the city had doubled in size in the same period—were reduced to standing and watching New York burn, and to pouring brandy into their boots to prevent their feet from freezing.

Nearly the entire town south of Wall Street, the mercantile heart of not just the city but the nation, had become a fiery cauldron. Street after street was engulfed in flames. Merchants who had rushed to their premises threw whatever they could salvage out the windows, only to find that the draymen and carters who had converged on the scene were demanding more than the goods were worth to drag them away. Firemen unable to do the job for which they were such proud volunteers helped instead to empty warehouses of tons of silks and satins and laces, only to see the huge piles they made in the streets ignited by blowing cinders and flaming bits of paper before they could be removed.

The burning debris hurtling through the air was both fed and transported by the howling wind. Later there would be reports of roofs that caught fire as far away as Brooklyn and Newark, and of firefighters as far south as Philadelphia and as far north as New Haven who saw the sky glowing red and turned out, thinking it was the outlying parts of their own cities that burned.

By three A.M. on Wall Street the supposedly fireproof Merchants' Exchange had gone up, the greedy flames devouring even stone and iron. When the sixty-foot cupola crashed to the ground, the seven men who had been trying to rescue the life-size bronze statue of Alexander Hamilton had to jump out of the way to save their lives, and Hamilton's statue was smashed to pieces by falling chunks of marble. By four the Tontine Coffee House, three blocks to the east, was ashes as well.

Men working for the city's newspapers raced not just the flames but the sparks, sometimes beating out smoldering bits of their own clothing as they pursued their quest for bits of information that would set their next day stories apart. One reporter would tell of hearing the foreman of Eagle Engine No. 13 say that if the wind shifted and the fire jumped Wall Street, the rest of the city would burn as well, though the journalist was never able to say for sure whose idea it was to blow up two buildings in the fire's path and deprive it of fuel.

In the face of such catastrophe anything was worth trying. Militiamen sent to patrol the streets and discourage looting supplied the gunpowder and the gambit worked. Thousands cheered the brutal, self-inflicted destruction. The barbarians were indeed at the gates, but the city had found a weapon with which to fight back.

Men desperate to do something ransacked the arsenals, tearing open cartridges however meager their yield, while officers and sailors from the Navy Yard in Brooklyn were sent for to do the demolitions, and a boatload of marines manhandled a path through the ice-clogged river to the powder house at Red Hook Point and ferried back twenty-five kegs of gunpowder.

The inferno raged uncontrollably from Maiden Lane to Coenties Slip and from William Street to the East River—those thirteen acres burned for all the next day and the following night and would smolder for two full weeks—but all the rest, everything north of Wall Street, was saved by using demolition to create a firebreak.

The lust for information about so huge a cataclysm was boundless. The penny press dug deep and mined stores of inventiveness. The first day after the fire the *Sun's* morning run was twenty-three thousand copies. A few hours later they published an "extra" of another thirty thousand, a single day's circulation for one paper that shattered all records. The *Herald* used illustrations for the first time to map the area of destruction, and a few days later included in one edition a two-column woodcut of the remains of the Merchants' Exchange.

However cleverly they did it, what they reported was bleak. Four thousand clerks were abruptly out of work, along with thousands of cartmen and porters. Seven hundred buildings had been totally destroyed. Nothing south of Wall Street and east of Broad, whether made by man or installed by nature, was whole and entire. The losses were estimated at close to twenty-six million dollars, more than three times the cost of building the Erie Canal a few years before. Twenty-three of the city's twenty-six fire insurance companies were instantly bankrupt.

There were, however, only two fatalities from among the thousands present at the fire, and the rule of law had not been entirely overturned. There were four hundred arrests for looting.

And repeated over and over again, as many times as needed to put heart into a demoralized population, was the best news: all the rest was saved.

The new and north-facing city that was marching up the Manhattan wilderness had reaped the wind and inherited the future.

Book Two

1836—1837

Chapter Fourteen

"I CANNOT CONTINUE to live with him, Papa."

"Carolina, he is your husband. How can you possibly make such a preposterous statement?"

"But I told you, he is—"

"You told me he is involved in some sort of dalliance. My dear child, it is shameful that you should come and discuss such a thing with me. It is still more shameful that after almost three years of marriage you are not wise enough to know that all men stray occasionally. If your mother had lived, she would no doubt—"

"Did you, Papa?"

"Did I what?"

"Stray occasionally."

Wilbur Randolf turned away from his daughter and walked to the long casement window of his study, an outsize pane of glass made possible because the glaziers were so clever these days. He had a fine view of elegant Washington Square Park. Constructed, he knew, above a potter's field in which God knows how many paupers had been buried. It was in the nature of man to want clearer sight of things, but also to cover over his sins.

"Carolina, you have no right to ask me such a thing. No decent woman can pose such a question, least of all to her own father." He had not looked at another woman from the first moment he set eyes on seventeen-year-old Penelope James until the day she died, but it would only make things worse if he told Carolina that. He turned back to her. "Surely you have not been so unwise as to confront your husband with your suspicions."

"They are not suspicions, Papa. I had suspicions for many months. Now I have certainties. I saw him with her and her child and the child's nursemaid the night of the fire. She is a foreigner, one of the China people in his houses on Cherry Street. As for confronting Samuel, he has given me no opportunity to do so. He has barely been home at all since that dreadful night."

"But he was there on Christmas day, Carolina. At luncheon with you and me and little Zac."

"Because he knew you were coming and you would expect him to be there. He left before you did, if you recall."

"Carolina, Samuel is an important man of business and a member of the Common Council to boot. The city has undergone a calamity. It is in a terrible state. A man like your husband has considerable responsibilities at a time like this."

"He has responsibilities to me and to his son!" She had promised herself she would not shout or cry. Now she was doing both. "He does not love me, Papa. I doubt he ever did. I don't think he loves Zac either. I waited until after the festivities of the season because I didn't want to upset you, but—"

"I expected you at my New Year open house yesterday. I was quite disappointed that you did not come. Even at a time like this, it's important that we keep up the old traditions, Carolina."

"How could I come when I had no husband to escort me?"

Randolf sighed and looked with some longing toward the drinks tray in the corner. Too early. And in the matter of his daughter, too late. He should have married Lucy and given the girl a mother, perhaps some brothers and sisters. Instead he'd over-indulged her and contented himself with whores. "Stop weeping, my dear. I shall help however I can."

"Then Zac and I can move in with you? There's plenty of room in this big house, Papa. And I can bring the nursemaid and even Dorothy. I will see that your comforts are not in any way compromised, I promise."

"Carolina, have you been listening to a word I've said? You are Samuel's wife legally and before God, and he is the father of your son. You cannot simply up sticks and move out of his house. The scandal would be immense, and you would be prejudicing young Zachary's future in the most irresponsible way. What will society make of him as the son of divorced parents?"

"But—"

"No more buts, Carolina. Go home and be the dutiful wife and loving mother you were raised to be. And mind you, show Samuel no coldness in the matter of . . . of his marital rights. I've no doubt this whole business probably started in just that way. A man has needs, child. It is your duty to be available, nay, welcoming, to meet those needs. You will do the situation no good if you withhold yourself as some sort of punishment for what you perceive to be his sins. Give Zachary a little brother or sister, the sooner the better. Be the best thing for all of you."

"Papa, I . . ." How could she explain about Samuel's utter lack of interest in sharing her bed. "Never mind. I shall go home. Exactly as you say I must."

"There's a good girl. And I meant what I said, my dear. I shall find some sort of solution for you. I'll make some discreet inquiries. If indeed it's warranted, I'll have a quiet word with my son-in-law. Quite to be expected that is. Quite the proper thing to do."

The infant slept with Ah Chee in the room behind the kitchen, at least when Samuel was there. If it became necessary to feed Mei Lin during one of her father's visits, Mei-hua disappeared. To that same little room in the back, Sam supposed. He didn't care where, as long as he didn't have to observe the process. He'd toyed with the idea of finding a wet nurse, but decided it wasn't practical. There was no guarantee of discretion for one thing, and for another Mei-hua would probably balk. Particularly since whoever he found would of necessity not be Chinese.

Ah Chee was equally aware of the inappropriateness of the situation. She, not the plum blossom's mother, had given Mei-hua suck. Eighteen years before, when the plum blossom was born, Ah Chee's breasts were not dried-up hanging-down raisins like now. And because the plum blossom's mother, the Mei Lin for whom this little girl was named, was for a short time Di Short Neck's favorite, she had no time to attend a squalling infant. Even one as perfect as Mei-hua had been. Perfect little baby this time too, but no way Ah Chee could wrap the plum blossom's breasts and stop the milk from coming so she would be quickly as before for her lord. Not unless the infant was to be starved. Sometimes on the sampans that happened with girl babies. When it was decreed there were too many of them. Not this girl baby.

When Ah Chee was not holding Mei Lin and hugging her and rocking her, Mei-hua was. As long as her lord was not present. And after the fire he was in this house many more hours than before. The Lord Samuel came every day and sometimes slept all night beside his supreme lady *tai-tai*. On those occasions Mei-hua would creep into the kitchen the moment she heard Mei Lin whimper, and sit under the picture of the kitchen god and allow the baby to drink her fill.

Once the Lord Samuel came to the door and stood and watched *tai-tai* feeding her daughter. Mei-hua's eyes were closed and she was humming a little song to her child and she did not know the Lord Samuel was there. They looked at each other, the lord and Ah Chee, and neither said anything, but next day when the Lord Samuel told the old woman the three-month-old infant must be weaned she was not surprised. "I will give you extra money every week," the lord said. "Buy milk for her." Extra money for Ah Chee's secret treasure purse. Special good idea now she had both the plum blossom and the plum blossom's daughter to protect.

Mei-hua did not want to stop giving suck to her baby. "Is she an animal that she should drink animal milk?"

"How they do things in this place. The Lord Samuel very angry if you keep on sharing your breasts with baby. Breasts get to be hanging down like this old woman's. All men same in every place, don't like hanging-down breasts. That's why I fed you. So beautiful mother of plum blossom have stand-up stick-out breasts for honorable father." She never said stinking dog turd river pirate aloud when Mei-hua could hear. Important that the gods know the plum blossom honored her father as she should. Never mind that he sold her to a *yang gwei zih* foreign devil, so now they were in this foreign devil place where a civilized wet nurse could not be found for the plum blossom's little bud. "Here they give milk from cow. Very much not bad milk."

Ah Chee had seen large urns of milk in the market, frothy, fresh and obviously prized by the women of this place, but she had no idea what it was used for. Nothing she knew how to cook required it. Now she understood. It must be that all women in this place gave milk from cow to babies. "After fire the Lord Samuel here more time now," she said. "Want supreme lady *tai-tai* all for himself. Plum blossom's little bud can drink cow's milk."

Mention of the fire reminded Mei-hua of a concern greater than whether she could go on suckling her precious doll. "Who was she? Why did she come here? Try to give ugly coat to the Lord Samuel. Who?"

Ah Chee shrugged. "Big ugly yellow hair. Maybe servant from where Lord Samuel does his business. Never mind." She had been saying the same thing right along. If she tried to tell one part of the story, it would all come out. Very much better if she not have to tell the plum blossom that the yellow hair concubine had given the Lord Samuel a son when his *tai-tai* produced only a daughter. Better to convince the plum blossom that her Ah Chee knew no more than she did. "Big ugly feet. No reason to think about her."

Mei-hua had been on her way out of the kitchen. Now she stopped and turned around and looked hard at Ah Chee. "How you know about big feet? How?"

"Flop-flop walk like a man," Ah Chee said. "Besides, all the women in this place have big ugly feet. I tell you that many times."

"When I asked you how you know she had yellow hair you tell me you saw under that hat thing. I did not see yellow hair. Now big feet. How?" If Ah Chee had not been holding the baby, Mei-hua would have flown at her.

Ah Chee had arranged a box lined with many cloths of silk and soft cotton beside the kitchen fire. Now she put the baby into the box and without saying a word went to the window and raised it. The air that rushed into the room was icy cold, but you could smell the burning, and wisps of smoke could still be seen rising into the sky. "Fourteen days and still some fire. Worst ever in this place. That's what they say in the market. Over and over I tell you. Worst ever fire."

"How you know about—"

"I tell you what I know. When whole city maybe burn up like a paper fan fall into the stove, *tai-tai*'s lord come here to be with supreme lady *tai-tai* and her daughter and even this old woman. Come so fast he not even wear something keep him warm. What difference about yellow hair big feet? What?"

"She is concubine." The words came out of Mei-hua's mouth even though she had promised herself she would not speak them. Now she had said them aloud, and the enormity of the truth was there in the room between herself and her servant. "She is concubine and never comes here to pay respect to supreme first lady *tai-tai*. My lord does not bring her for my approval, and talk to me about whether his concubine should have a room in this house or—"

"No room in this house. Sleep where? Where?" Ah Chee knew she had confessed her guilty knowledge and admitted the truth the plum blossom spoke. Too late to change that. The only important thing was that the plum blossom never know about the big stone house and the servants and the garden across the road. "Where?" she asked again. "On floor downstairs with Leper Face and Taste Bad and all the rest? Where?"

"I am *tai-tai*, she is concubine."

"Yes," Sam said. "Exactly. I have told you and told you."

"Then why you not bring her here and—"

"It's not how things are done in this place, Mei-hua. You are my supreme first lady *tai-tai* and I am your lord. It is not right that you keep asking me this. Not right."

Mei-hua moved in the bed so she could look up at him, her sea-colored eyes made still larger by the sheen of tears. "Why does my lord need a concubine when I am still young? Why?"

"Mei-hua, you must not cry. It is how things are done here. I have explained. I need to have a white woman sometimes. For business."

"Women help in your business?" Her astonishment was so great it interrupted her tears.

"No, not exactly, but I must be seen to have a white woman."

"A woman with yellow hair and big feet? To make business?"

"In a way."

Mei-hua settled into the crook of his arm while she took a moment to assimilate this information. Then she pulled away and sat up. "You do not make clouds and rain with her?"

"Clouds and . . . Oh. No, I don't wish to do so." It was true as far as it went. The whole truth would only make her more unhappy.

The covers had slipped to her waist, and Mei-hua was bent forward, supporting her head on her knees, looking sideways at him with her black hair hanging like a curtain over one side of her face. Her breasts were fuller than he remembered and the still swollen nipples quite excited him. Sam reached out and touched one. "Why would I want to do that with any other woman when I have you? Why?"

She giggled.

"Why are you laughing? Why?"

"Because my lord speaks exactly like a man of the Middle Kingdom, but the words come out of a *yang gwei zih* mouth."

"If that makes you laugh, you must fill the *yang gwei zih* mouth with something else." Sam drew her forward, and Mei-hua came eagerly, but then he stopped, holding her away from him and studying her face. "You do not give the child suck any longer? I told Ah Chee you must not."

"No more, my lord. Never once since you said I must not." Mei Lin had rejected the animal milk at first, turning her head away when Ah

Chee tried to spoon it into her mouth and making fists of her tiny hands and screaming so fiercely her face turned bright red. Then they got the idea of soaking a cloth in the stuff and letting the infant suck on that, and she was pacified or maybe too hungry to refuse any more. Never mind. It was good to learn very young that no woman could have everything she wanted. Not in the Middle Kingdom. Not here.

"Only for you now," Mei-hua said as she held her breast to his mouth. "Only for my lord."

"Pectoriloquy, gentlemen. The differences in what you hear should tell you what's physically there." Nick bent forward to demonstrate the process, pressing the black stethoscope first to one place on the man's chest, then moving it an inch or so to the right. "Different sound," he said, standing up and stepping out of the way. "You try, Dr. Chance."

Monty Chance glanced at the student standing next to Nick. Ben Klein, naturally. The Jew was a great favorite of Dr. Turner; he had been made Turner's laboratory assistant a couple of months back. Fair enough. Chance hated the stink of the formaldehyde and the putrefying flesh, and doing research, as they called it, wasn't the way to get ahead in a place like Bellevue. More important to make friends. Even with the likes of Frankly Clement and one-eyed old Jeremiah Potter. Even with Jews. Chance nodded in Klein's direction and slightly raised an eyebrow. Turner, the look said, was all right, but perhaps a bit of an eccentric. Klein stared straight ahead and seemed not to see. Damned sheenies. Not to be trusted. Do a Christian dirt any opportunity they had.

"Come, Dr. Chance, we've not got the whole day. Have a good listen and tell me what you think of what you hear."

Chance pressed his stethoscope to the patient's chest in the same place as Dr. Turner, then moved it in what seemed to him exactly the same fashion. "The lung sounds clear to me, sir," he said after a long few moments of attentive listening. "I hear none of that gurgling sound of consumption."

"Quite right, Dr. Chance. The patient is not a consumptive." Then before the junior doctor could bask in the confirmation, "But there's something else to be learned. You try, Dr. Klein."

The patient understood no English. He stared stoically straight ahead. Klein leaned forward with his stethoscope, moved it twice, just as both the fully fledged doctors had done, and took no more than a few seconds over the exercise. "There is tissue in one area, Dr. Turner, and a cavity next to it. What we hear illuminates the physical structure of the organ."

"Exactly. Well done, Doctor."

Monty Chance kept his face immobile.

Nick explained further how clinical practice could inform and enliven what the laboratory revealed, then gave it up and dismissed them. Apart from anything else, the ward's stench was getting to him. He'd asked for a few more women from the workhouse to augment the cleaning staff of the hospital, but Grant sent him prisoners instead. Slatterns. Swished a mop over the middle of a floor and called it done. Mind you, given the crowding of the place, little more was possible. He had to thread his way through a dozen men on floor pallets to get into the hall.

The air out there was a bit fresher but not much. He'd step outside for a bit and see if that helped. Not a great deal, probably. When the wind came from the south, the whole city still reeked of smoke. Nonetheless, he needed a breath of whatever sort of clean air he could find.

He was a few steps from the front door when it opened to admit Manon.

"Cousin Nicholas. I hoped I'd be able to find you today, and now yours is the first face I see."

"I've been hoping to see you as well, Cousin Manon, to wish you the joys of the season and inquire after your well-being. I trust the fire did you no personal damage."

"None. Though I can't help but think where I'd be if I hadn't so recently sold the house on Wall Street."

"Burnt out, like so many others. Come, step in here a moment." As usual, the director's office was empty; Tobias Grant spent almost no time in the hospital. "Tell me how you've been."

"Well," Manon said. "And you, Cousin Nicholas? You look a bit worn."

Because of how badly he'd been sleeping, no doubt. "Nonsense. I'm very well and all the better for seeing you. We've missed you over the holiday period."

"Yes, well . . ." Manon was not inclined to tell him how she'd spent the days from Christmas to New Year. "I'm here now. Nothing's changed, I'm sure."

"In this place nothing ever changes."

"You sound discouraged, Nicholas. That's not like you."

"It's such an uphill battle. I want this to be a decent hospital, but there's so little I'm able to do."

"Yes, but that's the same as it's always been. Come, we agreed fully a year ago now. You will use the opportunities this place provides to further your research and wait until the time is right to do something more. There's an increase of talk, you know, about how bad Bellevue is. Tobias Grant is bound to be called to account sometime soon."

"I hope you're right. Incidentally, that's not all there is to talk about. What do you think of this Maria Monk and her revelations? I thought with all your Catholic connections you'd have an opinion."

Her Catholic connections. Manon turned her head as if he might read guilt in her face, though she had no idea why she should feel guilty. "It's utter twaddle, Nicholas. I'm sure it must be."

"That's what I think as well. Never mind that it's supposed to have taken place up in Canada. Nuns made to be the mistresses of the priests who confess them, babies buried in the walls. When you think of Mother Louise and Sister Mary and the others we know, it sounds ridiculous. Still, for it to actually be a published book . . ."

"Not just in a book," she said brusquely. "They printed bits of it in the *Sun,* and as you might expect, in the *Protestant Vindicator.* But I don't think something is true, Nicholas, simply because it is written down and a lot of fools believe it. But enough about salacious gossip, tell me about you. I insist you look tired. You have been working too many hours, I suspect."

"Some late nights in the laboratory perhaps. But it's the thing that keeps me sane in this place."

Manon cocked her head and studied him. "Nicholas, I hope the fire did you no personal harm . . ."

He did not answer immediately. He had not seen Carolina since he had taken her home that dreadful night, getting her maid to put her to bed and ordering hot tea with laudanum as a sedative. He'd returned the next day, but she wouldn't receive him and sent word she was indisposed. It was the same on three more occasions. "No, no personal harm. Now I must go. But I wish you a happy new year, Cousin Manon."

"And I you. The happiest possible, Cousin Nicholas. With all the good things you deserve."

Manon watched him leave. Late nights in the laboratory indeed; something more personal she'd warrant. He looked utterly exhausted. Perhaps she was not the only one who had somehow missed out on peace on earth and good will to men.

The hewers of wood and the drawers of water . . . Manon had used those words to describe Catholics when she took Nicholas Turner to St. Patrick's Orphan Asylum. The flotsam and jetsam of society, that's what the immigrants were these days. Wreckage washed up on the shore. Not, Manon thought, the finer sort of seeker of a new life who used to come in her papa's day.

God forgive her. She'd never thought of herself as a snob.

Mother Louise would say it was the Devil tempting her not to go inside St. Joseph's Church.

It was dark and cold at not quite six in the morning on this frosty January Wednesday. The church on the corner of Sixth Avenue and Waverly Place in Greenwich Village was only now emerging from the deep night shadows. It had been built to serve the mostly Italian contractors and builders who lived in the district, decent working men, not the rowdy sort of Irish immigrants who—

She must stop this. Get thee behind me, Satan. If God were to be found in St. Joseph's Church, then what did it matter what sort of people might be in the pew beside her? If. A very big condition indeed.

Come along, my girl, take yourself in hand. Straight up the broad stairs to the pillared entrance and through the tall double doors.

She knew what was customarily done with the stone basin beside the inner doors, the ones leading to the sanctuary. Dip the forefinger of your right hand into the water—blessed by the bishop on the night before Easter Sunday, Holy Saturday as Catholics called it, so said Mother Louise—and sign yourself with the cross while saying silently, *In the name of the Father and of the Son and of the Holy Ghost.* The nuns' holy water stoup beside the chapel at St. Patrick's was the first she'd ever seen. Spotted that spring Saturday afternoon three years past when Mother Louise gave her a tour of the place. It was Manon's first visit and she had arrived with a basket of baked goods. Because, she said, she'd seen the sign outside and thought perhaps the bread and cakes might be welcome. Welcome indeed the nun had said, and wished her the blessings of God and invited her in, and smiled at the way Manon was staring at her clothes, and began the first of many explanations of all things Roman.

And that had led to this, her furtive entrance into a Catholic church to hear Mass.

A woman had entered just ahead of her and performed the little ritual with the holy water quickly, as if she were not really thinking about it. *It's a sacramental, my dear Mrs. Turner. A small thing that brings us closer to God. We don't think the water miraculous, whatever some may say. It puts us in mind of Him and the water of our baptism.*

And would a bolt of lightning come and strike Manon because she put into the blessed-by-the-bishop water two fingers, not one? The same two fingers that had been stained with Eileen O'Connor's blood? Probably not.

Her first Mass was on Christmas Day, at the quite splendid St. Patrick's Cathedral on the corner of Prince and Mott streets. Except for the sermon that dwelled (as did every sermon preached in the city that day) on how all must look to the counsels of religion to strengthen them after the calamitous fire, she found the service utterly bewildering and frankly boring. A lot of bowing and scraping and ringing of bells and mumbling of prayers in Latin, a language of which she understood not a single word. Meanwhile the air was filled with the smoke of so many candles and the smell of so much incense she thought she might be present at some mysterious pagan rite.

It was certainly not particularly uplifting. Not even the moment when, according to Mother Louise in a talk of which she had forgotten not a single word, the wafers and the wine on the altar were transformed into the actual—the nun's very word—the actual body and blood of Jesus Christ. "Why would we not take Him at his word, my dear Mrs. Turner? If He is indeed the Lord and Savior we proclaim Him to be, truly our Emmanuel, God with us, would He lie? This is my body. This is my blood. That is what He said. Even Protestant bibles have it so. We Catholics believe that is what He meant. Yes, it's difficult. 'This is a hard saying, and who can listen to it?' John, chapter six, verse sixty," she'd added, never having gotten over her Protestant habit of citing the provenance of any bit of scripture she quoted.

Manon had looked up the chapter as soon as she got home. Her King James Bible said, "This is an hard saying, who can hear it?" Same thing really. And exactly the same about the body and blood part. She could find no argument against the nun's claim that those were the Gospel words.

But neither did she have any reason to believe such an extraordinary statement was meant to be taken literally. *This is my body. This is my blood.*

I am Ruth amid the alien corn, she thought as she quietly took a place in the rearmost pew. She could not overcome the feeling that nothing occurring up front on the altar had anything whatever to do with her.

But she had come five times in the three weeks since Christmas Day, twice to St. Patrick's and three times to St. Joseph's. Totally puzzled by her own behavior, but thankful that each of the eight Catholic churches in the city were in parts of town where she knew no one and no one knew her. Each time she knelt in the rear, neither sitting nor standing when the others did, certainly not approaching the communion railing, alone with her thoughts.

Joyful, my dearest, are you a saint in heaven? Mother Louise says that since you were a good man you must be, that all who go to heaven are saints, and it doesn't matter that you were not a Catholic. She says there is some loophole in their Catholic laws that allow non-Catholics to get in. She has a twinkle in her eye when she says it, but she does take these things very seriously. My love, you must tell me what to do. Samson Simson tried to see me recently. I know you always liked him, but I turned him away quite rudely. He wants back what he entrusted to us all those years ago. And I'm entirely unsure if that is the right thing to do. Because Mr. Simson is aligned with Mr. Astor, and Mr. Astor became involved in bringing opium into China, and you would have hated that so.

But no matter how carefully she listened, Manon could not hear a reply, neither from Joyful nor from God.

A pink dawn was just breaking when the Mass ended. She crept out of the church after everyone else was gone, drawing her dark cloak close and keeping her eyes on the ground so that the broad brim of her black bonnet shaded her face. Ridiculous to feel so much like a criminal. What had she done except attend a worship service in a church?

On the opposite side of Sixth Avenue in the deep shadows of a large elm tree, Addie Bellingham had her hand pressed to her mouth so she wouldn't scream aloud the words that wanted to rise up and fly free in the morning. Harlot! Satan's whore! Popery is the Devil's own tool!

Addie had first suspected, then knew. She'd found a bit of paper in Mrs. Turner's room with the words "St. Patrick's Cathedral" written on it and an address. Not that she was snooping, mind. Addie was simply being kind and tidying up Mrs. Turner's dresser top. But then Mrs. Turner refused Addie's invitation to accompany her to Reverend Finney's service on Christmas Day. Since the French Church was damaged in the fire, Addie said. And later, when Addie asked where dear Mrs. Turner had gone to services, she had just sort of waved the question away.

So Addie knew. In her bones. Manon Turner had gone to the Catholics. The shame of it made Addie tremble. Mrs. Turner was leading them both into black sin, what with giving all this money to women with children and no husbands. A hundred dollars last month, doled out in ten-dollar portions, as Addie knew because after all—Lord have mercy on her—she kept the books. So those women would never understand that they must do what the Bible said and live upright lives, and not go on having more little bastard babies, and then they would be saved. And now—had she not seen it with her own eyes?—Manon Turner was practicing popery.

She should get right out of the lodgings on Vandam Street. But where would she go? She had a little money saved, it was true, but if she gave up the dollar a week Mrs. Turner paid her for her work for the Society for Poor Widows and Orphans, and was left with only what she could earn from any paid sewing she managed to find to do and had to pay her own rent in the bargain, she'd be back in the almshouse sooner rather than later.

She couldn't. God in heaven—the just Protestant God to whom she prayed—help her. She just couldn't.

If it had not been so icy cold, Addie might actually have felt the hot tears of frustration and anger coursing down her cheeks.

According to the newspapers Mrs. Turner frequently brought up to their rooms—the *Union* and the *Workingman's Advocate* as well as the *Herald* and sometimes the *Sun* (to which pile Addie Bellingham sometimes surreptitiously added the *Protestant*, which always had lovely things to say about Mr. Finney), fully two-thirds of the workingmen in New York City were now members of one or another union. Plus, they stated with shock or pride (depending on the paper's point of view), all of them were now bound together in the GTU, the General Trades Union. Fair wages for fair work, the papers that supported the GTU said. While according to the *Herald*: "In this land of law and liberty the way to advancement is open to all. Labor unions are a foreign idea unworthy of real Americans."

Addie was sure that must be correct, since the *Herald* supported Mr. Finney, but fair wages were certainly a good thing. Sewed till her fingers were bloody, she did sometimes, and earned only a dollar or two. Not that the General Trades Union would do her any good. Women were not allowed to join; the GTU treated them the same as the nigras. That didn't seem right to Addie. Leastwise, not when a woman had no choice but to work to earn her keep. But whichever side she supported, it was still true that she couldn't sew her way out of depending on Manon Turner. She had to continue sleeping in the little bedroom just next to Mrs. Turner's. Even the added dollar a week from her job at that wretched charity wouldn't be enough to allow her to move out and rent a room of her own. Not with prices the way they were these days.

She repeated those truths to Lilac Langton every time they shared one of their pleasant outings. Today, because she was so upset about that other business, she said more than usual. "There's nothing I can do. Even though I actually saw her go into a Catholic church."

"A Catholic church? You never did."

"Oh yes, I did too. Saw her with my own eyes."

"When? You never told me anything."

"A few weeks past, right after the fire. In January. And I didn't like to say. It's embarrassing, sleeping practically in the same room with a Catholic."

"But you sleep next door, Addie. And you said she wasn't one."

Addie shrugged. "Said she didn't used to be. But if she's going to their church, that must mean she's one now."

Lilac shook her head in sympathy. "I simply don't know what to tell you. It's not as if I have room to ask you to live with me. Of course I would if I could, but . . ." She had never actually invited Addie Bellingham into her rooms on Christopher Street. In order to get to her living quarters they would have to pass through the sitting room, where her clients waited to purchase the anticonception powders and pills she made up in her little kitchen, and the treatment room, where Lilac used her lady needles to restore a woman's peace of mind. Didn't come into it that Addie would think Lilac's suite of rooms positively lavish, nor what she would say if she knew how much Lilac earned from her activities. It would please Lilac to see the look on Addie's face if she told all that, but Addie might tell Mr. Finney, and if Mr. Finney knew what Lilac did to earn her living he might take back her conversion, say she wasn't saved after all. Take away all her peace of mind that would. Not much point in supplying it for others if you couldn't have it yourself.

So it was much better to meet Addie Bellingham in one of the little cafés in her neighborhood. Like today.

It was nice to be with someone who didn't know anything about her except what Lilac chose to tell. And considering the family her Mrs. Turner had married into, it seemed to Lilac that Addie had a sort of connection to the world of medicine, which wasn't a million miles away from what Lilac herself did, if you looked at it with an open mind. So these pleasant little outings always promised the possibility of new and important information. Of course it wasn't easy to come by. Addie wasn't straightforward about such things. But now that Addie had said that about seeing Mrs. Turner go into a Catholic church, Lilac realized, she was clearly working up to saying something more.

Lilac raised her hand and signaled the waiter to bring two more of the tiny cups of strong coffee so favored by the Italian workmen who lived in the area.

"You have another coffee if you like," Addie said. "I don't think I—"

"Nonsense. Of course you must have another. One's hardly enough when they're so small." The coffee was served in little glasses set in metal holders that allowed you to pick them up no matter how hot— Italians didn't seem to understand about proper cups—and another was definitely in order. Addie looked positively constipated with things she wanted to say but hadn't managed to spit out just yet. "Don't you worry, Addie dear. It's my treat."

Addie smiled. Then she started to cry.

"My dear Adelaide, whatever is the matter?"

Lilac took up her lovely rabbit fur muff (gloves just weren't enough in this frosty January weather) to look for a handkerchief, but Addie quickly produced one of her own and dabbed at her eyes a few times. The waiter appeared and put their coffees on the small and rickety round table and offered them a bowl filled with lumps of brownish sugar. The cheapest sort on the market, but still two cents a lump, even in this unpretentious little café. "Have two lumps, Addie dear," Lilac said grandly. "My treat, remember."

"Well, if you don't mind."

"'Course I don't." Lilac helped herself to three lumps, then waited until the waiter left. "Whatever's troubling you, my dear? You can tell Lilac."

Addie looked around, before leaning forward. "It's just . . ."

"Yes. What?"

Addie dropped her voice so low Lilac had to lean forward as well to hear her. They were sitting with their bonnets almost touching when Addie said, "All this Maria Monk business, Lilac. I wonder if Mrs. Turner . . ."

"*Priests, Nuns, and the Confessional*," Lilac said, sighing out the words. "Gives you the chills just saying it, don't it?"

"Makes my blood run cold," Addie said with a shiver. "I could never stay with her, no matter what, if she's anything to do with dead babies. Even if it means being on the street. You understand, don't you Lilac?"

Lilac sat back and dabbed at her mouth with the handkerchief her friend hadn't needed, lowering her head at the same time so Addie wouldn't notice how those words had brought a flush to her cheeks. "Of course I do. But dead babies . . . I really think it's unlikely your Mrs. Turner knows anything whatever about that."

Chapter Fifteen

A YEAR IT had been after his Penelope died giving birth to Carolina before the hunger burst upon Wilbur Randolf. It arrived with an urgency that could neither be denied nor sated with any shameful rubbing and twisting in the bedclothes, while pretending the sort of half-satisfactory relief such actions brought to be something that had occurred while he slept. He was no longer a pimple-faced youngster having to endure until he could afford a whore or take a wife. He was a man and he wanted— nay, desperately needed—a woman.

He tried once with Peg the parlormaid. She was willing enough, God knows, but Wilbur suspected that Carolina had seen them, and he resolved never again to indulge in such dangerous behavior. A short time later, in desperation, he'd gone to the third tier of the elegant Park Theater.

Everyone knew that Jacob Astor, who owned the theater and was said to be landlord of a few of the nearby bordellos, had instructed the ushers to keep that tier in almost complete darkness and ignore whatever went on up there close to the painted ceiling and far above the stage. So when, during the second act of Shakespeare's *The Taming of the Shrew*, while Bianca was insisting, "Of all the men alive I never yet beheld that special face which I could fancy more than any other," a creature whom he could hardly see but who was definitely female reached over and put her hand on his crotch, Wilbur was not surprised. This was precisely why he'd come. Minutes later she'd undone the buttons of his fly, hiked up her skirts, and straddled him.

At first Wilbur was so conscious of the others around them—many of whom were grunting and groaning in such a way he knew them to be engaged in the same activity—he was afraid he could not perform. The woman knew exactly how to deal with that. "Three dollars rather than two," she whispered in his ear, "and I'll suck you dry. Guaranteed." The thought of such a waste of money spurred him on, and he obtained the relief he was after in the customary manner, later sneaking down to the main floor as the ticket he'd purchased entitled him to do and leaving in the company of fashionable Knickerbocker society, as the old Dutch elite called itself. The Beekmans, Bayards, Kents, Livingstons, and Van Rensselaers who were the Park's regular patrons would have professed total ignorance of the activity in the third tier even in the face of the Spanish Inquisition.

Randolf went to the theater a few more times that lonely winter but soon realized he did wish to be a face fancied more than any other. Or at least one that was recognized. He determined to bear the expense and went to one of the cheaper bordellos. There he at least got to choose the woman he wanted and spend twenty minutes or so with her in a proper bed. But beyond the most elementary level he wasn't satisfied with this arrangement either. He would, he realized, have to face the expense of a better class of parlor house.

That spring he began spending ten dollars a week to have one evening when for an hour or two he had the company of a pretty and well-spoken young woman promised to be disease free, as well as an enthusiastic and inventive bedmate. After about ten years of this he drifted into an arrangement with a lady called Jenny Worthington. Eventually he helped her acquire a house of her own on Bleecker Street where other ladies could book rooms in which to entertain gentlemen friends, but only on nights other than Tuesday or Friday, because those nights were reserved for Mrs. Worthington to receive Mr. Randolf. On these occasions the two of them passed the time until well after midnight enjoying each other's company in every way possible. It was in fact because the journey up the town from Bowling Green to Bleecker Street and back again became tedious, particularly in bad weather, that after Carolina's marriage Wilbur sold the house that had been his and Penelope's and moved to Washington Square. It was a ten-minute walk from there to Jenny's place on Bleecker.

On the Tuesday after Carolina's disturbing visit Wilbur asked Jenny to make some discreet inquiries on his behalf. "A bordello," he said. "I've no idea what sort. But down the town in the area of Cherry Street. One that has Asian ladies, or at least one such."

"Asian?" Jenny was obviously perplexed.

"Yes. Ladies from China, I think. Who paint their faces and put ribbons in their hair."

Jenny's eyes widened. "Well, I never. I mean it never occurred to me. Do you wish to . . . ?"

They were having a late supper in Jenny's pretty dining room, where everything was yellow and white, complimenting Jenny's white lace wrapper. Wilbur leaned forward and covered her hand with his. "Of course I do not, my dear. Why should I when I have you? It's a business inquiry. Look into it for me, will you?"

Jenny said she would, and today, when they were once again at supper, she made her report. "Nothing, Wilbur. Not even a hint of anything. I'm told there are some lodging houses on Cherry Street where Chinee men are accommodated and that one old woman has been seen among them, but no other lady of any sort." She did not mention that she'd also been told the houses in question were owned by Wilbur's son-in-law. He probably knew that, and he'd perhaps prefer that she did not. "And someone said that old man Astor has a Chinese servant, also an old woman," she continued. "But not another one in the town. And none I can discover at any bordello or parlor house."

"Chinee men but no women? Except for these two old servants?"

"That's what I'm told. Perhaps the men are . . . you know . . . like sailors who are a long time at sea."

"Sailors a long time at sea have few choices as regards their behavior. Men who emigrate without women and do not subsequently send for any? That seems to me another matter."

Jenny considered the fact that there were bordellos in the city which offered young boys exclusively and were patronized entirely by older men, but she thought it best not to mention that either. Jenny Worthington was nothing if not discreet. "More port, Wilbur?"

Wilbur allowed her to fill his glass, but he emptied it in one go and pushed away the last of his pheasant pie. "It's late, my dear. I must leave."

It was considerably earlier than he usually left, but Jenny knew her place. She accompanied him to the front door, kissed him good night, and resolved never again to mention the matter of the Asian lady with the painted face and ribbons in her hair. It was not, however, the sort of thing she was likely to forget.

Most of the men charged with policing the town, whether constables working under the High Commissioner, marshals appointed by the mayor—two per ward—or a member of the night watch called leatherheads because of their helmets, took the job because they were fitted for little else. Here was a way to flex your muscles, sometimes even brawl, and earn money doing it. A few were clever enough to take advantage of ways to increase their income on their own time. Since Wilbur Randolf supplied the raw material to the workshops that made most of the leather helmets, he had no difficulty finding such an after-hours entrepreneur.

The man he chose had been christened James Michael Flannagan. Irish but not Catholic, from a Belfast family who had sent their sons to the New World soon after the American Revolution. The other Flannagans had become grocers and tavern keepers. James Michael swung a billy. Fearless Flannagan he was called, not as a compliment and not because of any grand courage shown in the face of real gangsters who fought with broken bottles and iron chains. A few years back, when the Common Council tried yet again to outlaw the pigs that roamed the city's streets, there was another of the hog riots that occurred each time the Council tried to enforce a similar ordinance. The working-class women who kept the pigs as the only source of meat their families could afford, and boarded them in the streets where the animals could feed on free scraps and garbage, defended their bacon with every scrap of energy they could muster. Fearless earned his nickname by beating two of the women senseless, leaving one blind for life. Short, peculiar-looking men with shaved heads and braids down their back were exactly his sort of opponent.

By the time the others found Fat Cheeks in a nearby alley and brought him to Taste Bad, he was half dead and his queue had been cut off and forced up his rectum. The *yi* treated him by cleaning and bandaging his many cuts and bruises and using judiciously placed tiny needles to alleviate the pain of his worst injuries, but Taste Bad was at a loss to know how to deal with any possible repercussions. "He talks very little the *yang gwei zih* talk?" he asked, in an attempt to ascertain how much damage might have been done. "True? True?"

"Not true," someone said. "Fat Cheeks was a year on the ships with *yang gwei zih* sailors. Now here in New York almost a year. Work on docks with *yang gwei zih* carrying men. Not true. Fat Cheeks learn much *yang gwei zih* talk."

It was worse than Taste Bad first thought. He conferred with Leper Face, and together they decided the wisest course was to say nothing and adopt a wait and see approach to the problem. The Lord Samuel was their conduit to the city and the alien world in which they found themselves. He was also the only reason any of them could imagine why one of their number would have been beaten in a quest for information. But what could Fat Cheeks know that would be of value to an enemy of the lord? Something about the Devrey ships maybe. Something that happened on the docks or during a voyage. Nothing that went on in these so ordinary two houses, nothing that Fat Cheeks could know anything about, could possibly be important enough to get him half killed. Wait and see. That was best.

"You are quite sure?" Wilbur repeated.

"Positive." Fearless sat in a chair across from the man who had offered him five dollars to find a young Asian woman, probably a whore, with a painted face and ribbons in her hair. He was not to approach her in any way, simply to discover where she was and report back. "Lives on the top floor of number thirty-nine Cherry Street," Fearless said. "Never goes out the door neither. Has a servant, an old woman. She goes out sometimes. Young one has a baby daughter. 'Course, she don't venture out neither, being only a few months old."

"You didn't speak to her! The young woman, I mean. You didn't—"

"Never a word to either woman. Didn't even see 'em."

"Then how can you know—"

"I was told. By what we in law enforcement call an informant."

"But perhaps your informant wasn't telling the truth. You can't be sure."

"Yes, Mr. Randolf, I can be certain sure." Little slant-eyed bastard would've told on his grandma and his three sisters by the time Fearless Flannagan was done with him. Some o' the constables working among the porters on the docks knew how it was. *Can't never go home again if they ain't got them braids in place. Threaten to cut it off and you'll get whatever you're after. 'Course, you'd best soften 'em up a bit first.* That's what Fearless had done, soften him up. And when he waved that knife near his head the little bastard sang like a bird. In the end Fearless cut the braid off anyway. Put it where the Chinee wouldn't have no trouble finding it neither. "Certain sure," he repeated.

"Very well." Randolf reached into a drawer, produced a five-dollar bill, and pushed it across the desk. "Thank you."

Fearless made no move to take the money. "There's a bit more. 'Course, I can't be sure it's what you want to know."

None of it was what Wilbur Randolf wanted to know. He'd clung to the hope that the woman was simply an exotic whore. If she was not, the whole matter was a good deal more serious than it first seemed. All the same. "If there's more, of course I want to know it. Five dollars is a not inconsiderable sum, Mr. Flannagan."

"Five dollars for finding her, you said. I done that."

The bill, drawn on the New York branch of Mr. Biddle's Bank of the United States, lay on the polished wood between them. Neither man touched it. "Don't hold with paper money," Fearless said finally.

"For God's sake, man, a bank can't issue paper unless it has sufficient specie, silver or gold, to—oh, never mind. Coins then." Randolf swept the bill back into the drawer and produced a handful of change and began counting it out. "There. That should do it. Cash money."

"That's another silver dollar, ain't it? In your hand there?"

Wilbur glanced down. "It is."

"Put that on the pile and I'll add a bit to what you know."

"Add a bit! We had an arrangement."

"So we did. And I kept my part of the bargain."

Wilbur put the silver dollar on the table with the rest of the coins, but he kept his finger on it, ready to slide it back if he deemed the additional information not worth the price.

"Young woman's been here four years now. Brought over special to marry a white gent as keeps her."

"Marry? What do you mean, 'keeps her'? Who said—"

"My informant, like I told you. Didn't use those words o' course."

"Perhaps he didn't mean—"

"Oh no. He was sure enough about the married part. Didn't say keeps her. Said this white gent married her soon as she arrived, and now he comes to see her regular and pays for everything. She lives there on Cherry Street. Has a sort o' palace on the top floor. Full o' furniture come all the way from China when she did."

"Four years you say?" The words came out with no hint of the mix of rage and astonishment roiling in his belly.

"That's right. That's all I know, Mr. Randolf. So I'll be taking me money and going now." Fearless leaned forward and scooped up the original five dollars' worth of coins. Randolf still had his finger on the silver dollar. "Nothing more to tell, sir. Like I said." The fact that the white gent was Sam Devrey and Randolf's son-in-law wasn't anything Fearless Flannagan had any intention of selling for five dollars or even six. Anyways, Randolf probably knew it already. Had to be why he was interested in the first place. All the same, might come a time when Fearless Flannagan could sell that information somewhere else.

Randolf released his finger and watched his silver dollar disappear into the Irish thug's pocket. For once he was too shocked and disappointed to care about the money. Four years meant that the woman had been part of Sam Devrey's life before he married Carolina, probably before he met her. And it was entirely possible that Devrey was a bigamist.

Since he wasn't on duty, Flannagan was wearing a proper stovepipe hat. He polished the shiny top with the sleeve of his old-fashioned narrow-cut swallow-tailed coat, put it on, and tipped it politely before he left.

❧

"I am not a bigamist."

"God damn you to hell, Sam Devrey. Bigamist or not, you're a cad."

"By your lights perhaps. Not by mine." Sam leaned back in the chair. His office was on the fifth floor of the remarkable new Devrey headquarters. A large square window glazed with a single sheet of glass looked out on the world below. Not much of a view today, however. It was snowing a bit and heavily overcast, indicating that it would snow more soon. "You look quite pale, Father-in-law. You should have that drink I offered."

Randolf shook his head. Drinking with the man would truly sicken him. "Am I?" he asked.

"Are you what?"

"Your father-in-law. Legally."

"Of course you are. I just told you. I am not a bigamist."

"My understanding is that you married this young China woman." There were shelves built to the side of the large window looking toward the harbor. Numerous jade statues on the shelves. Strange Chinese deities he thought. Sam Devrey had been too damned long in those foreign parts. That should have warned Wilbur of what Carolina was getting herself into. Not that he'd ever been able to stop her doing what she wanted once she'd made up her mind. "Is that true? Were you married before you and Carolina met?"

"I wish you would tell me who gave you all this information. I expected Carolina to go to you in the light of what she saw, but surely she did not—"

"Carolina merely conveyed to me her great sadness at discovering her husband, the father of her son, in the company of a foreign woman of dubious reputation."

"There is no way on earth Carolina could have said anything of the sort. Who told you I had this other association?"

"Then you're admitting it?"

"I am doing no such—Very well." Sam realized he would have to tell his father-in-law some version of the truth. "I was party to a Chinese ceremony giving me possession of the Chinese girl about whom you've made these inquiries."

"What kind of ceremony? And what do you mean by possession of her? Are you saying she's your slave? That's against the law here in New York now."

"She is most certainly not my slave, and the ceremony is unknown here, though it means something among the Chinese. She's my mistress, Randolf. I am hardly the first man in New York to have one. Mine is Chinese and lives on Cherry Street. What of it? Others can be found all over the town. Even on Bleecker Street I warrant."

"How dare you! Besides, my wife has been dead for twenty-two years."

"And mine—my only wife, my legal wife before God and man—is very much alive and the mother of my son. I assure you, Carolina will never see Zachary again if she is so foolish as to bring an action for divorce against me."

Randolf had already decided that was not a viable option. Carolina's dirty linen spread all over the penny press? It was unthinkable. "Divorce is not a solution, Devrey."

"Very well, I'm glad we agree on that. May I ask what you do consider to be a solution?"

"That's simple. You must stop seeing this Chinawoman. Send her back where she came from. Put her on one of your ships bound for Canton. The servant and the child as well, of course."

"No."

The answer was not a surprise to Randolf. He had considered the possibility of a flat refusal to put things right. It had always struck him as being in Sam Devrey's character. "You force me to take drastic steps. I shall go to Mr. Astor."

"There's no point in your doing that, Father-in-law. I already have."

"Surely Astor doesn't approve of such behavior by the man—"

" . . . he relies on to operate a large and important business interest," Sam finished for him. "He doesn't give a damn about my personal life, Randolf. Why would you assume Astor to be so squeamish, considering the activities on the third tier of the Park Theater?" Sam saw with satisfaction the way the other man blanched. It was a lucky shot and it had hit home. "Astor doesn't care about such things and neither should you." Sam's voice was silky now, smoothed by the satisfaction of knowing he had won and Randolf had lost. "Carolina has an entirely respectable position in the town and considerable personal comfort. The rest is none of your affair."

It was not the end of the conversation. But by the time Randolf left, there was no further talk of divorce or running to John Jacob Astor with the tale. Sam had promised to do his best to placate Carolina, buy her something nice, some new jewels, perhaps. Spend a bit more time at home. And in the matter of the foreign girl, he would be discreet. In return, for the sake of his daughter and his grandson, Wilbur Randolf would not make any sort of scandal.

Mentioning the third tier of the Park had been a brilliant stroke, Sam told himself when his father-in-law left. And not a difficult guess. The man had to have done something in those years after his wife died. As for Carolina, it was entirely predictable she would run to her father once she saw Sam with Mei-hua. Also that Randolf would threaten him with revealing the entire business to Astor.

Astor loathed public scandal. It didn't matter how well Sam managed Devrey's or how hard it would be to replace him. The old bastard would swat him as if he were a troublesome mosquito. When a man had that kind of money, there was nothing to stop him doing whatever he wanted and simply spending whatever it took to fix any unfortunate consequences. Astor could buy himself another shipping manager. Hell, he might buy another shipping company and merge Devrey's out of existence.

The only thing to do, Sam had realized from the first, was to brazen it out.

Unless of course he chose to give up Mei-hua. He had considered that alternative well before it was mentioned by Wilbur Randolf.

He could send her back to Di Short Neck. *I am returning the goods, pirate. I no longer desire them.*

But he did. Oh Christ Jesus, he did. He could not imagine life without Mei-hua. She was the silken thread that tied him to the man he'd been, young, with hopes and ideas and boundless courage, and all of China waiting to be conquered. Mei-hua allowed him to keep sight of his dreams.

Sam was quite certain he had succeeded in averting disaster, but he would have to make sure. Raise the stakes and give Wilbur Randolf still more to protect.

"She's in her bedroom, sir. Said she didn't want any dinner." Dorothy hadn't prepared any either. Why would she, when Mrs. Devrey said she didn't want none and Mr. Devrey hadn't been home for a proper meal in so long she couldn't remember the last thing she'd fed him? "I've a bit of cold meat pie downstairs, and I could boil some potatoes. Wouldn't take too long."

"Never mind, Dorothy. I'm not hungry. I'll go straight up and see my wife."

It was just past four o'clock, but the few times he'd seen her since the fire she'd looked weak and sickly. He thought he might find her undressed and in bed, make it quick at least. But when he let himself into Carolina's bedroom, he found her fully clothed and standing at the window with her back to him. She turned at the sound of the opening and closing door. "Dorothy, I told you I didn't wish to be— Oh. It's you."

"Yes." He slipped out of his jacket and began at once to untie his stock.

"What are you doing?"

"Getting undressed. I'd suggest you do the same."

"Get out of my room. You must be mad. I can't imagine how you can—"

"Imagining has nothing whatever to do with it. Reality is the order of the day, dear Carolina. The reality you and your actions have thrust upon us. Take off your clothes. You're my wife. You cannot refuse me."

"I can and I will." She reached for the bell.

"Put the bell down, unless you wish to be put on display in front of the hired help. Perhaps even your child. I imagine Zachary is old enough to remember such a spectacle if you see fit to provide it."

She took her hand away from the bell. Sam had removed his shirt and sat down and began pulling off his boots. She could not look away, could not forget the months she'd longed for him. "What do you want with me? Why now?"

"I want another child of you. I believe you once pointed out there was only one way to get one." He stood in front of her wearing only his trousers.

"You have another child," she said. "With her."

"You are never to mention her again. Not her or her child. Never." He slapped her, once either side of her face, so both cheeks were left imprinted with the mark of his hand. He knew she would resist, and he knew he would force her. Indeed, he suspected forcing her was the only thing that would make what he intended possible. Nothing else about her stiffened his cock. Looking at those red streaks on her white face did it. "Take off your clothes and turn down the bed."

In the end he waited only until she had removed her frock and stood before him in her chemise and corsets, all the things white women layered over their flesh. They disgusted him. She disgusted him. Even the small spark of desire was gone until he slapped her twice more, and she tried to get away. Then he was able to force her back onto the top of the silken quilt and push up her petticoats and get the job done. Afterwards, ignoring her sobs, he stated his intentions.

"We shall have these encounters every day for a week, then wait and see if you are with child. If not, we shall have to repeat the performance until you are. Once you conceive, I will not trouble you unless you go running to your father with any more tales of woe. If you do, I will denounce you publicly as a trollop and a whore. I'll say you've been carrying on with Nick Turner. And I'll turn you out of this house. Needless to add, you will afterwards be forbidden to see your son."

Chapter Sixteen

WHEN THE FINANCIAL heart of New York burned to the ground, it was not a local catastrophe. The city was the economic engine of the entire nation; help to rebuild must come from state and national government. That was the opinion of Cornelius Lawrence, the first mayor to have been directly elected rather than appointed by the council. He was a gentleman but not a Whig, though that was the newly formed gentlemen's party—a coalition of groups which had in common principally that they opposed the populist excesses of President Andrew Jackson. Lawrence was a Democrat, supported by the political club known as Tammany Hall. Which, for all its Catholic Irish rank and file, was run by men of business who were both influential and Protestant.

The embers of the blaze still smoldered when Lawrence's committee of one hundred twenty-five met, first to thank their neighbors in Brooklyn and Newark for fire-fighting help, then to do something about emergency relief. Both were worthy aims quickly achieved, but no one doubted that the committee's chief responsibility was to find the money needed to rebuild. Neither President Jackson nor the Congress rose to the mayor's expectations, but Albany quickly floated a loan of six million dollars, the largest sum ever allocated for disaster relief. It was then possible to offer destroyed businesses loans at a modest five percent rate of interest. Increased availability of credit meant as well that existing loans could be extended rather than called. Fewer bankruptcies were the result, and the Erie Canal Commission saw fit to shift another million into the city's banks.

The scent of opportunity replaced the stench of smoke.

The town was awash in money. Moreover, it had gained a sudden supply of the scarcest of urban commodities, space. Taming the island the Indians had called Manahatta, the place of high hills, had never been easy, not when the project was begun by the Dutch in 1624 or when the English took it over in 1664. These modern times were no different. Turning Chelsea, an area hard by the Hudson River, from one gentleman's estate into a district of fine homes for many gentlemen required digging down twelve feet for a distance of a mile in order to run Eighth Avenue at a reasonable level. Over on the east side of the city, where north of Corlear's Hook dry land finished at Second Avenue and a series of jagged cliffs ended in a band of swamp edging the East River, the cost of draining and filling had put off even wealthy landlords until one of them, a descendent of old Peter Stuyvesant, committed the money required to develop a section known as Tompkins Square. Fine houses lined the streets there now as well.

Still, before that fiery December of '35 no one had imagined that the oldest parts of the town, the southernmost tip of the island, where crooked streets and cobbled alleys had been laid atop paths originally cut through the forest by red men in moccasins, would suddenly become a blank canvas upon which New York money could draw a picture more in keeping with its idea of itself. And while it wasn't possible to impose the strict grid of the rest of the city on the old town, they could make streets wide enough for modern transportation and eliminate little alleys and byways going nowhere. It required only will and imagination. These were the sort of men who had both.

With the Tontine gone, the Stock Exchange was homeless, but it resumed trading four days after the blaze. Meanwhile unemployed laborers were set to work clearing the still warm rubble, and the prosperous silk merchant Arthur Tappan told the employees he assembled the day after the fire, "We must rebuild immediately." Then he sent one to find an architect and the rest to fit up interim quarters. By midday the *Journal of Commerce* announced the company open for business on the corner of Pearl and Hanover streets. Other merchants were almost equally quick off the mark. Hundreds of them set up shop in temporary accommodation, causing rents down the town to double and triple overnight. Money, more than ever before, was pumping through the city's veins and arteries with a freedom that had been unimaginable only a few weeks earlier.

In 1827 the Swiss brothers Delmonico had opened a six-table café and patisserie on William Street and developed it into the city's first public dining room not connected to an inn, or a tavern, or even a hotel. Delmonico's was a *restaurant français,* where chefs found from among the city's French immigrants cooked food never before seen in America, and it was possible to order *à la carte,* to select from a menu that offered choices rather than set meals. The whole enterprise had burned to the ground.

The brothers swiftly bought a triangular plot fitted into the junction of Mill, Beaver, and William streets and set about building a fairy-tale palace adorned with marble pillars, crystal chandeliers, and velvet banquettes. Their new Delmonico's had two floors for dining in see-and-be-seen splendor, and a third for private parties where intimate rooms offered chaises longues as well as tables and chairs, available for whatever reason a lady might wish to recline before, during, or after dinner. Below ground level was a vault that could accommodate sixteen thousand bottles of wine, and between the building and the street, foot-thick brick walls that would act as a firebreak in case, God forbid, there was another fire.

It was a possibility they must all consider. The new Merchants' Exchange was to be erected on the site of the old, but this time it would cover a full city block and, be constructed almost entirely of Massachusetts granite with not a splinter of wood. There would be an eighty-foot glass dome above a vast central hall and accommodations for insurance companies, bankers, brokers, the Chamber of Commerce, and the Stock Exchange, as well as a reading room where newspapers and periodicals from around the world could be found. A very New York sort of place, just as John Jacob Astor, for all that he still had a thick German accent, had become a New York sort of man.

A peculiar kind of caution had built Astor's fortune; he had a talent for taking over other men's failed dreams and using money to make them succeed. Now he conceived a different sort of venture. The area around City Hall was no longer on the periphery of the town, instead it was the new center, a place where theaters, churches, and businesses—especially newspapers—were clustered around what had been known as the common, but was now called City Hall Park. The almshouse was gone, and the bridewell scheduled for destruction if ever the new prison on Centre Street was finished. The area was attracting the best sort of people these days, not just from all over the country but the world.

Trust John Jacob Astor to know that a city which had been entertaining upwards of seventy thousand visitors each of the last few years would see still more after this frenzy of growth. Time, Astor decided, for New York's first luxury hotel. Something far grander than his own workaday inn, City Hotel, near Trinity Church. Something to surpass Boston's classically opulent Tremont House.

He already owned the ideal piece of land. The once remote site on Broadway between Barclay and Vesey streets where his private residence had been before he built a new one up the town became Astor House: five stories built around a central courtyard, with three hundred and nine rooms that could house eight hundred guests. There was the unheard-of convenience of bathing and toilet facilities on each floor, and gas lighting throughout was supplied by the hotel's own plant. There was as well a *table d'hôte* restaurant that didn't aspire to the excess of choice of Delmonico's extravagant *carte* but offered American merchants and their guests hearty fixed meals based on oyster pie, joints of beef, and roast wild duck.

As long as you were not a workingman on a set income, and able to survive the spiraling inflation brought on by so much cheap money, '36 was a very good year. By the end of it six hundred new buildings had replaced those that had burned, and according to the papers they were all devoted to doing business.

Making money. Making New York. There was now scarcely a private residence or a boardinghouse south of Wall Street. A very good year.

A year when Carolina Devrey also discovered it was possible for good to come of evil. Contrary to what she expected, the child born of the most hateful behavior was from the first moment the babe was put in her arms as precious to her as the one she'd imagined to be born of tenderness. Samuel insisted on naming the infant Celinda after his wretched mother, but even so Carolina adored her baby daughter. She thought of her not as the child of her shaming but of her release, because once it became obvious she was truly expecting, Sam had left her strictly alone. After their daughter's birth he asked nothing of her in the bedroom and little in terms of the household. Sam spent the barest minimum of time at three East Fourteenth Street and had apparently given her liberty to live her own life. Best of all, Carolina no longer pined for Samuel or thought herself in love with him. Tiny little Celinda Lucy Devrey, born in October of 1836, had set her free.

Sam had gotten away with lying to his father-in-law about what Jacob Astor knew and didn't know, but he did not fool himself that would always be the case. Only if he could take back what should have been his birthright, control of Devrey Shipping, would he be free of Astor's fearful shadow. If Danny Parker, the shipwright who had most of Devrey's business, knew of that ambition, he never mentioned it. He and Sam Devrey met frequently, but always they talked about ships, the how and the why of them, not who owned them. When the conversations concerned Devrey ships Danny was servicing, they usually took place down the town at the biggest and oldest Parker shipyard at the foot of Montgomery Street. When Sam asked

Danny to meet him at the smaller Thirty-fourth Street yard, they had conversations of a different sort.

"It's all in the bow," Danny said. They were alone in the uptown shipyard, the plans of the *Ann McKim* that Sam Devrey had produced some two years back spread once more on the table between them. Cod's head and mackerel's tail had been the conventional wisdom in the making of merchant craft for two hundred years, but according to the plans the *Ann McKim* had a bow that was not broadly rounded in the manner of the head of a cod. Hers was considerably narrowed, almost tapered. Danny tapped the drawing at that point. "Bow like this has to make her handle easier sailing into the wind."

Sam nodded agreement. "True enough, but it's precisely that curve of the hull that forces everything else." The ship was only twenty-seven feet in the beam, the prime reason she was less than five hundred tons burthen. Other ships of her length could carry twice as much cargo. "Danny, what if the slope of the keel were different?"

"Different how?"

"I'm not entirely sure yet."

There was a tiny room on the ground floor of number thirty-seven Cherry Street, the building next to the one that housed Mei-hua and Mei Lin and Ah Chee, which Sam had claimed for himself. A place where he was absolutely certain John Jacob Astor had no spies. It was not really a room so much as an oversized and windowless cupboard, but he forbade any of his lodgers entry. The room contained a tank full of water and an assortment of bits of paper and slivers of wood. Sam spent a good portion of his time in the yellow light of an overhead lantern, testing the shapes of many a hull. One thing he'd definitely established was that longer objects offered less resistance to water than shorter ones. And if the base of an object was triangular its whole distance, there was less resistance still.

The keel of the *Ann McKim* sloped downward from eleven feet at the bow to seventeen feet at the stern. "How could you make it a sharp V-shape the entire length?" Sam asked.

"You couldn't." Danny had been leaning over the plans. Now he straightened and reached for his pipe. "Not as long as you're building your ship out of God's own wood and not some miracle material the Devil might provide."

"So, Benjy, a real doctor now, *ja?* At the University of the City of New York they said so?"

"Yes, Papa. That's what it means that they gave me my degree from the department of medicine. I can write M.D. after my name and I'm a real doctor."

"Excellent, excellent." Jacob Klein helped himself to another piece of his wife's savory potato pudding. At this October Friday night meal celebrating the start of the Sabbath, even an ordinary potato was made special. "You will need a consulting room then. I have been looking at premises right next to the shop. Of course these days everything is very dear, but if—"

"It's all right, Papa. You don't have to take on any additional expense. I won't need a consulting room just yet."

"No consulting room?" Frieda Klein had just returned from the kitchen with a replenished platter of chicken, roasted in the brand-new coal-fired cookstove her husband had bought her. With an oven yet. So there was no need to turn a bird on a spit in front of the fire. She put the dish down between her son and her husband, meanwhile hushing her two daughters, who were ignoring the men and giggling between themselves. "But you must have a consulting room. Where will you see patients, Benjy?"

"I'm not going to see private patients, Mama. Not right away." His parents stared at him. His younger sisters, sensing something important afoot, did the same. "I'm going to stay at Bellevue for the time being. Dr. Turner has persuaded Dr. Grant to add a second resident to the permanent staff and he's offered the privilege to me. Isn't that wonderful?" Even to himself the confidence in his voice sounded forced and insincere.

"I see." Jacob reached for another piece of chicken. "And am I to go on paying seven dollars a week to the almshouse so you can have this great privilege?"

"Jacob! It's the Sabbath. No quarreling. And no money talk."

"It's all right, Mama," Ben said. And to his father, "No, Papa, Bellevue will now pay me. I get a hundred dollars a month." It was not an inconsiderable sum.

"But the future, Benjy. You need to earn more than a hundred—"

"What is the matter with both of you? On the Sabbath money we don't talk. And are you going to keep that piece of my delicious chicken on your fork in the air, Jacob? Like a flag? Eat. Later, when it's not the Sabbath, then you can talk to Benjy about earning a living."

Jacob could not wait that long. Only until the women were in the kitchen, putting the dishes in the soapy water they had prepared before sundown, laughing and talking so he knew they would stay there for a while. Only until he and his son were sitting with small glasses of schnapps and the little dry sweet cakes called *kichelach*. For Jacob, talking to Benjy about his future could wait only until then. "Benjy, a hundred dollars a month is good for just starting out, I agree. But if—"

"Papa, if I opened a private practice with a consulting room, I would average a dollar a patient. There is literature on the subject. And being new, how long would it take for me to have a hundred patients a month?"

"You've thought about this, I see," Jacob said.

"Of course, Papa. Carefully. The way you have always told me."

"*Ja,* but I think you thought about it for me. So you would have points to make in the argument. I think for yourself you are thinking something entirely different."

Ben was holding a *kichel,* but he hadn't taken a bite. "No, Papa, I really—"

"Benjy, you are the first American Jewish doctor here in New York. No, don't interrupt. I know about Mordecai Singer and Chaim Gold, but they are old men trained in the old ways of the Rhineland and Bavaria. How long do you really think it will take for you to have a hundred patients?"

Ben put the cake down. It was no longer so enticing. "Not long, Papa."

"And considering that Samson Simson is ready to be your patron, it is—"

"What do you mean, my patron? I haven't seen Mr. Simson for almost a year. Not since that day after *shachris*."

"I know. Mr. Simson came to my shop again last week. He has another nephew getting married so he needs another *kiddush* cup. And after he congratulated me on having a son who is now a real doctor, he said also that he and the elders at Shearith Israel were all proud that one of us was among the first group of doctors to be graduated from the University of the City of New York Medical College. He mentioned that he was sure many of the members of the congregation would be looking forward to the opportunity to consult you. That you should come and talk with him about it. Considering."

"He means considering that what he wants to talk to me about is Mrs. Manon Turner. I have nothing to tell him, Papa. I told you both that. She's a nice lady and she comes to nurse the poor. What is there to tell?"

"All right. To Mr. Simson maybe nothing. But to me? Maybe what to tell me is why you want to doctor poor *goyim* rather than make a living looking after our own kind. I don't mean to be heartless, Benjy. Sick is sick and caring for the sick is a *mitzvah* whether it's one of us or one of them. A bigger *mitzvah* when you do it for charity. But for charity you are a volunteer, a few hours every week maybe, like your Mrs. Turner. To make a living so some day you can support a wife and children of your own, *Hashem* should grant you such blessings, for that you need a consulting room and a private practice."

One of the Sabbath candles—lit by his mother before the Sabbath began, so there would be light for the meal without it requiring any of the family to do the work of making light—guttered out. Ben couldn't see his father's face when he said, "It's because of Dr. Turner, Papa."

"Yes. I thought so. Only what exactly about Dr. Turner? That's the part I don't understand, Benjy."

"It's the research, Papa. I want to go on working with Dr. Turner in his laboratory and doing research. Only at Bellevue is that possible. At least for now. Later I can have my own laboratory maybe."

"Research." Jacob had already had the conversation with his son in which he heard about the possibility of curing all disease for all time. A miracle to be achieved by cutting open poor Irish people who were already dead. It was only because he knew there were unlikely to be any Jews at the almshouse that he had not vigorously objected to the practice. Since it had been a condition of the original Jewish settlers being permitted to come to New Amsterdam that they never be burdens on public charity and always look after their own, Jacob could hold himself apart from such thorny moral dilemmas. "Research," he said again. "In a laboratory of your own. Tell me, please, Benjy, who is going to pay you to do this research?"

"Right now, Bellevue, Papa."

"A hundred dollars a month. I know. But in the future, Benjy?"

"I don't know. But I have to do this, Papa." The last candle flickered out, and the room was in total darkness. The kitchen was quiet as well. Mama and the girls had apparently retired. "I have to, Papa. It's what I was born to do."

"And I, *Hashem* help me, am apparently born to support you and your wife and children forever."

"But I don't have a wife and children, Papa."

"I know. That is a big part of the problem. Come, Benjy. Time for bed."

Chapter Seventeen

THE WIDOW TURNBULL ran nothing grand enough to be called a restaurant. She prepared one meal a day for a few local gentlemen whose business required them to be in this part of the island so far above the proper city when the four o'clock dinner hour arrived. Her plain and decent cooking was served to no more than the six who could fit around the table in the front room of her farmhouse on what was now grandly called Twenty-ninth Street and Second Avenue, though it looked little different from when it had been simply the Turnbull farm. The land had been in her dead husband's family since his people arrived from England before the Revolution. Most of the original acreage had been sold off to speculators convinced it would someday be part of a bustling city. Maybe so, but Mr. Turnbull preferred a dollar today to the promise of five dollars tomorrow. So now that she was a widow, thanks to her husband and the speculators, Mrs. Turnbull wasn't poor, but what was left of the farm could support only a few chickens, a couple of cows, and a plot of vegetables alongside the farmhouse. Cooking for strangers was a sensible way to make use of those remaining assets.

It was first come first served at the Widow Turnbull's, except for her regulars like Nick Turner and Mr. Harvey, whose job it was to ride through the woods, checking on the street and avenue markers indicating the future grid and report monthly to the council. Then there was Mr. Cranston, a widower who lived nearby and operated the ferry that brought farmers and cattle across from Long Island to the stockyards and abattoir on Twenty-fourth Street and Third Avenue, the section known as Bull's Head Village. Lately those three regular diners were joined at least once a week by Danny Parker the shipwright, come to check on his secondary yard located where so-called Thirty-fourth Street spilled into the river.

That yard, as Nick recalled the first time he was introduced to Parker, was where he had met Sam Devrey when Devrey felt the need to explain about his exotic second household on Cherry Street. Did Danny Parker know about that arrangement? Maybe he did and it didn't matter since Devrey Shipping was probably one of Parker's biggest clients. Not his worry, Nick reminded himself, though it did grieve him to think how awful it would be for Carolina if the story ever got out. On this particular February day he was glad to have the conversation at Mrs. Turnbull's table entirely occupied by talk of the stevedores who en masse had put down their tools and refused to work unless their wages were raised. Shut down the entire port. Mayor Lawrence had to call in the Twenty-seventh Regiment of the militia to get things back to normal.

"Seems to me," Harvey said, "since they call it a strike, that's what they should get. Bring back flogging. That'll put a stop to all this nonsense."

"Not unless Lawrence is prepared to whip pretty much every workingman in the city." Parker reached for one of Mrs. Turnbull's hot and flaky biscuits. "A few years ago there wasn't one of these labor unions anywhere in New York that I'm aware of. Now they're everywhere."

"A man has to protect his livelihood," Cranston said quietly. "If businessmen are going to buy marble quarried by Sing Sing prisoners who work for no wage at all, what are law abiding marble-cutters to do about it? They can't possibly match the Sing Sing price."

"But if Sing Sing marble isn't sold to defray the cost of operating the penitentiary," said a Mr. Graves, who had ridden down from Westchester and was stopping the night at Mrs. Turnbull's, "what will? And what are the alternatives? Hang them all instead? Or decent citizens having to pay higher taxes to keep them?"

"The marble-cutters are decent citizens as well, with families to support just like the rest of us," Cranston said. Nick was mildly surprised to discover this radical side to the ferry operator's character.

"Nothing to do with marble-cutters," Parker mumbled, his mouth full of stewed beef and onions. "It's the stevedores what went on strike."

"But they're all in it together, aren't they? This General Trades Union organization claims to speak for 'em all. Flogging's too easy. Hang a few of the ringleaders, that will make the point." Harvey was excited enough to stand up and wave his glass of ale at the rest of them.

"Now, now gentlemen." Mrs. Turnbull arrived to calm the troubled waters, carrying a steaming dish of something that smelled marvelous. "You mustn't get yourselves all excited. Lose your appetites you will. And I've made you baked apples with maple syrup."

There was a good bit of silent eating after that, though the strain of the argument flowed like an underground river among them. Nick took a last spoonful of baked apple and stood up. It was a short walk back to the almshouse, but it was easier while there was some light left, particularly in the cold of winter.

"Going so soon, Dr. Turner?" The stranger from Westchester patted his mouth with a napkin and stood up as well. "I had hoped to show you something of interest. At least I expect it would be, since you're a medical man."

"What's that, Mr. Graves?"

Graves went over to the satchel he'd left beside the door when he arrived. "I call it Somnus. For the god of sleep." He produced a tightly corked metal canister about ten inches high. "A few whiffs and your patients will slumber peacefully, and whatever you do, they will feel no pain."

"If you're speaking of nitrous oxide or laughing gas, I heard of it years ago in Providence. It provoked uncontrollable silliness, even euphoria. But as a medical analgesic it wasn't much use."

"My Somnus is not nitrous oxide, Dr. Turner. I can promise you that. It is quite different, as I'm prepared to demonstrate."

Nick spied Mrs. Turnbull watching them intently from her place beside the door to the kitchen. Whatever it was Mr. Graves wanted with him, the man had known to find him here because the Widow Turnbull had disclosed that Dr. Nicholas Turner regularly came to her farmhouse for his dinner. "Demonstrate how, Mr. Graves?"

"I will prove to you that Somnus produces a deep slumber that prevents the feeling of pain."

"And what exactly is this Somnus?"

"I'm not prepared to say at this moment, Dr. Turner. A man has to protect his right to earn from his labor, doesn't he?"

"Fair enough." Nick reached for his greatcoat and muffler, which were hanging on a hook beside the door. "But I'm afraid you've come to the wrong man. We can't afford such luxuries at Bellevue. You should talk to the doctors down the town at New York Hospital. Private charity for the deserving poor may stretch a bit further than the budget the council allots to the almshouse."

"I do indeed intend to visit New York Hospital, Dr. Turner, and a number of private physicians, but I wanted to speak with you first because I'm told you're a true man of science. Forward thinking. Not everyone is, as I'm sure you know. There's some that object to any kind of research as being against the laws of God and man."

That long, hard look, Nick realized, was intended to be conspiratorial. Damn. Impossible to keep anything quiet, not in a place like New York. "Forward thinking," Nick said. "I shall take that as a compliment."

"What I propose, Dr. Turner, is that what I have in here"—Graves indicated the metal canister—"would allow a man to come under the surgeon's knife while still alive and feel nothing."

There was a gasp or two from the others. "And afterwards?" Nick asked.

Graves shrugged. "Afterwards the patient would wake up, and things would go on as they would have in any case."

"It's a remarkable claim, Mr. Graves, but difficult to prove in these circumstances. If you care to come to the hospital sometime and—"

"I can prove the truth of my words here and now, Dr. Turner. I will be your patient. I believe Mrs. Turnbull can supply us with a sharp knife. I'm prepared to allow you to make as deep a cut as you like on any part of my person."

Mrs. Turnbull meanwhile had produced a large carving knife and was holding it in full view. "With that," Graves said, nodding towards the knife. "And with these other gentlemen as witnesses."

"He sat down," Nick told Manon the next day. "Then Mrs. Turnbull pulled the cork on the container of this Somnus and dampened a cloth with whatever was inside and waved it under his nose. Next thing you know, Graves has taken a couple of deep breaths and gone out as quickly as you'd snuff out a candle. Couple of the others slapped his face and called his name, but didn't get any response."

"And did you then cut him, Cousin Nicholas?"

Nick shook his head. "No. I couldn't bring myself to cut into perfectly healthy flesh simply to prove a point."

"Well then?"

"I'm not sure. The crafty widow wanted to cut him herself—they're obviously in league over this—but I wouldn't let her. So the other men pinched and pummeled him a bit more. No response whatever. He woke up after about fifteen minutes. It was like a deep faint, Cousin Manon, one that can be induced at will. It could be marvelous. For necessary surgery, of course." And for research. He didn't dare say it aloud, but the possibility of opening up a live patient and seeing the organs actually function . . . Every time he thought of it he was both chilled with terror and dizzy with excitement.

"My husband took laughing gas once," Manon said. "He told me about it. He was very young, only sixteen, and on the ship coming from Canton to New York to study medicine. Some of the passengers had the stuff and they would hold parties. For the silliness. But when Joyful took a whiff, he passed out and hit his head and he didn't feel a thing."

"Did he ever use it medically?"

"I don't think so. At least he never said. I don't believe he'd have known where to get this laughing gas."

"Those skilled in chemistry can produce laughing gas I know, but Mr. Graves assures me his Somnus is something entirely different. He's not prepared to say what, only to sell it already made up."

Manon cocked her head. "And have you then bought a supply of Mr. Grave's secret mixture?"

Nick nodded. "I couldn't resist. Don't know if I'll have the nerve to try it on a real patient, but I do have some if the proper opportunity comes round."

Little Annie Jablonski arrived in his hospital two days later.

Annie was not an orphan, but her mother had been caught stealing a loaf of bread and there was nothing the Police Justice could do but send her to the women's prison in the almshouse. That necessitated putting six-year-old Annie in the gentle care of Warden Frankly Clement.

"A rat bite, I expect," Monty Chance said when he showed the gangrenous leg to his chief. "She must have been bitten a week or so ago."

"At least that, probably longer," Nick said. The small leg was black and putrid and swollen to well up the calf. "The bite was simply ignored, the way everything usually is over there. Damn both Clement and his wife. If there's any justice there's a place in hell with their names on it." Little Annie stared up at him. Though she spoke almost no English, she seemed to have picked up something from his tone. Big tears rolled down her cheeks, though she didn't make a sound.

"Leg has to come off, doesn't it, sir?"

"Yes, Dr. Chance, it does. Above the knee. She hasn't a chance otherwise."

"Not much of a life afterwards, a girl like her, with only one leg."

"It's certain death with two. The more immediate problem is how to be sure she will live through the surgery. She's wickedly malnourished and very ill. The shock of the pain is likely to stop her heart."

"I can see if old man Potter has any laudanum in the dispensary, but last time I asked, he had none. And who's to pay if he has?"

"We'd find the money." Nick would pay, as he always did. "Thing is, if we give her enough laudanum to really deaden the pain, that might kill her as well."

"I've not seen laudanum kill anyone."

"It might, Dr. Chance. Look how thin she is."

"Just as you say, Dr. Turner. I agree. What do we do then? Allow her to die, I suppose."

"Absolutely not, Dr. Chance. Tomorrow we are going to put her into a deep sleep and cut off her leg before she wakes up. She will not feel a thing."

"Not even when we saw through the bone?"

"Not even then."

"Sounds like magic, sir."

"Not a bit of it, Dr. Chance. It is science."

Somnus might be science, but as far as Nick actually knew, it might as well be witchcraft. He went to the Widow Turnbull's the next day but found a notice tacked to the door saying that Mrs. Turnbull regretted having been called away and promised to serve dinner again the following day. So forget for the time being his only connection with Mr. Graves of Westchester.

He had to administer enough to keep the child asleep for at least half an hour; no way he could do this sort of surgery any faster than that. Graves had taken two deep whiffs and been out fifteen minutes. As for how much it would take to insure little Annie Jablonski painless surgery, Nick could do nothing but guess.

There was no proper operating theater at Bellevue. One had been planned when the original hospital was conceived in 1816 and even slated to be enlarged during additional building in 1825, but the budget constraints of the city and the greed of men like Tobias Grant had overrun the planners' good intentions. The operating theater had become a ward like any other, and now most surgeries were performed wherever the patient lay. Not this one. Nick decided to cut off Annie Jablonski's leg in the director's room off the ground floor lobby. He'd asked Manon to find him a blanket he might lay over the desk and perhaps a pillow for the child's head. She brought both from her lodgings on Vandam Street as well as a pair of lanterns and a large supply of scrupulously clean rags. "There's bound to be a lot of blood. I thought you might need these, considering how short of bandages this place always is."

"Indeed I will, Cousin Manon. Thank you. The lanterns will be useful as well." The hospital was supposed to have been piped for gas lighting the previous summer. Nick was not in the least surprised that it had not happened. No doubt the funds had provided a brace or two of fat pheasant for Tobias Grant's table.

"I thought they might do," Manon said. "And I've an extra supply of whale oil. In case it takes longer than you intend."

"Hard to know with surgery," Nick agreed. "You're a wonder, Cousin Manon."

"Don't flatter me, Cousin Nicholas. Grant me a privilege instead."

"Whatever you like," he said. "Though I can't think what would possibly be in my gift that's of any value to you."

"Allow me to observe."

"Observe the surgery?"

"Exactly."

"My dear Cousin Manon, you're an indomitable woman, as I well know, but surgery of this sort . . . it's no place for a lady, I assure you."

"It's little to ask, Cousin Nicholas, and I might be useful. I'm not a bad nurse, you know."

"But why?"

"May I be present, yes or no?" She had no intention of telling him her reason for asking.

"Yes, very well. But you are to stand near the door so you can slip outside if you feel faint. It's a bloody business, dear Manon. And while I have hopes, I can't promise the child won't be screaming in agony."

"Two o'clock is it?"

"Two sharp," he concurred. "Dr. Chance and Dr. Klein are to assist me."

Judging by the crowd trying to get in at the door of the director's room a few minutes before two, all of Bellevue had come to watch. Nick spotted half a dozen ambulatory patients, the three medical students currently working at the hospital, the warden of the orphanage, even the one-eyed apothecary who ruled the dispensary. In nearly two years he'd never before seen Jeremy Potter above his basement dungeon. "What are you all doing here? Go away. I can't—"

"We are here to see a miracle, Dr. Turner." Tobias Grant himself and a strange man with him. The stranger stayed just inside the door, but Grant pushed his way through the jam and came to stand almost nose to nose with his Senior Medical Attendant. "It is my understanding that's what you've promised. A miracle."

"Dr. Grant, I never—"

"One that is to take place at—" Grant pulled his watch from his waistcoat pocket and flipped it open—"two sharp. Ah, here is your patient."

Manon came in carrying the child wrapped in a blanket, and laid her down on the desk, hushing the little girl's sobs. "She's feverish, Dr. Turner. I gave her willow tonic and it helped some, but she's still quite hot."

"Salicylic acid," Potter intoned. "Make it up myself from willow bark. Best thing for a fever."

"Yes, well, that will help I'm sure. But I can't perform this surgery with an audience."

Grant turned to the patients and the medical students. "Everybody out!" With some grumbling the crowd of observers left. "Now, Dr. Turner, your patient is technically in the care of Mr. Clement here, seeing as he's warden of the orphanage. Mr. Potter prepared the medicine the child has recently received. This gentleman is Mr. Henry Morrison; he is my guest. And I, as you well know, am responsible for everything that happens in this institution. So we all have a reason to remain. With the exception of Mrs. Turner, of course."

Manon stood at the top of the desk, cradling Annie's head and shoulders in her arms. Nick hesitated a moment then said, "She may stay. Annie appears to take some comfort from her presence. Are you willing to remain where you are, Mrs. Turner?"

"Certainly, Dr. Turner." Manon shot him a grateful look.

"Very well," Grant said, "that gives you an audience of the lady, myself, my guest, the director of the dispensary, and the warden of the orphanage. Not too many, I trust." Grant shut the door with a decisive slam. "Proceed, Dr. Turner."

"Very well. But I won't be responsible for any weak stomachs among you."

Monty Chance had laid out the instruments: four scalpels of different sizes, two saws, a number of needles threaded with catgut, a pair of retractors, and a couple of probes. An old metal washtub would receive the diseased leg once Nick had cut it off. It was a dark gray day, but everything in the temporary operating theater was bathed in the yellow light of the lanterns suspended from the ceiling.

"Dr. Klein," Nick murmured.

Ben Klein stepped forward with a clean towel and a basin of water, in which floated a lump of strong brown soap. Nick and the other two doctors, having already taken off their coats and rolled up the sleeves of their shirts, scrubbed and dried their hands.

The canister of Somnus he'd purchased from Mr. Graves of Westchester was in the pocket of Nick's coat, which was hanging on a hook beside the door. He had to push between Grant and the mysterious Mr. Morrison to get it. He felt their eyes on him all the while. "Take this please, Dr. Klein. Remove the stopper as quickly as you can, and I shall put this cloth over the opening straightaway."

In the farmhouse Graves had used his handkerchief, one of Manon's rags would do today. Nick clamped it on top of the canister as soon as Ben had removed the cork. A sickly sweet smell filled the air straightaway. "Dr. Chance, the window."

Chance cracked it slightly and cold air rushed into the room. Nick put the cloth dampened with Somnus under the little girl's nose. Annie opened her mouth as if to scream or sob, then lifted her hand to push his away but only half completed the gesture. Her arm fell limp to her side, her eyes closed, and her head lolled against Manon's breast.

Nick mentally ticked off ten seconds, which felt like an hour, then took the cloth away and pinched the little girl's cheek as hard as he could. The mark he left was bright red, but she didn't so much as sigh. A pinch to her arm and another to her thigh had the same effect. The open window had cleared away the sickening smell. "Very well, gentlemen. Let us begin. Please tie a tourniquet right here, Dr. Chance."

He indicated a spot some two inches above the girl's knee, and Monty Chance tied a leather thong around it. "Tight as you can, Doctor," Nick said. The tourniquet would cut off as much as possible of the supply of blood to the rest of the leg, and inhibit bleeding from severed veins and arteries during surgery. "Excellent. Now the linen bandage." That went just below the tourniquet. Later it would help to roll the skin in place over the stump. "The leg, Dr. Klein." Ben took hold of the child's heel and raised her black and swollen leg into the air. "Very good, hold it absolutely steady, Doctor." Nick turned to his knives.

He selected a four-inch scalpel from the array and made the first incision, starting on the underside of the leg and drawing the knife towards him in a half circle that ended at the midpoint of the diameter of the thigh just above the knee. He had heard grown men shriek for their mothers when the cold steel of a scalpel first bit into soft adipose tissue. Annie Jablonski didn't make a sound.

The tourniquet meanwhile was doing its job. Blood pooled around the wound he'd made, but it oozed rather than spurted. Monty Chance sopped what there was with a wad of rags.

Nick heard someone gagging behind him. He cut again, once more starting from under the leg, but this time drawing the scalpel in the opposite direction. The second incision met the first with precision. A clean circular cut now separated the skin of the upper thigh from that just above the knee. Back when he was a student and later as a doctor in Providence, he'd never considered himself a particularly skilled surgeon, but he'd had plenty of practice since coming to Bellevue; the destitute were always arriving at his door with one or another limb crushed beyond hope. These days the scalpel felt like an extension of his hand, but until this moment only the dead had lain silent beneath his knife. The child's chest was rising and falling in a steady rhythm, and her eyes remained closed. "All right?" he murmured to Manon, who still held the girl's shoulders in the crook of her arm.

"Entirely all right," she whispered back. "A miracle after all."

Nick smiled and returned to his task. The muscles had to be severed next, but first, "The linen roller, Dr. Chance." Monty Chance put both hands around the circle of cloth he'd tied below the tourniquet and used it to help him draw back the skin the incision had loosened.

Saving as much skin as possible to stitch over the stump was the key to an amputation that did not later fester. Among Nick's most precious possessions was a journal written by his four times great grandfather; back in 1670. As long ago as that, old Lucas Turner the barber surgeon had noted the need to save skin when amputating. "Very good, Dr. Chance. Hold the leg absolutely still, Dr. Klein." Nick took up his largest scalpel and with two more semicircular cuts severed the muscle all the way to the bone. There was much more blood now, but Monty Chance had both hands occupied in protecting the skin. "Dr. Klein," Nick said. He spoke quietly because it was one of the surgeon's jobs to keep the operating theater calm and focused. Chaos was a deadly enemy when scalpels and saws were involved. "Sop the blood with your free hand, please, Dr. Klein. But don't lose your grip on that leg." Nick turned to the instrument array, seeking the retractor. Manon, relying on nothing but instinct and her powers of observation, had already picked it up and was holding it out to him. Moments later, when it was time for the large triangular saw, she held that out as well.

Nick looked at Annie one more time. She still slept. He began to saw.

Bones have no feeling. So every medical student was told when he began the study of surgery. *It's the ratcheting back and forth of the saw, the friction to the wounds you've made with your scalpel, that causes such intense pain. Be as quick and as decisive as you can; that's in the best interest of your patient. Make sure your tools are sharp and well oiled, and cut with the attention you'd apply to the last log in the world's last forest.* Not that this particular amputation would require much effort. Still, quick was best. Nick leaned forward and put his back into it.

He heard someone retching behind him.

He heard, as well, Annie Jablonski moan.

"She's coming round, Dr. Turner," Manon said, an edge of panic in her voice.

Nick felt panic too. After years of cutting in the midst of howling agony he had, in just a few minutes, become accustomed to the wonder of an operation performed without screams. He stopped sawing, took a step closer to the child's head, and grabbed his black stethoscope and pressed it to her chest. A steady enough heartbeat. Rapid, but that was to be expected. He lifted her hands. They were caked with grime, but he could see no sign of blue beneath her nails. His patient was not in shock. The mysterious Somnus was simply wearing off.

Nick grabbed the canister, prized out the cork, and shoved it below the child's nose. Manon took it out of his hand. "I'll do it."

"Count of twenty," he said.

This time the small room reeked of the sickly sweet smell of the stuff. It was making him lightheaded, and he could hear someone behind him struggling with a hacking cough. Manon put the cork back in the canister. Nick went to the window and threw it wide open. Fearsome cold, but it felt refreshing. "Deep breaths of fresh air everyone. We don't all want to go to sleep."

He went back to sawing. A few seconds more were all that was required and the lower half of the leg was free. Ben Klein caught it as it fell, and turned and plopped the thing into the washtub. There was more retching from one of the observers, then the sound of the door being opened and shut. Good riddance. Please God it was Tobias Grant.

Nick began trying off the arteries and blood vessels with catgut ligatures, instructing Monty Chance to continually loosen the tourniquet so that more would be revealed as the flow of blood returned to Annie Jablonski's thigh. Finally he rolled the reserved skin over the stump and stitched it carefully in place. Through it all the little girl didn't so much as murmur.

He put down the last of his instruments. "Done," he said. "Thank you, gentlemen. And you, Mrs. Turner."

His assistants, all three including Manon, were grinning at him. He was grinning as well, he realized. All of them as satisfied as cats with a bowl of cream. Painless surgery was a thing longed for since the days of Hippocrates. At last it had happened; they had witnessed a miracle. Nick turned to see if the sense of wonder had spread to the onlookers. Tobias Grant, he noted, looked pleased, though he wasn't actually smiling. Mr. Morrison had a notepad and a stub of pencil and was busy scribbling away. Frankly Clement looked positively grim. Not one of them seemed to have any idea of what an astounding sight they'd seen. Jeremiah Potter was gone. He'd been the retcher, then. That would teach the hateful old troglodyte to venture from his cave.

Grant mumbled something that sounded like congratulations and hustled his guest and Clement out of the room.

Manon lifted Annie into her arms. "I'll take her back to the ward now, if that's all right?"

"Yes, excellent. Can you stay with her for a bit? I've no right to ask when you've already done so much, but—"

"Of course. I'll let you know as soon as she wakes, shall I?"

"Please do, but don't climb the stairs. Send someone."

Manon said she would, and that she'd get word to Mrs. Jablonski in the women's prison wing. "She deserves at least to know Annie's alive."

It turned out there was a great deal more noise down the town that February day than there had been in Bellevue Hospital. Women, unable to feed their families because the cost of flour had risen from four dollars a bushel to over twelve, had converged five thousand strong on City Hall Park. What started as a peaceful demonstration against the merciless inflation let loose in the year spent recovering from the fire became a pot-banging, screaming, whistling stampede. The women's wrath turned the premises of half a dozen prominent grocers into rubble. "No looting!" the organizers yelled. "Punishment, not theft!" Punishment wasn't going to fill hungry mouths. Not a woman went home without as much flour as she could manage to carry.

Despite the hopes of Henry Morrison of the *Sun*, his paper, like much of the penny press, got out a special late afternoon extra, but they trumpeted the tumultuous flour riot, not the silent surgery performed at Bellevue.

At eight in the evening there was a tap on Nick's door. "Come."

"She's still asleep, Cousin Nicholas. I cannot rouse her."

"Manon, I'm sorry, I'd hoped you wouldn't have to climb the stairs. Was there no one to send to—"

She shook her head, dismissing his concerns. "I'm fine. It's Annie I'm worried about. It's six hours and she's not yet awake."

Nick did a rapid calculation. "More like a bit over five hours since we administered the last dose of Somnus. And that was a heavy one."

"Twenty seconds," Manon agreed. "Directly from the canister."

"Damn! Excuse me, Cousin Manon. I'm simply frustrated because I know so little of what to expect from the potion, whatever it may be. Fact is, I just got back from the Turnbull's farm. Walked over to see where to find this fellow Graves and make him tell me more."

"No luck?" she asked, knowing the answer before he replied.

"Less than none. For him as well, poor devil. Seems that a few days ago, on his way to peddle Somnus to the doctors of New York Hospital, our Mr. Graves was knocked down by a runaway horse, had his skull crushed by a wagon wheel, and died. Mrs. Turnbull was at Graves's funeral yesterday when I tried to find her." Nick reached for the stethoscope that lay on a nearby table. "Come, I'll go down with you. I intended to visit Annie again at any rate."

The child lay on a bed in the prized window corner of a ward as crowded as all the others at Bellevue. Many of the patients slept, others called out to Nick and to Manon as they threaded their way through the thicket of prone bodies, a few moaned in pain. But at Annie's bedside there was only silence. "I was mad to try it," Nick murmured.

"You were no such thing. When I think what you were able to spare that child . . . I can find no words strong enough to express my admiration for your courage and what you achieved."

"But she is not yet conscious. And for all we know, she might never be again." He put his hand on her forehead. "She's relatively cool."

"Yes, I believe she has had no fever for the past few hours."

Nick bent over Annie, pressing one end of the stethoscope to her chest and the other to his ear. "Her heartbeat is strong and steady."

"Well then, I presume we must just wait."

"Years ago," he said, "I heard of a case of a man who was struck on the head by a falling object. He went to sleep and never woke up again. He lived for two weeks and didn't once open his eyes. Died finally of a lack of food and water."

Annie Jablonski muttered some words in Polish just then and struggled to sit up. Manon bent to her immediately, and for her concern was rewarded with a shower of vomit.

Chapter Eighteen

IT WAS THE first week of March, the month that ushered in spring, and the wind was howling while a brooding sky promised more snow on top of the crusted drifts and icy ruts that already made the streets nearly impossible to navigate. The omnibus ended its bone-shattering run where Sixth Avenue did, at Cornelia Street. Nick had to trudge through half a dozen more of the narrow, twisting streets of Greenwich Village on foot before he arrived at Manon's lodgings on Vandam Street. He was frozen to the marrow, but a cheery open fire waited for him in her small sitting room, and hot tea and fresh biscuits with ginger butter, and an egg custard topped with sugar. Life soon looked better. "This is delicious, Cousin Manon. I'd no idea you were such a splendid cook."

"I bribed the landlady to let me use her kitchen. As for cooking, I was accomplished once, but that's ages ago." All these years alone, so long since she'd cooked for Papa and later for Joyful. She'd felt almost giddy when she set about preparing a small repast for Nicholas. It had turned out well. "I'm glad you're enjoying the refreshments, Cousin Nicholas."

"I am. Immensely. And I very much appreciate your invitation to tea, but—"

"You wish I'd not chosen one of the coldest days of the winter to drag you down the town."

"I never said that. Though I'm sure if this was purely a social invitation you'd have waited for better weather. So tell me what this is all about."

"Two things," she said with her customary directness. "First Annie Jablonski."

"She's doing very well, Manon. But it's been two weeks since the surgery, and I can't continue to keep her in the hospital." He knew she intended to ask him not to send the child back to the orphanage, but he had no choice.

"You can't feel good about returning her to the kindly care of Frankly Clement. It's an appalling notion."

Nick nodded. "Yes, it is. But there is no alternative. Unless . . . Manon, do you know someone who might adopt her? That would be a perfect solution."

"Not exactly." She saw the change in his expression. "But there is an alternative to Frankly Clement."

"St. Patrick's Orphan Asylum."

"Exactly."

"It's out of the question."

"Why? Give me one good reason, Nicholas, why the child should not be taken there? She is Polish, and all Poles are Catholics."

"My dear Manon, you could make the same argument about fully two-thirds of the children in the almshouse orphan asylum. Perhaps more. That's precisely why the town established an orphanage at Bellevue. To be sure that the children of the Catholic poor are rescued from popery."

"Cousin Nicholas, I admit there's a great deal of silliness and nonsense in the Catholic religion, but Mother Louise and the Sisters are good to the children. You know they are. Rescued from popery so they can have the vicious Clements instead. How absurd!"

There was a loud clatter from somewhere in the hall. Nick started to rise, but Manon waved him back to his chair. "It's all right. Miss Bellingham's in her room. I imagine she dropped something."

"Miss Bellingham? The secretary of your society?" Nick glanced in the direction of the door Manon indicated. It wasn't entirely shut.

"Yes, that's right. Now, about Annie."

Clearly Miss Bellingham had been eavesdropping. And just as clearly Manon must know about it. If she didn't care, it was no business of his. "My dear Manon, I can't conspire to—"

"Nicholas, look what you've already done for her. In this instance you need do nothing so courageous. She will simply disappear. Given the circumstances in your hospital, that would hardly be a surprise. As for the Senior Medical Attendant, he would have every right to assume the child had been sent back to the Clements. In which case he would do nothing."

Nicholas hesitated only a moment. "Nothing. Yes, I suppose I can manage to do that."

"Excellent. Now there is something else."

"I thought there would be."

Manon's manner changed. She seemed less sure of herself. "When you called me indomitable, Cousin Nicholas, did you really believe it to be true?"

"I think I said that when you wanted to watch the surgery. I certainly believed it was true, Manon. And you proved me correct."

"I shall need to be indomitable if I've any hope of making my idea a reality."

"What idea is that?"

"A dispensary for poor women and their children. Somewhere women who can't afford private physicians can go to get medical care for themselves and their young. What do you think?"

"It's a fine idea. Certainly it's needed. I presume your dispensary would see only ambulatory patients."

"Yes, at first. Later one might expand to some sort of residential patient care. I suppose any building should be planned with that possibility in mind."

"A building. That's a grand scheme, Manon. I'm told land is selling

for upwards of four hundred dollars an acre as far up the island as
Bloomingdale Village."

"To rich people, Nicholas. For country estates along the Hudson."

"Even here in Greenwich Village, it's going to be hugely expensive. I'd
no notion your society was moving the hearts of wealthy donors quite
so well."

"Ha! I assure you it is not. I'm fortunate to raise a hundred or two
in a month. But I've other resources. Of course, if my Wall Street house
had escaped the flames and I'd sold after the fire rather than before, I'd
have gotten a far better price. One of my old neighbors sold his house
recently. I heard he got sixty thousand dollars. That's three times what
I was paid."

"Exactly. Property's a tricky business."

"I agree, Cousin Nicholas, but I believe I will be able to persuade a
wealthy donor to make a gift of a suitable lot for our dispensary. And
perhaps build it as well."

"Sounds as if your donor is rich as Croesus."

"Indeed. Another biscuit, Cousin Nicholas?"

She clearly wasn't going to tell him who she had in mind. "Yes, thank
you."

"Now," she said, passing him the ginger butter, "leaving aside the
issue of location, would you assist me in training women to staff such a
dispensary?"

"You're thinking of women as the providers of this medical care?
What an extraordinary idea."

"You must not think me foolish, Nicholas. I would count on men,
proper doctors such as yourself, to volunteer a bit of their time. But any
decent woman who has charge of a household is accustomed to nursing
her family. With just a small amount of more advanced training, such
skills could prove extremely useful. The women of Five Points. . . . They're
so battered and beaten, Nicholas. Even the most elementary things are
beyond them. In the conditions they live in even simple cleanliness is
impossible."

"And you think a better class of women might be willing to take time from their own families to staff a dispensary for the poor? It wouldn't be the same as occasional visits to the homes of the respectable needy, Manon. There must be structure. You would require to be open at particular times of the day. Women with households of their own . . . it's a lot to ask.

"I know all that," she said stubbornly. "I believe women are quite capable of organizing such a thing. Look at Mother Louise and her Sisters of Charity."

"But their motives are religious. Ordinary women, Protestants . . ." He hesitated, then decided to plunge. He'd have no better opportunity, and apart from his affection for Manon, the main reason he'd come out on such a miserable day was to get what news he could of Sam Devrey's wife. "Cousin Carolina, for example. Might she be . . ."

"Oh, I realize it wouldn't be possible for someone like Carolina with a new baby."

"A new baby? Cousin Carolina? I didn't know."

"Did you not?" She busied herself pouring him another cup of tea, pretending not to notice how the news had unnerved him. "She and Cousin Samuel have a new daughter. Baby Celinda Lucy Devrey, named for Samuel's mother and Carolina's aunt. I can't think the Celinda part pleases Carolina very much." He was staring into his cup of tea looking as morose as ever she'd seen him. Manon hunted for a change of subject. "I take it you still have no idea of the composition of Somnus."

"None. I've made inquiries at the patent office, but they know nothing. Either Mr. Graves didn't intend to patent his potion or he hadn't yet gotten around to doing so." Then, after a moment's hesitation, "How old is Carolina's daughter?"

"Well, she was born in October of last year, as I recall. That would make her five months old."

He did the numbers quickly in his head. Had to be a child conceived after the night of the fire. Why in hell should that surprise him? From Carolina's point of view it was extremely distressing that her husband had a mistress and deeply shaming that Nick Turner had been with her when she discovered the fact, but Sam Devrey wasn't the only man in the city unfaithful to his marriage vows. Only one thing for it. Put her out of his mind. Carolina Devrey was the mother of two and totally off limits.

"Cut off her leg they did," Addie said. "And she didn't feel a thing."

"I don't believe it." Lilac held her glass of coffee in midair, too startled to take another sip. "I never heard of such a thing. It can't be true."

"It is. I heard them talking about it. Mrs. Turner and her cousin, the Dr. Turner who runs the Almshouse Hospital."

"Didn't feel anything when they sawed off her leg? Well, I never." Lilac's hand trembled. Imagine if she could use the lady needles on women who didn't feel a thing while she did it. The line outside her door would reach round the corner and back again.

"That's not all neither," Addie said.

"You're mumbling, dear. I can't hear you." Lilac leaned forward so as not to miss a thing.

"Now," Addie said, "they're going to give her to the Catholics. Going to spirit that little girl away to the Catholic orphan asylum. And Dr. Turner says he's not going to do a thing about it."

"You mean he's a Catholic as well?"

"That's not what I said."

"Then what is?" Steady on, Lilac told herself. Nothing to be had from Addie if Lilac didn't remain patient. "Doesn't feel like winter's ever going to be over, does it?" And when Addie agreed that it did not, "March, and I still need my furs." She had a mink skin wrapped around her neck with the animal's tail made to hook into its mouth, and a matching muff. The very latest thing. *Absolutely painless help for women's troubles.* That's what she'd say in her advertisement. Or maybe *Positively painless* would be better. She'd probably have to move to a bigger place. "Addie, how could that little girl sleep through something like that?"

"I don't know, and Dr. Turner don't know neither. The stuff he used came from some man that went and got himself killed, so now there's no more of it. Anyway, I'm not talking about that. I'm talking about the little girl."

"You mean this man's secret died with him?"

"I told you, I don't know. Dr. Turner said he was looking for more of whatever it was. Though how he can want to do anything so wicked is beyond me."

"What's wicked?"

"Trying to change the laws of nature. I asked Mr. Finney about painless surgery and that's what he said. It's wicked to try and change the laws of nature. Anyway, it's the little girl I'm concerned about."

"What about her? You already said about Mrs. Turner taking her to the Catholics. It doesn't seem to me there's anything you can do about that."

"No, there isn't. Not if Dr. Turner's going to do nothing."

"Then I don't see why you—" Lilac broke off. There was no point in scolding Addie. That just served to make her clam up. "It's not your fault, dear. How can it be?"

"I know it's not. But that poor little girl. They sold her soul to the Devil so she wouldn't feel pain, and now they're going to make her a Catholic."

"But if she's a Polish child she already is one. And I don't think you can go to Hell twice, can you Addie?"

"I suppose not." Addie took a sip of her coffee, then she put the glass down and stared into space with a dreamy expression.

Lilac had seen that look before. "What is it, Addie? You can tell me."

"It's this."

Lilac followed the motion of Addie's head and looked down. An object wrapped in dark blue velvet had appeared on the little round wooden table between them. "And what is that?"

"I'm not sure. That's why I've brought it for you to see."

"Very well. Unwrap it then. Or should I do it?"

"Oh yes, please. Mind no one sees," Addie added, leaning forward and speaking in a whisper. Then, seeing Lilac's expression, "I mean, you never know, do you? In a place like this."

Addie's caution was contagious. Lilac scooped up the bundle and made it disappear onto her lap. Then, using her muff to provide the cover the other woman seemed to think necessary, she removed the thing from its wrappings.

Hard. About the size of a large walnut. Round but not smooth. Rather like a jewel, though far too big to be one.

"Well," Addie said.

"Well what?"

"Aren't you going to look at it?"

"I'm feeling it. Good lord." She had taken her hand out of her muff and laid it on the table between them. What was there in the curve of her kid-gloved palm was a diamond. It shimmered and shone like nothing she had ever seen. Every bit of light in the room appeared to be reflected in the many facets.

"Do you think it's real?" Addie demanded.

Lilac's heart was racing, but she made sure her voice sounded calm. "Where did you get this?"

"From her. I wasn't prying, mind. I would never do such a thing. But I do sometimes tidy her room. Out of friendship, you understand. I'm not a servant, not a maid."

"Yes, yes. I know. Had she just left it out in her room? In plain sight?"

"Well, not exactly. I opened the cupboard to put something away, and it fell out at my feet. I couldn't ignore it, could I? Something like that?" The waiter was coming close. "Put it away!" Addie whispered urgently.

Lilac made a fist around the extraordinary stone and pushed it back inside the muff. The waiter passed by without looking at them. With her free hand Lilac picked up the tiny glass of coffee and drank it down. Scalding hot, but she hardly felt it.

"You must tell me what you think," Addie insisted. "I know it looks like a diamond, but is it real?"

"How can it be? A thing that big. Where would your Mrs. Turner get something like that?"

"That's exactly what I've been thinking. Where? You don't suppose it came from that Maria Monk person, do you?"

"Maria . . . The one what said she was a nun and had to do terrible things with all the Catholic priests?"

"Yes, exactly."

"But it was all lies. They said so in the papers. Her mother came forward like they say and explained that her daughter hadn't been right in the head since she was a little girl." The stone seemed to be growing heavier in her grasp. Best thing to do was keep Addie talking while she thought out what to do next.

"Well, people will say anything, won't they? That doesn't make it true."

"Yes, exactly."

"So what if this Maria Monk gave—"

"Addie, whether or not that book told the truth, what's it to do with this?"

"I don't know." Addie was growing impatient. She had come to rely on Lilac Langton's being more worldly and knowledgeable than she, but this time Lilac wasn't being much help. "It just seems as if it might be possible. Because of her going into that Catholic church. And if it came from something wicked and sinful like that, babies murdered and buried in the walls, well, it would be my duty to get it right out of the house, wouldn't it? I couldn't sleep under the same roof with something so—so evil, could I?"

Ah yes. Lilac felt tension easing as she saw the way forward. A bird in the hand, as Joe used to say. Quite literally in the hand in this case. "I'm sure you're right, Addie dear."

"Thank you. I feel better knowing you agree with me. But that still leaves the same question, doesn't it?"

"What question is that?" Heavier and heavier. And on fire in her hand now.

"Is it real? A real diamond?"

"I don't see how it can be, Addie dear. Diamonds are little things as fits in finger rings. Or earrings maybe. Have you ever seen a woman wearing a diamond as big as a large walnut?"

Addie shook her head. "No, I'm sure not." She had not, in fact, ever seen a woman wearing any sort of diamond, but there seemed no reason to say so. "Then it's not real?"

"Unlikely," Lilac pronounced. "But I tell you what I can do. I have a friend, well, more of an acquaintance really. She's married to a man come over from Russia. Has a shop where he sells fancy things of all sorts. Silver and gold, even pearls sometimes. I can have my acquaintance take me to her husband's shop and I'll ask him."

"Oh, would you? I don't want to be any trouble, but it does seem to me to be a very wise idea. I knew I could rely on you, dear Lilac. Now you just give it back to me and I'll keep it until—"

"But how is the gentleman to tell me whether or not it's real unless I show it to him?"

"Well, then, perhaps we could go to your friend's husband's shop together."

Exactly what Lilac had expected Addie to say. It all seemed to be happening very slowly now. Giving Lilac plenty of time to figure things out. "Of course we could, except that my acquaintance is a real lady. She would be, wouldn't she, married to a gentleman like that? And the way I got to know her . . ." She leaned forward and spoke even more softly. "She was having a problem. Being in a family way, you know." Addie's eyes opened wider and she nodded. "Thing is," Lilac continued, "she once heard me say I knew someone who . . . you know," she added for the second time.

Innocent as she was, Addie did know. The women in the almshouse talked about such things all the time. "I think so, yes. But that's wicked."

"Of course it is. But we can't be responsible when people make bad choices, refuse to pick themselves up by their bootstraps, as Reverend Finney always says. Not our fault, is it dear?"

Addie shook her head. "No, it's not." That's how she managed to go on working with the Society for Poor Widows and Orphans. Kept reminding herself it wasn't her fault if other people made bad, sinful choices.

"That's what I think as well. But with this business . . . if we both show up at this man's shop along with his wife, he'll think it mighty odd, won't he? His wife having two women friends he's never heard of. And neither of them married women she might have met somewhere doing her duty as his wife. It might cause him to ask more questions. I can't ask her to help me if it's going to make her husband ask embarrassing questions. That's quite impossible."

Addie agreed that it was. And that the stone, which was anyway probably just a piece of pretty glass, would remain with Lilac Langton until such time as she could get the husband of her acquaintance to tell them whether, against all the odds, it might just be a real diamond.

"It's ether, sir. Sorry to burst in, but I was sure you'd want to know."

Nick was in his shirtsleeves, standing at his laboratory bench, bent over his microscope. "What is ether? Listen, Ben, these slides you prepared of the tissue surrounding that boil are first rate."

"Somnus, sir. It's a chemical compound called sulfuric ether. Here, I wrote down the formula."

Nick straightened and took the piece of paper Ben offered: CH_3-CH_2-O-CH_2-CH_3. "Where did you get this?"

"From someone I knew when I was at the university, Dr. Turner. He's a chemist. I brought him the canister. You'd left it up here, sir, and since we both thought it was empty . . . I suppose I should have asked, but I didn't want—" He broke off, suddenly looking sheepish.

"Come along, speak your mind. What didn't you want?"

"To encourage your hopes, Dr. Turner. I knew how disappointed you were when we couldn't get any more."

"So I was. Please go on."

"Well, it occurred to me that since we could still smell the stuff when we took the cork out of the canister, there might be enough Somnus left for a chemist to analyze. There was. And it turns out sulfuric ether can be made in any laboratory. My friend says there can't be any patent on it because it was discovered hundreds of years ago. That's why—"

"Why we had no luck tracing Somnus through the patent office. You're a genius, Benjamin Klein. And so is your friend the chemist. Come!"

"Where are we going, sir?"

Nick was pulling on his coat and running his fingers through his hair since he didn't want to spend the time to find a comb. "To see Dr. Tobias Grant. We are going to strike a deal with the devil, Ben. In the interests of medical science."

"What makes you think I might be interested in your proposal, Dr. Turner?"

"Because, Dr. Grant, I believe you see some profit in being the place where painless surgery is first performed."

"Profit?"

"For Bellevue, of course. I've no doubt your motives are entirely selfless, Dr. Grant."

Nick and Ben Klein stood in front of Grant's desk in the room he called his study in the luxuriously appointed house known, with a good deal of understatement, as the director's cottage. "Your guest, Mr. Morrison," Nick continued, "he was a reporter, was he not? You invited publicity, so I must presume you hoped the hospital, the entire almshouse perhaps, would benefit from it."

Grant had lately affected the exaggerated muttonchop side whiskers that were the current fashion. He tugged at the left one now, meanwhile leaning back and regarding the two men. "So now that you know what this Somnus is, you are prepared to write up what has happened here for a medical journal. Why now and not before?"

"Because," Nick explained, "for a professional journal to be interested we must replicate our results as science demands. We must do two or even three painless operations. Now that we know what Somnus is and that we can make more of it, we can and we will."

"Replicate your results," Grant said.

"Exactly. There's bound to be a great deal of interest, even excitement, among men of medicine. It will reflect enormous credit on Bellevue Hospital and the council will surely consent to build—"

"You'll write an article. In a professional journal."

Nick wished the man would stop repeating everything he said like a trained parrot. "Sir, if you'll just consider—"

Grant held up his hand and rose and walked to the window. "Today is March fifteenth. The Ides of March," he said. "A date to beware, according to Shakespeare." He turned to face them. "And today on Wall Street Joseph and Company collapsed."

It seemed to Nick, to whom one Wall Street firm was pretty much like another, to be a complete non sequitur. Ben Klein said, "But Joseph is the American agent for Rothschilds. Surely a firm of such—"

"You mistake my meaning, Dr. Klein. I refer to the physical building. The premises of Joseph and Company fell to the ground earlier today. Brand-new and built entirely of granite after the fire. I suspect, gentlemen, that it presages the kind of financial disaster Dr. Klein thought I referred to. The price of cotton has plummeted in Europe, and the New Orleans cotton merchants are defaulting in droves. Those who have given them credit are, as I'm sure you're aware, all here in our city."

"But what has that to do with Bellevue?" Nick knew it would be wise to understand a bit more about the world of finance, but money bored him. "The poor in this place can't get much poorer, whatever happens on Wall Street."

"My dear Dr. Turner, if the bankers and brokers and factors are beggared, so must be the city treasury." Grant returned to his place behind the desk and took his seat, flipping up the skirt of his stylish full-skirted knee-length coat as he did so. "This institution will be allotted less money by the council, not more. So your research laboratory, this place where you and young Dr. Klein here may do God knows what, does not seem to me likely to be funded, whatever you might publish in some professional journal."

"Dr. Grant, surely however dire the financial consequences of the affairs you describe, they will be temporary. Even I know that such things always are." Nick put his hands on the desk and leaned forward, pinning the other man with a direct gaze. "Disease is always with us, and crushed limbs and kidney stones are a commonplace, as much for the aldermen of the Common Council as for the rest of humanity. Do you honestly think, whatever passing financial constraints they might face, they would ignore the immediate and personal benefits they might gain from such progress as this? Painless surgery, Dr. Grant. The philosopher's stone, the holy grail. Good God, man, to go under the knife and feel nothing. It's possible. You know it is. You saw it with your own eyes."

"So I did. You have made my point, Dr. Turner."

"And what point is that?"

Grant leaned back, tented his fingers, and stared over them. "The point that seeing, gentlemen, is believing. If your scheme is to have a chance of success, Dr. Turner, you must put aside all talk of publishing in a professional journal. Once you do, I expect dozens of doctors will be using this ether to achieve the same results. It will become a commonplace."

"As well it should."

"Yes, Dr. Turner. Of course. But if Bellevue Hospital is to benefit from it having been discovered here first, we—"

"Introduced," Nick corrected. "It was discovered hundreds of years ago."

Grant sighed. "Very well, introduced. No, let us say put to use for the first time here at Bellevue. If that is to be to our advantage, the introduction must be much more awe-inspiring than simply publishing an article in some dreary journal read only by the medical profession."

"I take it you think the penny press would—"

"I know it would. If we make it dramatic enough to avoid being pushed aside by a bunch of fishwives clattering on about the price of flour."

"What do you suggest?"

"A live demonstration, Dr. Turner. Precisely as you provided for me."

"With due respect, sir, that was never my intent."

"But it was your effect, Dr. Turner. I am listening to you right now because of it. And if we go to City Hall and let them see an operation—"

"City Hall! I am not a performing monkey, Dr. Grant. Neither are my patients to be sacrificed for the entertainment of idiots who—"

"Calm yourself, Dr. Turner. I thought the sacrifice of patients was exactly what we were seeking to avoid. The aldermen are to witness a surgery conducted in the most peaceful way possible, with the patient sound asleep and feeling nothing. What can be wrong with that?"

"What's wrong is that you're making medical care a traveling circus. I won't—"

Ben Klein cleared his throat. Then did so a second time. Nick and Tobias Grant stopped shouting at each other and turned to him.

"It's only a suggestion, sir," Ben said, "but perhaps Dr. Grant could bring the members of the Common Council to us. They could witness an operation performed under ether right here in Bellevue Hospital."

"I've asked Dr. Turner if I may bring you, Addie, and he says I may. Since members of the public are in any case being admitted to watch."

"The aldermen, you said."

"That's right, Addie." Manon went on with her darning while she spoke. "Along with you. Because Dr. Turner said you may."

"But why would I want to? I don't want to go back to the almshouse."

"Don't be ridiculous, Addie. You're not going back to stay. Only to observe an operation performed painlessly. It's truly remarkable."

"Even if it is, I don't want to."

"Why not?"

"I mentioned about that little girl. At church."

"Oh yes?"

"About her sleeping right through having her leg sawed off. I told Reverend Finney and some of the others."

Manon bit through a length of thread and rolled it into a knot with her thumb and forefinger. Addie Bellingham frequently drove her mad, but the woman had nowhere else to go, and having taken her on, Manon could see no way to get out of being responsible for her. Addie must be incorporated into her plans for the dispensary which, Manon realized, Addie already knew about because she listened at keyholes. Nonetheless, it would be best if she was convinced it was in her best interest. Manon saw herself giving up these rooms and living in the dispensary once it got started, so Addie must live there as well. "And what did they say at your church, Addie?"

"That man is meant to suffer. That it's God's law. That the little girl had to have been paying for her sins, and that we shouldn't be trying to change everything to suit us rather than God."

"Well, leaving aside the matter of a six-year-old paying for her sins, suppose you do as I ask and come along and watch. Just this once. Then you can decide for yourself what you think to be the law of God."

According to Tobias Grant seven aldermen had consented to attend, so the director's room off the lobby wouldn't be large enough. "Leave that to me, Dr. Turner. I will arrange a proper location for your demonstration. You just select the patient."

Nick already had. He was Patrick Shaughnessey, a porter thrown out of work by the fire. He had a growth on his shoulder so big it reached almost to his ear and forced him to hold his head to one side all the time. By the time the town's recovery had made work for porters plentiful, the tumor had become so unsightly no one would hire him.

"Observe, gentlemen," Nick had told the other doctors and the medical students the first time he examined Shaughnessey, "this tumor, if such it is, is movable." He could shift it slightly with his fingers. "That means it is not an osteosarcoma. What would it be if it were? Can one of you students tell me?"

"A cancer," one of them said.

"Exactly. Cancer from the Greek for crab, *karkinos*, because of the swollen veins resembling the legs of that creature. 'Osteo' is also from the Greek, from *osteon* for bone. But here on Patrick Shaughnessey's shoulder we have, as you can see, no swollen veins, simply a rough-textured and blackened series of bumps that have formed themselves into one ugly whole. And since the thing moves enough for me to all but get my finger underneath it, it cannot be connected to the bone. It is not properly speaking a tumor, gentlemen, it is a cyst. A sac attached to muscle and skin that is filled with sebaceous matter, fatty stuff produced by the body itself."

Nick leaned over his patient. "What do you say, Patrick? Will you give me permission to take off this thing?" He didn't need to ask permission. Nick could administer any treatment he thought necessary for a resident in the almshouse. Still, on this occasion he'd rather not have Shaughnessey dragged kicking and screaming to the operating table. "I can promise you won't feel a thing."

"Sure and it's hard to think how much worse things could be, Dr. Turner. If you can get this thing off me neck, I'd think meself blessed by all the saints, however much I suffered in the doing of it. If it's to be painless, well . . ."

Nick had already taken a brief whiff of the canister of sulfuric ether supplied by Ben Klein's friend the chemist. It was Mr. Grave's Somnus, no question. "Absolutely painless, Patrick. You'll sleep through the entire thing and wake up with the lump gone and only a bandage on your neck. I guarantee it."

He needed only one assistant for this sort of surgery. Nick chose Ben Klein. Monty Chance wouldn't be pleased, he was after all the more senior of the two residents, but if it were not for Ben the whole thing wouldn't be happening. The younger man deserved a share in the glory. "Someone has to be in charge of the hospital while we're operating, Dr. Chance. Your greater experience makes you the man for that job."

"I hear you're to do the surgery in the director's cottage."

Nick grimaced. "So they tell me. I wanted it to be here in the hospital. But it's all of us in the director's cottage," he said, "and you, Dr. Chance, in complete charge of the hospital while I'm away."

"Who would think there would be any place looked like this at the almshouse?" Addie spoke in hushed tones of wonder. The front parlor of the director's cottage had been cleared of much of its furniture, but the windows were curtained in dark blue velvet trimmed with gold tassels, a flowered Turkey carpet still covered the floor, and a dozen gilt and damask chairs had been set in front of a long table spread with a floor-length satin cloth. Addie pointed to the table. "Is that where he's going to do it?"

"It appears so," Manon said. "Though I cannot imagine a less appropriate arrangement. Come, Addie. We're to watch from this little cloakroom. That was the agreement."

"Not in here?" Having gotten a look at the grand front parlor, Addie did not wish to be immediately banished from it.

"Definitely not. That's why we had to come early. The aldermen would be shocked to see women present at a surgery. We must be discreet."

Two chairs had already been placed in the cloakroom, which was apparently also a staging area for the operation to come. There was a table below the small room's single window spread with surgical equipment. Addie stared at the array of knives and other things to which she could give no name and went quite pale. "To think of human flesh being butchered in such a—"

"It's nothing to do with butchery, Addie. It is life-saving medicine. That is the Somnus," Manon pointed to the metal canister. "It allows the patient to be put to sleep before the surgery begins. It's quite wonderful, Addie. A miracle. I so wish you would understand. Here, you look quite pale. I'll open the window and let in some fresh air."

It was considerably milder now that it was almost April and spring had officially arrived. The cloakroom was in fact close and stuffy. "Sit down, Addie." Addie did so, averting her eyes from the array of scalpels positioned exactly at her elbow. "There, that's better." Manon spied a pile of blankets and a pillow. "And that's what's meant to cover the operating table, not that ridiculous silk cloth." She went to the door; there was still no one in the front parlor. "I'll just nip out and arrange things."

Manon picked up the blankets and a pillow and left the cloakroom.

Addie considered for a moment, possibly two. Then, with no further hesitation, she pulled the cork from the metal canister and emptied the contents out the open window, after which she replaced the cork and put the canister back where it had been.

Chapter Nineteen

TEN MINUTES INTO the surgery. Nick had used a four-inch scalpel to cut around the diameter of the sebaceous cyst in the place where it was connected to the shoulder and the neck. He'd heard gasps from his audience as soon as he'd begun, and someone retching when there was a spurt of blood before he managed to clamp off an artery. Other than that he was able to ignore the roomful of onlookers and concentrate on his work.

Just oozing blood now, and Ben Klein deftly sopping that. Nick took the bulk of the lump off in slices, dropping each into the basin Ben held close to the table. Interesting to get a look at those under a microscope later.

He'd spotted the reporter, Henry Morrison, with his notebook and his pencil in the back row. Grant's idea no doubt. Still trying to get the tale into the papers.

Movement behind him. Someone had taken a step closer to the operating table. One of the less squeamish of the aldermen probably. "Here," a voice said, "how do we know it isn't a corpse he's cutting?"

"You'd not think so if you had arrived when we began, sir." Tobias Grant, from his vantage point in the back row next to the reporter. "The patient was ambulatory before the operation began. He walked into the room and climbed up on the table on his own."

"True," someone else said.

Shaughnessey was peaceful, breathing quietly. Christ with this sort of procedure who could tell if a man went into shock? "The stethoscope, Dr. Klein. If you please."

Ben took his stethoscope from his pocket and pressed it to Shaughnessey's chest. "Slow and steady, Dr. Turner," he said after he'd listened for a bit.

"Excellent. Thank you."

A miracle indeed. Let the tight-fisted members of the bloody Common Council get a gander at this. Envy of the medical world this would be. And while they were about it, the aldermen could note as well the luxury of this house compared to the squalor everywhere else. Maybe after the operation was done he'd invite them to tour Bellevue. Grant wouldn't like it, but what could he say? Particularly if the invitation was made while Nick and Ben were basking in the congratulations sure to come. But finish the job first.

Nick reached for his smallest scalpel, a triangular blade only an inch long, and began delicately to cut the thin skin of the neck just below the ear. Absolutely marvelous to be able to take his time, to cut as slowly as care demanded, not swiftly so the patient could withstand the agony. Not just a miracle, a blessing for all concerned. When he completed this last process the visible part of Patrick Shaughnessey's lump would be gone. After that, time to excise the root of the sac lodged in the intermuscular membrane of the shoulder itself. Give it five, maybe six, minutes of careful cutting; with the time needed to tie off the veins and arteries and sew up the wound, say another fifteen minutes. Then—

His patient moaned softly. And a second time. "Dr. Klein, more ether."

"Yes, sir." Ben put down the basin holding the pieces of the cyst and reached for the canister. He pulled the cork and grabbed the wad of bandages he had used previously. Nick stopped cutting, waiting for Ben to put the patient back to sleep.

Ben was acutely conscious of being watched. He tried not to look concerned. He'd thought the canister lighter than it should be when the operation began, but it was too late then to say anything, and it was anyway remarkably light to begin with. Very volatile, his friend the chemist had explained, lighter than water and highly flammable. Important not to allow anyone to smoke when there was ether around. Smoking, *Hashem* help him, was not the immediate problem.

Ben turned the canister upside down over the folded cloth and shook it. Nothing seemed to be coming out. Dr. Turner looked at him. Ben avoided his glance and stared over his chief's shoulder at the aldermen and Dr. Grant and the man he now knew to be a reporter for the *Sun*. *Hashem* help him and Dr. Turner and poor Shaughnessey the patient, who was moaning more loudly now.

Everyone was watching him. Ben was careful to keep his face expressionless.

Patrick Shaughnessey moaned a third time. And opened his eyes.

Ben gave the canister one last shake, then held the cloth over the lower half of the Irishman's face, pressing it firmly into place over the nose and the mouth. "Take deep breaths," he murmured. "Deep as you can." The Irishman complied, or at least he seemed to, but he didn't immediately go back to sleep, just moaned again. Forcefully enough this time so that the sound could be called a groan. Ben grabbed the canister itself and held it right under Shaughnessey's nose. "Inhale," he said in an urgent whisper. "As strongly as you can."

Shaughnessey did as he was told. His eyes closed.

Nick breathed a sigh of relief and went back to work with his scalpel.

Patrick Shaughnessey emitted a scream loud enough to wake the dead at home in faraway Galway.

❧

"I told you to stop, but you did not."

"I had a man lying on a table with his neck and shoulder sliced open. How in holy heaven could I stop? He could have died if I hadn't finished. Aren't you doctor enough to know that?" With each word Nick was conscious of how much he was making things worse. Grant's eyes became more opaque and his face more frozen in an expression that had passed mere disapproval and become rage.

"You embarrassed me in front of seven aldermen and a reporter. I invited distinguished guests to witness a painless surgery, and they finished up listening to a man howling in agony. If they wanted to hear such things, they would have become doctors themselves. Damn you, Turner, you could have stopped and finished later."

"I got Shaughnessey's permission to continue. You heard me do so. If I had waited he might—"

"His *permission*? What do I care for the permission of a convicted felon who then disgusted all present by vomiting on my carpet?"

"Vomiting after the inhalation of ether appears to be the norm, Dr. Grant. We shall make proper provision for it in future. And I believe Mrs. Turner prevented there being too much damage to your carpet."

"Mrs. Turner! Indeed, as if everything wasn't already bad enough, to have a woman come running out of the cloakroom. A woman thought to be a lady, no less."

"As you know, she's an experienced nurse. She wished to be of what help she could while Dr. Klein and I were occupied with the surgery."

"Ah, yes, Dr. Klein. And what do you have to say about all this?"

"I've already explained, sir. There wasn't enough ether in the canister when we began operating, only I didn't realize that. It's liquid but it's very volatile, sir. That means it acts like a gas. I can only think that the cork wasn't tightly enough in the canister after I collected it from the chemist yesterday and the stuff evaporated."

"This chemist is a friend of yours, isn't he Dr. Klein?"

"An acquaintance, Dr. Grant."

"Another Jew is he?"

Ben had been looking Tobias Grant straight in the eye. The way Papa always told him an honest man should behave when talking to anyone, whether higher or lower in status. Now he forced himself to look at the wall over Grant's shoulder so he could control the urge to punch the old fool in the face. "No, as it happens, Dr. Grant, he is not."

"I don't believe you. I think he must be a Jew. And everyone knows your kind will do ill to Christians any opportunity you get. You will leave the employ of this hospital immediately, Dr. Klein. And you, Dr. Turner, should consider yourself on probation until I—"

"If you discharge Dr. Klein," Nick said, "I resign from my post. You keep us both or lose us both. Your choice, Dr. Grant."

Ben was horrified. "Dr. Turner! You don't have to do that, sir. It was my fault. I should have told you the canister felt light before you started."

"Be quiet, Ben. We must give Dr. Grant an opportunity to consider his options. How important is it to have the latest of a long line of Doctors Turner running his miserable excuse for a hospital? How much is that kind of cover worth to you, Grant? Surely as much as the employment of one young resident. Both of us or neither of us. It's up to you."

"Get out. Both of you. Pack your things and leave Bellevue."

"I gambled," Nick said, "and I lost. It's as simple as that."

"But it's not simple at all." Manon had sent Addie to Vandam Street on her own and waited for Nick in the hospital. "What will happen to this place if you leave?"

"It will go on, Manon. It can't be much worse than it is."

"Oh yes it can," she said grimly. "You don't know what it was like before you came. You've made a great difference here, however much Tobias Grant tried to tie your hands. Where is Dr. Klein?"

"He left straight after the meeting. I said I'd send his belongings to his home. Poor fellow's distraught. Blames himself."

"That's not fair."

Nick shrugged. "No, but it's natural, given his youth and inexperience. It's Tobias Grant who is the idiot. He's the one who didn't understand that working with something so new is bound to involve some setbacks. He was a fool for insisting we do what was only our second painless surgery with an audience. And I was doubly a fool for agreeing to it."

"You did what you thought best. And I know it was wrong for Dr. Grant to discharge Dr. Klein, Cousin Nicholas, but you're so much needed at Bellevue. Can't you reconsider?"

"No, dear Manon, I cannot. Not under the conditions that exist at the moment. What this place needs is a complete top to bottom turn-out. And if it makes you feel any better, Cousin Manon, I have lost the battle, but not the war. I do not intend to give up."

Here it was then, the reason for coming to number three East Fourteenth Street that he'd been unable to find in the sixteen months since the fire. Though not the one he would have wanted. Nick rang the bell.

Apparently the forbidden to pass order placed on him previously had been lifted. Dorothy showed him into the front parlor and left to get her mistress. Minutes later Carolina arrived.

"Your visit is a surprise, Cousin Nicholas."

What had happened to the less formal Cousin Nick? Burned up in that bloody fire like so much else. "I'm sure it is, and frankly, I didn't send a note because I feared you'd tell me not to come."

Carolina had turned to close the double doors to the hall and she hesitated briefly before swinging round to face him. "Now why ever would I do that? Shall I send for tea?"

"No, dear Carolina. Don't trouble yourself. I shan't stay long. I'll get to my business straightaway, but first tell me how you are, how you've been." She wore dark gray today, with her fair hair drawn back in a strict bun. It was the first time he'd not seen her in the lovely rich colors that so suited her. Beautiful still, but different.

"I am well, Cousin Nicholas. And I'm sorry not to have seen you in such a long time. I was confined last year. Perhaps my husband told you." She did not look at him when she spoke.

"I haven't seen Cousin Samuel either." He started to say that he'd not seen Devrey since he last saw her, then thought better of it. "But I did hear that you've a new daughter. Congratulations."

That, at least, was rewarded with a direct glance and a bright smile. "Thank you. We call her Ceci. She's princess of the house, I'm afraid. Even little Zac adores her."

"Yes, I'm sure." She had crossed the room and come to stand close enough for him to smell her scent, a flower or flowers he could not name but would recognize anywhere now and always associate with her. "Can we sit down? Only for a few minutes, I promise."

"Yes, of course. I'm sorry to be so rude. Here by the fire, Cousin Nicholas. Perhaps a glass of sherry wine?"

"Nothing, thank you."

Carolina could not think of another thing to say. She sat across from him and folded her hands in her lap the way Aunt Lucy had always told her a lady must. Though it was hard to imagine that Nick Turner could still think her a lady. If her own husband valued her so little, as Nick above all people knew to be the case, she must surely be to blame. "It's a bit milder now, isn't it? Such a welcome change after the long winter."

"A bit milder, yes. Still quite a nip in the air, however."

Carolina caught herself making pleats in the fabric of her gray wool gown and made an effort to stop. Dear God, he has not come here to discuss the weather. A lady never lets a gentleman feel socially awkward. What topic could Carolina now introduce? *That time soon after the fire when Samuel violated me night after night. When slapping me wasn't enough and he brought a riding crop to my bedroom, shall we discuss that? Samuel was careful to leave no marks where they would show, and he knew I would be too mortified ever to let anyone see them. Would he find that a proper subject.* "I'm sorry to have no interesting conversation, Cousin Nicholas. I don't go out in society much these days. I'm afraid it's made me quite dull."

"You could never be dull, my dear Carolina."

She turned away. "Don't be kind," she whispered. "I cannot bear it."

"Carolina . . ." He stretched out a hand, then snatched it back.

"Please, Nick. Whatever you've come for . . . please just tell me and go."

"Yes, of course. Carolina, do you remember the first time I came here to see you?"

"Yes, I remember."

"I asked you to witness something I wrote. I hope you still have it, because I need it now."

"Of course I have it." She jumped up and went to her correspondence case and came back holding the folded pages she'd sealed three years before with pale lilac wax, her initials, and the date. And the mark of her wedding ring. "Here it is. I take it this means you've had some sort of altercation with the odious Dr. Grant."

"One of many. But this time he's given me the sack." And when she looked as if she didn't understand the modern euphemism, "I've been discharged."

"Oh, I know what it means. I simply don't understand. Cousin Manon said you were safe for as long as you wanted to be. That simply by being who you are, a Turner, you give that wretched Bellevue a cloak of respectability."

"That's true as far as it goes. Or I should say as far as it went. I'm sorry, it's really too complicated to explain just now."

"Very well," she said. "You owe me no explanations of course."

"I didn't mean—"

"I know you didn't. And Nick, you mustn't think I told Cousin Manon or anyone about that." She nodded toward the document in his hands. "I never did. Manon told me about you because she knew I was interested in your well-being."

"Are you really, Carolina? I'm glad. For I am very interested in yours." He stood up, put the pages in the inside pocket of his coat, and though he knew he should not, reached for her hand. "There isn't a day that goes by that I don't think about you."

"Don't, Nick. You must not."

"I can't help it. The thoughts simply come."

She shook her head. "Not that. I mean not only that. You must not . . ." She withdrew her hand from his. "We must not. It's impossible. You realize that, I'm sure."

"Yes."

"Good. Now I think you must go."

"I shall, but there's one more thing. Carolina, has Samuel mentioned anything about what's happened? I ask because this latest trouble between me and Dr. Grant . . . some of the aldermen were involved. Not Samuel directly. But I wondered if he might have spoken of—"

"No, nothing." She looked away again, this time embarrassed for him rather than herself. "Though I do know there was a story in the paper. The *Sun,* I believe. Something about an operation gone bad. My mother-in-law mentioned it to me."

No doubt Celinda Devrey would take delight in fanning the flames of the old Turner-Devrey feud. Any shame attached to the name of Turner would delight her. "It didn't go bad exactly. In fact, from the patient's point of view it was entirely successful. Just not entirely as advertised. To the aldermen, I mean. But I am seeking an opportunity to address the council. I thought maybe Samuel . . ."

"I'm sorry I can't help you, Nick. Truly I am. But these days . . . my husband spends very little time here with his family. Perhaps you should try and see him at his place of business."

He would not, Nick decided, seek out Sam Devrey in that impressive cathedral of commerce that was the five-story marble headquarters of Devrey Shipping. On Canal Street his cousin would be cloaked in all the power of his position, and Nick, the disgraced physician, would be a supplicant. Complex as their relationship had been since he came to New York, Nick did not believe that at this moment Sam Devrey wished him well.

Nick would go where the power had been his, where twice he had saved the life of the young woman who apparently meant more to his cousin than did his wife. Faced with imminent danger, when no one knew how far the blaze would spread, Sam Devrey had rushed to Cherry Street. Fair enough. That's where Nick Turner would go as well.

❦

In the full light of a sunny April afternoon the room was more extraordinary than it had been the two times he'd seen it by the light of lanterns and candles. The grand and imposing furniture was crammed into a room far too small for it, but it impressed nonetheless. Everything was painted red and black and gold, and decorated with drawings of strange beasts and exotic gardens, and peopled with figures dressed, as was Sam Devrey, in embroidered robes. Funny smell in the place as well. Not unpleasant, but definitely odd.

"It's incense," Sam said, seeing his cousin sniff the air. "The Chinese believe in one supreme god, The Jade Emperor, and a raft of lesser gods who serve him. They burn incense in honor of the minor gods."

"Like the Catholics and their saints."

"I've never thought of it like that, but I suppose so. What are you doing here? I don't imagine you've come to discuss religion."

"Not exactly, no. How is your . . . Mei-hua?"

"She's fine. Thank you, but I don't think she's what you've come about either."

"No, you're quite right. Can we sit down for a moment?"

"If you wish."

The robe his cousin wore today was red satin with gold embroidery. A fire-breathing dragon curled its tail at Sam's feet and spewed fire from somewhere near his shoulder. Sitting in the throne chair with the gilt canopy over his head, Devrey looked as alien as everything else in the place. "Look, I expect you've heard what happened last week at the almshouse."

"No, I have not. I don't spend much time in the sort of places where New York City gossip is exchanged."

"It was in the *Sun* as well," Nick said. Sam waved a dismissive hand. "Very well, let me get straight to the point." He stopped speaking when a child appeared in what must be the door to the kitchen, and toddled laughing into the room. She was followed by the serving woman. The child—Nick quickly calculated she must be a year and a half—evaded Ah Chee's grasp and threw herself into her father's arms.

"My daughter," Sam said. He spoke a few words to the little girl that Nick did not understand, then kissed her before handing her back to Ah Chee. "Her name is Mei Lin. It means beautiful grove."

"It suits her. She is indeed beautiful." Nick never recalled seeing Sam Devrey with his son by Carolina, and since she said her husband was seldom home these days, he could have little to do with their five-month-old daughter. The thought made the rest of what he had to say easier. "I want you to arrange for me to address the Common Council. As soon as possible. Next week for preference."

"About the almshouse, I presume. What shall you say to them?"

"That's none of your affair."

Sam shrugged. "Probably not. I suppose that you're going to tell them that Tobias Grant is a thief and the affairs of the almshouse are mismanaged."

"Something like that." Nick took a card from his pocket. "I'm staying in lodgings on Eighth Street just now. Please send word as to the time of the council meeting and I'll be there."

Sam took the card but didn't look at it. "You won't prevail, you know. I've told you before, Grant has friends. The sort generally referred to as friends in high places."

"That's as may be, and if true it's my worry, not yours. I'm only asking you to arrange the meeting."

"You're not asking, though, are you? You're telling me."

"If you choose to see it that way, I suppose so."

"Do you care to tell me as well why it is that you presume so much power?"

"Cousin Samuel, I didn't come here to threaten. What I'm asking is simple enough. I could petition the council for a hearing on my own, but that might take months to arrange. I wish to deal with the matter sooner than that, so I've come to you."

"And if I refuse?"

"Why should you? It will cost you nothing to do as I request. Whatever else, you are Jacob Astor's man and as such have a certain unofficial authority. They won't refuse you. But since you ask, you did tell me on at least two occasions that you relied on my discretion, did you not?"

"So we come to the heart of the matter. Yes, I did, and I have relied on it. So I am going to do as you ask, Cousin Nicholas, because, as you point out, it costs me very little to do so. But for the future I would prefer that there be no misunderstanding between us, so allow me to be completely frank. If you try to use against me anything that has happened in these rooms, anything about my relationship to Mei-hua or her daughter, I will make a great deal more trouble for Carolina than you will make for me. At least trouble she will feel far more acutely."

"Carolina! What kind of a cad are you?"

"The kind who knows how to protect himself, Cousin Nicholas. If you make any attempt to expose me in this matter, to expose Mei-hua or Mei Lin, I will file papers seeking a divorce from Carolina claiming you as the man with whom my wife has committed adultery."

"That's not only despicable, it's utterly untrue. How dare you—"

"My suit shall say as well that while I question the paternity of both of Carolina's children, in good conscience I cannot allow a woman of her sort to bring up two innocents. They will therefore be removed from her care and she will not be allowed to see them again."

"You do realize that if you do anything so ruthless and evil, all this"—Nick jumped to his feet and waved his hand to include the entire menage on Cherry Street—"will be exposed as well. The penny press will have a field day with the whole business."

"Indeed they will, Cousin Nicholas. But that will mean nothing to

Mei-hua or anyone here since they can neither read nor understand English. As for me, who do you think will suffer the upheaval and its results more, me or Carolina?" Sam stood up and went to the door. "Go away, Dr. Nicholas Turner. Go back to your lodgings on"—he glanced at the card—"Eighth Street. I will do as you ask. After that I propose we each forget the other's existence."

Chapter Twenty

NICK WAS SURPRISED by Mulberry Street. He'd thought he was headed down the town into the notorious Five Points, where most of his patients—correction, his former patients—lived. Mulberry Street did indeed extend that far, but the block between Broome and Grand streets seemed entirely respectable. The Kleins occupied the third floor of a four-story building, and the stairs Nick climbed to reach their door were dark and uncarpeted but clean and well swept.

A young girl answered his knock. About fifteen, he thought, with long black braids and a shy smile.

"Hello, I'm Dr. Turner. I've come to see Dr. Klein. I believe he's expecting me."

Ben appeared from somewhere in the interior of the house. "My youngest sister, Esther, Dr. Turner." The girl bobbed a curtsy. Ben himself opened the door wider. "Please, sir, come in. But you didn't have to trouble yourself, I would have come to you."

"I thought it best to come here." It was mild enough today for Nick not to need a greatcoat, but he gave his hat and his gloves to the girl. "I am glad to be here, Ben." He followed the younger man into what appeared to be a combined parlor and dining room. An older man, who could only be Ben's father considering how much alike the two looked, stood to greet him. "I thank you for receiving me, sir," Nick said. "You are, if I may be frank, why I wished to come to Ben's home. I believe his father should hear what I have to say."

"I am glad of the opportunity to meet you, Dr. Turner. I am Jacob Klein." The man offered his hand in a firm grip. He had, Nick noted, a more pronounced German accent than his son, but his English was fluent and clear. Not easy to learn a new language that well, so the senior Klein was clever. No doubt the source of his son's equally quick mind.

"My Benjy has spoken very highly of you, Dr. Turner, ever since he went to study at Bellevue."

"Ben is a fine doctor, Mr. Klein. You should be very proud of him."

"I am. Very proud. Though I did not approve of his decision to remain at Bellevue after he became a real doctor. It seems I was right."

"That's one of the things I came to say. Nothing of what has happened is Ben's fault, Mr. Klein. It is entirely mine."

"No, sir, that's not true!" Ben jumped to his feet.

"Benjy, I think Dr. Turner has come to talk, not to listen. But first we should all be calm. Please, Dr. Turner, I can offer you a schnapps?"

"Thank you."

Mr. Klein poured drinks for them all, then raised his tiny glass. "We say, *L'chayim,* Dr. Turner. It means to life."

"It's a good toast, Mr. Klein. I am happy to drink to life."

Nick watched his hosts toss their drinks back in one gulp and did the same. The liquor burned going down but landed in his stomach with a welcome warmth. Father and son were now looking at him expectantly. "I have arranged to address the Common Council at six o'clock on Monday evening," Nick said. "I am going to explain what happened in the matter of the surgery they witnessed."

"I will come," Ben burst out. "I will tell them it was my fault. They will have to reinstate you."

"You will say no such thing," Nick said. "Whatever happened was my responsibility and mine alone. Moreover, I was very foolish to agree to perform only our second attempt at painless surgery before an audience."

"The audience," Ben said miserably. "That was my idea as well."

"It was not. Grant insisted on an audience. You merely suggested that we invite the aldermen to Bellevue rather than perform the surgery at City Hall. It was a good idea. You shouldn't be ashamed of it."

"But as I understand it," Jacob Klein said, "you did not do this painless surgery in the hospital."

"No. In the director's front parlor."

"Because Dr. Grant didn't want the aldermen to see what a terrible shambles the hospital is," Benjy said. "They would know he was misusing the funds they appropriate for the almshouse."

"A terrible shambles," the senior Klein repeated, addressing his remarks to Nick, not his son, "but my Benjy was determined to be a doctor there rather than allow me to assist him to establish a private practice. I told him, Dr. Turner, that to do acts of charity is required of a righteous man. But also a righteous man must earn a living. We are not, as you see, rich people, still I could manage to assist him in building a future. But Benjy would have none of it. He thinks you are going to rid the world of all sickness, Dr. Turner. He thinks it is possible for a man to sleep through having his neck and shoulder cut open."

"He would have, Papa, if the canister hadn't leaked."

Nick nodded in affirmation. "That's true, sir. What happened was a setback but not the end of the experiment. I firmly believe that painless surgery is now a reality."

"In my smithy, Dr. Turner, I can make silver do remarkable things. I am not being immodest, only truthful. I can produce a goblet like that one over there"— the senior Klein nodded toward an elaborate cup in a case with a glass door—"with bunches of grapes dripping off the sides. Or a plate like that one that looks as if it were made of lace. But I cannot turn silver into gold. I cannot produce a miracle."

"Neither can I, Mr. Klein. I can do only what the laws of nature allow. My hope is that I can in some small way help to discover some of those laws we do not yet fully understand."

"Me too, Papa. That is what I want to do."

Klein nodded, then stood up. "It is past time I should return to my shop. I take it what you have actually come here for, Dr. Turner, is to ask that my son attend this meeting with the Common Council."

"Yes, sir. I will not permit him to accept any blame for what went wrong, only ask that he attest to the fact that the first surgery we performed using sulfuric ether was entirely successful and contribute evidence as to the conditions at Bellevue. Also, I came because I wanted to apologize to Ben and to you. Any mistakes and their consequences are my fault."

Ben started to speak, but his father held up a restraining hand. "Your apology is accepted, Dr. Turner. I have no doubt that you are a fine doctor and a good man. My son is not a fool and I trust his assessment of your character. And of the lack of character of this man Tobias Grant. I am therefore sorry that I cannot permit Benjamin to do as you ask. He will not be present at the meeting with the council."

"Papa! I must."

"Enough, Benjy. I have made up my mind. And you are my son, living in my house. This time you must do as I say."

The council chamber in New York's City Hall was a large room resplendent with marble pillars, an elaborate ceiling, and an intricately carved balcony where overflow crowds could be accommodated. On this Monday evening the balcony was empty and so were most of the seats in the chamber. Neither were all the chairs taken at the long table on the raised platform at the front of the room. Nine aldermen had bestirred themselves to attend the special session. Nick noted that Sam Devrey was not among them. As to whether any of the others had been present in the director's cottage when he operated on Patrick Shaughnessey, he'd paid too little attention on that occasion to know. Shaughnessey, however, was here; Nick had arranged for one of the porters to bring him. They could all see for themselves that the man was alive and well, and no longer had a grotesque lump on his shoulder. Frankly Clement and his wife were here, as was Jeremiah Potter, and sitting between the Clements and Potter was Tobias Grant. Nick counted on Grant not making any public fuss about the presence of Shaughnessey, because if he did, it would simply draw attention to how easily a man serving a prison sentence at the almshouse could walk out the door if someone took a mind that he should.

It was up to the alderman in the chairman's seat to bang his gavel and call the meeting to order. So far he had not done so. One of his colleagues was reading a newspaper. Two others were deeply engaged in a whispered conversation. The rest just looked bored. Nick turned and craned his neck to see what was happening behind him. Dear Manon. She was sitting in the back under a gaslight so that she could see to work on the embroidery she'd brought with her. She looked eminently respectable and wholesome in this gathering of thieves. He'd told her not to come but she'd insisted. "I cannot allow you to go alone into the lion's den, Nicholas. Besides, I have valuable evidence to offer. Presuming anyone cares to hear it." He had protested that if Grant carried the day she would be ever after banned from nursing at Bellevue. "Oh, that doesn't matter so much anymore," she'd replied. "I am determined to have my dispensary, and when I do, nothing Tobias Grant thinks will matter to me one whit." She saw Nick looking at her and smiled and nodded, then returned her attention to her needlework.

Nick swiveled to inspect the other side of the auditorium. Another woman stood way in the back, though he couldn't imagine . . . Dear God, it was Carolina.

But just then the chairman of the aldermen banged his gavel three times in rapid succession. "Hear ye, hear ye, this special and extraordinary meeting of the honorable Common Council of the City of New York is hereby called to order. Let anyone who has business with this body approach and state his case."

Nick felt a tap on his shoulder and heard a man's voice. "Stand up and tell them why you're here. Hurry. Otherwise they'll gavel the meeting closed and be rid of you that way."

The chairman peered into the gloom, then raised his gavel preparing to do exactly as the stranger said. Nick jumped to his feet. "I have business with you, gentlemen."

"And you are?"

"Dr. Nicholas Turner."

"You're not from here, are you, Dr. Turner?" The alderman who'd been reading the newspaper spoke. "From Rhode Island, I believe. Not a New Yorker."

"I was born and raised in Providence, yes. But I've been here since 1834."

"Three years isn't very long."

"I believe Dr. Turner has earlier and deeper roots in this city," one of the other aldermen said. "Is that not so, sir?"

So he had at least one friend at court, perhaps two. He was intensely conscious of the man sitting behind him and of Carolina in the shadows at the rear. "It is indeed so. My family came to New York when it was New Amsterdam."

"We don't put one class ahead of another here, Dr. Turner." The chairman spoke. "Don't matter if you're one of the old families as call themselves Knickerbockers. This here's a republic. Every man is equal."

Nick felt a tug on his sleeve. "Tell them about Christopher and Andrew."

"The Turners have never been wealthy, gentlemen, and while I believe the Knickerbockers claim Dutch descent, we Turners do not. Lucas Turner was a barber surgeon, an Englishman, though he arrived by way of Rotterdam. His grandson Christopher Turner was a celebrated surgeon as well and in charge of the Almshouse Hospital under the British. My grandfather was Andrew Turner, a hero of the Revolution, a remarkable surgeon, also head of the Almshouse Hospital in his day and a member of this council."

"Very well, Dr. Turner. We take your point." The chairman was leaning on his elbow, looking a bit bored. "You've established your bona fides, as they say. Now state your business."

Nicholas took a deep breath. "A great injustice has been done in the name of this honorable council, gentlemen. It is being repeated every night and every day."

"You mean because you got the sack, do you?" The alderman who'd first brought up Providence.

"No, sir. Not that. At least not only that." If he was going to produce the letter, this was the time. *I will file papers seeking a divorce from Carolina and name you as corespondent. The man with whom my wife has committed adultery.* Nick gripped the back of the chair in front of him. "I have been aware of conditions at the almshouse since I arrived in 1834, long before I was dismissed from my post."

"And you've waited three years to tell us anything about them? That's hard to believe, Dr. Turner."

"It is nonetheless the truth. It has been my hope that by remaining in my post I might mitigate—"

There was flurry of activity behind him: Sweet Jesus Christ, Monty Chance was walking down the aisle.

"I can tell the council why things are as they are at Bellevue," Chance said, pointing an accusatory finger at Nick. "Dr. Turner has mad notions about what's important. Always on about us washing our hands when we've barely enough time to treat the sick. And upstairs in his private apartment he—"

A loud ahem cut him off. Grant was on his feet. Of course. The old bastard didn't want any mention of the laboratory or the dissections. Flagrant breaches of the law at Bellevue Hospital would ultimately be his responsibility. "Thank you, Dr. Chance. I'm sure the council take your meaning."

Monty Chance made his way to sit beside Grant and Potter and Clement. Nick started to speak, but the chairman held up a forestalling hand. "You were saying, Dr. Turner."

"That the situation at the entire almshouse is a disgrace. The taxpayers' money is being wasted while—"

"Dr. Turner,"—the alderman who was clearly gunning for him—"is that true? You have folks wasting their time on hand-washing nonsense when you're supposed to be curing folks as is sick so they can go back to working for their keep?"

"Indeed I do. Because of germs. They can't be seen by the naked eye, but I believe them to be the cause of much illness."

Nick caught sight of Manon moving toward the front of the room to confront the aldermen. "I can attest to what Dr. Turner says. I frequently visit Bellevue to nurse the poor and—"

"We are not accustomed to hearing from ladies in this chamber, madam. Please take your seat."

"But I have important evidence to offer."

"Take your seat, madam."

"But—"

The chairman banged his gavel. "Sit down or I'll end this meeting right now. Ladies speaking in this chamber without being called. Ain't never heard of such a thing. Sit down!" Then, turning to Nick, "Seems to me, Dr. Turner, all this talk of invisible stuff that makes folks sick is a diversion. You're here for the very reason my colleague stated originally. You've come to complain because the man who hired you, believing you would be a trustworthy and competent Senior Medical Attendant for Bellevue Hospital, found you to be wasting the taxpayers' money on pie in the sky nonsense such as hand-washing and surgery that causes no pain. And as was his duty, he fired you. So you've come to complain. Isn't that true, Dr. Turner?"

"No, it is not."

"I say it is."

A number of the others were nodding and murmuring assent. The one alderman Nick thought to be on his side leaned forward. "Suppose my colleagues and I all keep quiet for a bit"—glaring down the table as he spoke—"and you tell us exactly why you're here, Dr. Turner."

"Thank you, sir. Gentlemen, a terrible injustice is being committed. The taxpayers' money is indeed being wasted, but not by me. It's being siphoned off for his own use by that man there." Nick swung round and pointed a finger at Tobias Grant, then turned back to face the aldermen.

"The conditions at the almshouse are a disgrace, gentlemen. A travesty of any kind of human decency. There are not enough beds for the sick in the hospital, medicine is compounded not to cure disease but to enrich the chief apothecary, who incidentally sits over there as well. And tiny children are flogged almost to their death in that appalling institution that calls itself an orphan asylum when it is no asylum at all but quite simply an antechamber of hell."

The passion of his accusations stunned his audience into silence. Then Tobias Grant was on his feet, along with Potter, Clement, and even Monty Chance. "Gentlemen, I have been blamed for heinous crimes. I insist on being heard." Grant's voice was the one that carried, though Potter and Clement were also clamoring for recognition.

The chairman banged his gavel. "Your turn, Dr. Grant. What do you have to say?"

"I hired Dr. Turner precisely because of the distinguished lineage he mentioned. Naturally it was my hope that he would bring honor to our city and our venerable charitable institution. Instead he brought disgrace. I believe some of you witnessed the fraud he perpetrated last week. And if you did not, you were able to read about it in the newspaper. Painless surgery indeed. Those who were there heard the patient's screams of agony when they had been promised a dignified—"

"Hey!" Patrick Shaughnessey had broken free of the restraining hand of the porter who brought him and was on his feet. "It's me what was doin' all the screamin', and thanks be to Almighty God I was. Dr. Turner here worked a miracle. Ask anyone who seen me before about the bloody great lump on me shoulder what wouldn't let me hold my head straight. Ain't got it now, has I? Just this here bandage on me neck, and that'll be comin' off soon. All thanks to Dr. Turner."

"That man is a prisoner! He has no business being here," Potter shouted. It was Tobias Grant, Nick noted, who pulled him down to his seat. As he'd expected, the director didn't want the porous nature of the almshouse custodianship brought to the attention of the council.

"Dr. Turner." The man behind Nick took advantage of the commotion to again offer advice. "Ask Shaughnessey if he was asleep during the early part of the surgery."

This time Nick didn't hesitate. "Patrick Shaughnessey." He bellowed the man's name and Shaughnessey jumped to his feet. "Tell these honorable gentlemen if you felt any pain when the surgery began."

"Absolutely none whatever. So help me God." Shaughnessey was obviously delighted to be called on. "Slept like a baby I did. At least at first."

"Then what happened?" one of the aldermen who had not yet spoken asked.

"Then I woke up."

"And suffered the terrible agony of the surgeon's knife. Is that not correct?"

"Yes, but—"

"So calling it painless surgery is a lie of the basest sort."

"No!" Nick shouted. "It's a simple enough procedure now that we know what went wrong. We just didn't have enough of the sulfuric ether for our needs. Next time we will."

The alderman leaned forward, peering across the table at Nick. "Next time," he repeated. "Perhaps, Dr. Turner, perhaps. Now I would like to ask another question. Are you a papist, sir?"

"A papist? What has that got to do with anything?"

"I'm told, sir, that you have introduced Jews into the management of the hospital. That's perhaps unwise given as how they need watching or they'll steal you blind, but it is not so dreadful a thing as popery. Popery, Dr. Turner, is a religion founded on lies. It seems to me therefore relevant to this discussion. Are you a papist, Dr. Turner?"

"I am not a Catholic, no."

"Then how is it that you spend so much time at St. Patrick's Orphan Asylum? Perhaps the charms of the ladies who run the place are the reason. I'm sure we've all heard of Maria Monk."

"The Sisters at St. Patrick's are fine and admirable women. And that book is a pack of lies." Nick broke off because it was clear the aldermen were no longer listening. "Gentlemen, please!" Nick tried again.

"Don't waste your breath," Nick's anonymous advisor murmured quietly. "They've got the excuse they've all been looking for. You're known to consort with Jews and papists, therefore nothing you say can be trusted."

"But—"

"No buts. Look."

Nick turned his attention to the platform. The chairman raised his gavel and brought it down with a decisive smack. "There is nothing to say except that Tobias Grant has acted exactly as he should and has the complete trust of this council. The meeting is declared closed."

Chapter Twenty-one

THE MAN HAD obviously been waiting; he approached Nick as soon as he left City Hall. "Dr. Turner? My name is Samson Simson. I'm an attorney. Here's my carriage. Please join me."

Nick saw a silver-haired man who carried a walking stick and wore an old-fashioned cloak that swirled about his shoulders as he moved. "You were the gentleman seated behind me, weren't you?"

"I couldn't represent you in any public way. Whispered advice was the best I could offer."

"It was good advice. I'm in your debt."

"Hardly. Nothing I said had the least effect on the outcome."

"I fear that was decided before I ever came here to City Hall."

"Precisely so. Now, if you will, Dr. Turner." Simson pointed his walking stick at the waiting rig.

"That's very kind of you, but there were two ladies . . ."

"So there may have been, but there are no ladies here now."

True enough. There had been no sign of either Manon or Carolina in the auditorium when the hearing ended, and they were nowhere on the street now.

"Dr. Turner," Simson urged, once more pointing to the carriage. Nick took a last look around, then swung himself up. Simson entered behind him, leaned forward, and tapped on the window that separated him from the driver. It slid open instantly. "Take us to the Astor. That will do, won't it, Turner? You look as if you could use a bit of supper."

"I'm not very hungry, I'm afraid."

"Nonsense. A young man like you should always be hungry. Now I propose we postpone our discussion until we are in more salubrious surroundings."

Twenty minutes later they were seated in the dining room of the Astor House, sipping a quite decent claret and waiting for oysters and cold pheasant pie. Simson's choice, since he apparently followed the homely custom of having a main meal at four and a light supper later. "Now, young Dr. Turner, I imagine you are curious as to why I turned up in your hour of need, as it were."

"Frankly, I'm still a bit too bewildered to have thought about it. Those men represent the governing body of this great city, and they had their minds made up before I ever opened my mouth. It's beyond belief."

"My dear boy, it is no such thing. Not if belief is tempered with wisdom. Ah, here's the food. Tuck in."

Nick slurped down a couple of oysters, then took a forkful of the pie. He looked up to say how good everything was and found Simson observing him over the rim of his wine glass. The plate in front of him was untouched. "I thought you were hungry, Mr. Simson. It's really quite good."

"No doubt. But I am a Jew, Dr. Turner. I am forbidden to eat oysters under any circumstances. And since the pie will not have been prepared under our dietary laws, I must forego that as well."

"I don't understand. Why are we here, and why have you ordered all this if you cannot eat it?"

"To make a point, Dr. Turner, about Jews in general and myself in particular. We refrain from oysters because in the holy book of Deuteronomy it says, 'You may eat all that have fins and scales. And whatever does not have fins and scales you shall not eat; it shall be unclean for you.' We are not, you will note, trying to make oysters forbidden food throughout the world."

"'Unclean for you.' I suppose you take that to mean for the Chosen People only, yourselves."

Simson smiled. "So the rabbis tell us. Frankly, considering our history, being chosen sometimes seems a dubious honor. My point, however, is that our laws apply only to us, Dr. Turner. We are capable of cooperating with those who are not enjoined to follow them. You and I can sit as equals in this fine dining room, and you can take a nourishing supper while I sip a glass of wine and we discuss our common interests. Our differing religions do not enter into the matter."

"Look here, Mr. Simson, that's a fine republican way of thinking, but what's this all about?"

"The future, Dr. Turner. The past, as you learned this evening, is not something that can be changed."

"I'm not sure what my future is to be. Though I do feel damned bad about Ben Klein. He's a fine young man and on his way to being an excellent doctor. Now, thanks to me—"

"Thanks to you, and I may say Dr. Tobias Grant, however much in spite of himself, Ben Klein will grow to be a man with an excellent position in society. His prospects are enormously improved now that he has been freed from his misplaced loyalty to the Almshouse Hospital."

Nick put down his fork. It seemed he had little appetite after all. "His loyalty was to me, and I let him down. Ben wanted to be involved in research. I promised him he would be."

Simson waved away a hovering waiter and poured more claret for himself and his guest. "Let me tell you something else about my religion, Dr. Turner. We prize scholarship and study. Of the holy and divine word first and foremost, but of all things in creation as well. In that I believe we are quite different from most Christians. It does not seem to us to be a violation of the divine law to try to understand more precisely what it is. Particularly when such study leads to the good of mankind."

Nick sat back and took another sip of his wine. "Just where is all this theology taking us, Mr. Simson?"

"Forgive me, I've been rambling. I have an offer to make, Dr. Turner. I wish you to set up in private practice with young Dr. Klein. The cost of establishing that practice, a quite decent office and a serviceable laboratory, will be arranged. A loan to be paid back on just and mutually acceptable terms. I can assure you that a number of the most respected and respectable members of the community are waiting to consult you both."

"Do you refer to the Jewish community?"

"Yes. I have no doubt you will soon enough have Christian patients as well, but our people will start coming to you immediately, providing a firm base on which to build. So to speak."

"Why involve me at all? Dr. Klein is now fully qualified."

"He is. But he is also very young. Your experience will temper his youth, for one thing. For another, I've no doubt the pair of you will continue to spend some time in this research to which you are equally devoted."

"You don't think we'll spend time in the laboratory rather than see patients?"

"I doubt that. There will be the matter of the repayment of the debt to keep you on the strait and narrow path. You are an honorable man, Dr. Turner. I have no doubt you will be sufficiently attentive to business to see that your monthly obligations can be met. Further . . ."

"Yes?"

"While I think this matter of painless surgery must perhaps be forsworn, since the fiasco of last week was so publically aired, if you and Ben Klein were to make other useful discoveries, Dr. Turner, it is very much in the interest of the Jews of this nation that those beneficial advances redound to our credit. If Dr. Klein is working with you and can make an honest claim, that will happen."

"Ben has a lively and inquiring mind. Given the opportunity, he may do grand things in research with or without me."

"Fair enough. I am, however, offering the opportunity to you both. A practice with Dr. Klein, Dr. Turner, yourself to be the senior partner as befits your age and experience. Are you interested?"

"Do you have Ben's agreement in all this? More important, do you have his father's agreement?"

Simson smiled. "How, Dr. Turner, do you imagine I knew about this evening's council meeting?"

"So, Mrs. Joyful, for some time I have wished you would come to see me."

"Have you, Mr. Astor?"

"*Ja*, I have. Because the last time it was not so good a meeting. Always I have felt bad about that."

Manon wanted to say that it was a thoroughly awful meeting. Because John Jacob Astor insisted on making money by smuggling opium into Canton, which her dead husband would have protested with every fiber of his being, as did she on his behalf. No point in saying any of that nineteen years later. "Let us then begin anew, Mr. Astor. I believe you and Mr. Simson would now like to have returned what you entrusted to my husband before his death."

"Entrusted to both of you, Mrs. Joyful. It was the cleverness and good intentions of both of you on which Mr. Simson and I relied. But now, what you are thinking, it is not entirely correct."

"Is it not? How so?"

"Mr. Simson and I, no longer we are working hand in glove, as the saying goes. Our interests have diverged. That is the English word, is it not?"

"It is."

"So, if Mr. Simson has approached you to recover what is in your keeping, that is not any affair of mine."

"Mr. Astor, are you asking me to believe you have no interest in something so extraordinary?"

Astor laughed. The dark eyes were every bit as piercing as they had been when she first met him, and the brain seemed just as active. Never mind that he had to be well over seventy. Perhaps having such incredible wealth kept him young.

When Manon visited him that first time, soon after Joyful's death, Jacob Astor still lived on Broadway and Barclay Street in what was now the resplendent Astor House. She'd not been to the hotel, but she remembered Astor's home as a palace. This one far up the town was if anything more grand. It overlooked the part of the East River known as Hellgate because of a confluence of currents, Eighty-eighth Street according to the grid. They were in a long parlor off the front hall. The walls were paneled in rare rosewood, on the ceiling was an elaborate mural of the Garden of Eden (three artists were said to have spent a month on their back to complete it), and seven enormous crystal chandeliers would of an evening cast shimmering light on furnishings of marble and gilt and intricately carved woods, the names of which Manon did not know.

"A little more wine, Mrs. Joyful?"

"Thank you, Mr. Astor." She should refuse, but his Madeira was delicious. Besides, she needed fortification at least as much as a clear head. "You are not telling me you've no interest in the treasure, are you?"

"No, no. Much interest I have. Always. But with you it was infinitely more safe, Mrs. Joyful, because no one would expect you to have it. Lately my mind it has changed a little. Only I want to know why, since apparently you refused to give it to Mr. Simson, you are prepared now to give this thing to me."

"I didn't say I was, Mr. Astor."

"No, but why else would you come here? Something you want, Mrs. Joyful, that you believe I can give to you and Mr. Simson can not. That is correct, no?"

There was no point in sparring with him. Joyful always said the man had a mind like a bear trap, wickedly sharp and always ready to spring. She must not make the mistake of thinking age had changed him. "Yes, Mr. Astor, that is correct."

"Good, then you will tell me what you want and I will see if I can provide it for you. If I can, we will arrange to trade. *Ja?*"

"*Ja.* I mean yes. I didn't intend to—"

Another burst of explosive laughter. "It is not to worry, Mrs. Joyful. In the Five Points there are one-eyed beggars who better than I speak the language. But still they are beggars, while I . . ." He shrugged. "My English to me has not been a hindrance, and sensitive about it I am not. Now, the terms."

No hindrance indeed, at least not to the amassing of enormous wealth, which should make her request for land and a dispensary a trifle. Particularly considering what she could give him in return. Manon leaned forward and began speaking.

Astor insisted he would take her home in his carriage. "On Vandam Street you are living now." She had not told him she'd moved, but Manon was not surprised that he knew. "So," he continued as he helped her into her cloak and gathered up his hat and his gloves and his walking stick, "together there we will go and you will give me the Great Mogul diamond, *ja?*"

She had not heard it called by its proper name since her father died. To herself she thought of it only as a millstone, a responsibility she could not shake and did not know how to discharge. "I'm not entirely sure I should, Mr. Astor."

"But you said—"

"I have no hesitation in giving you the stone. It has been nothing but an enormous worry to me ever since my husband died. But how can I be sure about the rest of our bargain?"

All the effusive bonhomie disappeared from Astor's expression, and

Manon had some sense of the darkness of the man's true character. Things were very bad in the town this spring, particularly for the working class. Astor was the landlord for a great many of them, and he was said to be putting at least a dozen families a day on the streets, as well as foreclosing on vast numbers of the mortgages he'd taken on in better times. Why not? He was rich enough to wait out the inflation-born depression and sell again later at an even greater profit. "You think I will cheat you?" he asked.

"I think my husband would suggest that I should have any promise in writing," Manon said.

"Here you wait," he said, and disappeared to another room. When he came back, he was carrying a piece of paper, blowing on it to dry the ink. "A fine lot it is," he said, after he'd handed her the document. "On Waverly Place and Fourth Street, and a three-story building I am promising to build for you."

Manon glanced down and read quickly. "But the lot is not in Five Points," she protested.

"Of course it is not in Five Points. Forgive me Mrs. Joyful, but foolish you are being. You think you will get any nice respectable ladies like yourself to come and work in your dispensary if in Five Points it's to be? Please, tell me how many of them go with you to be a nurse there now."

She didn't have to say that none did. Obviously he already knew. "This document isn't signed," she said instead.

"A lawyer maybe you are," he muttered. "When I have the Great Mogul, then I will sign it. Now please, give it back to me and let us go."

"Addie, this is Mr. Jacob Astor. My companion, Miss Bellingham."

Addie jumped to her feet so quickly the sewing spilled off her lap onto the floor. "Mr. Astor," she murmured. Heaven help them, were they to be put into the street?

"Close your mouth, Addie, and get on about your business. Mr. Astor hasn't come to foreclose on us and he won't be staying long." Then, to Astor, "Follow me, please."

Since she was bringing him into her bedroom, Manon left the door open. Her clothes cupboard stood against the opposite wall. She opened the double doors and began removing the hatboxes from the top shelf, taking them down one by one and stacking them on the bed. Silly to still have so many when nowadays she only ever wore a plain black bonnet in winter and an equally plain gray one in summer. The bonnets in the boxes were leftovers of another time and another life, like the one in the very last box she removed from the shelf, all pink straw and pale green satin streamers and a bunch of purple pansies stitched to the side. It had been a favorite of Joyful's. She had opened the box only once every year since he died, to check on the thing wrapped in the blue velvet cloth.

"Have you thought how extraordinary it is that we should have such a thing, Mr. Astor?"

"I have, Mrs. Joyful."

"What shall you do with it?"

"I am not entirely sure," he admitted. But to possess the world's largest diamond, for the time being that would be enough.

Manon did not remind him that years before, he and Samson Simson had said that someday this fabulous jewel might be important for the country's future. Now, she thought, it would be only about money. She reached below the pink and green bonnet to where the precious bundle had been hidden all these years. Foolish to give it to Astor perhaps, but surely to create something as much needed as a dispensary for poor women and children, it— "Oh."

"What 'oh'? What is the matter, Mrs. Joyful?"

"It's not here," Manon said. She tipped the hatbox upside down on the bed, pawing through the tissue and sending little motes of dust dancing in the May sunshine streaming through the window. "The diamond isn't here!"

"When is the last time you saw it?"

"Right after the New Year. I checked on it as I always do, once every year. Then I put it back."

"Maybe in another box you put it."

"No, it's been in this one at the back of my cupboard ever since—"

Manon stopped speaking when she heard the thud from the sitting room. Addie Bellingham had fainted.

Chapter Twenty-two

"**WHO DID YOU** give it to?" Manon demanded. Addie clamped her lips into a thin line. "It's thievery, Addie, the act of a common criminal. I would never have expected it of you."

"It fell out of the cupboard, like I said. I was looking for a bit of sewing cotton in that odd shade of yellow, and the thing fell at my feet."

"Ridiculous," Astor said. His normally ruddy complexion was ghostly white, and his hands were balled into fists at his sides. He seemed far more upset than Manon Turner. "All the way at the back of the top shelf, the box was. Underneath a hat. Never it could have fallen at those feet." He looked down at the sturdy workaday boots of Addie Bellingham. "And as Mrs. Joyful says, it is robbery. If Jacob Astor also says so, do you think in the police court the Police Justice will have any doubt? To the women's prison in the almshouse you will go for sure, Miss Bellingham."

He had unwittingly said the words she was most afraid of hearing. Addie shrieked.

Manon recognized their advantage and pressed it. "The almshouse for at least five years, I should think, Mr. Astor. With no possibility of getting out."

"Not five years. Ten more likely. I will tell the Police Justice ten years at least."

Another shriek. Then, "My friend Lilac Langton, she's the one who has it. Going to take it to a Russian man with a fancy-goods shop. To see if it was real. We never thought it could be, a thing that big. We never thought—"

Jacob Astor was staring at Addie as if seeing her for the first time. "Lilac Langton," he said. "Certain you are that is her name?"

"Of course I'm certain. We met at Mr. Finney's church on the Anxious Bench. Both of us giving our lives to Jesus the same night. Been friends for quite two years now. You don't know her, do you?"

"Knowing her is maybe not how you would say it. I know who she is. The busiest and most popular lady to do abortions in all of the city."

Addie shrieked again.

"Mr. Astor," Manon asked, "how do you know this?"

"Because I am her landlord."

Addie swayed, on the verge of fainting a second time, but Manon picked up a vase filled with water and spring flowers and dumped the contents over the other woman's head.

No one answered the door to Lilac Langton's rooms on Christopher Street. They knocked a number of times, then Mr. Astor sent the driver of his carriage to his countinghouse on Little Dock Street to get the duplicate keys he kept there. He looked his age now, pale and drawn and with a thin blue line around his mouth that Manon found quite worrying. She looked around for someplace they could wait until the driver returned. "I think I saw a café around the corner. We can go there for a short while, Mr. Astor."

Astor shook his head and sat down on the steps of the building next to the one where Lilac Langton lived. "Here we can wait. Please to stop sniveling, Miss Bellingham. It annoys me."

Addie blew her nose loudly, then was silent.

"I hope whoever lives here doesn't mind our sitting outside their front door," Manon murmured.

"It doesn't matter if they do," Astor said. "This building also I own."

She should have known, just as she should have known that Addie Bellingham was more than a snoop who listened at open doors. A woman hurrying down the street went straight to Lilac Langton's front door and knocked. Exactly as they had done. Manon jumped up and went toward her. "Excuse me, please."

"Yes?"

"You're looking for Mrs. Langton, I take it."

The woman, younger than Manon, but well dressed and respectable-seeming, looked embarrassed, then lifted her chin defiantly. "I am. You as well, presumably."

"Yes, I was. I mean I am looking for her. Do you have any idea where she might be?"

"None whatever. I came round to see her last week as well and she wasn't here then. I suppose I'd better go to someone else now. Heaven knows the papers are full of advertisements for similar services. Mrs. Langton will lose all her custom if she continues to behave this way."

Manon watched until the woman had walked away, then returned to Mr. Astor and Addie. "Mrs. Langton's been gone for days and days. At least that's what it looks like. That woman came to look for her a week ago and she wasn't here then either."

Addie again began to sob. Astor turned to her. "So, you told me you gave to your friend Mrs. Langton what did not belong to either of you a few days ago. This was maybe not the exact truth?"

Addie sobbed louder.

"The almshouse prison," Manon said, "is far worse than the workhouse. Even I was afraid of the women in the almshouse prison."

"Three weeks it is since I gave it to her," Addie said between gasps for air. "I been round here every day for the last ten looking for Lilac, and she hasn't been here. We was going to share. If it turned out to be real, I mean. But she—"

Astor's carriage drove up and the driver jumped down carrying a ring hung with numerous keys.

Neither Astor nor Manon nor even Addie Bellingham was surprised to find Lilac Langton's rooms stripped bare. There was nothing anywhere that might give them a clue as to where she'd gone.

It was dark beyond the windows of the Vandam Street lodging house. It was dark inside Manon as well, but within her was not the balmy softness of a May evening, but the bitter, soul-destroying cold of winter. "It was a wicked, wicked thing to do, Addie. I trusted you and tried to help you and you betrayed me. I'm afraid we can no longer live together. I want you to leave."

"Now? But where will I go? I—"

"Tomorrow morning first thing. And I don't care where you go. You are very fortunate it will not be prison."

Not even a man as vindictive as Jacob Astor had any desire to explain how it was he knew where the world's largest diamond could be found, or why all these years he'd allowed it to remain hidden in a widow's hatbox. Manon had realized from the first that he would not press charges against Addie Bellingham. As for her, she had never considered the Great Mogul diamond as being her possession, so she could not imagine claiming she'd been robbed of it. Only because Addie Bellingham understood none of those things had she been so frightened by their threat of a return to the almshouse, to the prison wing no less.

"You have some money put by, I know, Addie. And I shall give you a hundred dollars." She could not turn even Addie Bellingham into the streets without some means to survive. "There are some quite inexpensive boardinghouses here and there in the town. I'm sure you can find one. Along with your income from sewing, if you're prudent, you will manage, Addie. Now please go to your room. Frankly, the sight of you makes me quite ill."

"And that's it?" Nick asked. "No sign of the stone?"

"No sign whatever," Manon said. "Mr. Astor was quite sure he knew which fancy-goods merchant this Mrs. Langton likely had in mind, a Russian merchant on Broadway near Wall Street. He went there immediately. The man's shop was shuttered closed and no one has seen him for days. Mr. Astor said there was a rumor he had taken ship for Europe. With a lady friend, according to some of the neighbors."

"Your Mrs. Langton, no doubt. Incredible." Nick sat back in the large chair behind the sizable desk that occupied his book-lined consulting room. He had already shown Manon the similar chamber for Ben Klein, the examining and treatment room they shared, and the small but impressively equipped laboratory in the rear of the suite on Crosby Street. He and Ben were now engaged in the practice of medicine in an area that had twenty years earlier been a rural fastness. These days the neighborhood was home to rich Jews of the old guard, bankers and moneymen who considered themselves entirely different from the latest wave of German Jewish tradesmen and entrepreneurs. It was home as well to Catholics of French and Spanish descent, who of course saw little to connect them to their Irish coreligionists. Both groups considered it fitting to make their home in the shadow of the very imposing Shearith Israel Jewish synagogue or, for the Catholics, close by St. Patrick's Cathedral. The neighborhood was for Nick a world so far removed from Bellevue as to make it seem like fairyland. Manon's extraordinary tale was of a piece with it. "A diamond as big as a pigeon's egg," he repeated.

"It was extraordinarily beautiful, Cousin Nicholas. To look into such a stone . . . I'm sorry I never showed it to you."

"So am I. Cousin Manon, may I ask how you came to have such a thing?"

"No, dear Nicholas, you may not. It's an incredible story involving Canton and intrigue among thieves and runaway slaves, and you probably wouldn't believe me if I told you, though I assure you it was painfully real when we were living through it." Unlikely either that he would believe she'd once been beautiful enough for someone to want to spirit her away on a pirate ship. "Anyway, it was really my husband's story. I only told you as much as I have to explain why I'm looking for somewhere to rent. To open a less ambitious version of the dispensary I originally planned."

"Astor wouldn't make good on his promise?"

"Not once it became clear I could not make good on mine." *To be a bargain both sides must do what is offered, Mrs. Joyful.* She shrugged.

"Wretched woman," Nick said, unwilling to mention Addie Bellingham's name. "And after you'd done so much for her."

"Wretched indeed. And one of the things I've learned these past years is that if one does the right thing for the sake of being thanked, much less loved—well, it seldom works out that way. Now I must go, Nicholas. I see that your location here is far too grand for what I have in mind. But if you hear of anything, you will keep me in mind?"

"Of course I will." He got up to see her to the door, then paused, "Cousin Manon, the night of the hearing at City Hall, Carolina was there as well wasn't she?"

"I believe so, yes. For a time."

"How do you suppose she knew about it?"

"I told her, Nicholas. I knew she would be concerned for you, as was I." She smiled and nodded her head to indicate the luxury of his surroundings. "We couldn't either of us know how splendidly you would land on your feet."

St. Patrick's Cathedral had a three-story-high vaulted ceiling, gothic-arched windows of elaborate stained glass, and a truly enormous marble altar backed by an exquisite reredos, a screen worked in gold. The eye Manon's goldsmith father had trained recognized workmanship of the highest quality, but it gave her no joy. What in this place seemed appropriate to the memory of the humble carpenter's son? She caught the faint scent of the incense used in the morning devotions, the whiff, she sometimes thought, of corruption and decay. This religion with its overelaborate buildings and ancient rituals and its insistence on speaking a language dead to most for hundreds of years . . . but where else could she go to pour out her complaints?

Manon had sounded quite resigned when she spoke with Nicholas. But, oh, inside, in her deepest heart, she was not resigned at all. How could a God of justice permit such a thing to happen? And why come here to seek consolation?

Because after everything, my Manon, here—for you—is where I am to be found.

The voice spoke in her head, she knew she had not heard it aloud. But it was nonetheless a voice. And she had heard it.

All these months and years. All this grieving and guilt and rage at what had been meted out to her. All those prayers wrenched from a dryness that seemed it would never be anything other than an arid wasteland of unknowing. And now this.

For you, my Manon, here is where I am to be found.

She felt as if she floated beneath that magnificent ceiling, though she knew quite well she knelt still at the altar railing where she had come almost shaking her fist in anger and despair. She had as well a different and equally real awareness. That of love pouring into her, meant for her, filling every gap hollowed by years of loneliness and loss.

Manon caught her breath and held it. Then she exhaled. And everything was wonderfully and simply and beautifully clear.

It had been ten-thirty when Manon left Nicholas and walked the short distance to St. Patrick's church. Now she came out and stood trembling with quiet joy in the midafternoon sunshine. A nearby clock chimed three times. It was late, much later than she had realized. Long past time. But at least now she knew exactly where she must go and what she must do.

"This is my last visit, Mother Louise."

"Oh, I am distressed to hear that, Mrs. Turner."

Manon shook her head. "I'm sorry, I am not being clear. I mean it is my last visit as a guest. My last time choosing my own way. I must return to my lodgings and arrange my affairs. Tomorrow, if you will permit it, I will come to stay. Shall you have me?"

The nun smiled. "There is a long road to travel, my dear. And many pitfalls and temptations along the way, but of course we will have you. I have in fact been expecting you for some time."

Book Three

1842—1844

Chapter Twenty-three

ACCORDING TO BO Big Belly, who had left the Middle Kingdom just after the Lantern Festival in this year of the Tiger, white-smoke-swallowing-clouds war was done and over. Big guns of English ships had flattened junks and sampans of Imperial Chinese Navy. That was why now, when Ah Chee came back from the market and opened the door of number thirty-nine Cherry Street, she did not smell man stink or shit stink or little-bit-better stink of food cooking. Instead she smelled little-bit-sweet smell she thought she had left behind when she said goodbye to the Pearl River sampans of the pirate Di Short Neck. "*Ya-p'ien* legal now," Big Belly reported. "Soon everybody in Middle Kingdom swallow clouds, feel all the time happy."

"Ha! Swallow clouds and get nothing done. No time to work. Only smoke." Ah Chee had not forgotten that on the pirate sampans the fingers were cut off anyone who smoked the ya-p'ien. Food was put in their bellies by trading silver for the sticky black balls the English brought from somewhere very far away, and the pirate sampans sold the black balls to other Chinese, who got still richer by selling it to the smoking fools on the mainland, while the English used the silver to pay the Hong merchants, who would accept nothing else for their tea and silk. But on the sampans, no smoke. No smoke. All the fingers on one hand first. All the fingers on the other for a second offense. The third time no head.

"No work. No work," she said now, and kicked at the baskets of rubbish and spent ashes lining the hall by the front door. "Why you not bring this mess outside? Right now. Before the Lord Samuel comes and beats you all to death. Right now."

That should have been a threat with teeth. The Lord Samuel was on Cherry Street most days for at least a few hours. Many times he slept the whole night beside his *tai-tai*, and in the morning played with his daughter Mei Lin. But Ah Chee was aware that somehow the lord didn't seem to care that at thirty-nine Cherry Street there was the stink of white smoke in the downstairs hall. Not too much outside the rooms of those who had lived longest in the building; Leper Face and Taste Bad and the rest of the old-timers didn't swallow clouds. "Very much too bad thing," Leper Face said one night when Ah Chee was with them playing cards. "Too bad."

The game they played was called *Ya Pei*, and that night, Ah Chee was invariably the first to lay down a run of plum flower or orchid or bamboo or chrysanthemum cards and take all the coins in the middle of the table, chortling with pleasure when the men cursed her luck. "Not enough incense burned in these rooms," she had said, sniffing the air. "Not enough attention paid to Fu Xing happy god or even Matsu sea god. Not enough."

"Matsu very important when at sea. Not so much important here on land," Taste Bad said. "Anyway, back in Middle Kingdom is where they need to burn more incense. Build more temples to Guan Sheng Di war god. Maybe not lose every time and give away little pieces of kingdom to stinking dog turd English."

"What little pieces?" Ah Chee demanded. "How?"

"Hong Kong now have English rulers," Leper Face explained. "In Hong Kong stinking dog turd English people now do whatever they want, don't have to obey Middle Kingdom emperor."

"Stinking no good island anyway," Ah Chee said. "Not to worry if English have it. Bo Big Belly say Chinese sampans all blown away by stinking English warships," she added, turning the subject back to the topic of most interest to her. "You think every one blown up? Even dog turd river pirates on Pearl River?" If Di Short Neck was dead, the plum blossom must burn incense in his memory.

The men could not, however, answer her question. Maybe yes, maybe no they said. Though it was important to bear in mind that the war began when the emperor sent his army to the Pearl River to throw all the chests of *ya-p'ien* into the sea. Who had lived and who had died? Very much impossible to say for sure.

Better to err on the side of caution, Ah Chee decided. So for the next four days she instructed both Mei-hua and Mei Lin to burn five sticks of incense to Chuan Yin, who was the goddess of compassion as well as fertility. "Help father and grandfather be happy in new crossover place. Much incense. Much incense."

Mei-hua had no happy memories of the man who had fathered her. Nonetheless she understood the need to show respect to her father's memory so as not to make the gods angry. It was she who guided the hand of her seven-year-old daughter when Mei Lin offered the stick of burning incense at the altar set up to honor her grandfather, Di Short Neck, who had sold her mother for a few chests of *ya-p'ien*. Never mind. Show respect.

As for Mei Lin, she did not find it difficult to do as her mother asked. At least it was a new distraction. She was only rarely allowed out of the rooms on the top floor of thirty-nine Cherry Street, and when she was—always in the company of Ah Chee—she was unhappy and intensely conscious of the way people stared at the old woman with the funny feet and the funny clothes and the little girl at her side. The little girl who, unlike her elderly guardian, understood every derisive word she heard.

Both things—the size of Mei Lin's feet and the fact that she spoke English—existed because Sam Devrey had made them so. Each morning that she could remember, her father spoke to Mei Lin in English. From the day she started to speak, she answered him in that language, though when Ah Chee or Mei-hua talked to her she replied in Chinese. They were not two separate languages to the little girl, simply a bigger language in which it was appropriate to use certain words some of the time and other words at other times.

It was also her father who decreed that Mei Lin's feet not be bound. He did not, however, discuss this with Mei-hua or Ah Chee ahead of time, and he was not in the house in 1838, when for the first time Ah Chee had bent back the big toes of three-year-old Mei Lin and wrapped them tightly in cotton bindings. He did not hear Mei Lin's screams or the soothing words of Mei-hua, who smiled with satisfaction even while she offered the little girl sweets and kisses as comfort for her pain.

Mei-hua had chosen that particular occasion to begin the binding because she knew the lord would be away for a little time. In the past she had never known when he would come and when he would leave, but since these days the lord was almost never gone two nights in a row, he had informed Mei-hua that she would not see him for perhaps seven nights, and she was not to worry. Mei-hua had shared this information with Ah Chee and said it was an excellent opportunity to begin the foot-binding. Not because she anticipated any objection from her lord—however tired and distracted he might be, Mei-hua could still make him rock hard simply by rubbing her tiny silk-wrapped feet on his crotch—but because she knew Mei Lin would at first cry and scream. The lord must not be subjected to that annoyance.

Mei-hua broached the possibility of breaking Mei Lin's tiny arches right away so that too would happen when the Lord Samuel was not there to hear the screams. "No can," Ah Chee muttered, taking the child's tiny feet in her old and wrinkled hands. "No can. Not again. Not now." She remembered how it had been before, how inflicting such pain was, she was quite sure, worse for her than for Mei-hua who had to bear it. "Wait maybe until next time the lord is not here."

"Very much too bad this house so small," Mei-hua grumbled. "No proper women's quarters." These days that was the closest she came to complaining about what she had seen on the one occasion she had left her house, the day the Lord Samuel drove her to the place where her son was stolen from her womb. She no longer pressed Ah Chee for details of what the old woman saw when she went outside to buy food or other necessary things such as cloth to make their clothes. The Lord Samuel had come to be with them the night the city burned, and ever since he spent very much more time with her than with the big ugly yellow hair with floppy too big feet. Never mind that he would not let clouds and rain happen while he was inside her. Never. Never. And never mind that Ah Chee had burned the hollow bamboo thing Mei-hua used to make Mei Lin. No more blown up delicious duck. No more babies. Never mind.

But a daughter with floppy too big ugly feet? Who would want such a thing? How could Mei-hua know her lord would be overcome with rage when he came back and saw what they had done or that he would rip off the binding cloths with his own hands? Mei Lin, who had been crying less and less since the wrappings went on, now screamed in agony as blood rushed into the cramped toes. "You cannot bind her feet," the Lord Samuel said. "Not in America. It is impossible."

"Who will want her if she does not have golden lilies?" Mei-hua demanded. "What kind of husband will you find for her if she has big ugly floppy feet like a man?"

She did not notice Ah Chee's look of satisfaction. Very too much in her mind that in all the years they were here she had never seen a *yang gwei zih* woman with golden lilies. Very too much possible that in this place it was better if Mei Lin not have them. But not her place to make such a decision. Better if the lord did so. And as long as the arch had not been broken, the choice could still be made. Whatever the plum blossom who understood so little might think.

"No binding," the Lord said. "Never. Never. No binding."

Sam Devrey was already deeply conflicted about the question of who would marry his half-Chinese daughter, but that was not a problem he could discuss with Mei-hua. He could only do his best to give the child a few tools with which to survive. That's why he had originally made it his business to see that she spoke English, and having set about doing that, had fallen entirely under the spell of this child born of love, while he had no particular feelings for Zachary, the son born of duty, or Celinda, the daughter born of calculation. He said none of this to Mei-hua, only thanked God he had come back before they broke her arches, and made it a matter of his law, which reigned supreme beneath this roof, that Mei Lin's feet be allowed to grow naturally. And in 1840, when she was five, he issued another not-to-be-questioned decree. Mei Lin must go to school. "There is a place not far. I will arrange it."

In fact, though Sam told Mei-hua that sending young children to study outside the home was the norm in New York, it was not entirely true.

The New York rich tutored their children at home until they were old enough to be sent to boarding schools or private day schools. For the offspring of artisans and journeymen, the part of society now frequently referred to as being from the middle walks of life, there were a few free schools and some that charged a nominal fee.

All taught elementary reading, writing, and arithmetic, but there were never enough to serve the thousands of children born to paupers and the laboring class. Consequently those same subjects were included in the many Sunday schools active throughout the city, basic instruction to accompany lessons in the Word of God. The Evangelical churches, with their belief in democracy and republicanism, soon had sixty such schools meant to teach "the depraved and uneducated part of the community." And while the Episcopal Church did not share the radical social ideas of the Evangelicals—abolition and women's rights and the rest—they established a dozen schools of their own. In both networks excellence was rewarded with certificates which could be saved until the student had enough of them to exchange for a bible.

In addition to private funds, some money to support both the free schools and the Sunday Schools was provided by the Common Council. After a time the Free School Society objected to sharing the small sums available. Using taxpayer money to support Sunday Schools run by religious institutions, they said, was a violation of the separation of church and state guaranteed in the Constitution. Aid to the denominational schools was promptly cut off. In 1826, having won that battle, the Free School Society became the Public School Society.

Education, they insisted, must be not charity but a right. Nonetheless their resources remained so limited that public schools were opened only in areas considered to be quiet and orderly.

The nearest public school to Cherry Street was a bit up the town in the somewhat better-class neighborhood of Hester Street. That was where Sam Devrey enrolled his daughter under the name Linda Di, giving her the surname of Mei-hua's pirate father since he could not bestow his own.

Hester was too far from Cherry for a five-year-old to walk alone. Sam decided that Bo Fat Cheeks would escort the child each morning and pick her up at one when classes ended. He chose Fat Cheeks precisely because the man's queue had never grown back properly after it was cut off. Growing hair long enough to be braided and allowed to hang freely down the back was a young man's game. Fat Cheeks, in his forties now, had only a scrawny little one-inch braid at the nape of his neck. It was easy enough to hide that and his shaved skull under the knitted hat he usually wore with the checked shirt and oiled pants of the tar he'd once been.

Sam did not, however, reckon with the amount of trouble that would be caused by the fashion sense of Mei-hua and Ah Chee.

Mei Lin was sent to school on her first day wearing a knee-length red silk robe over a long red silk skirt. Both garments were lavishly embroidered with flowers and dragons picked out in gold thread, work done for her daughter by Mei-hua's own hand. Sam eyed the outfit with some trepidation when he kissed the child goodbye, and resolved he must find some way to have proper Western clothes made for her as soon as possible. His good intentions were too little and far too late. That first day Mei Lin came home from school with her clothes torn to shreds and most of her hair hacked off. The girls in her class had cut off her hair, she explained to her father when eventually she stopped crying.

"Where was the teacher?" Sam demanded.

"Looking out the window. She is an ugly old woman with a mustache, and the girls took her scissors to do this and she didn't tell them not to."

"And your clothes? They don't look as if they were cut with scissors."

"The boys tore my clothes. Outside while I was waiting for Fat Cheeks to come."

Mei Lin was not again sent to the free public school, and the matter of her American schooling was dropped. Mei-hua and Ah Chee thought the Lord Samuel had forgotten all about the insane notion that the child should be sent out of the house to be educated, particularly since Mei-hua was herself instructing her daughter in reading and writing Mandarin, playing the *gu zheng*, and skills such as embroidery, which Mei-hua had acquired because the Lord Samuel had insisted upon it when he was preparing her to be his supreme lady *tai-tai*. As for whose *tai-tai* Mei Lin would be, that was now a matter for the gods. Both Mei-hua and Ah Chee would burn so much incense that when the time was right a proper husband would be found. Despite the fact that the girl would have big ugly feet. The right man would look at her exquisite eyes and not notice her feet. Much incense. Much incense.

The day in 1843 when Ah Chee returned home to the smell of white smoke in the downstairs hall and the bins of unemptied rubbish by the door, she was not expecting to have to deal again with this very much too crazy idea about going out of the house to school. She let herself into the rooms on the top floor and stopped when she saw Mei-hua and Mei Lin holding each other and rocking back and forth and crying. "What happened? What? What? Quick tell this old woman before my heart stops. What?"

It was Mei Lin who managed to stop crying long enough to explain that her father had told them that the next day she was to be taken to another school. "Different he says. Taught by people who will not stand and look out the window if other children are mean to me. But," she added, beginning again to wail, "I do not believe it."

"She will be fine, Cousin Carolina. I am quite sure little Ceci does not have the croup, only an ordinary cough associated with her cold."

"Thank you, Cousin Nick. It was good of you to come. You always make me feel much better."

"That, my dear, is what doctors are supposed to do."

Carolina laughed. "Years ago you told me you had no skill with bedside manners. Look how you underestimated yourself."

"Not really. I merely get by. It's Dr. Klein who has all the ladies of Crosby Street and points north lined up to consult him."

"How is he? And his growing family?"

Ben had married Bella Markus a few years earlier. Nick had been invited to the wedding and found it extraordinary—singing and clapping even during the ceremony. "Ben and Bella are both splendid. Two children already. I was invited to dinner recently and told that another was—" He broke off when he saw her head swivel toward the parlor door.

"Excuse me." Carolina had heard no bell and no sound of Dorothy coming up from downstairs, but the front door had opened and closed. Apart from her, only Samuel had a key. She went quickly to open the door of the parlor. Her husband was standing in the hall, holding a small valise. "Samuel, I thought it must be you. Cousin Nicholas is here."

"Is he? Oddly, I don't find that a surprise."

She flushed and hated herself for it. "He came to see Ceci. She has not been well."

Nick observed the exchange from the parlor. There was not just tension between them, he thought, there was a palpable animosity. "She has a bad cold and a cough, Cousin Samuel," he said. "Cousin Carolina feared the croup, but it is nothing so dire."

"I am glad to hear it. And I suppose I should thank you for coming all the way from Crosby Street to tell my wife such good news. Particularly since there are perfectly competent doctors closer by."

"Naturally, Samuel, I prefer someone I know and whom Ceci knows. I—"

Sam cut her off with a gesture. "I've some things to get upstairs. Don't let me interrupt your consultation."

He started up the stairs. Carolina turned back to Nick. "I'm sorry. He must be tired. I'm sure he wouldn't—"

"There's no need, my dear. Not with me."

The soft words were almost her undoing. Carolina turned her head, and when Nick said he would be going, she simply nodded. "I've left you a salve to rub on Ceci's chest three times daily, and a tonic," he said. "She's to have a spoonful morning and night. Let me know if it's doing her any good and I'll arrange for more."

"Thank you, Nick."

He pressed her hand and left.

❧

Surely whatever Samuel wanted from the upper floors of the house would be in his bedroom, the one across from hers, though he slept in it seldom and as far as she knew there were few of his personal belongings there. When Carolina heard his voice coming from Ceci's room, her heart lifted a bit. He must have gone in to see how the child was feeling. Carolina, keenly aware that for all practical purposes her children had no father, hurried in to see if she could contribute anything to better relations between Samuel and his daughter.

"Wasn't it good of your papa to come and see you since you're ill, Ceci? You must thank him properly and—" She broke off when she saw her husband standing in front of the cupboard containing Ceci's dresses and pulling them out one after the other. "What are you doing?"

"I'm taking these four frocks." Ceci was over a year younger than Mei Lin but bigger and taller. Ah Chee would have no difficulty altering the clothes. "What are the appropriate undergarments?" And when neither the girl nor Carolina answered, "Petticoats, I imagine. Chemises as well. Where are they? In this chest?"

"Papa, that blue frock is my favorite. Will you bring it back?"

"No. What do you wear beneath it? Tell me quickly, please."

Ceci's lower lip began to tremble. Carolina sat beside her on the bed and pulled the girl close. "It doesn't matter, darling. We'll have another blue frock made. I saw some lovely material in one of the shops. As soon as you're well, we'll—Not that drawer." Samuel had started pulling out all the chest drawers and rifling through them. Ceci was a fastidious child, and all this rummaging through her things was bound to upset her. "Those are nightclothes," Carolina said quietly. "Petticoats and chemises are indeed what you want. They're in the drawer below." She held Ceci close all the while, feeling her grow hotter by the moment. The child's fever was rising again. Let him take what he came for and get out.

Sam made a pile of the things he wanted, then began methodically putting them in the valise. "Shoes," he said suddenly. "I suppose I should take shoes as well." Mei Lin wore silk slippers in the house, straw-topped wooden clogs made by one of the lodgers on the few occasions she went outside. There were two pairs of boots with tiny buttons and patent leather dress shoes with a ribbon tie in the cupboard. He gathered up all three pairs. Ceci wailed.

"Don't cry, Ceci," Carolina said more sharply than she intended, as if it were the child making her feel this lump of rage that started somewhere in her stomach and spread fire throughout all the rest of her. "Don't." She stood up and went to stand beside the door to the little girl's room. "There is nothing in that valise worth one of your tears. Your grandfather will see to it that you have new shoes. I promise."

Sam started to leave, then paused and looked directly at his wife for the first time. "Yes," he said. "I'm sure he will. Or perhaps they will be supplied by . . . what does she call him? Uncle Nicholas perhaps? That's the custom among women who take lovers, or so I'm told."

"How dare you." She could not prevent the words, not even though she knew her six-year-old child was listening. She had suppressed too much for too long. "How dare you come here and speak to me like this? How dare you take the clothes of your lawful child for the bastard of your concubine? That's what she's called among the heathen orientals, isn't it? I've made it my business to learn about such things. A concubine is the name for a Chinese whore, is it not?"

"Not precisely," Sam said quietly, "they are somewhat different. But in this instance it will do. Except that you've got one thing wrong, Carolina. She is my wife. You are and always have been the concubine."

Les Religieuses du Sacré-Coeur du Jésus, The Religious of the Sacred Heart, came into existence in secret in 1800, in a France still shuddering from the effects of the Reign of Terror, which after the Revolution of

1789 had lopped off the heads of most of the ruling class and until the coming of Napoleon had left the country in the control of *les citoyens*, the great unwashed. The role of these women Religious of the Sacred Heart, in parallel with that of the Society of Jesus, the Jesuits, would be to educate to the highest Christian standards what remained of the children of the better classes. Thus, transformed by virtue, the higher-born might return to the power that was theirs by right. *Les Religieuses du Sacré-Coeur de Jésus* were, in other words, founded to educate the girls who would become the women who would rock the cradles of those who would rule the world. At least the Catholic world.

The Madams of the Sacred Heart was how the nuns were known in English, in 1840 when they arrived in New York City, having established their first American convents in Saint Louis and New Orleans. They came at the invitation of New York's recently installed third bishop, John Hughes, the first Irishman to hold the office. The Madam sent to take charge of the society's first convent in the east, a large house on the corner of Mulberry and Houston streets given to the congregation by the bishop, was a woman her community privately called, *la formidable*. She was Mother Aloysia Hardey, born in Piscataway, Maryland, and herself educated by the Madams in Louisiana.

"We have a separate school for the poor, Mr. Devrey," Mother Hardey said. "Such children do not board here at the convent but come to lessons a few hours every day. Perhaps your ward would be better off being educated in that manner."

"She is, as you say, madam, my ward. She is therefore not poor." Sam cast a quick glance at Mei Lin sitting in the chair by the door to which she had been assigned. It seemed that Ah Chee had altered the blue frock perfectly well, and he had himself tied the child's long, straight black hair back with a blue ribbon. "Does she look poor to you?"

"It is not, perhaps, Mr. Devrey, a matter of appearance." Appearance, she knew, was superficial. Nonetheless, this child had most peculiar eyes. Not only an extraordinary shape, but a quite remarkably intense gray-blue, while her skin was the color of pale honey. Some might find her beautiful. No one would say she was not distinctive.

"If not her appearance, what then?" Samuel asked. "Why should you be reluctant to take her into your school?"

"I simply meant . . . Your ward is unusual looking, Mr. Devrey. Was she born here in America?"

"Eight years ago, right here in the city of New York, madam." She'd told him she was to be addressed as Mother, but that seemed to him as preposterous as her outfit. She wore a long black woolen dress that swathed her from neck to ankles; a long black veil, and a stiffly pleated white ruff that encircled her face. "I suspect," he said, "here in New York many people would think you unusual-looking as well."

Mother Hardey permitted herself a small smile. "I grant you are correct in that, Mr. Devrey. Nonetheless, I must be concerned for the good of all our students at the convent, as well as the best thing for your ward. Is she intelligent?"

"Very." He toyed with the notion of mentioning that the child was fluent in Mandarin as well as English.

"Nonetheless, I do think that in your ward's best interests, Mr. Devrey, we—"

"She is, as you say, madam, my ward, and it is therefore my responsibility to decide what is best for her."

"There are other schools, Mr. Devrey. And you are not, as you tell me, a Catholic. Nor is the child."

"In other schools there is not, I think, such a high standard of discipline. A child who is, as you yourself point out, different, is liable to be teased. Even persecuted."

Aloysia Hardey was not the sort of woman to let such a statement pass without saying what she thought of such behavior. "No one, absolutely no one, will be treated so under this roof, Mr. Devrey. You can be entirely certain of that. Persecution of any sort would never be tolerated."

"So I believe." Sam's eyes had been opened to the possibility this new school presented by the story he'd heard from a business acquaintance, a wealthy Portuguese who had been willing to bring his family from Lisbon only now that he could send his three daughters to an appropriate Catholic school. The little girls lived five days a week with the nuns, the

Portuguese said, where they were taught to the highest possible standard and kept under the strictest imaginable discipline, enforced by women from the finest possible backgrounds and the most prominent families, women who, once they gave themselves to God, never left their convent. *Pure hearts and iron wills, Senhor Devrey. That is how we Catholics will eventually take over. We shall start with our wives and daughters.* He'd laughed when he said it, though Sam had no doubt the man meant every word. "I have brought my ward here precisely because of that guarantee of control."

"But she is not a Catholic," the nun repeated.

"Then make her one if it suits you." Sam reached into the inside pocket of his frock coat. "I was told the tuition is one hundred dollars per term. This will cover the first three terms." He put the check on the table between them and saw the nun examine it in a darting glance before once more looking straight at him. "There's a bit extra," Sam said. "A contribution to your good works. Perhaps you can use it for that school for the poor you mentioned."

"All our students wear uniforms," Mother Hardey said. The check for a thousand dollars had already disappeared into the drawer of her desk. "They are to be made at Mr. Stewart's emporium on Broadway. No private dressmakers are allowed. That way we are assured there will be no deviations. Here at the Convent of the Sacred Heart, Mr. Devrey, we frown on deviation."

"He said that I was his concubine and she was his wife, Papa. To my face and in Ceci's hearing."

"My dear, I—"

"It's all right, Papa." Carolina stood up and gathered her things. "I know very well you will not support me in divorcing Samuel. You have repeatedly made that clear. I only think you should be aware that since in his opinion I am a whore"—she did not stop, even though she saw him wince—"it follows that he considers your grandchildren to be bastards. That seems to me important information for you to have."

"You are right and I will not forget," Wilbur said quietly. "Now where are you rushing off to? Stay a while. Take a meal with me."

"Thank you, but I can't. I'm meeting Dr. Turner." The conversation with Samuel had freed her. She would choose her own company and worry less about what anyone might think, but she was equally determined that she would never seem to be hiding around shadowy corners or behind half-closed doors. "Ceci is almost entirely recovered, but Cousin Nicholas believes I should be dosing her regularly with a restorative tonic. I'm to collect it."

Not the worst excuse he'd ever heard, but Wilbur Randolf knew that if Nick Turner prescribed a tonic for Ceci there was no real need for Carolina to collect it in person. Besides, he'd been a number of times at Carolina's when Nick was present. There were always good excuses for those visits as well, but Wilbur had seen the way the man looked at his daughter. "As you wish, but be careful, my dear. Society does not afford women the liberties it allows men. People can be very cruel."

Indeed. And she had never told him about the riding crop. "I know that, Papa. You need have no concern on that score."

It was not entirely true that she had a rendezvous with Nick. Only that she hoped she had. *I shall be at Mr. Stewart's dry goods store,* Carolina's note had said, giving the date and the time. *Perhaps you might meet me there, and bring another bottle of that tonic that seems to be doing Ceci so much good.*

She had specified the department dealing in cambric, easy to find since one of the things that made this the most popular store in the town was that it was a model of orderliness. The different fabrics—satins and laces and silks as well as sturdy wools and gabardines—were all on display, with the prices fixed and clearly marked. Carolina Devrey was not the only New York lady relieved not to have to haggle over the cost of what she wished to purchase. No wonder there was talk of Mr. Stewart opening an even bigger store.

Cambric was on the second floor in the rear; it was being offered at what was tagged as a greatly reduced price, two dollars and seventy-five cents per yard. Quite economical, but not exactly the right shade of blue. She had promised Ceci a dress the same color as the one that had been taken, though they had agreed that it would be made to a new style pictured just this month in *Godey's Lady's Book*. The publication was issued in distant Philadelphia, but arrived by mail every month. Carolina knew three dollars an issue to be an extravagance, but it was such a pleasure. Particularly now that Ceci was old enough to enjoy it with her.

"Hello. I like that color," Nick pointed to a golden bronze. "It reminds me of the gown you were wearing the first time I saw you."

He could always make her blush. "Thank you for meeting me, Cousin Nick. I hope it wasn't inconvenient."

"Did you for one moment doubt that I would come?"

"I hoped you would," she said softly. She had removed a glove the better to test the drape of the fabric, and her bare hand lay on the display counter. Nick covered it with his own. Carolina allowed a few seconds to pass, then snatched hers away. "I'm shopping for Ceci," she said, the words coming quickly, as if they were of enormous importance. "She wants a particular shade of blue, and there's nothing exactly like it here. I think perhaps I must buy velvet or taffeta instead."

"Very well. Lead the way to the velvets and taffetas, milady. I have no doubt you know exactly where they are." He offered his arm with exaggerated politeness.

"Such fabrics are dearer, I'm afraid; they will be downstairs on the first floor. Mr. Stewart always tempts you with his best goods before you must exert yourself to climb to the floors above." She started for the broad stairs in the center of the selling floor, then stopped abruptly.

Nick followed her glance.

One of the Chinamen stood a few feet away beside a sign that proclaimed school uniforms would be made to the precise specifications of the particular institution. There was a little girl with him. She was dressed in dark green calico and being measured by a shop assistant. The child stood very still, arms akimbo, directly facing them.

"That's her, isn't it?" Carolina spoke in something less than a whisper, but Nick heard each word. "Samuel's . . . That's her."

"I think so, yes." Actually Nick had no doubt. The eyes were the same remarkable color as those of her mother. The same shape as well, though her skin was a lighter shade of gold, and while delicate boned, she was already almost as tall as the man standing beside her. Long black hair as well. Quite lovely.

"That's Ceci's dress." Carolina almost hissed the words. "She's wearing Ceci's boots as well."

All the color had drained from her face. Nick drew her arm further through his, gripping it with so much firmness that he was almost carrying her. "Let's go. You don't want a scene, Carolina. Not here."

She said nothing, just took another long look at the child, who looked back implacably. As if she were accustomed to being stared at, Nick thought. Finally after one last glance over her shoulder, Carolina allowed him to lead her from the store.

"It's not the child's fault, Carolina. She didn't ask to be born."

"You're right, of course. I know that. But—" She broke off and took another sip of wine. Nick had insisted on bringing her to Delmonico's. Very grand, very elegant. She had wanted to come for years and never thought it likely she would have the opportunity. Now she was too upset to appreciate it. "You know the whole story, don't you?" she asked him suddenly. "The night of the fire Samuel said, 'Why have you brought her here?' He wasn't surprised to see you. Only me. I've always puzzled about that. I'm sure you know more than I do."

Nick was past dissembling. "Yes, I expect I do. Drink your consommé, my dear. It will revive you." She had allowed him to order for them both, and he'd thought a nourishing broth a wise idea. "It's uncommonly delicious, Carolina. You must try it."

"I shall, I promise. But you must not change the subject. Tell me what you know, Nick. It's past time I should have all the details."

He shook his head. "I'm a doctor, Carolina. I owe my patients confidentiality. You know that."

"I know that Samuel Devrey has lied to me and cheated me, apparently from the first day of our marriage." She stopped speaking long enough to lift the two-handled cup of soup and drink most of it, though she tasted nothing. When she put it down, her hands were again trembling, though she'd thought she had regained her calm. "Shall I tell you what my husband said to me last week? Just after you left. Had you stayed a few minutes more I've no doubt he would have said the same thing in your hearing. Lord knows, he has no thought of protecting me or his children."

"Carolina, you need not tell me anything."

"No. I want you know. My husband told me she—the woman we saw that night—Samuel said she is his wife. I, he said, am his . . . his concubine." If she'd any tears left she might have shed them now but she simply sat, white-faced and numb with something that was either pain or shock, though she wasn't sure which.

"Whatever else," Nick said, "that's not true. You are his wife." The child's mother had been his patient; Sam Devrey never was.

"How do you know? How can I know?"

"It's what I thought as well originally," Nick said. "But whatever else Devrey may be, he's not a bigamist. Not by the laws of the United States at any rate."

"How can you possibly know?"

"Because he told me." They had not been in a sickroom when Devrey described the way things were between him and the Chinese girl, and under the circumstances, Nick's promise of discretion seemed to have run its limits. "He said the girl had been given to him in some sort of Chinese ceremony. He married you in St. Paul's. No pagan rite would supercede that."

Carolina sat for a moment, assimilating his words. "You're sure?" she asked at last. "Absolutely sure?"

"Absolutely. I give you my word that is exactly what he said."

"Thank you. I have been grieving as much as anything over the fact that my children might not be legitimate. You have given me a great deal of peace of mind."

He wasn't a lawyer and he wasn't as sure as he would like to be that what he'd told her, though literally true, was accurate. Civil marriages were, after all, legal in New York. But looking at her, seeing the color begin to return to her cheeks and the way she smiled at him, Nick didn't give a damn.

Chapter Twenty-four

"IT'S CALLED LIFE insurance, dearest." Wilbur Randolf's voice was exceptionally subdued. He obviously did not enjoy the discussion, though it was he who had raised the topic.

Jenny Worthington stared at the document covered in the finest sort of print. No way she could read anything but the heading—Mutual Life Insurance Company—not these days, not without her spectacles, and she never put those on in front of Wilbur. "Life insurance? Wilbur, I quite understand insuring against a ship sinking or not sinking or a fire happening or not happening. But death, that is the one sure thing in the world for us all. What kind of a fool would offer insurance against it?"

"Indeed the company must eventually pay, but they are gambling on the possibility that before they do, you will have paid more in premiums than they pay out in settlement. Actually, it's a clever idea. Particularly if enough people can be persuaded to purchase the policies. I'm surprised they haven't been offered before now."

"But what earthly good is the settlement to do you if you must be dead to collect?"

"It's not done for yourself." Wilbur took her hand. "You name a loved one as beneficiary. You do it for those you care most deeply about, to see them right after you're gone." That was the answer being given to the preachers who insisted that such insurance was, like so much else in modern life, contrary to the law of God. Wasn't prudence a virtue? Could it be right to leave those for whom one cared in life to the mercy of cold charity after one died? "I'm not getting any younger, Jenny dear."

That's what was on his mind, Jenny knew. Those weak spells he'd been having of late, the times when he said his heart seemed to race ahead of his ability to breathe. "And you're quite sure this is genuine?"

"Quite sure. You are named as beneficiary of this policy, Jenny. I always told you I would provide for you, my dear. You've this house free and clear and in your name, and when I die you will receive five thousand dollars. It will all be quite discreet and no one to say you nay. Now put this policy away and don't think about it again until you must."

She could hardly think of anything else. Not while they were up in the bedroom and Wilbur was doing his business and she was, by force of long habit, making the accustomed noises and wriggling her hips in the expected manner, and not afterwards while they ate one of her delicious cold suppers in the yellow and white dining room that was now heated by steam from a coal furnace in the basement, so she'd been able to wall over all the first-floor fireplaces, though they were still required for the upper stories. Particularly not when she kissed him farewell before opening the door and allowing Wilbur Randolf to go happy and satisfied and with an apparently clear conscience into the pleasant crispness of the October late evening.

Five thousand dollars. Always presuming it was actually paid out and didn't turn out to be only another way of taking money from fools who knew no better. Though heaven knows, when it came to business, Wilbur Randolf was no fool. Still, five thousand dollars when he was worth a hundred times that. Maybe a thousand times that. And all so he wouldn't have to put her name in his will and embarrass his precious Carolina. Whose husband, as Jenny had made it her business to know, had virtually moved out of that fancy Fourteenth Street house her father had given her—far grander than this place on Bleecker Street—because

Carolina's husband preferred to live with his mistress on, God help us, Cherry Street. Five thousand measly dollars.

Some weeks later when the knock on the door came, she was ready for it.

"Mrs. Worthington, I believe?"

"You believe correctly, Mr. Devrey. Come right in."

Sam was only slightly startled that she knew his name.

"I am told it is you who has set a Mr. Fearless Flannagan to watching me," he said over tea in her pleasant parlor, "and I believe it. But so there can be no misunderstanding between us, I would appreciate your confirmation."

Jenny refilled his cup, congratulating herself on having the prescience to use her best silver teapot. She had acted on the assumption that he was not here to say something about propriety and his children, at least those living up the town with Carolina, or to chide her for being Wilbur's mistress, much less for running a part-time bordello. He was here as an ally, though of what sort she had yet to discover. "A Mr. Flannagan watching you, Mr. Devrey? Whatever for?"

"Let neither of us waste the other's time, Mrs. Worthington."

"Very well. I know a Mr. James Michael Flannagan, Mr. Devrey. Is that the man of whom you speak?"

"I suppose it is." Sam took out his pocket watch and examined it. "I remind you that time, Mrs. Worthington, is worth money. In less than an hour, for example, you must turn over this parlor to the first of your expected customers."

"The customers of my lodgers, Mr. Devrey. Nothing to do with me." He opened his mouth to say more, and Jenny knew she had pushed him as far as she dared. "Very well," she said before he could speak. "I hired Mr. Flannagan, yes."

"Why?"

"Now it's you who is wasting time. You know why. I have an alliance with the father of your wife. The wife on Fourteenth Street," she added, and had the pleasure of seeing him wince. "An alliance that has now lasted quite a good few years but that affords me no legal protection and nothing to assure me a comfortable old age. I endeavor to find advantages, Mr. Devrey. I accumulate them and set them aside. Like a nest egg, you might say."

"I take it, Mrs. Worthington, that I am part of your nest egg."

"In a manner of speaking, Mr. Devrey." She shrugged. "Though now you know about Mr. Flannagan, perhaps a less important part. Might I ask how you found out?"

"Do you really need to ask?"

"Money," she said.

"Fifty dollars, to be precise. You came at a steep price, Mrs. Worthington. So I ask again, what value do you suppose I shall be to you?"

"To be frank, Mr. Devrey, I've never been exactly sure. As I said, I am simply accumulating opportunities. And I expect that your arrival rather means there is to be one."

Sam placed his spoon across the top of his cup in that old-fashioned gesture of gentility that indicated he wanted no more tea and sat back, tenting his fingers, and looked at her over them. She had been a good-looking woman once. Now her jaw sagged and face powder had collected in a pair of wrinkles either side of her nose. "Perhaps, Mrs. Worthington. Tell me, please, since I see very little of him of late, how is my father-in-law's health?"

He knew he was being a bit obvious, but there was no help for it. Time, Sam had lately come to realize, was running out.

The American Institute, headquarters of marine architecture, had recently put on display a small-scale ship that was eerily similar to the design he'd been playing with for half a dozen years. Her bow was sharply angled to cut through the water, and the stern was rounded. Sam saw at once what was gained by such a design. The water displaced by the sharp and narrow front of the vessel would slide easily past its broader curvaceous rear; the conventional wisdom of cod's head and mackerel's tail was reversed. Such a craft, Sam knew, would be amazingly fast, and thanks to the breadth of beam, it could carry as much as any merchant craft presently afloat. Perhaps more.

He spent a good many hours at the institute, studying the new design, watching others come in and out to gaze and to comment, listening to talk of how it would be impossible to plough through the fifty-foot waves off Cape Horn in such a vessel. Damn fool idea most of his competitors said. *Swamped for sure, soon as those waves come crashing over the decks. Lose all the crew and all the profit, for an absolute certainty. Agree, don't you, Devrey? Man of your experience, you've got to see that. A damn fool idea.* Sam always indicated that he was in complete accord.

All the while his gut was roiling with the certain knowledge that the puzzle had been solved and that sooner rather than later someone was going to build such a ship and become as rich as Astor as a result. Rich enough to buy the old bastard out of Devrey's all together. Or maybe Astor himself would become convinced the new ship design was brilliant, despite what Sam Devrey said to put him off the scent. What then? Sam Devrey's single hope of reclaiming what was rightfully his would be gone.

In a burst of feverish activity Sam collaborated with Danny Parker to make a model similar to that on display at the Institute, and took it back to thirty-seven Cherry Street, the house next door to Mei-hua's, to the tank, where sometimes in these last few months he had taken to smoking the occasional pipeful of opium to relax himself and clear his mind. The stuff had made its appearance on Cherry Street a few months back, with the coming of a new man they called Lee Big Belly. The opium trade was booming now that the British had crushed the Chinese government's resistance. No point, Sam had decided, in his attempting to resist a small amount of white smoke winding up here. If nothing else it insured the ability of Big Belly and a couple of the other newcomers to pay their rent. They offered the Lord Samuel the occasional small wad, enough for one pipeful, as a courtesy. He would be churlish to refuse.

After some weeks of smoking a bit of opium and simulating high waves in his tank, Sam became certain that it was possible to find ways to navigate through them without the ship being swamped. The key was the length of the vessel. She must be long enough to move at the greatest possible speed, since he was convinced that length did contribute to speed. Then, with a first-rate captain, she would survive rounding the Horn. At least in theory.

Danny would have none of it. "Steam," he muttered. "That's what's coming. They've already got engines that can take a packet cross the Atlantic. Everybody said that wouldn't happen neither, but it did." He looked bleak when he said it; Danny Parker was a man who had been born to the glories of sail.

"Not for the China trade," Sam insisted. "They'd need to tow a second ship just to carry all the coal. It's halfway round the world, Danny. All the way if you consider the return journey." But sweet Christ, the profits for the making of each such journey. These days it wasn't only the traditional Canton trade. The peace treaty that ceded Hong Kong to the British had opened up the ports of Amoy, Fuchow, Ninghsien, and Shanghai, and the British couldn't keep the Americans out. Better still, these days both here and in England the rich wanted not just China's tea and silks but her cinnamon and porcelain, her furniture, even her firecrackers. "Ships like this," Sam said, pointing to the model, "they're the future, Danny. Don't you want to be part of it?"

"Aye, I do. But I have to be paid first. Can't afford the future otherwise."

The future, Sam realized as he sat drinking tea in Jenny Worthington's front parlor, was apparently also the problem most worrying her. "My father-in-law's health," Sam repeated. "Are you concerned?"

"Well, to tell the truth," Jenny said, "it does worry me a bit. Care deeply for Mr. Wilbur Randolf I do. And sometimes he seems to me quite poorly."

"I've wanted to visit before now, Cousin Manon—if I may still call you that—but I was told that you'd been spirited away to Maryland to make what was called your novitiate and that no gentlemen visitors, not even cousins, would be allowed."

"I am officially Sister Marie Manon, since they could find no proper saint who corresponded to my odd French Protestant name. But everyone calls me simply Sister Manon. And indeed, after forcing me to become a Catholic, they locked up all of us novices in a great brick fortress and fed us bread and water until we learned to do as we were told."

"You're joking, aren't you?"

"Of course I'm joking. Anything to make you look less like a startled rabbit and more like your old self. As for me, I know I look peculiar." She gestured to her ruffled black cap and to the unfashionable long black dress and short black cape. "But I am just as I always was. And so happy to see you, dear Cousin Nicholas. When I heard I was to be sent back to New York to St. Patrick's Orphan Asylum, it was one of the many things for which I thanked God. That I would be able to see you again and know how you've fared."

"As you can see, I've fared well. I'm a fortunate man. The practice thrives."

"And Dr. Klein? I hope he is well."

"Fighting fit. Ben and his Bella have three children, two girls and a boy, and a fourth on the way. There was a set of twins as well, also boys, but they lived only a short time—" Nick caught himself. "Manon, forgive me. That was thoughtless."

"No, it was not. I don't grieve so anymore, Nicholas. At least not in the same way. Now what about painless surgery? Surely you're well placed to do more testing of sulfuric ether."

Nick shook his head. "We don't touch the stuff. We promised Samson Simson we wouldn't, because so many see it as against the law of God. Simson says that the Jews probably wouldn't be of that opinion. But"—he shrugged—"I can understand them not wanting more criticism."

"From Catholics as well as Protestants, I must say," Manon said briskly. "We're just as prejudiced about the Jews. More so, perhaps." She was pleating and unpleating the skirt of her habit in a nervous gesture for which the novice mistress had many times reprimanded her. "Tell me, Nicholas, do you hear any talk of any kind of dispensary? The sort of thing I had in mind before."

"There's still nothing like it in New York, though we're to have something new. The Association for Improving the Condition of the Poor."

"So I've heard."

"Judging by your tone, you don't approve of it. I thought you would."

"It's more of the same, Nicholas. Rich bankers and businessmen who say they want to help the deserving poor but then find so few of them deserving. And they continue to insist that the reasons for poverty are to be found in the paupers themselves. If they would only—"

"—adopt moral habits and pull themselves up by their bootstraps," he finished for her. "Their lot would improve. Yes, I know what you mean."

"And you know it isn't true, don't you? It's the same businessmen and bankers that keep the poor from having any opportunity to make a decent life."

"My dear Manon, I do believe the Catholics have made you a socialist."

Her burst of laughter sounded just like the old days. "If you only knew, Nicholas, how far that is from the truth. The Holy Father and the bishops are appalled by socialism. No, it's simply a matter of following Our Lord's instruction to feed the hungry and clothe the naked."

"I'm sure Protestants want to do that as well."

"Yes," she admitted. "I know they do. It's which poor and which naked, and how to go about it. That's where the quarrel lies."

"Manon, why couldn't your Sisters of Charity establish such a dispensary as you envision? I remember your telling me how wonderful they were during the cholera epidemic back in '32. It would seem a natural progression."

She smiled. "Yes, it would. Nothing of the sort is yet planned, Nicholas, but you have discovered my secret. I intend to pray it into being. Now tell me what you do in your practice, since you abstain from painless surgery. Infected fingers and wheezing coughs and swooning ladies and runny-nosed children?"

"All of that."

"And it's to your liking?"

Nick looked sheepish. "You know me too well, Cousin—Sister Manon. Ben Klein and I do see such patients. A great many of them, since we must eat and pay our bills. But there is also the laboratory. It is the challenge that keeps our minds active."

"Indeed. Nicholas, where on earth do you get cadavers on which to experiment?"

She had lost none of her directness, he liked that. He'd never felt it necessary to understand her religious impulse, that was no business of his. But the lively mind and the clear thinking, he'd have hated to see that disciplined out of her. "There's less need of cadavers for the work we're doing now," he said, being as forthright as she had been. "The interior of a body is no longer the mystery it once was. There's a large amount of literature on the subject these days. As for Ben and I, what we're studying is diseased tissue, the flesh around a suppurating boil or an inflamed toe. That's the sort of thing we cut away any number of times in the ordinary way of seeing patients." He would not tell her of their other source of human tissue: they had a steady supply of the foreskins of infant males since Ben had been inspired to make private arrangements with the *mohels*, the providers of the Jews' ritual circumcision. "You know my theory of germs," he said instead, "and their importance in the spread of disease. I'm learning more about germs every day."

"And now, with running water just about everywhere in the city, you can truly insist on all the hand washing you recommend."

"I can. Here too, I hope. You've running water now, haven't you?"

"Spigots in three places in this building and two next door," Manon said with a touch of wonder. "I caught a glimpse of some of the overhead construction when we arrived. They tell me the aqueduct runs forty miles from the Croton River and finishes at a reservoir in the woods at Eighty-sixth Street."

"Forty-one miles," Nick corrected. "And the Eighty-sixth Street reservoir isn't the end of the chain, it's only a holding tank. The distribution reservoir's nearer, though still a fair distance from the city, at Forty-second Street and Fifth Avenue. From there Croton water is fed into a series of underground pipes, and—I can see the glaze of boredom in your eyes, dear Manon. Suffice to say the town's finally got running water. It's even in parts of the Five Points, you'll be happy to know."

"I am."

"And there's no more Night Watch, you know. They've abolished all the marshals as well."

Manon raised her eyebrows. "How wonderful that New York has become the Garden of Eden and there is no more crime."

"More crime than ever," Nick said cheerfully. "But now we have police, though the law says we're never to have more than eight hundred of them. Everyone calls them coppers, because of their star-shaped badges. Fancy blue uniforms as well. Makes them look like butlers if you ask me."

"And do they keep the peace?" Manon asked.

"Well enough, as long as there's not real trouble. It's still the militia of the Twenty-seventh they call out to break up the riots."

"Do you know the French expression *Plus ça change?*"

"*. . . plus c'est la même chose,*" Nick said. "The more things change, the more they're the same. Yes, exactly." He paused. "I wasn't sure I should mention it, but I saw your Miss Bellingham not long ago."

"Whyever not mention it? Where did you see her?"

"I didn't want to upset you. She was in a tavern."

"A tavern! Addie Bellingham? I don't believe it."

"It's true. The Crowing Cock on Broome Street. It's not far from the office and I go there for a bit of supper sometimes."

"Nicholas, for a woman to go to a tavern. She's not . . . I mean, Addie wouldn't have fallen to the point of . . ."

He chuckled. "I'm teasing you, dear Manon, which is very bad of me, especially now you're a nun. She was indeed in the Crowing Cock, but her purpose was entirely moral. Apparently Miss Bellingham is now an active member of the American Tract Society."

"The people who go about distributing pamphlets with excerpts from the Bible?"

"Exactly. Miss Bellingham and another woman came in and gave everyone a tract, then wished us the blessing of God and left."

"Do you think she recognized you?"

"I don't know. She didn't let on if she did. In any event, I refrained from asking her about a missing diamond. Though the thought crossed my mind."

Manon glanced at the clock on the wall. Only five minutes of the half-hour visit left. She had been a Sister of Charity for four years—they'd made her wait a year after she became a Catholic before she could officially enter the congregation—and she no longer chafed under such restrictions. "We've only a little time left, Nicholas. Tell me about Carolina. You do still see her occasionally?"

He flushed, looked away, then looked straight at her. And knew from her expression, however fleeting, that she had seen his reaction and knew a great deal, probably everything, without his having said a word. "I do. Occasionally. Carolina is as lovely and as charming as ever. But she has much to bear."

"Samuel."

"Yes. He is no husband to her and no father to her children."

She had thought to ask him if there was any woman in his life, any chance he might marry, as she'd been urging him to do for years. Now she did not waste her breath. "She is nonetheless his wife," she said.

"I know, but—"

Somewhere a bell rang. Manon—Sister Marie Manon, as she truly was now—instantly rose to her feet. "It is time for prayers. I must go. Thank you for coming, dear Cousin Nicholas. I look forward to another visit whenever you are able." But first she would ask permission to write to her cousin Carolina Devrey and tell her that the woman now known as Sister Marie Manon was once again in New York and Sisters of Charity were entitled to a monthly visit from any member of the family.

January of 1843. As bitter as hard winter could be, Sam Devrey thought, and not just because of the cold. It was looking to be the winter that strangled his dreams.

Years before he'd gone to Maryland to see the *Ann McKim* in her home port—that was the week when Mei-hua and Ah Chee had bound Mei Lin's feet—and convinced himself that beautiful as she was and fast as she was, the *Ann McKim* was not the answer to steam he'd thought she might be. She simply could not lade enough to be more than a rich man's toy, and there was no way, given the specifics of her design, that Sam could see her adapted to carry more. He'd advised Astor against bidding on her when she went on the block after McKim's death, and it had never worried him that Devrey competitors William Howland and William Aspinwall bought her and brought her to New York. The *Ann McKim* frequently was the first ship back in port with the spring harvest of China tea, but she couldn't carry enough of it to satisfy the market. Plenty of profit left for the merchant ships that came after her, so no grief there.

Now, however, Howland & Aspinwall had commissioned a new ship to be built at one of the town's busiest yards. No chance of keeping anything secret in such a place; her keel was stretched out for all to see. A ship as huge as anything crossing the Atlantic, with a sharply pointed bow and a narrow beam, while aft she was as rounded as an apple. Jacob Astor was among those who went to see the incredible vessel his competitors looked close to launching.

So, Samuel, you think maybe we should commission Mr. Parker to make for us also such a ship? My son thinks we should in shipping not now invest more. I am not so sure. What do you think? William Backhouse Astor, the old man's second son but his true heir, was busy expanding their real estate empire; the shipping business was an afterthought as far as the younger Astor was concerned. *Shipping remains as profitable as ever, Mr. Astor. You've seen our accounts and you know that. But this new ship, the* Rainbow, *is to have masts as tall as a three-story house. She'll founder in the first decent swell. Head straight for the bottom with all who sail on her.* He should, Sam thought, offer himself to P. T. Barnum as an actor, perform at Barnum's American Museum. He sounded, even to his own ears, as if he actually believed what he was saying.

But convinced as he was that these new ships were the future, Sam believed something to be not quite right about Howland & Aspinwall's

Rainbow. The critics of her design were mostly old-timers who couldn't see a thing of genius as it materialized under their noses. Still, as the weeks passed and Sam watched her ribs rise and her hull take shape, he knew in his bones that some part of the puzzle was yet missing. The *Rainbow* was nearly perfect, nearly the ship of his dreaming, but not quite.

As for the two Bills, as Messrs. William Howland and William Aspinwall were known, they backed down in the face of persistent criticism. *Ain't no ship with a pointed nose and a fat ass going to get anywhere on the China run.* The Bills heard the remark once too often, and in that February of 1843 called a temporary halt to the building of the *Rainbow* while they sent to England for the opinion of yet another set of marine architects.

The delay turned out to be little comfort for Sam Devrey. In March A. A. Low & Brothers laid another keel at another yard. Just as long, just as narrow, just as sharp at the bow and broad at the beam, but without the sloping V-shape keel of *Rainbow* and nearly everything else afloat, certainly everything else considered seaworthy for a long and testing ocean journey. The ship of the brothers Low had a flat bottom, and the men who commissioned her had stronger stomachs than Bill Howland and Bill Aspinwall. Hang the criticism, the Lows said, keep building.

"It's the flat bottom, Danny," Sam said. "That's the thing that will make it work." They met in the all but deserted Thirty-fourth Street yard for a Sunday afternoon consultation, the latest in a long series of such meetings. Danny Parker sat calmly smoking his pipe, while Sam Devrey was as agitated as ever the shipwright had seen him. "She's to be called the *Houqua*, named for a Canton merchant who has vowed to fill her stem to stern with the first crop of tea that comes down from the hills of Lumking and Mowfoong. Bring it all home while it's still pristine-fresh and sweet as the day it was picked, before it's had any chance to mold. What do you imagine that will bring at the Exchange?"

"A fair bit, Mr. Devrey. Quite a fair bit."

"A hundred thousand, Danny. Good God, it could be a hundred and fifty. What if I were to offer you a twenty percent interest in the first three cargoes my new ship brought home? Might that influence how much you had to have in ready cash before you started to build?" If he was right, and if Danny took him up on the offer, it meant he'd see no profit for two years, maybe three. But without a new ship, wholly owned by Sam Devrey, the dream was finished. Whatever their owners might think, there was no doubt whatever in Sam's mind that the *Houqua*, probably even the *Rainbow*, would turn the shipping business on its ear. And while Sam might hold him off now, as soon as the results were in, Astor would make his move. He'd have more money to finance the venture than Low or Howland or Aspinwall. Devrey Shipping would triumph, but it would be forever beyond the grasp of the man who bore the Devrey name.

"How long is she to be?" Parker asked.

"The *Houqua*?"

"No, the ship you want me to build for you."

"My calculations say the optimum length would be one hundred and seventy feet stem to stern, and thirty-three across."

The ratio, five times as long as she would be wide, was highly unusual; four to one was the norm. But all Danny said was, "And she's to have one of these flat bottoms?"

"Yes. Concave sides that widen out as they rise above the water line, and below it a bottom as narrow as any keel, but flat, not V-shaped. I promise you, she'll sail closer to the wind than any ship ever built and do it faster and carrying more cargo than either *Rainbow* or *Houqua*, if either of them is ever actually finished and launched."

"And your ship will take more with her to the bottom if she founders."

"True," Sam said. "But if she does not founder she will be the finest thing ever seen afloat, Danny, and there won't be a shipwright in the country who can touch you. You can have two more yards, three more if you want. String them right round the island of Manhattan."

"Aye, maybe. Or I can lose everything."

"I'm not denying it. That's the thing about a dream. You win everything or lose the same amount. What do you say?"

"Pipe dreams," Danny said softly, tamping his pipe, "like clouds, aren't to be relied on. They blow away in a stiff breeze."

It was the first Sam knew of any talk of opium beyond Cherry Street. "This is no pipe dream, Danny. We're talking tea and silks, not opium." Sam gestured at his sketches. "We'll build her right here at the Thirty-fourth Street yard. Keep her under wraps at least until we raise the masts." Impossible after that, but by then it wouldn't matter.

"What about the men? They're bound to talk."

"Some will, but we'll offer a bonus for work that's not just flawless but speedy as well."

The pair of them had been hunched over the drawings for nearly an hour. Sam stood up. His head almost touched the ceiling rafters of the mean little room. The coal stove was losing the battle against the late October winds coming through the chinks in the rough walls. "Tell you what, we'll avoid union help. Only hire the born agains, the ones flocking to these revival meetings all over the town. Get them to swear secrecy on a Bible. What do you say, Danny?" he asked again. "In or out?"

A few seconds went by. "In," Danny Parker said finally. "For thirty percent of the first three cargos. And sixty thousand in cash money before we lay the keel. Thirty-four thousand deferred payment until the sale of the first cargo."

Ninety-four thousand dollars to build one ship. Madness. Except that Sam Devrey knew it was no such thing. "Twenty-five percent of the first three cargos," Sam said. "And two deferred payments, not one. Seventeen thousand each after her first and second voyages."

Danny closed his eyes for a moment, calculating. "Aye," he said when he opened them. "My hand on it, Mr. Devrey."

"And mine, Danny."

"The sixty thousand," Danny said after they shook, "how soon can you get it?"

Work on the *Rainbow* might be stalled until that second opinion came from London, but the *Houqua* was proceeding rapidly. Sam's ship had to sail soon after she did and race her to Canton and back, otherwise it would be many months before there would be a fresh tea crop to bring back and make their fortune. By then he'd be bankrupt.

"Start finding the lumber," Sam said. "You'll have your money in seven days."

God help him, he had to make it be true.

Chapter Twenty-five

THERE WAS ABOUT a teaspoon of the brown powder in a twist of ordinary paper lying on the table in Jenny Worthington's kitchen. And no one in the house except her and Sam Devrey, who had come in through the back door well after dark.

"You're sure he won't taste it?" Jenny asked.

"I'm told he will not. If he does, you simply toss everything out and say the tea must have molded and you're sorry. He will suspect nothing."

Sam had not himself gotten the poison from Taste Bad. He'd left that to Big Belly, after letting the man know that if he intended to continue encouraging white men to participate in the pleasures of smoking opium, he needed to make common cause with a white man who not only spoke proper English but had access to the sort of clientele who could afford the indulgence. Nineteen percent of the weekly earnings to come to the Lord Samuel. And to show good will, a business the lord wanted arranged with Hor Taste Bad. *And if you betray me now or at any time in the future, I'll cut open that fat belly and strangle you with your own guts.*

"When will Randolf be here next?" Sam asked.

"The day after tomorrow." Jenny's voice betrayed nothing of what she was feeling. After all these years . . . Still, a mere five thousand, and that dependent on some insurance company making good on a most peculiar policy. "How do I know you will keep your word? About paying me, I mean."

"You do not," Sam admitted, "and I'm not about to put it in writing. But here's a start." He pushed a wad of bills across the table. "Four thousand now, eight thousand when it's done." That committed the last penny of ready cash he could raise, with nothing on hand to meet Danny Parker's sixty thousand requirement.

His only other resource was the collection of jade. He'd taken them to the best of the numerous auction houses on Pearl Street, telling himself that building his ship was the only thing that mattered. Hell, after he'd gotten back his birthright he'd return to China, take Mei-hua and Mei Lin. It would be a fabulous journey. He'd buy all the jade he could stuff into a valise and bring it back. Build a new house someday, with a special room just to exhibit his collection of Oriental art. Make everything else worthwhile. Once he built a ship that would cross the seas as if she flew with the clouds everything would be wonderful.

The thought had been an enormous comfort while he watched the auctioneer take each piece out of its wrappings and examine it, finally running his exceedingly short and stubby fingers over a grinning monkey carved entirely of rose-pink jade and seated on a white jade throne. Mutton fat jade, the Chinese called the pale stone. The piece was not the rarest or even the finest example of the stuff, but it was exquisitely carved and enormously desirable. Sam had been ecstatic when he found it in Shanghai.

"Not the sort of thing most housewives fancy in their front parlors, Mr. . . . er . . . Smith," the auctioneer had said. "Not at all the popular taste."

"Of course not. These are uncommon, choice pieces. I've been collecting them since I was a lad. They're worth a king's ransom, man. This piece here," Sam quickly unwrapped an exquisitely carved dragon made of the rarest, most translucent pale green jadeite, "is thought to date from the Han Dynasty. That makes it almost two thousand years old. Worth a fortune."

"Only as much of a fortune as someone's willing to pay, Mr. Smith. Not a penny more or less." The auctioneer was re-wrapping the jade monkey in the bit of silk Sam had brought it in. "Dragons and monkeys. Not your average sort of Chinee curio. How much did you say you wanted to place as a reserve?"

"Sixty thousand," Sam said. "For the entire collection. There are thirty-two pieces." He'd held back only two, another Han piece, a carp carved of jadeite and one pink jade Ming Dynasty vase of which he was especially fond. "If we're to sell them separately I would think a reserve of between one and two thousand on each. I'd take your advice on that. Separately or as a single collection, I mean. You're the auction expert. I realize that."

"My advice, Mr. Smith," the auctioneer had finished wrapping the monkey god and pushed it back across the table, "as you're calling yourself today, is that you take these back to wherever they came from. I couldn't promise you'd raise more'n a hundred on the lot."

He'd gone to three more auction houses and got pretty much the same response.

Nothing for it then. The twist of brown paper was his only reliable course of action.

"No season more beautiful than autumn, dear Jenny. Crisp and invigorating. A man can't ask for more." Wilbur Randolf left his hat and his gloves and his walking stick on the table by the front door and kissed the cheek of his mistress. "We should go out for supper later. It's bound to be a glorious evening. Perhaps Delmonico's. You're always saying how much you want to go there."

"Indeed I do, and you always say we must be discreet."

"Fiddle on discretion, that's what I say now. I feel a new man, my love. Entirely new."

"Oh, and may I ask why that is, Wilbur dear?"

"You may not." He accompanied the words with a swift slap on Jenny's generous buttocks. "Suffice to say I have made arrangements that please me. And now I wish to be otherwise pleased."

"Do you now? Just what do you have in mind, you big strong man? Must I be punished for all my naughty ways when you're not here?" He hadn't wanted to spank her for ages, but Jenny Worthington had gotten as far as she had by always knowing what a man desired before he did, and it seemed her instincts were still sound.

"Absolutely," Wilbur was removing his frock coat as he spoke. "Severely punished. Now upstairs with you. And you will bring me the hairbrush yourself."

Afterwards he wouldn't let her be on top, though that too was the way things usually went these days. No, no, he insisted, she must lie yielding beneath him, and he would show her what a raging bull he could still be. He was, too, until he rolled off her and lay panting on the bed, red-faced and sweating.

"Oh my, Wilbur. That was really quite wonderful. I'd no idea you could still—"

"Frankly, neither had I. It's peace of mind that does it, Jenny. But I think we must forego a trip to Delmonico's this evening. I'm not up to it."

"Not to worry, dear heart. I've everything ready for a nice supper. What you need now is a nice cup of tea. Put the life back in you."

Wilbur agreed that it would and that he'd rest up here a bit while she went down and got the food ready. "Ring your little bell when everything's prepared and I'll come down."

Fifteen minutes later Jenny rang and rang and wondered if the tea would be more likely to taste odd if it cooled. "Do come, Wilbur," she called. "Everything is ready."

In the end she went upstairs to get him. Wilbur lay on the bed staring at the ceiling. Not moving and definitely not breathing. But he was smiling.

Jenny left Wilbur where he was and dumped the pot of tea outside where the chamber pots were usually emptied. Then she went upstairs and got Wilbur dressed. Quickly, before he stiffened. That done, she summoned the copper now on duty on her stretch of Bleecker Street. Fearless Flannagan, as it happened—or to put it more accurately, as she had arranged with the alderman who served her district. None of her doing that Fearless had been one of the first men hired by Tammany as soon as they set about forming the new force of city police. But once that happened, well, Jenny had never been one to let an opportunity pass her by.

"I've gotten him dressed, Fearless, but you'll have to get him back to his house in Washington Square. Then go up to Fourteenth Street and tell his daughter he's passed. Better coming from you than from me."

"No doubt about it," she would say later, remembering that smiling corpse, "Wilbur Randolf died a happy man." That was not, however, what she said to Sam Devrey. To him she described a horrific scene of agony and screams. "What I went through," she said, sniffling and dabbing at her eyes. "It's worth every penny, Mr. Devrey. Every penny." That last spoken while she made Sam's eight thousand in ready money, coin and paper in a small leather pouch, disappear down the front of her dress. "It was absolutely dreadful. Now I'm without my dearest friend and support, but you've got what you wanted."

"So have you, Mrs. Worthington," Sam said. "So have you."

"As security, Mr. Belmont, the deeds to two properties. Numbers thirty-seven and thirty-nine Cherry Street." Sam didn't like coming to the Jews for money, but he saw little choice. It had to be someone he knew was not in Astor's pocket.

August Belmont, a Prussian by birth, was the Rothschilds' man. Belmont had arrived in New York in May of 1837 just as the panic broke and the price of everything was tumbling, long before his employers back in Europe knew what was afoot in the New World. Within a day and on his own initiative the twenty-two-year-old Belmont began buying depressed bank notes and securities, using the Rothschilds' credit and gambling on their approval. It came. Fulsome praise, in fact, and a salary of ten thousand a year. These days Belmont, still in his twenties and ensconced in a Wall Street office, traded both for the Rothschilds and in his own name.

"And these properties are worth . . . What do you imagine, Mr. Devrey?"

"Twenty-five, possibly thirty thousand."

"Less, I think." Belmont's English was almost without accent. "Cherry Street is not the best part of town. But you are asking for a loan of sixty thousand. That is correct, no?"

"It is."

Belmont smiled. "I know your reputation as an astute man of business, Mr. Devrey. So I am sure there is other collateral, something you have not thus far mentioned."

Sam was not such a fool as to offer the jade. A man of August Belmont's perspicacity would immediately recognize the real value of the collection. And there was no way he would ever get it back once Belmont had his hands on it. And thanks to Sam's daring and Jenny's greed, he need not pay such a huge price to get what he needed. "There is another house, Mr. Belmont. Number three East Fourteenth Street. At the corner of Fifth Avenue. It is worth considerably more. I will produce the deed to it shortly."

"I see. May I ask why you did not bring it this morning? Along with these others."

"The Fourteenth Street house was a gift—or rather the promise of a gift—to my wife from her father, on the occasion of our marriage. My father-in-law has just died. My wife is his only heir. Therefore, as her husband, I will acquire the deed, which will come into my possession in the next week or two, as soon as the will goes through probate and his affairs are settled. When it does, I will give it to you. But if the venture in which I'm interested is to go profitably forward, I need the cash now."

"And your late father-in-law"—Belmont glanced at the notes Devrey had prepared for him, though Sam had the feeling he already knew much of what they contained—"was Mr. Wilbur Randolf. A landlord as well as the proprietor of a leather goods firm."

"That's a rather modest description of Mr. Randolf's position. He had a virtual lock on the whole of the trade in leather in the town."

"Yes, I believe I have heard that. But you, Mr. Devrey, have no interest in leather, I think. And no particular expertise in the details of your late father-in-law's enterprises."

"That's correct. I'm in shipping."

"Devrey's Shipping. Yes, of course. So the leather business will . . ."

"That remains to be seen. What counts, Mr. Belmont, is that once my wife inherits I will not require additional funds. It is to provide the funds I need now that I'm coming to you."

"On the strength of your . . . or perhaps I should say your wife's expectations."

"My wife. Just as you say. That is a technicality, is it not?"

"It is." Belmont reached for his checkbook. "Twenty-one days, Mr. Devrey. Then payment in full with twenty percent interest."

Extortion. Nonetheless. "Done, Mr. Belmont." Sam relaxed for the first time since he'd walked into the office.

Carolina had known Gordon James all her life. He'd been her father's attorney for as long as she could remember. He always came to the house to deal with Papa's affairs. This day was no different. They sat in Papa's front parlor, the one with the long windows looking out on Washington Square Park. The trees were all bare now. Soon the branches would be frosted with snow. Then it would be spring again. Life went on as it always did, except that poor Papa was in his grave.

"Probate in this matter will be more than usually swift," James said, looking across at the couple. Carolina was pale, a bit tired-looking, the lawyer thought. Mourning didn't suit her. As for her husband, Sam Devrey looked to James like a vulture. Black suit, white shirt, and white stock. Handsome when young, he was growing gaunt as he aged. His nose seemed sharper as his cheeks became more sunken. A bird of prey waiting to pounce. Well, Mr. Devrey, we shall see about that.

"Wilbur Randolf's will is exceedingly simple and very clear," the lawyer said. "In fact, he remade it shortly before he died."

"Remade," Sam said. "What was there to alter? My wife is his only heir."

"Not exactly, Mr. Devrey."

Good Christ Jesus, what if Wilbur Randolf left a bundle to Jenny Worthington after all? "But—"

James waved away the interruption and cleared his throat. "If you'll permit me to continue." He knew he was drawing it out longer than he needed to. Hell, he'd really had no reason to arrange this formal reading, the document was plain enough. He could have let Carolina know how things stood and been done with it. He'd done it this way because he suspected it's how Wilbur would have wanted it. Wilbur couldn't abide Sam Devrey, not these last few years. It would have given him enormous pleasure to see the man squirm. "I'm pleased you brought young Master Zachary with you, Carolina my dear."

Carolina touched her son's knee but quickly withdrew her hand. At eleven, a student at the Trinity School on Grand Street, Zac did not permit outward signs of maternal affection. Her pride was nonetheless apparent. He was almost as tall as she, but dark like his father. And sitting upright beside her, staring straight at the lawyer. *Look a man in the eye when you do business with him, son. That's the way to get on. That's how your grandpa's always done it and so should you.* Zac would miss Papa even more than she would. Certainly he'd been the strongest male influence the boy had known. Zac liked Nick, of course, always had, but it wouldn't be the same.

"Can we please get this done with?" Sam said. "I've other things to see to."

"Yes, Mr. Devrey. As you wish. As I said, shortly before he died, Wilbur Randolf made a new will. He was at my office and signed it the very day of his demise."

"And the terms of this new will are?"

James picked up the document and read aloud. "I leave absolutely nothing to my beloved daughter Carolina, not because—"

"But that's absurd!"

"I assure you it is not, Mr. Devrey." Then, reading again, " . . . not because of any lack of affection, for indeed she is as she has always been the great joy and consolation of my life. However, she made a poor choice of husband, and to my everlasting sorrow I did not override her decision. It is unthinkable to me that my son-in-law Samuel Devrey should in any way profit from the marriage vows he has so flagrantly violated. I therefore leave everything I possess to my beloved grandson, Zachary Devrey." James couldn't help himself. He paused for full dramatic effect. That's got him, Wilbur, he thought. His face is as white as his stock. You'd have been delighted.

Sam took only a few seconds to get his breath back. "That doesn't seem to change much," he said. "Zachary is a minor and I am his father. I will of course oversee his affairs until he reaches his majority."

"No, Mr. Devrey. You will not. Mr. Randolf expressly forbade that." James looked again at the copy of the will and read, "Everything I own is to be placed in trust and held for Zachary until he reaches the age of twenty-one. The sole trustee is to be his mother, my daughter Carolina Randolf Devrey." The lawyer raised his eyes. No one said anything, but Devrey's face had gone from white to bright red. "Your father has also decreed, my dear Carolina, that for the duty of oversight which he lays upon you, the trust is to pay you a salary of three thousand a year. You will not therefore be in any way dependent on your husband for the ordinary expenses of your daily life."

The lawyer stared at Devrey. Sam stared back, but it wasn't Gordon James who was on his mind. *A pox on your black soul, Wilbur Randolf. May you rot in hell. But the Hakka pirates couldn't outwit me, and neither shall you. Once my ship sails, I won't need a penny of your poxed estate.* "Fair enough," Sam said. "I'm glad to hear my wife is to have a decent income of her own, since I require that she and the children vacate the Fourteenth Street house within twenty-four hours."

"Samuel, we can't. The children—" Then, seeing that he stared straight ahead and refused to look at her, "Very well, but if we must go, surely you can give us more time, Samuel."

"No, I cannot. Under the terms of the marriage settlement the house is yours on your father's death. Acting as your husband, I now demand vacant possession. That is my right under the law, is it not, Mr. James?"

"Indeed it is, Mr. Devrey. Except for one thing."

"Which is?"

"Before he died, Mr. Randolf arranged the sale of the house. That right remained his. Also a matter of the terms of the marriage settlement, as I'm sure you know."

"And it was sold to whom?" The ice was now firmly lodged in Sam's belly, spreading its cold through every part of him. He could feel it reaching his heart and taking bitter hold.

"The Fourteenth Street house was sold to Master Zachary Devrey, who paid the sum of one dollar. That is correct, young man, is it not?"

"Yes, sir, it is." If he'd known that grandpa was really going to die he'd never have agreed. He'd have made him take it back. But he knew Grandpa did it because Papa was so mean to Mama and didn't deserve to have any hold over her. Not over him or Ceci either. The boy's chin came up. "It's exactly how we did it, sir. I bought the house from my grandfather for a dollar."

"Indeed you did, young Master Devrey. And it has now been made part of your trust, which your dear mama will oversee until you are twenty-one." He looked directly at Sam. "I myself filed the transfer of ownership at the registry of deeds yesterday."

Chapter Twenty-six

"IT IS GOOD of you to receive me, Mrs. Devrey."

"Not at all, Mr. Belmont. It is good of you to come." Carolina poured her visitor a small glass of sherry as she spoke. There had been a good many visitors making condolence calls these past weeks. Presumably that was the motive of this visit as well, though she'd not known that her father had business with August Belmont.

"I suspect you may not—" He broke off and nodded his thanks when she handed him the wine.

"May not what, Mr. Belmont?"

"May not be entirely pleased with what I have come about."

"I see. Well, in that case let us sit down and you can tell me what that is. I always prefer bad news in as direct a fashion as possible."

"I don't mean to convey the wrong impression, madam, and I realize you are in mourning. But I had some business dealings with your husband a short time past, right after the passing of your late father, as it happens. I thought Mr. Devrey might be here."

"I assure you he is not." Carolina took a small sip of her drink and studied her caller over the rim of the glass. Short, a square sort of body and an equally square face below an already much receded hairline, though she'd heard he was still in his twenties. Not yet married, and said to be exceptionally clever. No doubt he was. How else would he be so rich so young? It followed that Mr. Belmont knew as well as everyone in the town not only that Sam Devrey hadn't lived with his wife for years, but also the unusual terms of Wilbur Randolf's will. "Perhaps you would care to tell me whatever it is you intended to tell my husband, Mr. Belmont."

"Very well, perhaps that would be best. Three weeks ago I made a substantial loan to your husband. I took as security the deeds to two properties on Cherry Street, numbers—"

"Thirty-seven and thirty-nine," Carolina supplied. "I know the buildings."

"Yes, I thought you would. You will then know as well that their combined value is perhaps twenty-five thousand dollars. That did not collateralize the full loan, Mrs. Devrey. This house was to provide the balance of the security. Mr. Devrey naturally enough presumed it would come to you on the death of your father. And that as your husband, of course he could . . ."

Belmont allowed the words to trail away. He obviously felt it unnecessary to spell out the extent of a husband's control of his wife's property. A horrid law, Carolina thought. Women should rise up and insist it be changed. "Of course," she agreed. "But I am sure, Mr. Belmont, that you've been apprised of the terms of my late father's will. Nothing whatever has come to me. Everything has gone into trust for my son, Zachary. Including, as it happens, this house, which my father before his death sold to his grandson."

"For the sum of one dollar. An excellent bargain."

"Indeed. What then is the purpose of your visit, Mr. Belmont?"

"I understand you are the sole trustee of your son's estate." She nodded and Belmont continued, "I am also told that you are a clever and accomplished woman and that already you are taking steps to both guard and increase the fortune that has been left to the young heir."

"If you mean that I am selling the leather interests and holding the property, that is, I presume, public knowledge on Wall Street."

"It is, madam. Which is why I've come here today to ask if you wish to retire your husband's loan."

In a million years he could not seriously think she would pay Sam Devrey's debts. All New York knew she would not. Neither for love nor duty. "That is always a possibility, Mr. Belmont. Though, frankly, one that is remote. However, if we're to discuss it further, shouldn't you tell me the exact amount involved?"

"With interest, madam, I am owed seventy-two thousand dollars."

"A great deal of money, and scant collateral. They tell me you are a man of uncommon astuteness, Mr. Belmont. So perhaps you will tell me why you made such a loan."

Belmont had merely toyed with his sherry thus far. Now he drained the glass, refused the offer of a refill, and sat forward. A ray of weak winter sun wreathed his almost bald head, rather like a halo, Carolina thought. But she did not mistake him for an angel.

"Your husband, Mrs. Devrey, is John Jacob Astor's man. And Mr. Astor, despite his eighty years, remains a force to be reckoned with."

"The Astor fortune, Mr. Belmont, will always be a force to be reckoned with. Mr. Astor's son, Mr. William Backhouse Astor, can be relied upon to see that continues to be true. I do not, however, see what that has to do with me."

"I believe it has a great deal to do with you, madam. Because it is my belief that you mean the future Mr. Zachary Devrey also to be a force to be reckoned with."

Carolina smiled. "Pray continue, Mr. Belmont."

"I am sure it will not surprise you to learn that having made a not inconsequential loan to your husband, I made it my business to discover why he needed so much money so quickly."

"I am not surprised in the least."

"Apparently, Mrs. Devrey, your husband has embarked on a venture in shipbuilding. It's meant to be secret, but I have it on good authority that a new keel is already on the ways at a yard some distance from the town."

"Parker's auxiliary yard at Thirty-fourth Street," she said at once, making the rapid calculation that he probably already knew, and if he did not, it mattered more that she be seen as knowledgeable. "It has to be Parker's. They have been Devrey's shipwrights for generations."

"You are correct about the yard, but this ship is commissioned not by Devrey Shipping but by Samuel Devrey personally. That much I know, and it is what I find so interesting about the undertaking. I was, however, able to learn little about the ship itself. She is, as I said, being built under terms of strict secrecy. In any case, shipping, or more precisely the building of ships, is not my line of country, Mrs. Devrey. But seeing as how, given the name he bears, it is likely to be in some manner your son's . . ."

Belmont shrugged and once more seemed to count on her divining the rest of his sentence. A business technique, Carolina realized, a way of never saying more than he meant to. "Please tell me exactly what you are proposing, Mr. Belmont. I am, after all merely a woman. You must realize that such matters as these are not always entirely clear to me." *I can bat my eyes at you, Mr. August Belmont, as well as any debutante you meet at a ball, and were I not wearing this dreadful high-necked black mourning frock I should lean forward and give you a good look down my bosom.*

Belmont glanced at the clock on the mantel. "If that timepiece is correct, Mrs. Devrey, your husband's debt comes due in precisely four minutes." He removed two documents from the inside pocket of his frock coat. "At that time I am free to sell these two properties."

Good God! She'd expected Belmont to say he was the owner of the properties and in return for something—she wasn't sure what—he would turn out her husband's mistress and his bastard child and to all intents and purposes Samuel himself. A joy indeed. But that she might be able to do it herself . . . The surge of pleasure was so exquisite it made her palms tingle; Carolina had to fold her hands primly in her lap to keep them from trembling. "How much are you asking for those houses,

Mr. Belmont? Presuming, of course, the debt to you is not paid in the next four minutes."

"Three minutes now," Belmont said, glancing again at the clock. "I will take the princely sum of one dollar each, madam. Exactly as was paid by your son for this house."

"Why?"

"If I say for the love of mankind and concern for a newly bereaved daughter and grandson you are, I expect, unlikely to believe me."

"Entirely unlikely, Mr. Belmont."

"Very well, I am offering you the Cherry Street houses in return for two dollars, and ownership of the instrument of your husband's debt for thirty thousand more. Plus a twenty percent interest in this mysterious ship being built at Mr. Parker's yard."

"Please explain exactly what that means. Not the deeds, Mr. Belmont. I understand about the deeds." She would immediately sell both houses to Zachary and make them part of the trust. "As for the ship, I may be only a woman, but I know investors take a part interest in ships every day of the week." But for that to matter to her, first she must own one. There were intricacies here that could defeat her if she were not careful. "I need to understand the matter of my husband's debt."

"It's quite straightforward, madam. Here is the note your husband signed." Another piece of paper appeared on the table in front of Belmont. "I propose to sell it to you. In financial circles you would be said to have bought the paper that indicates Mr. Devrey's indebtedness. Of course it is not the paper that matters, only that by owning the paper you own the claim. Mr. Devrey would then owe, not to me but to you, seventy-two thousand dollars, less whatever you may realize from the sale of the two houses on Cherry Street."

"If I chose to sell them."

"Yes, of course. If you chose to sell them."

It had to be a truly extraordinary ship. Samuel would not otherwise have incurred such an enormous debt, and August Belmont would not be paying such a high price for an interest in it. "You say you know nothing of the vessel Danny Parker is presumably building for my husband, yet you are prepared to cancel a substantial debt for less than half of what you're owed, plus ownership of a fifth part of this same mysterious ship. May I ask why that is, Mr. Belmont?"

"Money, Mrs. Devrey. The entire waterfront is buzzing with stories of new sorts of oceangoing clippers being built at a few of the yards. Some say they're going to revolutionize the China trade."

"And what do others say, Mr. Belmont?"

"That the entire scheme is madness and these new ships will go to the bottom on their maiden voyages. But," he said, leaning forward again and looking directly at her (as if she were a man, Carolina thought), "I, Mrs. Devrey, believe it worth a gamble to have a piece of such a ship. If for no other reason than that I've no doubt Astor will, whether it's the son William or the father Jacob. I do not choose to be completely out of any game my competitors are playing."

Carolina took a long breath. "One more question, Mr. Belmont. If indeed I buy this paper as you propose . . . Can a husband be legally indebted to his wife in that way?"

Belmont smiled. "Frankly, I don't know, but I doubt it. However, I do not believe that to be your interest in this matter. And I do not think it will require a court to get you what you want once you are in possession of such weapons."

The narrow stairs were not well lit. Carolina drew her skirts closer as she climbed. Thirty-nine was the building the whore lived in. Nick had told her so, though he'd taken a good deal of persuading.

I do not like it, Carolina. Not any part of it. You are independent of him now. Zachary's birthright is protected, at least on his maternal side. Why should you seek revenge? It is beneath you, my dearest. And frankly, Mei-hua doesn't deserve it. None of this is her doing.

Very well, Carolina thought, but lord knows, it was all Samuel Devrey's doing. How could Nick understand? How could he have any idea of the extent to which her husband had shamed and degraded her? Though sometimes she thought he suspected that it was fear rather than morality that made her refuse to allow him to become her lover. Terror that Nick would take her in his arms and she would see not his face but Samuel's, and that his caresses would feel like the stinging pain of a riding crop.

The top floor of number thirty-nine, Nick had said at last.

She lives there with the old servant, the one you saw the night of the fire. Ah Chee she's called. The little girl as well. Her name is Mei Lin, she's almost nine. And Samuel? Carolina asked. Samuel also, Nick confirmed. At least so I believe.

The fourth-floor door was in front of her. Carolina took a moment to compose herself, then she lifted her hand and knocked.

Mei-hua half-rose from her chair and stretched her neck to see over Ah Chee's shoulder. She had expected the knock to announce one or other of the men. They did not disturb the *tai-tai* frequently, but sometimes they had business of some sort with the lord.

It was the big ugly yellow hair. The concubine. Mei-hua saw the top of the yellow hair's head over Ah Chee's gray one when Ah Chee opened the door. Surprise brought her all the way to her feet, then she realized what a loss of dignity it would be to stand in the big ugly's presence and sat down. Good thing she was sitting in the throne chair. Good thing the gilt canopy was over her head. Good thing she was protected either side by the dragon-claw arms. Never mind that she was holding them so tight her fingers hurt.

She was supreme lady *tai-tai*. The big ugly yellow hair was concubine. Her lord had told her so. "Tell her she is too late," she said. Ah Chee did not turn around or otherwise acknowledge the command. She was speaking to yellow hair in the strangle-sound words of this place, and they seemed to have stopped her ears. Mei-hua spoke again. At the top of her voice this time, to be sure Ah Chee would hear. "Tell her a concubine comes to pay her respect to supreme lady *tai-tai* before she goes to the husband's bed. Not good to come so long after. Tell her supreme lady will not receive her and she must go away."

Ah Chee ignored the steady stream of words coming from the throne chair behind her. Ah Chee did not believe big ugly yellow hair had come to show the plum blossom long overdue deference. She had come to do them harm. Ah Chee was not only sure of it, she knew why. Yesterday, when she was frying wonton, some drops of water got into the fat and it spattered all over. Couple of drops landed on the hem of the garment of Zao Shen, the kitchen god. She had known right away that something bad would happen as a result. She'd offered him three of the wonton by way of apology, not just the customary two, and burned five sticks of incense to prove how sorry she was. Much sorry. Much sorry. Didn't matter. Bad stuff happen anyway.

"What you want?" she asked, as she had been asking over and over since she opened the door. "What you want? What? What?" All the while trying to close the door.

Carolina could not understand one word the strange little creature spoke. "My husband," she repeated for the fourth or fifth time, enunciating the words as slowly and clearly as possible. "I have come to see my husband."

"What? What?" This time Ah Chee leaned her whole body against the door and closed it to within only the space of one of her gnarled old hands. "What? Go. Go."

Carolina put both her palms flat on the door and pushed back against the slight weight of the old servant. "Don't you dare close the door on me. I am your new landlady." It was not strictly true; she merely represented their new, underage landlord. But that was too complicated to explain. Besides, she had managed to force the door further open and she could now see inside the room. There was the whore with the ribbons in her hair, and over by the window Samuel's bastard daughter. She was sitting with her head bent, pretending, Carolina realized at once, to neither see nor hear a word of what was happening. Ceci would act the same way if she were frightened. "I wish to inspect the property," Carolina said. "And to see my husband, Mr. Samuel Devrey."

At the sound of the name mother, daughter, and servant seemed to startle, as if the barrier of language that separated them had suddenly been pierced. "My husband," Carolina repeated still more loudly and forcefully, "Mr. Samuel Devrey."

This time Mei-hua stood up. "*Guen, ni guen.*" Get out, roll away. It was the command made to an unwelcome dog. "*Guen. Guen.*"

Ah Chee was annoyed with the plum blossom for losing her dignity and addressing the big ugly directly. "Be quiet. Be quiet. I will tell." But it was a big mistake to take attention from the door and put it on the plum blossom. Big ugly push harder. She was in the room now.

"*Guen, ni guen,*" Mei-hua repeated. "Right now. Go. Go." Her heart was beating very fast. Why had yellow hair come after so much time? After Mei-hua made herself not think about the concubine, after she made herself believe what both her lord and Ah Chee told her, that things were different in this place. Not good. Not good. She turned away from the big ugly and looked at her daughter.

Mei Lin sat by the window where the light was better for the embroidery her mother was making her practice. *You eight-year-old girl, almost nine. Almost time be tai-tai. Who will want you when you make big clumsy stitches? Make big clumsy dragon breathe fire down instead of up. Who? Who?* Who would want her anyway? The Lord Samuel would not permit his beautiful daughter to have beautiful golden lilies, so whose *tai-tai* could she be? Another sadness for another time. Right now only getting rid of the big ugly mattered, and for that her daughter was required. "*Ni lai,*" Mei-hua said, summoning the child to her. "Mei Lin, *ni lai.*"

The girl put down the embroidery and came to stand beside her mother. Mei-hua put an arm around her shoulders but addressed herself to the yellow hair concubine. "*Ta bu zai,* Lord Samuel." He is not here.

"She does not understand, Mamee," Mei Lin said. "Does not understand Ah Chee either." A year and a half at the Convent of the Sacred Heart had made Mei Lin not only more fluent in multiple languages—under the tutelage of the Madams she was adding French to Mandarin and English—but given her some inkling of the mysteries of accent. "I will tell her what you are saying. Can?"

"Yes, tell her right now. Right now. Tell her go. Tell her supreme lady says go. Supreme lady will tell Lord Samuel to beat her very hard otherwise."

Sometimes when Mother Duquesne who had charge of the youngest girls turned her back for a moment and one of her classmates pinched Mei Lin really hard and Mei Lin squealed because she couldn't help herself and Mother Duquesne whirled around and demanded to know who had made that awful screeching sound, Mei Lin was tempted to open her mouth and say it was her and say why. But of course she did not. She was being educated to the highest standards. That meant learning when to tell the truth and when to fib. Not lie of course. A lie was a bad sin and must be confessed to Father; otherwise you would burn for all eternity in the fires of hell. A fib was what you said instead. It was a forgivable sin. Mei Lin dropped a quick and exceptionally graceful curtsy, the only kind Mother Stevenson permitted in deportment class. "It is kind of you to call, madam. But my mother says to tell you that Mr. Devrey isn't here."

Carolina caught her breath. The child's voice, clear and without the edge of anger and hostility she had heard in the voices of the two older women—of herself, come to that—was like a shower of fresh, cool water. And not only did she have excellent manners, she spoke perfect English. Why would she not? She had been born here, just as Ceci had, and not, as Nick repeatedly pointed out, through any choice of her own, also like Ceci, whom she had never blamed for the terrible circumstances of her conception.

"Do you know," Carolina asked, "where he can be found? It is very important that I see him. I shall have to wait here otherwise," she added in a burst of inspiration.

Mei Lin turned to her mother. "Take her next door? Can? Take her to see Baba? If I take her she will go. Otherwise stay here and wait."

Mei-hua looked to the statue of Fu Xing, the golden god of happiness who presided over this room. He was smiling. But Fu Xing always smiled. When she nearly bled to death after they stole the son from her womb and the red-hair *yi* came and saved her, Fu

Xing smiled. When that same red-hair *yi* pulled a live baby out of
her and transformed it from a son to a daughter, Fu Xing smiled.
When her lord took their daughter away to a school where they
caused her precious Mei Lin to think it a bad thing to show respect
to the gods—the child had absolutely refused to give moon cakes to
the kitchen god at the new year festival, and she wouldn't burn even
one joss stick—Fu Xing continued to smile. Now, Mei-hua realized,
if yellow hair big ugly stayed in this place, all the bad things she
could feel hovering around them would happen, and Fu Xing would
still smile. I am supreme first lady *tai-tai*. She is concubine. My lord
said so. "Take her next door," she said. "Go quickly, *mei-mei*," calling
the child little sister as a mark of affection and putting her hand
lightly and quickly on Mei Lin's cheek, ignoring the soft growl of
disapproval she heard from Ah Chee. "Do not be afraid, *mei-mei*.
Take her to Baba. Now. Now."

"Can you hear me, Samuel?"

"Carolina?" Sam raised his head and tried to focus. "It's you, isn't
it?"

"Yes, it's me." He was lying on a wooden bed, the mattress ripped in
places so she could see the straw stuffing beginning to poke out. There
were no sheets and only one pillow. In the old days, when he had slept
beside her most nights, Sam had insisted he must have at least two
pillows to be comfortable.

The room was so small there was barely room for the bed, a tiny table
beside it, and a large tank of some sort. The place smelled as well. Not
just from dirt and unwashed flesh, but something sickly sweet. "Are you
sure you can hear me, Samuel? It is very important I speak with you."

"How did you get here? How did you know where . . . Oh. Turner. It
has to have been."

"Cousin Nicholas has nothing to do with my being here. I have come
to discuss business. Can you please get up? It's very difficult speaking to
you when you are sprawled in that fashion."

Sam struggled to a sitting position. His ornate long-stemmed pipe was within reach, and he desperately wanted to smoke another blob of opium—he'd been doing little else since that poxed day of the reading of Wilbur Randolf's will—but he resisted. Whatever brought Carolina here, he had to deal with it. At least well enough to make her go away and leave him in peace. Time enough to smoke then. "What do you want?"

"Your signature," she said, reaching into the drawstring bag hanging from her wrist. "On this piece of paper."

"What is it?" He squinted to see, but it wasn't possible in the dim light. "Divorce papers? That's what you want, isn't it? So you and—"

"These are not divorce papers, Samuel. It is rather too late for that." Papa's words came back to her as clearly as the day nine years past when he first spoke them. *Think of Zachary's future, Carolina. What will society make of him as the son of divorced parents?* "Have you a quill?"

Sam stood up. He felt terribly dizzy for a moment, but he knew from experience it would get better if he could manage to stay on his feet. He reached out a hand and touched the wall for support. That helped. "I can find a quill if I need one. But not unless you tell me what you want me to sign."

I cannot think, Mrs. Devrey, that your husband will actually sign a document such as this. So said Mr. Gordon James. Maybe she should have gone to a different lawyer and not given yet another of the family's sordid secrets into the hands of the man who already knew so many, but that would have meant many more explanations. *I promise you he will sign, Mr. James. I am certain of it.*

"It is a bill of sale for the ship being built in Danny Parker's yard on Thirty-fourth Street. You are selling it to me for the sum of ten dollars."

Sam stared at her and wiped a hand over his eyes, but Carolina had not disappeared. She was not a dream, a cloud-induced mirage. "You're mad. You must be. How did you find out . . . No, never mind about that. How can you think I would—"

"Sell me the ship? Because it is in your best interest to do so."

The dizziness was increasing, and he felt sick, as if he might vomit. Perhaps all over Carolina's black mourning frock. He tried taking his hand from the wall and standing up to his full height so he could look down on her, but he staggered and had to put the hand back for support. "You're mad," he said again. "How is signing away my ship for ten dollars in my best interest?"

"Because I am offering you another consideration as well. You pay ten dollars and sell me the ship Danny Parker is building, and you secure the right to stay where you are. You and your mistress and her child and her servant—all of you may remain right here. You may even continue to collect the rents from your Chinese lodgers. At least for the time being," she added, wanting him to know that withholding those rents was yet within her power. "Otherwise I shall evict the lot of you."

"You can't. You don't have possession . . ." Then, as some bits of clarity pierced the opium fog, "The Jew, August Belmont. He's behind this, isn't he?"

"In a manner of speaking. He sold me these two houses, Samuel, which I have purchased on Zachary's behalf. They are part of his trust, and as you know, I am the sole trustee. So I have the power to put you all on the street, and I shall do it unless you sign this bill of sale for the new ship."

Samuel shook his head. "I won't. I'm your legal husband, and that means that whatever is yours is mine."

"You're not listening, Samuel. I don't own the houses, Zachary does, but it is I who control their disposition. I am also in possession of the note you signed with August Belmont."

He sagged as if the weight of something entirely too heavy to be borne had settled on his shoulders, and leaned against the wall to prevent himself from falling. "You're a witch from hell, Carolina Randolf. I should have known it years ago."

"Carolina Randolf Devrey," she corrected. "You gave me your name in St. Paul's Church, Samuel Devrey, and for the moment it suits me to keep it. As for being a witch, perhaps I am and what of it? You are in my debt, Samuel. More precisely, in debt to the trust I manage. However, I am prepared to forgive all in return for your signature on this bill of sale. If, on the other hand, you do not sign, I will put your Chinese whore and her bastard child and her servant on the street. Where will they go, Samuel? Who will take them in? Where will you go? I'm told Astor has already replaced you at Devrey's." She toyed with telling him of the note she'd sent to Astor, anonymously of course, about the menage on Cherry Street but decided against it. "If you try to return to Fourteenth Street I will set the coppers on you and make such a public stench as New York has never before had the opportunity to smell."

"You wouldn't. What about the children?"

"They are young. They would grow past it. You aren't young, Samuel."

Sam stared at her a moment more. "Hell witch," he said, then staggered a step closer to the tank and fell to his knees. Was he going to beg, she wondered? And why did she not feel more elation at the prospect?

The pen and the inkpot and his journal were under a loose floorboard. He kept them handy so that he could make notes of his experiments, but hidden so no one else could read the observations he'd been recording. His hands were trembling so it wasn't easy to prize up the board. He wanted to ask for her help, but he would not. Finally the thing lifted. He retrieved the pen and the ink and started to let the floorboard drop back into place, but Carolina extended the pointed toe of her leather boot to prevent it. "That book," she demanded, "in the hole. What is it?"

Sam had hold of the floorboard. Wreck of a man that he was these days, he could still summon enough strength to smash it down on her foot. He looked up at her and realized she knew that as well. Slapping her, once even blacking her eye, beating her about the legs with a riding crop. It used to help. Not anymore. The time when physical violence directed at Carolina somehow eased him was apparently past. Quiet, that's all he wanted now, and, if he told the truth, to swallow clouds. "I'll extend our bargain," he said. "The book contains all the secrets of the ship. You need the one as well as the other. I will give it to you in return for one thing more."

"What is it?"

"The little girl. My . . . Mei Lin." The words were thick and heavy in his mouth, and the smell of opium somewhere in the building was driving him nearly frantic with longing. "Mei Lin," he said again.

"Yes? What about her?" Surely he wasn't suggesting she adopt his bastard.

"She goes to school. Nuns. Madams of the Sacred Heart. They call her Linda Di. She must keep on going. Half Chinese. It's her only chance. You will pay her tuition."

"How much?"

"One hundred dollars a term."

She didn't ask to be born, Carolina. "Very well."

"Until she is eighteen?"

"Until then. You have my word." She moved her foot and stretched out her hand for the notebook.

Sam handed it to her.

When Carolina went outside, the child was waiting. Impossible to know how much she might have heard. "You're called Linda Di, I'm told."

Mei Lin curtsied. "Yes, ma'am."

"And you attend a school taught by Catholic nuns."

"Yes, ma'am. The Convent of the Sacred Heart on Mulberry Street."

Carolina took one of her visiting cards from the drawstring bag, which now held Samuel's journal and the document giving her ownership of the vessel under construction in Danny Parker's auxiliary yard. "Here," she said, handing the card to the girl. "This is my name and my address. I take it you can read."

"Yes, ma'am."

"Call me Mrs. Devrey." God knows what the child thought her mother might be called. "And if you need anything. Or if something happens to your father. Indeed, anything you think I should know about, come and see me."

Chapter Twenty-seven

"DOES SHE HAVE a name, Mr. Parker?" It was, Carolina knew, considered the worst possible luck to change a ship's name.

"Not yet. Owner's privilege to pick the name. I've been waiting for Mr. Devrey to say."

"Well, as you know, I am now the owner." She nodded at the document Danny Parker clutched in his hand. He'd kept hold of it all the while they surveyed the ship. The keel and the ribs were rising from stocks erected above ways headed directly into the river. That was the ordinary manner of such things, Carolina knew. What was not ordinary was that in this instance the whole affair was tented beneath a vast expanse of tarpaulin supported on thick posts, the frontmost set in the river itself. The arrangement might not have been necessary up here in the Thirty-fourth Street wilds, but obviously they had put a high price on secrecy. Besides, it kept out the worst of the November winds and thus helped the quest for speed. Carolina knew all about the *Houqua* and the race for Canton. It was now her business to know such things.

The soft slap of water lapping at heavily oiled canvas was the only sound to be heard. It would have been pitch black had Danny Parker not held a lantern. They stood amidships, the lantern's yellow glow illuminating the length of the vessel stretched either side. "One hundred and seventy feet stem to stern, not counting the bowsprit," Parker said. "And thirty-three feet across the beam. There's nothing larger afloat. Might never be. She'll lade eleven hundred tons."

"You're proud of her, aren't you, Mr. Parker?"

"Aye, I am. Mr. Devrey and I designed her. After his experiments, o' course."

She had spent hours poring over Samuel's notes of those experiments. "And you believe she will be the swiftest ship as well as the biggest? Because of her flat keel?"

Danny didn't let on how surprised he was that she should know such a thing. "I do. Her keel and her length," he added. "Those seem to be the key. Plus how much sail she'll carry."

"Eleven hundred tons of fresh tea that arrives soon after harvest. That will fetch a fair price at auction, don't you think, Mr. Parker?"

"Aye, it will. And twenty-five percent of the gain mine. That was the arrangement, Mrs. Devrey. I've a note signed by your husband."

"I will honor the agreement, Mr. Parker. You need have no fear on that score." Danny Parker's participation in the profit was noted in Samuel's book, so she was not surprised. August Belmont, however, would not consider himself bound by the agreement. Thus Mr. Parker's twenty-five percent share would come entirely out of her earnings. Fair enough. *Businessmen as let greed rule them are inevitably headed for ruin, Carolina.* One of the lessons she'd learned at Papa's knee, when Wilbur Randolf talked to her because he had neither wife nor son with whom to share his ruminations, back when it would not have occurred to either of them that one day she might own the majority share in the fastest ship afloat. "But, Mr. Parker," she said, "you must promise not to hold me liable if we lose our gamble and she founders."

Parker nodded. "That's how we laid it out. Me and Mr. Devrey."

"Then that will be our agreement as well. I will require a new note between you and me speaking directly to that. I'll have my attorney draw it up."

"Do that," he said. "I'll sign."

Cold as it was outside the tarpaulin, it suddenly seemed to Carolina very close in the damp dark beneath it. She took a handkerchief—edged in black lace because she was still in mourning for her father—from her muff and dabbed at her face. "That's it then. We prosper or fail together, Mr. Parker." Carolina held out her hand.

Danny hesitated a moment, then he took it. "So we do, Mrs. Devrey. What about a name for her, then? Seeing as you're the new owner."

She had toyed with Zachary Celinda or even a made-up combination such as Zac-Ce or Cezac. Then, the night before, she'd wakened from a sound sleep and known exactly what the name of the vessel was to be.

"She's to be called *Hell Witch*, Mr. Parker." Samuel had said she was a witch from hell; perhaps he was right. Perhaps it was entirely unnatural for a woman to be so exhilarated by these matters of business, but she had Samuel Devrey to thank for whatever she'd become. He had not permitted her to be the wife she'd longed to be. Now she and her ship would sink into oblivion or sail to glory together. "*Hell Witch*," she repeated.

"I fear it won't be easy getting a crew to sign on to sail a ship with that name, Mrs. Devrey."

"On the contrary, Mr. Parker. I think it will be very easy once she's seen to be the most beautiful thing ever to set sail from New York. Anyway, we will tempt them."

"With what?"

"Money, of course. Bonuses for getting her to Hong Kong and back in the fastest time ever made." So much promised to so many meant that her own profit, the profit accruing to Zachary's trust, might turn out to be little or nothing at least on the maiden voyage and perhaps the next one or two as well. But according to Samuel's notebook, a ship like this might make two round-trip voyages in a year. So they would sail on to fabulous riches together, Carolina Randolf Devrey and her *Hell Witch*. And would that repay her for everything she had suffered at Samuel's hands? Yes, because it must. "*Hell Witch*, she is," she said.

They took her down river to Parker's main yard at the foot of Montgomery Street on the evening of June 13, 1844, triple reefed but still catching all the breezes that customarily rose after sundown, and waited until sunup the following morning to send her into the inner harbor at the foot of South Street. Early as it was, a crowd had gathered. There was no way it could not be so. The tarpaulin had come off two months before, when the masts of *Hell Witch* rose a hundred and forty feet into the air.

Hell Witch. As long and sleek as a greyhound, with a razor-sharp bow and a rounded stern and a hull that rose above the waterline in graceful concave curves. Painted black she was, with a blood-red stripe, and her figurehead a woman with golden hair streaming in the wind. Modeled after Carolina Devrey herself, people whispered. But when Carolina's ship moved into the outer harbor and at last released her sails, they had something else to talk about.

Hell Witch rode beneath a cloud of canvas such as New York had never seen. The *Houqua* had sailed two weeks before and they'd thought her rigging remarkable. But this . . . *Never seen the like. Probably never will again. Not after she goes below the waves at the Cape.* Mainsail, topsail, topgallant, and royals, those were not strange sights to New Yorkers. But Carolina Devrey's ship carried as well a skysail so high it might, someone said, be a napkin to tie beneath God's chin. There was as well an assortment of other sails hung on extended yards either side of the normal rigging, and triangular sails between the masts, and still more hanging from the bowsprit. One by one, or so it seemed, they were unfurled and caught the wind, and the exquisite craft glided towards her destiny.

"There's never been anything to match her," Carolina murmured. "Never."

"Never," Nick agreed, putting his arm around her waist and drawing her close, something he could do only because they had total privacy inside Mr. August Belmont's carriage. Belmont had lent it to Carolina for the occasion, along with his driver, and they were parked hard by the

South Street dock that belonged to Devrey Shipping, peeping through the carriage's curtained windows. The ship—which did not fly the gold lion and crossed swords of the Devrey arms on the owner's pennant run up to mark the occasion, only the initials, *HW*—became a white speck on the horizon. The crowd began to disperse, all talking, everyone with an opinion. And each as good as the next for the moment. It would be months before the fate of *Hell Witch* would be known for sure.

Carolina squeezed Nick's hand. "Captain Paxos," she said, speaking aloud her greatest worry. "Do you think I did the right thing?"

"I think you followed your best judgment. There's nothing else you could do."

The captain is as important as the ship. So said Samuel's notes. *The right man can bring her through the Atlantic gales, the Cape's fifty-foot waves, or the monsoon winds, indeed the weather of any time of year. But he must be as finely tuned to his purpose as the vessel.*

Aristotle Paxos had presented himself to Carolina two months before, introduced by August Belmont, who claimed that the man had come from Athens by way of London, with a personal recommendation from someone Belmont claimed to trust totally in such matters. Paxos was almost as tall as Nick, dressed entirely in black, with a silver beard, and with a huge silver cross hanging round his neck. *I am a Greek, madam, born of the union of Poseidon and a naiad. The blood of Odysseus runs in my veins! I was born to possess your witch from hell. I shall make her my bride and she will yield to me and we will make your fortune.* She could picture him now standing at the helm, bellowing orders, not just to the crew, to the wind itself. "Perhaps," she said. "Nothing to do now but wait and see."

"Yes." Nick agreed. "No other choice."

In late July, a ship docked that had seen *Hell Witch* riding the Brazil current past the coast of Argentina and heading towards the stretch of ocean known as the Roaring Forties.

"They saw her four weeks ago, Nick." Carolina's voice trembled with excitement. "That means she reached Argentina only twenty days into her voyage." She had tacked a map on the wall of the back parlor on Fourteenth Street. She called it her office and from there administered all the things to do with Zachary's trust. "Where do you imagine she is now? Where shall I put the pin?"

Nick came and stood behind her. "Here," he said, and guided her hand to a position just west of the Cape of Good Hope. Though by now, if she had survived that peril, *Hell Witch* must be well around it. "Let's not tempt fate."

In late August they heard from a seaman who whispered a rumor that the next morning was heard first at the Astor House bar, where the shippers customarily gathered for breakfast, then repeated all over the waterfront. The tar said he'd been on watch in a fierce storm south of the Java straits and seen a ship on the horizon sailing in the opposite direction under more canvas than any sane captain would unfurl in such weather. *Heeled over so far she was it seemed she must be riding on the wind. A bloody miracle she wasn't swamped. But she wasn't. Not while I watched.* That was remarkable enough, but not all the tar had to tell. He claimed that four days after he'd seen the vessel that could only have been *Hell Witch*, his ship had passed the *Houqua*. She had left port two weeks before *Hell Witch;* now she was sailing in her wake.

This time it was Nick who moved the pin, positioning it just west of the Sunda Strait between Sumatra and Java. Seventy-eight days into her voyage, Carolina's ship was—at least she might be—an estimated two weeks from making landfall at Hong Kong.

The best tea was said to be the early spring crop from the lowlands; it was known as Heaven Pool tea. But in late summer came the tea called Dragon Fountain, *Long Jin*, grown in the mountains, where the plants leafed out much later after the last snows melted. "The first harvest of *Long Jin* tea from Hangchow," Carolina said. "If that's where *Hell Witch* is"—she pointed to the pin near Java—"it's possible, Nick. It is, isn't it?"

He stared at the map. "It would seem so. If the talk isn't only that."

But talk there was. Even Aunt Lucy, now a frail old woman, brought rumors to her niece. "I'm told your ship has taken but sixty days to arrive at Hong Kong, Carolina. Apparently that's very fast."

"If it were true it would be not simply fast but miraculous, Aunt Lucy. *Hell Witch* may have made the voyage in something more like ninety days, and that's remarkable time. If it's true. We can't know for sure until she comes back, of course."

"Ninety days? I shall be sure to correct the next person who tells me sixty."

"Please do."

"But that's not all I hear."

Carolina was stitching a bit of picot tatting to one of Ceci's chemises and went on with her work. Lucy would pass on gossip as long as there was a breath in her body. No encouragement was required.

"I'm told your cousin by marriage, Dr. Nicholas Turner, works miracles on Crosby Street. Absolute miracles. My friend Sally Whitaker's daughter had a plague of boils on her backside and he rid her of them after three treatments. Apparently it's this new Croton water that does it."

"Not because it's Croton water, Aunt. Because it's fresh water that runs." Sally Whitaker's daughter, as Carolina remembered her, was a slut, however much she was presumed to be a lady. "If one can be persuaded to bathe more frequently because of it, any sort of running water will be an aid to good health."

"So one hears," Aunt Lucy agreed. "They say these new mansions going up on Fifth Avenue are all being fitted with special rooms for bathing. And now I suppose there will be more."

"More mansions or more water?"

"More mansions, of course."

"Why should that be?" Carolina was as skilled a needlewoman as she needed to be. She did not need to concentrate so on the task of stitching the store-bought edging in place. Still she did not lift her hand from her task. Aunt Lucy was working up to saying something about Nick. Carolina was sure of it.

"My dear, you must get out more. According to Hannah Markus—I don't think you know her. Hannah's daughter Bella married Dr. Turner's partner, Dr. Klein. Jews you know, but the very nicest sort." She stopped to examine a bit of her needlework, then went on. "Anyway, Hannah Markus says there's talk of doing away with the parade ground at Twenty-third Street and making another park. Madison Square I believe they mean to call it, though I can't think why we must name anything for that dreadful president who got us into that dreadful Mexican war, and—"

"Whatever else, Aunt, the Mexican war brought us a fair amount of territory."

"California is nice enough, I'm told," Lucy agreed with a sniff. "But Utah and New Mexico are desert and nothing else. Anyway, it's all too far away to do us any good."

"Perhaps. What were you saying about your friend Mrs. Markus?"

Lucy licked the end of a length of black sewing cotton and threaded a needle while she spoke. "Oh yes, Hannah Markus. She says all the best people shall be flocking to live on Fifth Avenue once the parade ground's gone. Do you imagine Dr. Turner might build himself a Fifth Avenue mansion? I fancy he can afford it, given how every society matron in New York insists he's the only doctor to see. Perhaps he may even take a wife, Carolina. Hannah Markus was saying he's considered quite a catch, that he's been seen around town with this one or that and—What is it, dear?" That last in response to a loud exclamation by Carolina.

"I pricked my finger. Nothing to worry about." Nick hadn't mentioned anything about seeing young ladies, but he must, of course. Stupid of her to be surprised about that.

"Do be careful, Carolina. You don't want to get bloodstains on your work. Of course some people intimate all manner of things. Not enough to do with their time it seems to me. And I tell them so. After all, Dr. Turner is your cousin."

"Aunt Lucy, I have no idea what you're talking about."

"Oh don't be so obtuse, dear child. Everyone in town knows he dotes on you. These others, they're just a concealment. And given how the mothers pursue him, what else can he do? But when I'm asked, I remind people that he's your cousin."

"Yes, Aunt Lucy, he is."

"Though only by marriage. So if you were to marry him—"

"Aunt Lucy! What are you talking about? I am already married."

"Perhaps," her aunt said. "Perhaps, however, you are a widow."

"What? Wherever did you get such a notion?"

"My friend Jessie Farmer mentioned it to me last month."

"And what gave her that idea?"

"Jessie said she heard it from Isabel Downing."

"Aunt Lucy, such wicked gossip! How do they come to be spreading such a tale? I'm not a widow. Samuel is—"

"Samuel Devrey has not been seen in this town since anyone can remember. And you've been wearing mourning for nearly a year."

"I'm in mourning for Papa, Aunt Lucy."

"Oh yes, of course. But you've been in black nearly eight months. Not all daughters remain so obviously bereaved for such a length of time. Whereas widows . . . There, that's another one done." Lucy finished crocheting a black edge around another of her niece's white handkerchiefs. "That should see you through another few months. Then perhaps you will no longer need them. It will be a year in November, Carolina. You might properly come out of mourning then."

"Mourning for Samuel, you mean."

"I didn't say that. I'm simply reporting what I have heard."

"Aunt Lucy, where would your friends get such an idea?"

"Oh, I don't know," she said, with a shrug of her bent and exceedingly thin shoulders. "I suppose I might have whispered a word or two to some of them soon after that ship of yours set sail. Put down your sewing, dear child, and listen to me."

Carolina needed no encouragement. She hadn't taken a stitch since Aunt Lucy had mentioned Nick.

"You are a widow, Carolina, in everything except name, and you have been so for at least the eight years since Ceci was born, longer if I'm any judge. Though I don't doubt she's Sam Devrey's daughter."

"She is."

"Yes. She looks too much like a Devrey for it to be otherwise.

Nonetheless, no one has seen or heard from Samuel in—how long?"

"Aunt Lucy, Samuel is not dead. He does not live here with me, but—"

"Where does he live, Carolina? Is it anywhere the likes of my friends Mrs. Whitaker or Mrs. Farmer or Mrs. Downing or even Mrs. Markus the Jewess are likely to see him?"

Carolina shook her head.

"Anywhere your younger friends might see him?"

Carolina shook her head again.

"I thought not. So if you could manage to somehow shut the mouth of that wretched Celinda Devrey, you could—"

"Aunt Lucy, you are talking madness. But even if you were not, my mother-in-law is—"

"Interested only in money," Lucy said firmly. "You have a bit of that now, dear child. And if the rumors about your ship prove true, you could, as the old saying has it, stop Celinda Devrey's mouth with shillings, my dear. As many shillings as it takes."

Carolina refused to continue the conversation, and she never told Nick what had passed between her and her aunt. But nothing could make her forget Lucy's words. Particularly since she had little else to think about.

For three months they heard nothing more about *Hell Witch* or *Houqua*.

Until on Monday, November 18, shortly after two in the afternoon, word came from the Sandy Hook semaphore that *Hell Witch* was less than ten miles from New York harbor and would make landfall before dark.

In all of sailing history there had never been such a voyage.

"Seventy-eight days and fourteen hours sailing time, Hong Kong to New York," Captain Paxos said. "As Jesus Christ will be my judge, that's the truth."

Carolina required no such oath; she already had the proof. *Hell Witch*'s cargo of eleven hundred tons of perfect and fresh *Long Jin* tea had been sold at auction that afternoon for one hundred and ninety-eight thousand dollars. After the expenses of the journey were calculated, including handsome bonuses for Paxos and his crew, that meant August Belmont's share was thirty-six thousand. Adding that to what Carolina paid him previously, Belmont had now recouped what he'd loaned Sam Devrey, including the interest, and could look forward to fabulous profits on every journey *Hell Witch* made.

Then there was the share belonging to Celinda Devrey. Carolina would be paying her every time *Hell Witch* returned to port—and indeed any other ship in which she had a whole or a partial interest. Celinda had added that proviso after Carolina thought they had reached an agreement. "Five thousand cash money, my dear, yes, but I think I should look forward to that on more than just *Hell Witch*. I believe you shall not stop with that one vessel, Carolina. Your father made you more man than woman, that's why my son could never . . . an equal sum on the docking of every ship you own."

"For how long, Mrs. Devrey?"

"Why, until I die, Carolina. That is, after all, the reason I am giving you this undertaking of silence. To provide for my old age. So let us say that whether your profit be on the whole cargo or a part thereof, I shall be paid the same. Five thousand each and every time. I'm sure you wish to be that generous to your mother-in-law."

For her part Carolina was sure Celinda knew what hardly anyone else did—Samuel's actual whereabouts. Barnabas, the stable boy, had always kept Samuel's mother informed of the household's comings and goings; if Celinda wished to make trouble she could produce proof of her claims. So Carolina agreed, five thousand each time she sold a cargo. Which wasn't to say that she had made up her mind to follow the rest of Lucy's advice, only that Celinda Devrey was now part of the calculation of her earnings. Something on the negative side of the ledger.

Then there was Danny Parker. The shipwright's twenty-five percent share of the profit would apply to *Hell Witch*'s first three cargos. On this maiden voyage it came to twenty-two thousand. It was all relative, of course, but in his own terms Danny Parker must feel himself a man as rich as August Belmont.

Carolina had asked the shipwright to join them for this celebration dinner at Delmonico's, but while he thanked her kindly, he refused. She did not insist, knowing he might feel uncomfortable in such a place. Particularly since it was August Belmont who sat at the head of the table, playing host. *More appropriate him than me, Nick. Besides, I want to keep him sweet. I think I may have more business to transact with the gentleman.*

Belmont had chosen to have their gathering at one of the restaurant's second-floor private dining rooms. The walls were covered in flocked red wallpaper above ivory-colored paneling, the cherubs flying across the plaster ceiling were picked out in gilt, and the chandelier was three tiers of crystal teardrops, each reflecting a dizzying number of pinpoints of gaslight. The chairs were gilt and red velvet, and the table was draped in dazzlingly white linen. A line of silver and gold epergnes of various heights marched the table's length, each displaying an arrangement of exotic fruits and exquisite flowers. In the midst of all this splendor a procession of waiters came and went, presenting a succession of remarkable dishes. There was a whole fish glazed in shimmering aspic flecked with black truffles, vegetables Carolina had heard of but never tasted—artichokes and endive—napped in remarkably silky sauces that hinted of lemon and orange, a fillet of beef crisped almost black on the outside and pink within, served with yet another astonishing sauce. And with each course a new infinitely more delicious wine.

It was an evening and a setting far too glorious for the somber black of mourning.

Carolina, flushed with laughter and triumph, wore emerald green velvet, an off-the-shoulder gown with short puffed sleeves and a bodice so tight she could barely inhale—at least that was what she blamed for her breathlessness—and a skirt so full she had to support it with four petticoats.

"You are too beautiful to be real," Nick had said when he called for her. "I am with a fairy princess."

"You are with a thirty-one-year-old mother of two who will probably soon run to fat and wrinkles. But you are very kind to say you think I'm beautiful."

"Not kind. Truthful." And he had put his hands either side of her face and kissed her full on the mouth, with tenderness at first, and then something else.

Carolina had eased herself away, as she always did, and reached for the cloak that matched her gown, green velvet lined with the skin of a Chinese leopard. The outfit was a wild indulgence she had allowed herself some months earlier, just after her talk with Aunt Lucy about being a widow when one was not. She had put it away in hopes she would wear it for just such a celebratory occasion as this. "We must go," she said. "It won't do to keep our host waiting."

Now, after she had lost count of how many bottles of wine and how many dishes of food had been carried into and out of their private dining room, Mr. August Belmont was as delirious with pleasure and excitement as everyone else. He had spent most of the meal listening to Aristotle Paxos's explanations of where on the journey the wind softened, freezing them in place, and where it howled like a banshee come to send them straight to the bottom. He'd heard of the agony of trying to find any breeze in the doldrums, and of how after *Hell Witch* crossed the equator she met waves that plunged the bowsprit completely under but survived to encounter the northeast trades that sent them racing home with every man aboard knowing they would set a record for the ages.

"Enough my good friend," Belmont finally told the guest of honor. "I am seasick from simply hearing about it. We must have more champagne." A quick signal to the waiter hovering by the door and the glasses were once more charged with the Bollinger '36 recommended by Lorenzo Delmonico himself. *As remarkable as the feat you are honoring, Mr. Belmont. And like madame, if I may say so, a rosy pink.*

"To *Hell Witch*," Belmont said, standing and bowing first to Paxos, then lifting his glass in Carolina's direction. "And to the remarkable and exquisite lady who made this evening possible."

"He is quite smitten with you," Nicholas said later. It was close to midnight, and they were in the front hall of Carolina's house. It had occurred to him that he might have whisked her away to a discreet and distant spot, but where? Nick had no doubt that some men could have pulled off just such a romantic escapade, but he had never been such a man. He was skilled in science, not romance and seduction. Now his love and his longing would go unspoken one more time.

"August Belmont is not smitten with me," Carolina said. "And if he were, it would make no difference. I am not smitten with him."

"I'm glad to hear it. I thought he might . . ."

"Might what?"

"Might take you from me," Nick said softly, not quite meeting her glance. "At least as much of yourself as you permit me to possess," he added.

"Never," she whispered.

You are a widow in everything except name, and you have been so for at least the eight years since Ceci was born, longer if I'm any judge. So Aunt Lucy said, and she did not know as Carolina did how much the man who had tricked her into marriage despised her. While the man who loved her was here, standing with her in the dark and silent hall, close enough for her to feel his body warmth. But Nick was not Samuel. Nick would not take what she was unwilling to give, only what she freely offered.

Carolina reached for his hand, then raised it and placed it on the soft skin above her breast exposed by the green velvet bodice of her daring gown. She heard his strangled intake of breath. "Do not tease me, Carolina. I cannot bear it. If you do not intend to yield to me, then let me leave at once."

"I wish to yield." Her voice trembled on the word. "Oh God, I wish it so much. But I'm afraid, Nicholas. Dreadfully afraid."

"Afraid of me?"

"No, never of you. I fear the past."

"Then you fear what does not exist." He drew her close and kissed her. She tasted of champagne and the many glories of this magnificent evening but also of the eleven years since he'd first seen her, of all that had happened between then and now. Of herself. The only woman he would ever love. At first she was tense in his arms, then, at last, she melted against him. She was, he knew, finally his.

"Not upstairs," she murmured when he started in that direction. "And not in the front parlor." She would be swamped by ugly memories in either place. "Come." She took his hand and led him to her small and cluttered office, the place in this house where she was most herself, where there were no ghosts of the misery of her terrible marriage. She closed the door, then stood with her back to him. "You must help me. I can't manage by myself."

Her gown fastened down the back with a row of tiny buttons, and when he seemed to be taking forever to undo them, she said, "I can't wait, Nicholas. Tear it off me."

He pulled the frock apart and heard the soft plopping sounds as the buttons fell to the floor. Carolina stepped out of the gown, then the petticoats. "And I still don't come to you as God made me," she said, giggling softly, fumbling behind her back with the laces of her corset. "Fashion is not meant for lovers, I fear."

He laughed with her. Samuel had never once taken her with laughter, not even in those first months of their marriage, when she had suspected nothing of the sham and the lie she was being asked to live. Only Nick laughed, then crushed her up against him with an urgency that somehow seemed to include her rather than be directed at her. Only Nick kissed her neck and her shoulders and finally, when he had helped her loose the ties of her final undergarment, her breasts. Only Nick discovered ways in which she was somehow virgin, newly introduced to the meaning of what transpired between a man and a woman.

Carolina trembled in his arms and found herself whispering his name over and over again, a talisman to protect her against the shadows of memory, a promise to be forever his.

Then, when it was over, there was more laughter and soft kisses. And a new world.

Book Four

1848—1853

Chapter Twenty-eight

THEY CALLED IT Sunshine Hill, and though it was a house that ran more to gaiety than to grandeur, it had a large library on the first floor. Nick's consolation, Carolina said, for having to give up the site he'd found on the even more remote west side of Manhattan. She must, she said, look out on the East River, not the Hudson, because, as Nick knew without her saying so, that's where the Devrey docks and warehouses were. And despite all she had accomplished and all they had dared together, getting Devrey Shipping back for Zachary remained (after hopes for himself and her children) Carolina's dearest dream.

Sunshine Hill, however, was the dream they shared. They chose the name together after the house was built by a Baltimore architect who brought his plans and his craftsmen and laborers with him, and took them all away again when the house was done. The Hill part was misleading. The house's lonely position on what Manhattan maps showed as Seventy-first Street and First Avenue was in fact at the top of a heavily wooded cliff. The only access was a long carriage road that climbed steeply to the front door and was barred and gated below. There was a small cottage off to one side of the house, built with the idea that

Aunt Lucy should one day come and live with them—*Perhaps when I get old, Carolina dear, but right now I am not ready to leave the city*—otherwise they were entirely alone.

To the north there were woods and for a short distance still more cliffs, though the outcropping disappeared within half a mile on either side. Their nearest southerly neighbor was the Mount Vernon Hotel at Sixty-first Street, where the high ground ran out and the river lapped a gentler shore. The hotel served as a stopping place for travelers to the city from Westchester and escapees from the city's hubbub traveling up to the country on a Sunday afternoon.

Isolated enough, Nick had decided in '45, when they built the place, his caution intensified by the fact that now he had not just Carolina and Zac and Ceci to protect.

I am with child, my dearest.

During the year they had been lovers they'd been drifting, deciding what was best to do while Nick paid frequent visits to Fourteenth Street but maintained his Eighth Street lodgings. Carolina's news—no surprise except that joy had fogged his brain—sent him on an intensive search for a site where he could build a house in which to hide her away and keep them all safe from wagging tongues.

Two weeks after her announcement he bundled her into a hired carriage and took her far up the Hudson River shore to a spot looking across to what were called the Palisades of New Jersey. "What do you think? The view's magnificent, don't you agree?"

"I suppose it is. If you mean to spend the rest of your days looking at the Hudson River."

"I take it that means you do not."

"I would rather not," she amended, slipping her arm through his, "though I will live anywhere in the world, as long as it's with you."

"But? Come, Carolina, what is the rest of the sentence."

"Only that I entirely agree with your plan. It's how we must fix things. Zac must board at school, and Ceci have a resident tutor rather than go every day to Miss Alderson's Academy for Young Ladies, which anyway she loathes, and we must have a very private house."

"You won't be horribly unhappy, my love? You won't think I've caused you to give up all your newfound pleasures as an independent woman?"

"I will be more ecstatic than I am now, if that's possible. As long as we can hide away on the east side of Manhattan island, not the west." And a few days later, "I've seen the ideal place, Nick darling. Perhaps an hour and a half's journey into town, if we invest in a brougham and don't rely on my old buggy. You can see patients at Crosby Street a few days each week, though I doubt it will be practical to make the trip every day. Will you mind that terribly?"

He did not tell her that he exulted in the thought of more time spent with her and his books, and perhaps an experiment or two if he could find a corner somewhere to set up his equipment. Nick feared only that the site was not distant enough to protect her from the city's gossip. And there was the matter of the Astor mansion about a mile to the north, but the old man was pretty much a recluse these days. Ill, people said, and certainly past caring about Devrey household affairs, if he ever had. Anyway, it was the site Carolina wanted. So they settled on Sunshine Hill, just barely near enough for her and almost far enough for him, and where each, thinking the partner in this madness might come to feel deprived by the bargain, arranged the other's consolations.

It was Nick's idea to build a tower at the top of the house. "You can take a spyglass up there and have a view up and down the river, my darling. In Providence there are many such arrangements. Indeed, rooftop perches are a New England commonplace." He did not mention that in New England such lofty lookouts were called widows' walks. Because, since she was not legally his wife, she could never be his widow.

Carolina's Turret they called their top-of-the-house aerie. Nick commissioned a powerful telescope from the same company that supplied his exquisitely crafted microscopes. He mounted it himself while she was still abed recovering from the birth of their son Joshua, and carried her up to see it when the baby was two weeks old and he judged her still too weak to climb the steep stairs on her own. "Most men would buy a jewel to mark such an occasion," he told her. "But I know my darling Carolina." Her squeals of delight when she looked through the telescope and the inner and outer harbor both appeared as near as her hand were proof he'd been right.

That no gift could have been more prescient was proven on a cold March day in 1848, when Carolina draped herself in furs and a large black bonnet with a dark veil and went to stand in the Trinity churchyard as—shortly after his eighty-fifth birthday—they put John Jacob Astor in the ground. There was a great crowd present at the service and the internment; she need not have been so concerned about attracting attention. August Belmont, however, seemed equally interested in discretion. He moved quietly to Carolina's side just as the preacher was offering a final blessing to Astor's elaborate coffin. "My carriage is parked behind the Exchange," he murmured. "Ten minutes."

She had no difficulty identifying which rig was his. A large letter *B* was the centerpiece of the elaborate escutcheon mounted on the door, and the coachman was apparently watching for her. In what seemed the flicker of an eyelid he had the door open and had helped her inside. Mr. Belmont and another man were waiting for her.

Both tipped their hats as Carolina took her place on the velvet-covered bench across from theirs. She might not have been sure of William Backhouse Astor's identity had she not just minutes ago seen him standing beside his father's grave. She had never traveled in the same exalted social circles, not even as a girl. In his fifties now, Will had waited a long time to take full charge of the Astor empire. Having done so at last, he was apparently in a great hurry to consolidate what was at last entirely in his control. "Good afternoon," he said, not waiting for Belmont to introduce them. "I'm sure you know who I am, and I know that you are Carolina Randolf Devrey. I'm told you are interested in having the Devrey shipping company return to your family's control."

"My control, to be exact, on behalf of my son. No one else, even if a bearer of the Devrey name." It was, she was quite sure, clear to both men that she spoke of Samuel. Celinda had died the year before, having choked on a piece of mutton and fallen face forward into a plate of carrots stewed in cream.

Astor cleared his throat. A trick, Carolina knew, of many businessmen seeking a few seconds to phrase their next remark. "My understanding," he said when he was ready to speak, "is that the financing will, in part, come from Mr. Belmont."

"Yes, though the majority shareholding will lie with Zachary's trust. I was referring to familial control."

Astor looked hard at her, as if trying to discern the expression hidden behind the veil. "Some in the town say you're a widow, Mrs. Devrey. Others are not quite sure."

"People say many things, Mr. Astor. Most of them are not particularly important. The deed of sale is to be made over to the trust of Zachary Devrey. Those are my terms."

"And Master Devrey's father?"

"Is not of any concern in this transaction. I am the sole trustee of Master Devrey's estate. He will not reach his majority for six more years."

"But if at some point the boy's father should object? I mean if he is not, as some presume, already gone to his reward. There could be an exposure of the sort that is not in my best interest."

"There's little likelihood of that," Belmont said.

"Of what?" Astor had taken to studying his nails.

"Any objection by any third party," Belmont said.

Carolina did not doubt that August Belmont knew where Samuel Devrey was and how he was. It was one of the things she hated most about her situation, that at any moment someone who wished to hurt her or Nick or the children—Almighty God forbid—could wield such a weapon against them. *In business, Carolina, you have to be extremely careful. But also sometimes you have to trust.* Another lesson learned at her father's knee. "Mr. Belmont is correct," she said. "But I would say no likelihood. None whatever."

"So you say." Astor was apparently not going to budge until he got what he wanted, but she wasn't sure what that might be.

"I will indemnify the transaction," Belmont said, "as part of a separate agreement between us. With the provision, separately agreed with Mrs.

Devrey, that if I am required to act on that guarantee, the ownership of Devrey Shipping will then revert entirely to me."

William Astor smiled. "That would satisfy me, but will you agree to it, Mrs. Devrey?"

"I take it the indemnity would come into effect only if someone not a party to the agreement, an unknown third party, raised objections to the terms of the sale." Even so, she would be in thrall to Belmont. He could easily find someone to act as this unnamed third party, but years before he had told her that he had no knowledge of shipping as such, that he was interested only in the profit to be made from it. And they had so far made a great deal of profit together. *Trust, Carolina, is sometimes the most important thing in business.* "Is that correct, gentlemen?"

Both men agreed that it was. And when she pressed them further, agreed that the necessary papers could be drawn by her long-time attorney, Mr. Gordon James.

"Then I agree," Carolina said, "and I thank you," making her voice a little tremulous, because otherwise she was afraid her gleeful triumph would show. "I'm sure you understand that as a woman I need to be quite clear about these things, and that I rely on gentlemen I can trust."

The two men murmured appropriate comments, and Carolina formally shook hands with each of them. Her eyes remained cast down behind her veil so that they might not see them spark with triumph. God be praised! Unless she had entirely misread August Belmont (and she was sure she had not) only Samuel could ever cause this thing to come to grief. And she'd see him in hell before that would happen.

"You have been remarkably generous, Mr. Belmont," Carolina said, her arm in his as he escorted her to Nassau Street, where she'd left her own carriage.

"I have never failed to see a handsome return from our ventures together, Mrs. Devrey. I see no reason to think this will be an exception."

"Nor do I, Mr. Belmont. Here we are." She'd taken the four-in-hand with the coachman Nick had insisted they hire after Josh was born. Not because she agreed with Nick's objections to her single-handed sorties into the town. Because—though she hadn't yet told Nick—she was quite sure she was again with child. "Thank you again. Mr. James will deliver all the necessary papers to your office within the week."

Belmont tipped his hat again and walked on. The coachman helped her up. Carolina gripped the bar beside the carriage door with one hand and kept the other deep in her astrakhan muff, pressing it against her belly. Child of triumph, she thought. Child of wonder.

Was he, Nick wondered, the only man in America who had delivered all his own children and so fervently thanked God for what seemed like a providential choice of career? Their second child was a daughter they called Goldie because she arrived on the September day in 1848 when the *Herald* announced to New York that in far-off California gold had been discovered the previous July.

Nick read the intelligence aloud to Carolina as a distraction, since by then her contractions were coming every five minutes. "Listen to this extraordinary news from the West. 'The entire population of California has gone to the mines, many return a few days later with hundreds of dollars in dust and nuggets. Spades and shovels are selling for ten dollars apiece. Blacksmiths are making two hundred and forty dollars a week. Even a child can pick up three dollar's worth of gold in a day from the treasure streams.'"

"How extraordinary. If it's true. You always say the *Herald* isn't reliable."

"I don't know if it's true, but it makes a change from all Horace Greeley's ranting in the *Tribune*. Especially about the rights of women," he added slyly.

She felt another contraction beginning and panted her way through it, barely finding the breath to say, "Not now, Nicholas. I'm at an unfair disadvantage."

Carolina had vociferously supported the Women's Rights Convention organized the preceding year by Elizabeth Cady Stanton and Lucretia Mott, though given the situation of herself and Nick, she could make no open move. Carolina even thought women should be allowed to vote. Nick laughed aloud each time she mentioned the notion.

In a lull between pains, she grew serious. "Do you realize what this situation in California might mean, Nicholas?"

Nick said he did not, but they could not continue the conversation until a few hours later, because their daughter was suddenly in a great rush to be born. Carolina, however, did not forget. She'd no sooner taken the child to her breast when she said, "Droves will now head west, Nicholas. They are going to be in an almighty hurry, and no wagon train can possibly get them there fast enough. I shall build another clipper to accommodate them. And we shall call this precious little girl Goldie to mark the occasion." It was Nick who insisted that while Goldie was a fine name within the family, Gilda Turner was more fitting for the young lady she would grow up to be.

He took no part, however, in naming Carolina's second ship. She was called *West Witch*. Captain Paxos, still skipper of *Hell Witch*, which had by now made a dozen voyages to Hong Kong, produced a cousin, Socrates Paxos, to captain her. On her maiden voyage in August of 1849, *West Witch* took one hundred and twenty-two days to sail down the east coast and around the tip of South America at Cape Horn, then north by northwest to San Francisco. No earlier ship, not one of which had been a clipper, had done it in fewer than two hundred.

The birth of their third child, a boy born soon after the 1850 death in office of President Zachary Taylor, nearly killed Carolina, but she was nonetheless most agitated about what he would be called. "I've already got a Zachary," she said, "so we won't be unpatriotic by not giving this lovely boy that name. Must he be Millard, do you think?"

Nick shook his head. "Much as I dislike the shenanigans of Tammany Hall Democrats, I'm no Whig. And I don't think this fellow Fillmore will amount to much."

They called him Simon, for no reason other than that they liked the name. Nick gave Carolina pearls to mark the occasion, but what he celebrated most was that both his wife and his son lived. Carolina had labored two days and three nights and still she was barely dilated. In the end he'd pulled the infant out with his own two hands, literally plunging them both inside her. As a boy visiting a farm, he'd once seen a man deliver a calf that way. The procedure apparently made no difficulty for cows; it was not so easy for a woman. Nick had never seen such damage to the female organs and found it hard not to blame himself as being— twice over, so to speak—the cause. "There will be no more children, my love. And you must take at least a year to recover from this ordeal. No more dawn meetings with Danny Parker. I absolutely forbid it."

She'd agreed to that at once. Easy enough to do, he discovered three months later. Danny had retired—a rich man thanks to his quarter interest in *Hell Witch*'s first three cargos, and his son Seth Parker was now the yard's chief shipwright. Carolina met Seth at Thirty-fourth Street after dark on days when Nicholas went to Crosby Street and was himself late home to Sunshine Hill. "Strictly speaking, I did not break my word, Nicholas. The meetings were not at dawn and they were not with Danny Parker."

So Carolina built her third clipper, *East Witch*. She set out on her maiden voyage on September 14, 1851. Carolina was far too conscious of jinxing this marvelous new ship to say so, but Nick knew she thought *East Witch*, sailing with yet another Paxos relative at the helm, this one named Plato, would set new records.

It was, however, still too soon for her to be climbing up to the turret to watch through her telescope for *East Witch*'s return. Nick, however, now had the daily pleasure of a fully equipped laboratory in an outbuilding a short distance from the house. Carolina planned it for him with the same motives that had originally caused him to want the turret for her. What if he missed the old life too much? What if this exile made necessary by their unorthodox union seemed to come at too high a price?

"I thought first to put a laboratory in the cellar, dearest, but then, what with all the grisly things you study, a separate place of your own seemed wiser." It was in fact perfect. So too the library, which was on the ground floor across the hall from the room they called the long parlor and functioned as well as Nick's study. All his old books were close to hand, and the room's proportions were so generous he could order new books and periodicals without fearing he'd nowhere to put them. *The Boston Medical and Surgical Journal* had a prominent place on his shelves. He kept all the back issues, including the one that described the demonstration at Massachusetts General Hospital in October of 1846 which proved beyond doubt that sulfuric ether did indeed make patients insensitive to pain. The phenomenon was much discussed these days. No less a figure than the prominent physician and writer Oliver Wendell Holmes had lauded the practice and said it should be called "anesthesia" from the Greek for without sensation. Despite such endorsements, there was considerable argument about whether the use of ether or its derivative, chloroform, was a moral and ethical practice that should be further studied, much less used.

Bloody nonsense, Nick thought. Bloody clerics getting their oar in as always. Never mind. Science would trump that nay-saying form of religion when sufficient numbers of individuals were faced with the choice of going under the knife asleep or awake and made the to-be-expected choice. It wasn't the battle about anesthesia that most occupied him these days. Nick took as well the *Provincial Medical and Surgical Journal* from London, because it was in Europe that the argument raged loudest as to whether germs could be the cause of disease or were simply spontaneously generated as a result of it.

Carolina was always threatening to have the oldest copies of his magazines thrown out lest the family should have to move out to make room for all of them. Nick knew it to be an idle threat and ignored it. But scientific journals were not the only things cluttering up—Carolina's term—the library. Sometimes, living as they did in this isolated place, even Nick craved everyday sorts of intercourse.

He had developed a passion for newspapers and arranged to have seven dailies delivered to his Crosby Street office. He collected them when he was there and brought stacks home to be read at leisure. In fact, he'd just added a promising new one to his list, *The New-York Daily Times.* The first evening edition of the first printing was dated two days before, September 18, 1851. Like the other broadsheets, it had mostly news from Europe on the front page. Nick took special note of an announcement that on the seventeenth the Royal Mail steam packet *Europa* had arrived in Boston from London, and her mail had been sent on by the New Haven Railroad train which left Boston at nine P.M. and arrived in New York at ten the following morning.

"That's the new paper, isn't it?" Carolina had come in and was looking over his shoulder. "*The Times.*"

"*The Daily Times.* And you can probably answer a question that has just occurred to me. How long does it take a steam packet to travel between London and Boston these days?"

She turned from the paper and picked up the mail, also brought home from the Crosby Street office, and was thumbing through it while she spoke. "Rather depends on whether it's one of Mr. Cunard's austere Canadian workhorses or one of Mr. Collins's American luxury fillies. On average, on the voyage west, twelve days."

"And a railroad train can go from Boston to New York in thirteen hours."

"A letter from Zac at last," she said, without looking up. Her eldest had gone across the Hudson to Princeton in New Jersey for further education, and he did not write as frequently as his mother thought he should. "And to answer your question, yes, I believe it takes the steam train from Boston thirteen or fourteen hours to get here to New York. I also believe you are thinking my clipper ships will soon be obsolete."

"I admit the idea has occurred to me."

"Would you weep if that turned out to be true?"

"Only for you, my dearest. Only because I know what stock you place in your accomplishments in the world apart from Sunshine Hill."

"I do, Nick, I don't deny it. But nothing is more important to me than you or the children or our life together."

"I never thought otherwise. But you haven't said whether you think the clippers are to be overtaken."

"On the European run they already are. And if they ever manage to build a transcontinental railroad, I suppose it will be the finish of getting to California under sail." For a time they'd thought the end of the gold rush in '49 would mean a stop to huge numbers wanting to book passage on *West Witch,* but in 1850 California had been admitted to the Union as a free state. That caused the South to fear a free state majority in Congress and set off a political row that ended with the formal declaration that Utah and New Mexico were officially territories, meaning they could look forward to eventual statehood and that in neither place were there to be explicit restrictions on slavery. It was yet another of those compromises that was supposed to put the vexed issue of slavery behind the nation and allow it to move forward, but that somehow never did. The one thing Carolina was sure this compromise had accomplished was to encourage a stream of settlers to head west, for the time being at least traveling on the clippers. "But to China," she continued. "Unless people are to sprout wings and fly, I think we're unlikely to lose the clippers' superiority in sailing halfway round the world and back."

"I'm sure you're right," he said. "Anyway, a railroad right across the continent from the Pacific Ocean to the Atlantic seems a mad idea, doesn't it?"

"Absolutely daft. Though there was another story about it in the *Tribune* a week or so ago."

"I keep telling you, the *Tribune* is a dubious source. Mr. Greeley believes in socialism, vegetarianism, abolitionism, Irish rights, and that women should be allowed to vote." Nick held up a hand to forestall her explosion. "And, I don't doubt, free love."

She'd not give him the satisfaction of rising to the bait about women's suffrage. "I entirely agree about free love." She kissed his cheek and he patted her rump.

"As do I," said Nick, "as long as you are free only to love me."

Carolina laughed. "I absolutely promise that shall be the case. But now, my one and only *paramour,* you must get ready to go. You're to be at Cousin Manon's hospital at three this afternoon, and since we can't provide either a clipper ship or a steam train for the journey, you've not a chance of getting there on time unless you leave by half past one."

❧

Normally Nick hated leaving Sunshine House for any reason other than his practice, but this occasion was different. He was to attend a meeting to inaugurate a fund-raising drive at Manon's St. Vincent's Hospital on Thirteenth Street between Third and Fourth Avenues. The Sisters of Charity had opened the facility two years earlier in 1849.

"Not just a dispensary. Cousin Nicholas, it's to be a proper hospital. These last few years, with the potato crops failing in Ireland, the numbers of immigrants . . . well, we can do with nothing less. The bishop has given us the land, and kindly private citizens are contributing funds. Remember years ago when you asked me why there were not more wealthy Catholics to help the Catholic poor?"

"I do. And you told me that in New York Catholics were the hewers of wood and the drawers of water. Not so any more, I take it?"

"Not entirely. For one thing, Bishop Hughes agrees it's a good idea and will help us."

Nick remembered her telling him earlier that the New York Sisters of Charity had separated from Mother Seton's original congregation in Maryland because there were disagreements between what the Mother General wanted and what the bishop wanted. And that these days the group to which Manon belonged had as their superior the sister of Bishop Hughes. "Quite," he had said.

"Don't look like that. It's not just because of family connections. Bishop Hughes realizes that religious orders have their own ways of doing things. He's allowed the Redemptorists to establish Catholic parishes where everyone speaks German. He's even let the Jesuits in." And when she saw that this meant nothing to him, "Jesuits are said to have the ear of most of the crowned heads of Europe and be great political meddlers. Many bishops want no part of them, but Bishop Hughes has allowed the Jesuits to establish a college up near the village of Fordham, and a school for boys here in town on Sixteenth Street."

"Whatever you say."

"I am boring you, dear Cousin Nicholas."

"No, of course not. I'm simply tired. I was up late last night with a patient."

A likely enough excuse, but Vatican politics had obviously been making his eyes glaze over. "We have skilled laborers among the Irish immigrants now," Manon had said. "And enough work for them to earn a living. They are very generous to the church."

Nick was familiar with the Irish enclaves in the Bronx and Harlem and along the route of the Hudson River Railroad they had helped to build, but there seemed no fewer Irish paupers in Five Points, a worse hellhole than ever these days. Better not to say that; Manon had grown defensive about her adopted allegiances. "Must one be a member of your religion to receive treatment at this hospital?"

"Absolutely not. We will care for anyone who comes to us without respect to creed. Or color," she added pointedly.

"Be careful you're not branded abolitionists. You've enough to bear simply for being Catholics."

"I believe the word is papists in that context. Never mind, I think when one is sick enough and poor enough, such considerations seem to matter less. Nick, will you be a member of our board of prominent lay advisors?"

He had agreed, though he'd told her "prominent" was not a word he thought applied to him and that in any case he had no desire to be such. Manon replied that he was prominent whether or not he wanted to be, that his reputation had grown in spite of himself. She did not mention Carolina and said nothing about the illicit life Nick lived with her and their children, though he had no doubt she knew about it. However, it had never occurred to him that Manon had any knowledge of Mei Lin, Linda as she'd asked him to call her. Be that as it may, when Nick arrived for the board meeting at a few minutes to three Mei Lin was standing beside the hospital door.

"I went first to your office, Dr. Turner, but Dr. Klein said you were not seeing patients there today. He suggested you might be coming here."

Nick had long since taken Ben Klein into his confidence. As for Linda, she would be sixteen in a few weeks, and even dressed in her exceedingly modest school uniform he found her exotic beauty quite breathtaking, perhaps because he didn't see her frequently. Carolina tried to do the right thing, but she could never be easy with the girl; the memories were too bitter. Still, apart from a sense of duty, it was vital to both of them to remain informed about Sam Devrey and so Nick had taken over dealing with the Cherry Street situation. "I wasn't expecting your visit for another month," he said. "Otherwise I'd have arranged to let you know I wouldn't be at my office today. Is something wrong, Linda?"

"My father . . ."

"Yes?"

"He's very poorly. I thought . . . I mean my mother thought . . ." *The this-place-red-hair* yi, *he will fix. Go get him.*

Nick glanced at his pocket watch. The board meeting was to start in ten minutes. He could not get to Cherry Street and back in that time. "Is it urgent, Linda? Does he need a doctor at once?"

She shook her head. "No. He's been ill for some time. Taste Bad has been treating him, but he doesn't improve. My mother thought you might be able to help."

"Very well, I'll go with you back to Cherry Street as soon as I'm finished here. I've a meeting to attend. Come wait inside. It won't take long."

❦

Mei Lin was careful to sit as Mother Stevenson instructed in deportment class, hands folded in her lap, ankles crossed, and feet flat on the floor. She could not, however, manage to gain merit in heaven by keeping her back from resting against the chair for all the time Dr. Turner was gone.

The nun sitting behind the small table near the front door seemed indifferent to how Mei Lin sat. She bent her head over a ledger of some sort and did not once look up. Still Mei Lin was sure she was being watched. At school the nuns always knew everything that was happening, even when their backs were turned. Perhaps the ability to see without looking came with holy vows. Never mind that these were different sorts of nuns wearing a different sort of habit. Though they did seem a great deal less . . . ethereal, that was the word. The Mothers never seemed to touch the earth when they walked. Some of the girls wondered if they had to do ordinary things like use a privy. Maybe God took that need away when they entered the convent.

Mei Lin sighed. She was assuredly not ethereal. Right now she had an itch above her left ear under the straw bonnet fastened beneath her chin with a black bow tied precisely as the Madams of the Sacred Heart said it must be tied. Mei Lin tried to ignore it, but the itch got worse. *A young lady does not remove her bonnet in public,* mes enfants. *It is not permitted.* One of Ah Chee's chopsticks would be perfect, the long ones used for cooking. She could poke it up under the bonnet and scratch as much as she needed to. Never mind, she would say three Hail Marys and an Our Father, and if the itch hadn't gone away by then she'd just—

The door to the room at the end of the hall opened and a gentleman came out.

The meeting must be over. The nun quickly left her place behind the table and went to stand by the door, ready to open it for the distinguished visitors when they left. Mei Lin stood as well, but no one else followed the gentleman into the hall. He pulled the door of the meeting room shut behind him with an air of trying not to disturb the people still in the room. Mei Lin sat down again. The man walked towards her, stopped directly in front of her, bowed politely—he was carrying his silk topper under his arm, so he couldn't tip it—and said, *"Chi le fan meiyou?"* Have you eaten rice today?

Mei Lin's gray-blue eyes opened as wide as was possible. The man was white, but he had spoken to her in perfect Mandarin. An ordinary greeting, but apart from her father, he was the first white man she'd ever heard speak Chinese words, and his accent was considerably more natural than Baba's. *"Chi le. Chi le,"* she managed after a long moment. Eaten. Eaten. An equally ordinary and polite answer to his greeting. The man bowed again, then turned and left.

It was years since Nick had been on Cherry Street, and the first thing he noticed was that the neighborhood had changed. The houses were more run-down, the people on the street surlier and almost entirely men, the two women he did see looked very much like doxies. Another surprise was how many of the men were Chinese. He'd always had the impression that Sam Devrey's lodgers kept their heads down and traveled the city only to get to and from their jobs, but here on Cherry Street he saw idlers and small groups talking, a great many of them Chinamen and certainly more than could possibly cram themselves into the two Cherry Street houses. There was even a tiny shop with a Chinese shopkeeper selling sundries. That at least looked a respectable enterprise. "Mei Lin—excuse me, Linda—what does your mother think of all this?"

"You can call me Mei Lin if you like. It's only with white people that it matters." She suddenly realized what she'd said. "I mean, you're white, but . . ."

"It's all right. I understand what you meant. But there certainly seem to be many more Chinese people here than I remember. Does your mother find that unsettling?"

"If you mean how much more crowded everything is and how much dirtier, I don't think my mother notices. It's hard to see such changes from the window."

"Are you saying she still never goes out? Even with so many more of her own kind about?"

"Never. Not once since she arrived, as far as I know. Ah Chee gets her everything she needs. Ah Chee's too old to carry much, but one of the men goes with her to help."

Nick knew of at least one time Mei-hua had left her rooms, but that was not something he would speak about to Mei Lin. "It's hard to believe," he said.

"It's the Chinese way for a lady never to leave her house. At least, my mother has always believed it to be so among the—" She broke off and didn't look at him. He would think what she had meant to say very stupid indeed.

"Go on," he urged. "Among the what?"

She couldn't get out of it. "Among the highborn. My mother believes herself a princess, Dr. Turner. She thinks my father is lord of a kingdom."

Nick concerned himself with stepping over the piles of rubbish he had to navigate to get inside the door of number thirty-seven, where Mei Lin told him her father was to be found. "He almost never comes next door now," she explained. "I don't think he wants my mother to know how ill he is."

"But you said she sent you to get me."

"Yes. Taste Bad reports regularly to her. He comes to show his respect. They all do. At least the people who live in my father's buildings."

He wondered if the girl knew that the two houses no longer belonged to Sam Devrey, though the rents were still paid to him. Carolina thought that Mei Lin had heard and understood everything seven years ago, on the day of the final confrontation between herself and Sam. It was impossible to tell from the girl's manner or her speech. She was so utterly and carefully refined it was hard to discern a real person beneath her mannered *politesse*. The Madams of the Sacred Heart did their job well.

"My father is in here," Mei Lin said, opening the door of a tiny windowless room. The smell of disease and dirt—and opium—was overpowering. She stepped aside. Nick went in. Then she closed the door behind him.

Devrey lay on a straw pallet raised about a foot from the floor on a makeshift bedstead created from bits of wood roped together. Nick had to kneel down to examine him. If he had not known the man to be his Cousin Samuel, he'd not have recognized him. He was shrunken to the point of being skeletal, his skin yellowed and flaking. Clean shaven, however, which made it apparent how hollow his cheeks were and how black the circles beneath his eyes. They remained closed while Nick poked and prodded and used his stethoscope, a marvelous new one with a length of rubber between an earpiece and a flared listening trumpet. When Nick began to palpate the glands of the neck, Sam opened his eyes.

"Turner. What are you doing here?"

"Your daughter brought me."

Sam struggled to lift his head and see over Nick's shoulder. "She's not in here, is she? I don't want her in here."

"No, she waited outside. Who shaves you? Doesn't look as if you can manage that on your own."

"Leper Face, not that it's any business of yours."

"Brings you your supply of opium as well, does he?"

"None of your business," Sam said again. Leper Face would not touch opium, much less supply it. Big Belly brought him what he needed.

"It's killing you. I presume you do realize that."

"Wrong," Sam said. "It already has killed me. I'm a walking corpse. At least sometimes. Don't walk much these days."

"Why have you done this to yourself?"

"Why not?"

"Because you're a man. Because you've got a—"

Sam chuckled. It came out like a death rattle and betrayed the fact that he had few teeth left. "Started to say I'd a wife, didn't you? Which one did you have in mind? Carolina's your whore now, I imagine."

"I suppose you know I could snap your neck with my two hands."

"Of course. But you won't. You're a gentleman. A Christian. A doctor who took an oath to heal. All the things I am not, Nicholas Turner. But I'll be pissing on you from hell. You can count on it. I'm told she has a third clipper now. I lie here praying for the grandmother of all storms to take her to the bottom. I—" He coughed, then spit up yellow, blood-specked phlegm. "I won't die yet," he said when he could speak again. "Not until I hear about how Carolina's clippers have gone down."

"There's nothing I can do, Mei Lin. I'm sorry."

"I didn't expect anything else, Dr. Turner. I only came to get you because my mother asked me to."

"Yes, I understand. Shall I go up and tell her how things are?"

"No, it's better if I tell her. Dr. Turner, it's the opium, isn't it? That's why he's so ill."

"It is indeed. It's a vicious and fatal habit, my dear. I am sorry it has been so available to him. Providing the drug is a misguided kindness, I assure you."

"He doesn't get it from us, Dr. Turner, I promise you." She thought it best to change the subject. "Dr. Turner, there was a man who left the meeting at the hospital a few minutes before you did. Not very tall, stocky, fair hair. Do you know him by any chance?"

"Kurt Chambers," he said after a few moments' thought. "He joined the board recently. I know nothing about him except that he's arrived recently from Europe, London I believe, and he's been a generous benefactor to St. Vincent's. Why do you ask?"

"I saw him leave," she said. "And I just wondered who he was." Unless he asked her directly she would not tell him that Mr. Kurt Chambers spoke Chinese. It wasn't really a lie, just as not telling him that Lee Big Belly supplied the clouds for Baba to swallow was not a lie. Never mind that he did it with such a free hand Mei Lin, who knew *ya-p'ien* to be a source of considerable profit, was astonished. If she was not asked, not telling was permissible.

Chapter Twenty-nine

"YOU WILL TAKE some tea, Papa Klein?"

"Yes, Bella, I will take a little glass of tea."

Ben's wife brought her father-in-law the tea on a tray covered with a lace-edged white cloth, with a small dish of cherry preserves on the side. A silver spoon was placed invitingly beside the preserves. Jacob Klein had himself made the spoon; it was part of the silver service for twelve he had made for Ben and Bella as a wedding present. Next to the spoon was a silver dish, also his work, filled with her homemade cookies. Before Bella had married Ben, after a test in her kitchen so there could be no cheating, Frieda Klein had pronounced her future daughter-in-law an excellent cook. That had sealed the bargain, though there were things about Bella Markus's family which did not meet with Jacob Klein's approval. Never mind. The couple had been married fifteen years and Bella had given him seven beautiful grandchildren. The youngest, a girl named for Jacob's great grandmother Rachel of blessed memory, was just six months old. He thanked Bella for the tea and did not touch either the cookies or the cherry preserves.

"So, Papa Klein, you like the new house?"

"It is very nice, darling. Beautiful." What could he not like about a four-story brownstone house on the north side of elegant Hudson Square, west of Broadway, where rich people lived. Even, nowadays, rich Jews. "Only . . . Benjy doesn't find it too far to walk to synagogue on the Sabbath?"

Bella looked away, busying herself with something not quite right about the lay of the lace doily beneath the lamp beside her chair. "He doesn't find this location inconvenient, no. And to the office, only twenty minutes to walk on a nice day. Invigorating, he says."

"And on a day that is not so nice?"

"He takes the buggy." Something else on the table required her attention.

"Benjy will be home soon?"

"Yes, Papa Klein. By two always on Thursdays. He writes his reports on Thursday afternoons. In his private study on the second floor," she added, unable to resist this tiny bit of bragging. "He says the light is better here than at the office."

"So. Good light is important. I agree."

"That's why the older children aren't here. Sofie takes them to the park on Thursday afternoons. So Ben can have quiet." They had hired a woman, a free black, to help with the children after Bella lost their four-month-old twins to the croup and was for a time despondent. Sofie had been with them ever since. "Of course," his daughter-in-law added, "if we'd known you were coming . . ."

Jacob waved away the apology. "I was in the neighborhood. Delivering a pair of candlesticks to a customer." Not exactly. The customer lived ten blocks up the town. No, wait. According to his daughter Esther, these days he must say "uptown." "Up the town" was old-fashioned. Esther had married a man who owned an insurance company, and they lived in a house even grander than this one, uptown as Esther said, at Twenty-first Street on Gramercy Square.

"Please, Papa Klein, have a ginger cookie. I baked them myself just this morning."

Jacob put a hand to his stomach. "My digestion . . . Forgive me, Bella. I'm sure the ginger cookies are delicious."

"And my cherry preserves?" Bella could feel the heat of her reddening cheeks. She could sometimes control her temper but never her cheeks. "I made them myself as well. You've always loved cherry preserves in your tea, ever since I've known you."

"Yes, darling, but lately . . . I don't know—"

"My kitchen is *kosher*, Papa Klein. I would not serve you anything from a kitchen that was not *kosher*." She stood up. "How can you think I would do such a thing? That Ben would permit such a thing? How can you?" She did not add that it was so all the Kleins could eat in their house that she and Ben had determined to keep a *kosher* kitchen. "Are we *goyim* that we do not understand the importance?"

Jacob leaned forward and took a heaping spoonful of cherry preserves and dropped them into his tea. They shimmered like red jewels at the bottom of the glass. "I apologize, Bella." He put two ginger cookies into his mouth at the same time. That way he did not have to say what he was thinking she meant. The importance to him, not to her.

The door of the parlor opened and Ben came in. He and his father embraced. Bella offered to get fresh tea, but both men refused. "In that case," she said, "you'll have to excuse me. It's time to feed Rachel. Your newest granddaughter has an enormous appetite, Papa Klein."

Jacob made a point of kissing Bella's cheek before she left. Seven grandchildren: three girls and four boys, all healthy and beautiful. Never mind whatever he didn't like about her relatives. Some of the relatives of Esther's wealthy-from-insurance husband Jacob also didn't like. They were Bavarians, a group Jacob, who was from Prussia, had never fully trusted. But Esther and her husband and their two boys attended a proper synagogue. Indeed, they had been instrumental in founding a new one three blocks from their home. Not so with his son.

"Very nice, Ben," Jacob said. "Everything. Very, very nice."

"We were waiting to have you and Mama see the house when we were more settled. It's only been three weeks. Still everywhere boxes."

"I was in the neighborhood." With a shrug. "Anyway, I didn't mean the house only. Your Bella looks beautiful. I like when a woman gets plump and pink." When Ben married her Bella was thin as a rail and so pale.

Jacob had worried she might be sickly, but his son the doctor had assured him Bella was perfectly healthy. Apparently he'd been correct. "And little Rachel and Morris, I saw them as well. They are also beautiful."

"We're calling him Morrie, Papa. That will be easier for him. In New York. In America."

"I know where New York is, Benjy. Only I've been wondering do you?"

"Papa, what do you mean?"

"I mean that New York is not just geography. It is a place that *Hashem* sees. Like every other place."

Ben motioned to the sofa. "Sit, Papa. Tell me what you want to tell me."

"I shall, Benjy. With no fancy words, because you are my son and from me you should hear only the truth without any decorations. I am wondering if in two years, when it is time for my eldest grandson, your David, to be a *bar mitzvah,* if—*Hashem* permit me to live to see that day—I can stand next to him on the *bimah* and feel my heart swell with pride as a grandfather's should."

"Why would that not be the case, Papa?" Ben asked quietly.

"Because if David is to be a *bar mitzvah* at this Temple Emanu-El on Chrystie Street, presuming those idolaters follow even that much of the law, I cannot attend."

"Idolater is a very strong word, Papa. There are no golden calves on Chrystie Street."

"To worship *goyim*, to think that one must be like them in every possible way, what is that Benjy if not idolatry?"

Ben shook his head. "Worship *goyim?* Papa, where did you get such an idea? And I'm not a member of Temple Emanu-El."

"So tell me, please, where are you a member? To pray sometimes during the week and on the Sabbath, what synagogue do you walk to, Benjamin, my son? When your mother and I die, where will you go to say *Kaddish* for us?"

"Papa, there are almost fifty thousand Jews in New York now. It's not the same as—"

"Yes, that I know. Waves of them have come. And now, here in New York, there are five hundred thousand people all together. So from being a tiny drop in a not so big New York we fifty thousand Jews have become a big part of a very big bucket. And there are probably ten synagogues. I lost count some time ago. By the way, that's probably ten not including your Temple Emanu-El."

"Why are you not counting it? True, their synagogue is in space they rent only, but Shearith Israel began in a room behind a mill, so—"

"Shearith Israel obeys the law, Benjy. Maybe I do not like the prayer book they use or the way they do some things, but they follow the rules given us by *Hashem*. They do what Torah and Talmud tell us Jews are supposed to do."

"Torah yes, Papa. That is the authority. But Talmud is commentary only. Old-fashioned notions from rabbis arguing hundreds of years ago about the meaning of this or that. You don't know the exact date of a particular holiday, which way the moon maybe was or is going to be? You will then keep the holiday for two days. So you should not by accident make a mistake. In Exodus it says, 'Thou dost not boil a kid in its mother's milk.' From that you get a million laws about what you can put in your mouth and even your stomach, and how long it will take to digest so maybe you can put something else in your mouth. I am a man of science, Papa. I do not need rabbis from Babylon who have been dead already a thousand years telling me how long food stays in my stomach."

"From Isaac Markus you get these ideas. They can come from nowhere else."

"Isaac Markus! Papa, Bella's grandfather has been dead for thirty years, may his name be for a blessing. He never came to America. I never met him."

"But I met him. In the old country, in Prussia. He was a follower of Samuel Holdheim. Who called himself Rabbi Holdheim, but I don't think so. This reform of his is nothing that would come from a rabbi. Isaac Markus, he believed also in so-called reform. My question to you, my Benjy, my only son, is this, do you?"

"I'm not sure, Papa."

"Not sure. Very well. Can you then promise me that David will be a *bar mitzvah* at B'nai Jeshurun? So I can stand beside him?"

Ben hesitated, but not for long. "I'm sorry, Papa. Bella and I think ... I cannot promise that."

Countess Romanov Lilac Langston called herself these days. After all, she had actually been at the imperial court of Nicholas I, Tsar of all the Russias, in St. Petersburg, dressed up in an elaborate gown such as she'd never yet seen, much less owned. With a tiara. Never mind that later, when she tried to sell it, she found out the tiara was paste. She always knew the entire adventure was a sort of a dream. So when she woke up one morning to find Vladimir gone, she wasn't surprised.

There was no note, but he had left her a whole pile of rubles—not that she'd ever reckoned him to be entirely truthful about what they were paid for Manon Turner's diamond, which was now part of the Russian crown jewels—but she'd never supposed Vladimir to be the staying sort. In fact, he'd hung around two years longer than she'd have guessed. As for the money, he was a fair sort, no doubt about that. When they ran away from New York together, Vladimir told her he'd left the keys to his fancy-goods store beside his wife's bed. *I only took this tiara for you, Lilac darling. Because where we're going you will need it.* Grand it had been wearing a tiara and a ball gown and making a deep curtsy to the Tsar and Tsarina. A woman could get used to that sort of thing. So when she realized Vladimir was gone and she was on her own again, Lilac had instantly made up her mind that from then on she'd be Countess Romanov.

But not in St. Petersburg or anywhere in Russia. Not with them fierce winters they had, and their language being so difficult to learn. London or New York, that was the question. There were black marks against both: In London, even as Countess Romanov, she might find herself drawn right back to Spitalfields, lured by the old ways, and pretty soon she'd really be Francy again. In New York there were those who might think Lilac owed them something. Addie Bellingham for instance. Or Mrs. Manon Turner.

But when was Lilac Langton who had been Francy Finders and was now Countess Romanov not a match for the likes of Addie Bellingham or Manon Turner?

New York it was.

Only it turned out she changed her mind or had it changed for her. The steamship *Russian Empress* was supposed to stop in Oslo first, then Greenland, where seems like they didn't have any cities, at least none she could pronounce, then Halifax in Nova Scotia, and finally (wouldn't it be grand!) down the coast to old New York. But four days out of Oslo the ship developed engine trouble, and since Portsmouth was the closest port, that's where they put in. At least a week was needed for repairs, it turned out. And what with one thing and another, she never did get back aboard the *Russian Empress*.

There was a little cottage on the edge of the town, flowers all around, and even a few sheep grazing in a pasture out behind. And it was for sale. Like a country estate it was, like the *dachas* the rich Russians had. Perfect for Countess Romanov. Cheap, too. She had plenty of brass left after she bought it, but that's not what she planned to live on. Too clever for that she was, whatever name she called herself. Do a bit of business with the lady needles, real quiet and only for the gentry, that was her plan.

Then, when she was just getting started, two women—leastwise they were dressed like women, though she'd never seen ladies who looked so much like men—came and beat her silly. She was black and blue for days, and ever after missing one of her front teeth. *Don't do to cut in on business as is already established, love. Have to make your living, best you get 'em in the family way rather than out of it.* Later she found out they were called Sapphos, women as were lovers with other women, though God knows what they actually did. And in these parts it turned out, Sapphos had the abortion business stitched up tight.

Whores, however, were another matter. Always plenty of whores in a waterfront town like Portsmouth. Most lifted their skirts behind any convenient fence, but some aspired to a better class of activity and required a safe and discreet place to bring their johns. There were parlor houses aplenty in London, but in working class Portsmouth there was a real need, and Countess Romanov managed to fill it. The sheep became a real feature of the place. Some of the ladies dressed up like Little Bo-Peep sometimes. One or two of the gents thought that was the most exciting thing ever. You never could tell what would excite nobs, Lilac learned.

She might have ended her days in Portsmouth, thinking up new entertainments to titillate a better class of johns, except that in the autumn of 1851 Lilac took a trip to London on the brand-new Crystal Palace Railway to see the brand-new Crystal Palace in Hyde Park. Built entirely of wrought iron and great sheets of glass it was. Eighth wonder of the world, folks said. Lilac was quite looking forward to visiting it and seeing the Great Exhibition it had been built to house. But she never got there, because as soon as she got off the train at the terminus on Stewarts Lane in Battersea she read about chloroform.

In all the papers it was. How women could have painless childbirth by taking a few whiffs of this new gas and going to sleep, though some said that was against nature and no decent woman would consider such a thing. Some preacher had led a whole pack of protesters to object to the immorality of using chloroform to ease the agony of labor. "A parade of men from every walk of life," the paper said. As far as Lilac was concerned, no man should have anything to say as to whether a woman—

Good God Almighty. Painless surgery.

Lilac hadn't thought about painless surgery in years. Never heard a word about it in St. Petersburg. 'Course, she couldn't read the papers there. And in Portsmouth, well, it was a backwater sort of place when it came to science.

How much could she make if a woman could take a couple of breaths of something and go into such a sound sleep than she wouldn't feel the lady needles? A bloody fortune, that's how much. England was out of the question; didn't want to lose the rest of her teeth, did she? That left New York.

Addie Bellingham was in New York. And Mrs. Manon Turner. And Reverend Finney.

Same question as before. When had Lilac Langton who'd been Francy Finders in Spitalfields and survived to be Countess Romanov today not been able to deal with the likes of them? Right now her job was to find out where in London she could buy some of this chloroform, then arrange to take it to New York. Because with it Countess Romanov could well and truly be the most popular abortionist in the city as well as the richest. Maybe as rich as Nicholas I, Tsar of all the Russias.

It was thanks to New York's doctors and their dislike of competition from persons they called irregulars that abortion after quickening, generally believed to be in the fourth month, had been made illegal in 1828. If after that time an abortion was required to save the mother's life, two doctors must agree on the necessity for the procedure. That was the law, though throughout the 1830s no one paid it much attention. Indeed, there were those who argued that it was neither moral nor desirable for families to grow beyond their means, and that given how unreliable were most methods of birth control, abortion was a societal good.

In the 1840s, however, a few years after Lilac Langton had left the city, a man by the name of George W. Dixon, owner of a weekly journal, appointed himself guardian of public morals. Dixon was not concerned with the health of the mother or the life of the fetus; his interest was in female virtue. If abortions were easily obtainable, Dixon said, women might commit adultery without fear of detection. Indeed, a man who thought he was marrying a virginal maiden might, because of birth control and abortion, have not "a medal of sure metal fresh from the mint, but a base lacquered counter that has undergone the sweaty contamination of a hundred palms."

Dixon said nothing about the adultery of the thousands upon thousands of New York men who supported the many, many hundreds of prostitutes who flourished in the town. He did, however, set out on a vendetta aimed to make an example of a woman calling herself Madame Restell. She did such a thriving business in birth control pills and abortions that she could not avoid coming to his notice.

By Christmas 1851, when Lilac sailed into New York harbor on Mr. Collins's luxurious, steam-driven ocean liner *Atlantic*, Madame Restell had been in prison twice.

She was arrested the first time in 1841, when a man accused her of a botched abortion that killed his wife. After a few weeks in the Tombs she was tried for murder but convicted of only a minor infraction and went free to enjoy the added business brought on by the publicity. Six years later, after a trial witnessed by lawyers from all over the country and still more publicity, she was convicted of a misdemeanor and sentenced to a year in the penitentiary on Blackwell's Island. Word was that her supporters—many powerful men who counted on being able to bring a young friend to Madame Restell when necessary—insured a comfortable incarceration.

Given that it was the medical profession that pushed through the first antiabortion law, it surprised no one when the doctors continued to agitate for strict control of what was called female medicine. Particularly since in these modern times they had found lucrative specialties overseeing midwifery and the diseases of women and children. Feminists too, given their view of the laws that put women's entire lives in the legal control of their husbands, were opposed to easy access to abortion. One of the burdens women were supposed to bear in silence was the unrestrained philandering of their husbands. That behavior was bound to be encouraged by quick and simple methods of avoiding the consequences. As for those New Evangelicals who still held such sway in the city, the ones who promoted the notion of domestic bliss and women as saintly homebodies who shed light and grace on the world from the sanctity of their decorous parlors, they supported the new notion of prosecuting not only the abortionists but also the women who sought their services. They did not, of course, suggest that the men who impregnated the women be held to any account.

Those mothers-to-be, however, who either had no husband or had one who wasn't around and who could therefore take no joy in the thought of birthing a child, had few options. There was in New York no lying-in hospital that would take in unmarried women. To be accepted at the New York Asylum for Lying-In Women on Orange Street close to Five Points you had to prove you were married and produce references saying you were respectable.

There was not a single foundling home in the city. Only Bellevue would accept abandoned or deserted children, and it remained part of the almshouse. Infants too young for that institution's orphanage were boarded with poor women, who were paid less than the amount actually necessary to support the child. According to the records, nearly ninety percent died, as many as a thousand babies a year.

Lilac, or Countess Romanov as she preferred to be called, stepped off her luxury liner into this buzzing hornets' nest with only her wits, her bit of brass—a fair bit to be sure—and her chloroform. Never mind. She'd landed on her feet every time and she would again. And crikey, wasn't the old town looking grand!

One of the best places to get an eyeful of what had happened in New York since Lilac left fourteen years before was on the corner of Broadway and Chambers Street, from inside or outside the new Stewart's Emporium. What Lilac liked best was to stand across the road and gaze up at the place. Five stories tall like his earlier store, this one was built entirely of white marble. The street-level facade had fifteen huge glass display windows separated by ornate cast-iron pillars, and inside everything was arranged around a great glass dome that allowed each floor to be flooded with daylight. Every aisle was wide enough to allow ladies in the new hoopskirts to walk without difficulty, and God Almighty, wasn't Lilac glad to see those hoopskirts that had come over from Paris. It felt like being let out of prison not to carry the weight of four or five petticoats. But women wearing trousers like men, that was something else again.

That bad idea started right here in America, and Lilac wasn't surprised to learn the feminists were behind it. The outfits the papers called "bloomers" consisted of a dress that reached to just below the knee, with diaphanous pantaloons beneath. How were you going to wee in such a thing? In petticoats or a hoop, with proper crotchless pantaloons, you could lift your skirts, spread your legs, straddle whatever, and there you were. But in bloomers . . . make yourself all wet before you got the pantaloons down you would. All right for men with something they could pull out and aim, but women had needs of another sort. Lilac was not at all impressed by bloomers.

Everything else on Broadway, however, she deemed simply splendid, especially now with the town done up for Christmas and particularly after dark when the gaslights came on and the whole of the avenue sparkled like fairyland as far as the eye could see. Let the Russians have St. Petersburg and the English have London. She might call herself Countess Romanov these days, but there was nothing and nowhere she'd ever seen that lifted her heart the way New York did. And to think she'd almost let herself forget the city of her dreams.

Chapter Thirty

ONE OF MEI Lin's deepest desires—along with Baba no longer swallowing clouds, and at least one girl at the convent deciding to really be her friend—was that her mother and Ah Chee would become Catholics. Mei Lin worried constantly about the possibility that Mother Renault, who taught French, was correct when she insisted that not to be baptized a Catholic damned one to the eternal fires of hell. Mother Josephs, who taught religion, once came across Mei Lin weeping over this notion and had gone to great pains to explain about baptism of desire. *All who earnestly wish to know and serve God, and worship Him in sincerity, may be saved by His mercy, my child.* But Mei Lin was not sure that loophole was available when the worship, however sincere, entailed burning joss sticks to dozens of gods on dozens of different occasions, so that one way or another the rooms on the top floor of thirty-nine Cherry Street were always full of the smell of incense.

It occurred to her that if Mamee and Ah Chee could see an entire city decorated in honor of the birth of the Lord Jesus Christ they might have a better understanding of how He alone was the Savior. It was certainly worth a try. Particularly since that time Dr. Turner came to visit Baba he had insisted on giving her money when he left, and said she must buy herself something she'd like as a Christmas present.

"I have arranged a tour of Broadway for you, Mamee. Ah Chee too."

"How I go on a tour of Broadway?" Mei-hua pointed to her golden lilies. "I look out the window, I never see a litter in this place. Not one. Not one." Her tone in this most toneful of languages was one of scorn, but she could not keep the trace of longing from her voice. She was quite sure that at home in the Middle Kingdom even the most important supreme lady *tai-tai* went on tours sometimes. A tour would be exciting. "Who will carry me? Taste Bad and Leper Face and the others all too old. How? How?"

"I have hired a carriage, Mamee. For the three of us. No one needs to carry it. No one. Pulled by horses."

Mei-hua remembered the other time she had been in a carriage pulled by a horse. "No good. Everyone can see. I look out the window, I see this horse-pull litter. Open. No good."

"It will be good, Mamee. Promise, promise. You are thinking of a buggy with open sides. No buggy. Closed-up carriage with curtains on the windows. You peek out, but no one see in. Promise."

Mei-hua did not open her mouth to answer because she was afraid "yes" words would come out when she knew they should be "no" words.

Ah Chee, who had listened in silence to the whole conversation, spoke for the first time. "Very much true," she said. "Closed-up litters pulled by horses. No see inside. Never. All over the town. True. True."

Mei-hua looked for a moment at her old servant and her young daughter. "Yes, go," she said at last. "Go. Go."

Charles Tiffany and John Young started their stationery and dry-goods shop on Broadway in 1837. They survived the panic brought on by the post-fire inflation and soon enough saw the need to distinguish themselves from dozens of other shops exactly like their own. In the forties it became fashionable to buy imported goods from Tiffany &

Young, luxuries such as English silver and Belgian crystal and gold jewelry and watches from Switzerland. In 1848, Mr. Tiffany acquired the jewels of a deposed French queen: tiaras and brooches and pendants and earrings such as New York had never seen went on display in his shop. Henceforth Tiffany was known as the King of Diamonds. Better still, when a gentleman bought an expensive trinket for his wife or his sweetheart, the excitement began as soon as she saw the package, always wrapped in a distinctive shade of blue. Mr. Tiffany, it seemed, had caught the temper of the times.

Soon at least some of the spectacular jewelry he sold was made in his own workroom and displayed not just inside his shop but in a window facing the street. During the holiday season of 1851 Tiffany's window featured the crown August Belmont had commissioned for his young wife, Commodore Perry's daughter Caroline, to wear to the opera. It was made of finely worked gold and decorated with emerald and ruby flowers hung with diamond dewdrops. Crowds lined up to gawk, and two coppers armed with billies stood either side of the window lest anyone seriously consider a smash and grab assault.

Peeping from the curtained window of her carriage, Mei-hua spied the throng that was crowding the sidewalk for a full block. "All those people, what they look at? What? What?"

"Jewels, Mamee." Mei Lin tapped on the window separating them from the driver of the hansom cab, who was seated high and in the rear. There was a little flap she could push open so he could hear her, and she asked if he could get closer to the display.

"Not much closer than this, miss. But I can stay where I am for a bit if you and the others want to get out and have a look at the baubles."

Mei Lin looked at her mother pressing her face to the slit in the window curtains while Ah Chee struggled to see over her shoulder. "We get out here," she said. "A short while only. Just to see."

At first Mei-hua protested, but when her daughter hopped onto the pavement and lifted her mother out of the carriage, Mei-hua could not bring herself to seriously resist. "Down, down," she whispered urgently when it seemed Mei Lin might be going to carry her all the way to the window into which everyone was looking. "Down. I am supreme lady. Must have dignity."

Mei Lin dutifully set her mother on her own feet and turned to help Ah Chee, who had joined them. "What you think, this old woman can't walk, see what's there? Need help from little bud was shitting her pants yesterday only? Not need. Not need."

So the three women approached the line, each under her own power. Mei Lin wore the winter uniform of the students of the Convent of the Sacred Heart, a regulation bonnet and gray wool cloak over a gray dress; she might have been any respectable young woman out to enjoy what everyone these days called window shopping. Ah Chee wore a gray quilted tunic and long trousers and of course her conical straw bonnet tied under her chin with a sturdy piece of hemp. Mei-hua was resplendent in a short jacket that was a variation of the longer robe, the *lung p'ao*. This one was made from a length of silk her lord had given her when their daughter was born. It was scarlet shot with gold thread, and she paired it with a long, slim red satin skirt that was slit knee high on either side so she could totter with more comfort on her beautiful golden lilies, which were on this special occasion wrapped in satin ribbons of red and gold and black. Ribbons of the same color were twisted into her upswept hair along with the jeweled butterfly that was one of her favorite ornaments, and she carried a red and gold and black fan, though it was winter and the fan was more for show than for necessity. Never mind.

One by one the people waiting to get their chance to gaze at Mrs. Belmont's golden crown turned to look at this still more extraordinary sight. Mei Lin realized what a bad idea it had been to get out of the carriage and tried to whisper into her mother's ear that they should return, but Mei-hua was now taking mincing little steps along an open path created by the fact that acting as one, the crowd had fallen back to permit her to pass.

Mei-hua made her way along this pathway slowly, smiling and nodding, accepting the supreme first lady *tai-tai*'s due. She was aware that some of the stares of the big uglies either side of her were not friendly. Never mind. Her lord was the ruler of the kingdom. One of the rulers at least. She had come to accept that this was a very big foreign devil place and it was likely that the Lord Samuel did not rule it all. Still, she was a princess and supreme first lady *tai-tai*, and that's why the big uglies were hard watching, as if maybe their eyes would fall out of their heads.

She reached the window and looked for a brief time at the jeweled crown sitting on a black velvet cushion with two gaslights either side. "Nice. Nice," she said, when she had looked as long as she felt she must. "Now we go back inside the horse-pull litter." With this she turned and began walking back to the carriage.

Ah Chee and Mei Lin followed behind her, Mei Lin praying that they would get back inside the carriage with no incident and that she had not made some terrible error that would cause her mother and Ah Chee to be less likely than ever to recognize the one true Church.

"Well, I never!"

The loud exclamation came from somewhere to Mei Lin's right. Mamee and Ah Chee stopped walking, though the carriage was just a few feet away. Mei Lin stepped between her mother and Ah Chee and urged them forward to the safety it promised, even as she turned her head to see who had spoken.

Mei Lin and Ah Chee were looking as well.

So was Lilac Langton.

Mei-hua was the first to break the stunned silence. She screamed and threw her arms around Mei Lin, terrified that now the same terrible person who had stolen her unborn son and made her almost bleed to death was after her daughter.

Ah Chee recognized the devil woman who had taken her money, then did the stinking dog turd abortion anyway. She shook her fist in the woman's face and berated her in a stream of gutter Hakka Chinese, words she thought she had forgotten in the nearly twenty years since she left the sampans of the stinking dog turd pirate who sold her plum blossom to the *yang gwei zih*. Which transaction she also cursed, since now the Lord Samuel had swallowed so many clouds he didn't know better than to leave them on the street with no protection.

A low rumbling of discontent began among the onlookers. The strange and obviously foreign women had provided an unexpected distraction on an evening when most folks were out seeking only a good time, but now they appeared to be threatening one of their own.

A man stepped between the strange woman and Mamee and Ah Chee. "*Qi rang wo bang mang, tai-tai.*" Please allow me to help the supreme first lady *tai-tai.* He removed his topper and bowed repeatedly in Mei-hua's direction. "*Bu yiao ma fan zhiji.*" Do not trouble yourself. "*Qi bu yiao ma fan zhiji.*" Please do not trouble yourself.

Mei Lin was astonished. A word like "please" had no place in ordinary Chinese, where only the tone of speech conveyed politeness. "Please" as part of the spoken language was reserved for those to whom one wished to pay the highest honor. The speaker must have the language as deep as the marrow of his bones to understand such a subtle difference. Moreover, the polite words made it entirely acceptable that he took Mei-hua's arm and practically carried her to the waiting carriage.

Mei Lin opened her mouth, but words in either English or Chinese refused to come. The man who was now lifting her mother into the carriage was Mr. Kurt Chambers.

Ah Chee hurried along behind her plum blossom while urging the little bud to join them. "No stay here," she admonished. "Bad. Bad. Come. Come."

"It is good advice, Miss Di." Mr. Chambers spoke quietly without turning around, seeming to keep his total attention on Mei-hua. "Please come and join your mother and your servant. It would be the best thing."

It was the first time she'd heard him speak English. He had a British accent. Mei Lin moved forward. Mr. Chambers helped her into the carriage in the deferential manner he had used when he assisted her mother.

Chambers turned to face the restive crowd, calling over their heads to the pair of coppers who were uncertain as to whether they should remain beside Mr. Tiffany's window or were required to break a few heads and thus avert a riot. "Do your job, the pair of you. What do you think your billies are for?"

"Yes, sir, Mr. Chambers, sir." They spoke virtually in unison. Lead-tipped weapons in hand, they made a move in the direction of the two toughs who looked most likely to start trouble if there was to be any, but this time no trouble ensued.

The police returned their attention to protecting Mr. Tiffany's window, and the crowd turned theirs to the bejeweled crown of Mr. Belmont's wife.

Chambers surveyed the calming of the waters with satisfaction and turned to Lilac Langton, who was still standing in the spot she'd arrived at when she first caught sight of the ghosts from her past. Though they were not at all the ghosts she had expected. "Countess Romanov, I presume," Chambers said. He had put his topper on again and he merely touched the brim.

"That's me. And you're Mr. Chambers."

"That I am."

"I didn't know you spoke that Chinese."

"And I didn't know you would recognize it when you heard it, much less that I would have the opportunity to speak it when I arrived at our rendezvous. Now, madam, I think we have attracted enough attention. Shall we take ourselves off to somewhere we can talk in private?"

He offered his arm and Lilac took it.

On the Monday following the nearly disastrous outing, precisely at midday, there was a knock on the door of the fourth-floor rooms at number thirty-nine Cherry Street. Ah Chee hobbled over to answer it.

Mei-hua heard a few words of Chinese and craned her neck to see which of the men had come bearing what message. But before she could do so, the man left and the door closed and Ah Chee turned around. She was holding a package: a square about as long on each side as the distance from Mei-hua's tiny wrist to her dimpled elbow, a hand-spread deep, and wrapped in shiny red paper tied with a big green ribbon.

"Who? Who?" Mei-hua demanded. "Who bring this thing?"

"No one I know. Does not live here or next door. Brought this for the little bud."

"How can he not live here? Where does he live? He was a civilized person from the Middle Kingdom, no?" Mei-hua was quite sure the words she had heard were civilized words. "That man from the street? The *yang gwei zih* who speaks like a civilized person, it was him?"

"No. No. A civilized man. But he says he lives on another street. And his accent was not like ours. Toishan maybe. Not sure. Not sure."

"Never mind. Give me that."

"Not meant for you," Ah Chee said. "Meant for little bud." She had no reason to be fearful of giving the package to Mei-hua, but she was. She clutched it to her chest and kept repeating, "Not for you. Not. Not."

"Give," Mei-hua said, in a tone that permitted no argument. She held out both hands.

Ah Chee put the package into them, then shuffled away to the kitchen, intent on lighting a joss stick in honor of the kitchen god. Perhaps it would ease her sense of impending doom. It was a feeling she had not had before they went out in the horse-pulled litter, which was when she should have had it, but one she could not shake now that they were home and everything seemed to be back to normal.

Mei-hua held the parcel on her lap and did not immediately open it. The name written on the front was Mei Lin, not Mei-hua or Supreme First Lady, but it was not that which slowed her eagerness to tear off the paper wrappings and see what the package contained. She was *tai-tai* and the mother, and anything that concerned her daughter concerned her. Or that was how it should be, but here in this place it was not always so. Language had become a kind of wall between her and her daughter, and sometimes she felt her precious Mei Lin was disappearing behind that barrier. As long as they spoke in civilized speech her authority could not be questioned. But if, as was sometimes the case, a transaction must occur in the *yang gwei zih* speaking words, then Mei-hua was helpless and must rely on Mei Lin in every way. "Not right," she whispered. "Not right."

But it was how things were and she knew no way to change them. Now this.

Ah Chee returned to stand in the doorway between the kitchen and the main room. Mei-hua could smell fresh incense. "What Zao Shen going to do?" she asked with some surliness. "All this time we ask and ask for a husband for the little bud and none comes. Now it will be different?" She did not say what both of them knew, that it was the Lord Samuel's responsibility to provide a husband for his daughter, but he was too full of clouds to attend to that duty any more than he attended to most others. It was years since he had shared Mei-hua's bed. Not even her tiny golden lilies could harden his jade stalk after so much *ya-p'ien*. "No different. No different."

"Yes, maybe different," Ah Chee said. "Maybe."

Mei-hua did not need to ask what she meant. The man who came to their aid two days before looked like a *yang gwei zih* but he spoke like a civilized person. Not a *yang gwei zih* who had learned civilized words like the Lord Samuel. A real civilized person. Mei Lin was a real civilized person who looked—somewhat if not entirely—like a *yang gwei zih*. The possibilities were obvious to both women, though neither had yet mentioned them aloud.

"Unwrap," Ah Chee said. "Unwrap." She had decided it was better that they know what was inside before the little bud returned from the errands she'd gone to do. It would have been better still if the package had arrived when the girl was away with the ladies the little bud called nuns and Ah Chee thought of simply as black-white women.

When Mei Lin had first gone to the school on Mulberry Street, Ah Chee had spent many hours standing across from the building the little bud said was called a convent. She had spied out a fair amount simply by catching a glimpse or two of the inside each time the door was opened. Then, in the year of the Water Sheep, which the *yang gwei zih* said was 1846, the black-whites moved their convent to a place far away, to the country the little bud said. Too far. Too far. Way up to a section Ah Chee knew was called the Bronx, to a hill looking over a village Mei Lin said was called Manhattanville. Every Sunday evening Mei Lin took a train to get there—loud and noisy and puffing smoke, with the words Hudson River Railway painted on the side, which Ah Chee knew because once Mei Lin had read them to her—and every Friday afternoon the little bud took another puffing-smoke-train to return to Cherry Street. Too far. Ah Chee could not go to Manhattanville to watch from outside and be sure the girl was in a good place. Even so. Better if she were in Manhattanville today rather than home for this *yang gwei zih* Christmas festival. Which had already nearly gotten them killed, and which like nearly every festival in this foreign devil place lacked even a few fireworks.

But any too soon time the little bud would be here. And if it turned out that whatever was in the package was something she should not see, it would be too late to put it on the kitchen fire and say nothing. "Unwrap," Ah Chee repeated. "Unwrap."

Mei-hua continued to stare at the parcel.

Too late. The door opened and Mei Lin came in. "What is that? What?"

She had never before seen on Cherry Street anything quite like what was on her mother's lap. Carefully wrapped Christmas presents were part of her convent world, not this one. And she didn't get them, the other girls did.

"What? What?" she repeated.

"Don't know," Mei-hua said truthfully, nodding to the package. "Just come."

Mei Lin had by then gotten close enough to read the writing on the outside of the box. "It is for me. That's my name."

"Yes," Mei-hua said, starting to carefully untie the green ribbon.

"I should open it. I should."

"Bad writing," Mei-hua said.

It was true that the calligraphy on the outside of the box was not particularly good; the characters of her name looked to Mei Lin as if they had been formed by an unpracticed hand. Perhaps Dr. Turner or even Dr. Klein had sent her a present, but she had no reason to think that either of them knew enough about Chinese calligraphy to write it at all, even badly. Who then? "Let me open it," she repeated. But by then her mother had the paper off and was lifting the lid of the box and plunging her hands into a river of exquisite silk.

There were two pieces of clothing of shimmering silvery blue. One was a long, slim dress with a high neck and deeply slit sides, the other was a short jacket to be worn over the dress. The jacket was lined with silver cloth and embroidered with blue flowers. "Civilized clothes," Mei-hua said. "Made for you." The outfit looked as if it would fit perfectly.

"Who sent it?" Mei Lin asked, as she bent to retrieve the card that had fallen to the floor when Mamee took the clothes out of the box. "Who?" The truth was that she had a very good idea. Even before she read the note, written not in Chinese but in English, which said: *I would very much like to see you wearing these things. Please have dinner with me at Delmonico's this evening. It is not only for my pleasure, but in the best interest of your mother and yourself. I will send a carriage. Be downstairs at precisely seven o'clock.*

"Who?" Mei-hua demanded in her turn. Though she, like her daughter, had a very good idea who had sent the clothes.

"Mr. Kurt Chambers," Mei Lin said.

Ah Chee, who had said nothing, merely looked and listened, drew a short, sharp breath and hurried back to the kitchen to light another joss stick.

She expected that in a restaurant there would be a great many people; that was one reason Mei Lin had agreed to come. She did not know what to think when the man who greeted her at the door led her to a private stairway which entirely avoided the grand expanse of the dining room, and led to a small but elegant room with a table laid for two. Mr. Chambers was waiting for her.

"I thought you would be more comfortable here," he said, taking her hand and bowing over it. "A strictly educated convent young woman like yourself I'm sure prefers such discretion."

Mei Lin said nothing. Either Mr. Chambers thought she was as innocent as the other Sacred Heart girls—most of whom had no idea about sex—or he realized that having been raised on Cherry Street, where half-naked women frequently sat at a window displaying what they were offering to any passing male with a dollar or two, she would not be surprised by the presence of the red velvet chaise longue in the dining room for two. And either she was very foolish to have come here, or she was wise to have changed her mind and decided to come. Even though she would never ever do what the chaise longue had been put there to allow her to do.

She had made the decision after her mother went weeping to the bedroom because at first Mei Lin would not even agree to try on the beautiful clothes, and after Ah Chee drew her into the kitchen and said in a low whisper, "You go. Get dressed up in new clothes and go."

"I cannot, Ah Chee. You know what he expects. I cannot do that. Cannot."

"You think this old woman so stupid she wants you to give away for some food what is only for husband who makes you *tai-tai*? Not stupid. But you need to hear what he tells you. Otherwise how we survive in this place?"

"What do you mean? How we have always survived. Why not?"

"How long you think your *baba* will keep on breathing now he has swallowed so many clouds?"

"Yes, but—"

"No but. Little bud listen to her Ah Chee. Already the men in these two houses know *tai-tai* not going to be *tai-tai* much longer. Already the money each week is less than the week before."

"But Baba . . . he doesn't know how much is there anymore? Ah Chee telling me he doesn't know?"

Ah Chee nodded. "The old ones, Leper Face and Taste Bad and Fat Cheeks and the rest, they pay the same amount as always. The others pay only a little bit. Every week Ah Chee goes next door and the Lord Samuel says take the money on the table. Every week a little less money."

Mei Lin took only a moment to understand. "The others are joining with the strangers."

That was how they always referred to the new arrivals from the Middle Kingdom, a place Mei Lin had heard about for so many years she felt as if she had herself been there. The civilized men who came to New York when the clipper ships made their return journeys from California frequently stayed only until the next voyage back to the place they called *Jin Shan,* Gold Mountain, a name it had been given during the first gold rush days. Having seen New York, they found themselves a job on one of the clippers going back to California, the land of perpetual sunshine and no snow.

Such exploratory visits were frequently made by men from the province of Toishan. The Toishanese were clever and organized. In each village they drew lots to see who should go and who should stay, and the ones who went accepted certain obligations, as did those who stayed. They system made no allowance for simply deciding to remain in New York, unless there was a compelling economic reason. But there were other visitors who were not part of the rigid Toishanese arrangement, and some of them did find New York exciting and decide to stay in the city of winter cold and summer heat and not so very much sunshine. Enough for there not to be sufficient room in numbers thirty-nine and thirty-seven Cherry Street to accommodate them.

These days there were a few other lodging houses in the area in which civilized people lived. They paid no money to Baba and owed him no allegiance. The men in the two houses Mei Lin thought of as hers, who thought of her mother as the supreme first lady *tai-tai* and showed the utmost respect to her and to Mei Lin and even to Ah Chee, called the others the strangers.

"You think it is because of the strangers?" Mei Lin asked Ah Chee. "You think some of our people have joined with the strangers and that's why they give Baba less money every week?"

Ah Chee shrugged. "Not just that problem," she said. "That not such a big problem. Ah Chee make money stretch like silk thread." She did not explain that her secret treasure purse was available to supply any shortfall. Better the little bud not know everything all at once. "Other problem is what will happen to *tai-tai* when the Lord Samuel goes to his ancestors. She is still beautiful. Still the only civilized woman in this place." Ah Chee held out one gnarled old hand and tapped the palm. "Her golden lilies fit right here. Even in the Middle Kingdom no one has better."

"No," Mei Lin insisted. "No. The civilized men in this house, they will not let anything happen to her."

"More strangers than friends pretty soon," Ah Chee predicted. "Plenty more. Plenty."

"You think Mr. Chambers will protect Mamee when my father dies?"

"I think maybe. Little bud must go and talk, find out. Keep legs crossed and skirt down around ankles and find out."

Mei Lin had every intention of keeping her skirt down around her ankles, but sitting at the table across from Mr. Kurt Chambers she had no need to cross her legs, which would anyway be a terrible breach of deportment of which Mother Stevenson would not approve. Mr. Chambers was a perfect gentleman. "Have your French nuns made you familiar with French food?" he asked when a waiter presented the *carte*.

"Oh yes, Mr. Chambers. In the afternoon we have what is called *goûter*, a snack, and Sister Catherine often makes us little cakes that she says are from Burgundy, where she grew up."

"This is not that kind of French food."

"Oh, I'm sure it isn't. But at the Convent of the Sacred Heart we are all taught French from our first year at school. I can read the menu."

Mr. Chambers reached over and took the large and elaborate *carte* out of her hands. "Yes, I've no doubt you can. But on this occasion you must allow me the pleasure of ordering for us both." He nodded to the waiter hovering in the corner. The young man stepped forward.

"*Escargots*," Mr. Chambers said. "And *consommé à la tortue*. Then *sole normande* and after that *boeuf bordelaise*. And we will drink sherry with the snails and the turtle soup, then the Sancerre '49 with the fish, and finally the St. Emilion '44 with the beef." Reciting the wines was a mere formality. He had chosen them earlier and the bottles were lined up on a nearby sideboard. "You may serve the amontillado immediately," he said.

Mei Lin ignored the small crystal glass the waiter was filling with pale gold sherry. "Mr. Chambers, you must tell me why you asked me—"

He held up a forestalling hand. "Later. After we have dined. Now taste your wine."

Mei Lin took a sip. "It is delicious."

"I presume you have tasted plum wine." These days bottles of the potent Chinese wine were for sale in a couple of tiny shops on Cherry and Market streets. "But have you had sherry before?"

"Yes," she said. "But only a taste at the convent before Christmas. And not so good as this. Sister Catherine says—"

"I thought the Sacred Heart nuns were all called Mother."

"The choir nuns, the teachers, are called Mother. The ones who cook and clean are called Sister. Are you a Catholic, Mr. Chambers?" He shook his head, and she suppressed a small pang of disappointment. It had occurred to her that Mr. Kurt Chambers might be a gift from the Blessed Mother of God, an answer to the many prayers Mei Lin—who had taken the name Linda Marie when she was an eight-year-old child and the nuns had her baptized in a quiet and private ceremony—uttered with total confidence and pure love. Requisites, the nuns assured her, for prayers being answered. He was, perhaps, her future. She knew that was what Mamee and Ah Chee were thinking. But if Kurt Chambers was not a Catholic, that wasn't possible.

"I am a seeker of truth," he added, as if he knew that his not being a Catholic would be a cause of regret for her.

"Jesus Christ is the way, the truth, and the life," Mei Lin said.

"For some," he agreed.

She did not feel prepared to argue theology with Mr. Chambers. "Please, you must tell me. That day at the hospital, how did you know I would be there?"

"I had absolutely no idea you would be there."

"But you knew to speak to me in Chinese."

"I didn't say I did not know who you were, only that meeting you that afternoon was an accident, and I decided to take advantage of it." And before she could press him with more questions, "Ah, the *escargots*. Have you tasted snails, Miss Di?"

She knew he expected her to be shocked. Mei Lin lifted her chin. "No, Mr. Chambers, I have not. But I know they are considered a great delicacy in Burgundy."

"Indeed. See," he said, demonstrating as he spoke, "you use these tongs to hold the shell and take out the meat with the little fork." He watched while without a trace of hesitation she copied his actions. "Now eat and tell me what you think."

"Delicious," Mei Lin pronounced. They were a bit too chewy for her liking and tasted only of the garlic and butter surrounding them, but she would not say that.

Two hours later, when Kurt Chambers had in front of him a large snifter of cognac and Mei Lin had been served a tiny glass of something he called *eau-de-vie de Mirabelle*, which was the color of pale straw and tasted like sweet fire, Mei Lin no longer felt such a sense of urgency about her many questions. The food and drink and Mr. Chamber's amusing stories (of which she could not now remember a single word) had combined to make her feel mellow and quite relaxed.

The cut-glass decanters containing the two *digestifs* were on a small table next to Chambers. He sent the waiter from the room. "Now," he said, "I will tell you why I brought you here and how things are to be arranged."

"Arranged? I don't believe I have given you permission to arrange anything, Mr. Chambers."

"*Guai*," he said sharply, using the single word with which a Chinese parent reminded a child of the obligation to obedience and correct behavior. "You are too young to be in a position to give permission for anything. When I am ready, I will ask the *tai-tai* for permission. I expect by then it will be entirely up to her, because any day now Samuel Devrey will go to be with his ancestors."

"That is a cruel thing to say!"

"No, it is a true thing, which you know quite well. There are, however, other things you do not know, and I have brought you here to tell you about them. Not because I must, but because your happiness is important to me. So be quiet and listen."

Mei Lin folded her hands on the table and looked down, not letting any part of seething emotions show. The way she did when one of the Mothers reprimanded her.

"Better," Kurt Chambers said. "First let us establish the elements of the situation. Do you know that in the rest of New York the *yang gwei zih* are starting to call the street where you live and a small section around it China Village?"

Mei Lin shook her head.

"I thought you might not. But they do. There are now precisely one hundred and seventy-two civilized people living in the city, all within the three-block area of this so-called China Village. Before he became an opium addict your father had considerable control over many of them. Now he has none. The ostensible leader of the China Village is Lee Big Belly, but since I came to New York he has been working for me. I am the Kiu Ling. Do you know what that means?" Mei Lin again shook her head. "It is a Cantonese term. It means economic ruler. Remember it. Also understand why we are speaking in English tonight and not Mandarin."

Mei Lin said nothing, kept her head down, and waited for the explanation.

"In the world which you and I will share," Mr. Chambers said, "that we both speak perfect English will afford us the maximum advantage. It allows us to fit in when we must, and to communicate without other civilized people understanding. Both are sometimes expedient. So we will speak English together almost always. Note that I said almost. I will explain the exception at the proper time. Here and now I have determined that we should begin as we mean to go on."

"Begin? Mr. Chambers, what makes you think we are to go on in any way at all? You are presuming a great deal about my feelings, sir." The girls at school had been passing around a book and reading it secretly when none of the nuns were watching. The heroine said exactly that.

"I am not very much interested in your feelings."

Mei Lin brought her head up sharply and stared straight at him.

Chambers chuckled. "I mean the feelings you have now, while you are still a girl. Later I will teach you what feelings to have. As for presuming, I am merely stating the obvious. You are exquisitely beautiful, Mei Lin." It was the first time he had used her proper name in that way. It had a startling intimacy that made her feel as if she stood naked before him. "Particularly dressed as you are tonight," he added. "The dress is called a *cheongsam*, by the way. It is a daring new fashion from Hong Kong. Next time you must wear it without a corset. And I would venture a guess that this is the first time you have been permitted to wear your hair up."

That was true. Mei-hua had herself pulled the dark hair to the top of her daughter's head and twisted it into a great bun woven with silver and blue ribbons, and she had put silver earrings in the girl's ears, which Ah Chee had pierced with a sewing needle when Mei Lin was two. But she was not allowed to wear earrings at the Convent of the Sacred Heart. The earrings too were a first-time event marking the special character of the evening.

"I am content that you do not have golden lilies," Mr. Chambers said. "In our situation it is better so. But lovely as you are Mei Lin, to the *yang gwei zih* you are a mongrel. The men of the Middle Kingdom, even if there were here any of such a class as to deserve you, would think the same. So you are a thing to be scorned by civilized men and *yang gwei zih* alike. But you are perfect for me. That is why—"

"How can you—"

"*Guai,*" he repeated in the same stern manner as before. "You are perfect for me because you too have a foot in both the Chinese world and the white. China Village, which New York still largely ignores, is going to be much more important in the near future. There will be more civilized men coming to live here and do the bitter labor, the *ku li,* the whites do not choose to do for themselves. That is the source of our word coolie," he added. "Did you know that?"

Mei Lin shook her head.

"Now you do. You should also know that China Village will remain the source of opium, to which I believe many more of the *yang gwei zih* will soon enough be addicted. As the Kiu Ling I control all that. It might have been your father, if he had not become an addict himself. In which case I might have had to kill him. As it is, I need only wait for him to die."

Mei Lin jumped up. "You are a wicked man. I will listen to no more of this."

"Sit down. I have not yet explained about your mother."

She did not sit down.

"When I tell you to sit, I mean for you to do exactly that. *Sit down!*"

She was long trained in obedience to authority. Mei Lin resumed her place at the table.

"That's better. As I was saying, the supreme first lady is still young and still beautiful, and her golden lilies are a thing of wonder. She is, moreover, the only civilized woman in all of New York. When your father dies, the richer among the civilized men intend to play *Ya Pei* for the *tai-tai*. The winner of the game will take her as his concubine for as long as he remains in this country. But given that she is such a precious and unique commodity, the others are to have access to her one night every month. I presume you know for what purpose. When the man who has won her is ready to leave this place to return home to China, he will pass her to the next in line."

Mei Lin could not breathe. Her heart was pounding and her palms were wet with sweat. "No," she whispered. "No, no, no. They would not. Leper Face and Taste Bad and Fat Cheeks, they would not permit it."

"There is absolutely nothing they will be able to do to prevent it. The others are far too powerful. In fact, if they wished, they could come and take the *tai-tai* tomorrow or the next day. They have chosen not to do so because it is better for all if there is no fuss in China Village, nothing that will attract the attention of the coppers or any of the other powerful *yang gwei zih*."

Chambers paused to pour a bit more cognac into his snifter. Mei Lin's *eau-de-vie* remained untouched. "Have a sip of the Mirabelle," he said. "It will help to calm you. And do not look so frightened. What I have described to you is the plan of Big Belly and a few of the others. It is not going to happen."

"Why not? How can it be prevented?"

"I am taking the *tai-tai* under my protection. I have already bought a house for her uptown, but I believe she will be happier about moving after your father dies. So we will wait until then."

"Even then she will not wish to go. It will be very difficult to convince her—"

"It will not be difficult at all. I shall, after all, be her future son-in-law."

Mei Lin opened her mouth but no words came out.

Chambers chuckled. "What else did you think I intended? You are to be my wife, beautiful Mei Lin. You will be Woman Chambers, my supreme lady. Our house is ready and waiting. It is right next door to the one where your mother and Ah Chee will live. It is far enough uptown so there will be no near neighbors, no *yang gwei zih*, to make the *tai-tai*—I suppose we must call her first *tai-tai* once we are married—to make first *tai-tai* uncomfortable."

"You keep saying *yang gwei zih*, but you are one of them. You are white."

Chambers did not smile. "Only on the outside," he said.

When Mei Lin got home, dazed as much by what she'd heard as the wines and the Mirabelle, her mother had fallen asleep in the throne chair. It was Ah Chee who undressed Mei Lin and put her to bed, taking careful note of her privates while she did so. She nodded in satisfaction when she saw no sign of bruising or disturbance. Later the old woman made a careful examination of the blue silk dress. She could discover not a speck of blood.

She would light five joss sticks to each of the gods in the house. Very big dangerous all cash gamble to allow the little bud to go alone to meet the *yang gwei zih*. Big gamble. But Ah Chee was convinced she had won.

Chapter Thirty-one

"HERE," NICK JABBED at the magazine on his desk with a decisive finger. "I found the article I was telling you about."

"I don't yet have my hat off"—Ben removed it while closing the office door behind him—"and already you are shouting at me."

"I'm not shouting."

"Sorry. Talking in a loud voice. What article?"

"The one by Ignaz Semmelweis in Vienna. Discussing how many fewer women die from childbed fever when the doctors wash their hands between patients."

"Germs," Ben said.

"Yes, germs. You never doubted before. Why now, Ben? Why can't we publish?"

"It's a theory only. Why should we put our names to a theory? What have we got to offer that's new? Tell me that." He leaned over the desk and swung the magazine around so he could see it. "They've got the name wrong. It should be 'Ignac.' With a *c*."

"How do you know?"

"Because in Germany his name is spelled always with a *c*. And I read Semmelweis's article in the original."

"Why didn't you tell me?"

"You don't need more convincing about germs."

"Ben, what's going on?"

"Nothing is going on. Semmelweis says that in the midwife wards the women don't die from childbed fever. Only where the doctors are delivering the babies."

"Yes," Nick agreed, "but when he has all the young doctors wash their hands with chlorinated lime, then the incidence of death from childbed fever goes from forty percent to one percent. For years I've been thinking ordinary soap isn't enough. What more proof do you need? I've ordered a supply of chlorinated lime for the office."

"Good."

"Good? But if you don't believe—"

"I said only that it wasn't proven. In the midwife wards the women don't die without the chlorinated lime hand-washing. How do you explain that?"

Nick had no explanation. It was the piece of the puzzle he'd been trying to find for years, the one that would be definitive and end the argument. "I don't know," he said.

"That's why we don't publish anything," Ben said. "You don't know. And you know a great deal more about this and everything else than I do, so it follows that neither do I know. And we can't publish."

"The germs don't appear spontaneously," Nick said stubbornly. "Nothing in science is without cause or a reason."

"You already said you don't know."

"That's one of those arguments. About angels dancing on the head of a pin. Unprovable."

"We Jews would call it a Talmudic argument, though I think the angels were discussed by a Catholic saint. And I'm sorry I ever mentioned it. But you can't explain the midwives."

Nick sat back and clasped his hands behind his head. "My young colleague, I am the senior physician, am I not? Your guide and mentor in all things medical?"

"Most things."

"All right, most things. But I believe there is something you are not telling me. How can I guide if I do not have the facts?" He saw Ben grimace as if he were suddenly gripped by a gastric cramp. "There! I knew it. Your guilty expression betrays you." And a few seconds later, more seriously, "If you don't want to tell me, we'll drop it. But I think we should definitely start using chlorinated lime."

"I already agreed to that. Look, Dr. Turner, there is something."

They had been in practice together for sixteen years. At least once a month Nick said that Ben should call him by his given name and Ben always said he would. But he never did. Nick accepted that, just as he accepted that the other man had to tell a story in his own way. It was, he thought, a barrier Ben Klein had to cross each time: the Jew trusting the gentile was how Carolina put it.

"Mr. Simson was against it," Ben said now. "He said it was a disgrace considering. But the others wouldn't listen."

Nick wanted to ask what others and what was a disgrace, but he didn't. He waited.

Ben took a deep breath.

Nick prepared himself, the dam was about to burst.

"They're opening a hospital," Ben said. "Samson Simson donated the land. On Twenty-eighth between Seventh and Eighth avenues it will be. The trustees are Mr. Hart, Mr. Isaacs, Mr. Nathan, Mr. Davies, and Mr. Hendricks."

Nick knew every one of them and had treated a few. "That's excellent. The town needs more hospitals."

"They're all Jews," Ben said.

"Yes, I know."

"It's to be called Jews' Hospital. They don't want to let you see patients there."

He didn't understand at first. "Why should I want to see my patients anywhere I don't see them now?"

"The trustees don't want the hospital to serve only the poor. They hope ordinary people will come as well, and some of them think all the doctors who do anything there should be Jewish. So if anything good happens, we get the credit. Mr. Simson thinks it's a terrible idea. He said that because Jews were the objects of prejudice, that is not an excuse to start practicing it."

Nick took a moment. "Very well," he said finally, "but I think you should make sure they have a supply of chlorinated lime."

"Yes."

"And I take it that somehow your not wanting to weigh in publicly on the question of germs is connected to the matter of this Jews' Hospital."

Ben shrugged. "I only don't want to give them more ammunition."

"What else could I tell him?" Ben didn't wait for Bella to answer. "Half the trustees have consulted him about their own illnesses, their relatives' illnesses. But when they open their hospital, Dr. Turner can't be listed on the roster of doctors who see patients there."

"Have more tea," his wife said. "You'll feel better."

"No, I won't. It's a disgrace."

"But you told me they said the hospital must be available to everyone. Whatever their religion."

"Patients, yes. And Mr. Simson and most of the others think any doctor in good standing should also be welcome to practice."

Bella bit her lip. It was a way she had when she wanted to say something and didn't want to, both at the same time. "What?" Ben said. "Tell me."

"The some who don't want Dr. Turner to be welcome at this new hospital . . . Ben, don't be angry, but is it that they don't want all *goyim* or only Dr. Turner?"

Ben put down his cup because his hand had started to shake. "I never thought . . . You mean they know about him and Mrs. Devrey? Way up there on Seventy-first Street where no one lives but maybe some wild cats and some pigs?"

"People talk in this city, Benjamin. I think sometimes that's all they do. And she's been . . . well, not like most ladies."

"And he's very successful and well thought of."

"Exactly. It's mostly jealousy."

"Not entirely," he said. "It's prejudice as well. We have to stop this, Bella. If Jews are going to be successful in America, we have to be like everyone else. This afternoon, after I left the office, I went to see the rabbi."

"What rabbi?"

"On Chrystie Street."

Bella bit her lip again.

"What? What aren't you saying? We agreed. It has to be different here."

"You went to Chrystie Street to arrange for David to be a *bar mitzvah*," she said. It was not a question.

"Of course."

"At Temple Emanu-El."

"On Chrystie Street. I already said that."

"What about your father?"

"He will have to accept it. Or not accept it. I don't care, Bella. I cannot stand that things should not change. That a man like Dr. Turner should not be accepted because he's not Jewish."

"I told you. That's not why."

"I don't care about that either. Services in Hebrew when no one understands—"

"At Temple Emanu-El the service will be in English?"

"No, in German. And the women sit separately now, but some in the congregation think that should change. Someday you'll be able to sit beside me, Bella." He saw the expression on her face. "Your own grandfather was involved in the reform, Bella, back in Prussia. Papa told me. And you and me, we talked about it. You said you agreed."

"About some things only. And David doesn't speak any German. Not a word."

"He doesn't speak Hebrew either," Ben said. "To do it at B'nai Jeshurun he would have also to learn his *Torah* portion by heart." Papa would say that was Ben's fault. That it was shameful he had not seen to it that his son learned Hebrew.

Bella rang for the maid to come and take the tea things away. "It will be on a Sunday?" She did not look at him when she asked the question.

Among the reformers Sunday worship was preferred. In the countries in which they found themselves, they said, that's how things were done. Adaptation was the key to survival. So they would meet to pray on Sunday and there should be an organ, like in a church. Flowers also. Who could object to flowers and music? No man would wear a skullcap or the traditional prayer shawl, not even the rabbi. He would wear black robes like a minister, and the congregants would not cover their heads, because that was the custom in Western society. The Chrystie Street rabbi also mentioned to Ben that there was some question about whether a thirteen-year-old should be asked to commit himself to life as a Jew, if maybe fifteen or sixteen wasn't the better age. He wouldn't tell Bella that.

"I asked if maybe we could have the service on a Saturday. The rabbi said—"

The door opened. It was their eldest daughter, ten-year-old Rebecca. "I can take the tea tray away, Mama."

"Yes, I know you can. But why should you? Where is Liza?"

"She's busy."

"What do you mean, busy? And if she is, why didn't Sofie come?"

"She's busy too."

Ben wasn't paying a great deal of attention. Domestic things were entirely Bella's province, and she was wonderful at managing them. His household always ran smoothly. Except that right now Bella was looking . . . the only word was thunderous. Thunder from Bella was a great rarity and not something to ignore. "What are both Liza and Sofie busy with, Rebecca?" he asked. "I think you must tell us. Immediately."

"They're just busy." Rebecca attempted to take the tea tray and escape.

Bella put out a hand and stopped her. "Leave that. Yesterday when I came home from shopping and wanted someone to take my parcels, you came. Not Liza and not Sofie. That's what you said then, that they were both busy."

"Mama, I don't want to say any more. I promised and I can't break my word. You always say that's a terrible thing to do."

"Yes," Ben said. "Your mother is right. Breaking your word is a shameful way to behave, but lying to your mother and father, that is a sin."

"But I'm not lying! I never said anything. How can it be a lie if I don't say anything?"

"Rebecca Spinoza," he said under his breath. Bella, who for all her intelligence knew nothing about seventeenth-century Jewish philosophers, looked puzzled. His daughter tried again to take the tea tray and go. Ben stood up. "That is a sophistic argument, my darling Rebecca. And once we have settled this business about Liza and Sofie, I will explain what sophistry is and why I do not approve of it. Now put down the tray and take us to where whatever it is that is going on is going on."

There were a black man and woman in the cellar of his house, way in the back behind the coal bin. The woman was moaning, delirious. It was the effort to silence her that was occupying the Kleins' household help.

"Runaway slaves," Bella said, though it did not require saying.

"I didn't want to tell." Rebecca was in tears. "Papa made me."

Liza looked at the girl and shook her head. Sofie made a clucking noise that was, Ben thought, supposed to offer some comfort. He turned to his daughter. "Stop crying. That is a waste of energy and no one has time for it just now. Do the other children know about this?"

"Only David."

"Good. And is this the first time there have been such . . . such visitors in our cellar?"

Neither Liza nor Sofie looked at him, but Rebecca shook her head to indicate it was not.

"Very well," Ben said. "We will talk more later. Now go get your brother. I want both of you down here immediately. You are to bring my bag."

Bella took a step forward. "Benjamin, I don't know—"

"I know, Bella. Please, my dear, go upstairs and look after the rest of the children and the house. If anyone comes to the door, say I am out and you don't know when I will return. Say I've gone to visit a patient." He turned to Sofie. "Is anyone else likely to come?"

"Not nobody what's to do with us, if that be your meaning."

"It is." And to his wife and daughter, "Go. Both of you."

Though Ben found it hard to believe that anyone in this country still had a musket rather than a rifle, the delirious woman had a musket ball in her thigh. She'd been shot four days before, according to the man who had arrived with her. Not by the overseer of the North Carolina plantation they'd run from, but by some old man whose barn they'd hid in during their last night in Maryland. "Barn be wide open, like it was meant for us. Should've known that meant a bounty hunter."

They were married, the man said, and he'd carried her all the way from Philadelphia. "We had a mule before that. But it be dying soon as we crossed on out o' Pennsylvania. There was places we was s'posed to go where they be looking after us, but I couldn't find none of 'em. Lost my way like. 'Til I got here."

Ben knelt beside the woman he now thought of as his patient, therefore under his protection. The wound was inflamed and swollen, and she had a high fever, but the leg had not turned black. "I think we can save it," he said, with a nod at the handle of the kitchen knife poking out of Liza's pocket. "You're quite right. The musket ball must come out. Only not here."

David and Rebecca arrived with his bag. "I want you both to see what is involved in this enterprise in which you've implicated yourselves," Ben said. "David, you and I will carry her upstairs. And we must do so without any of the younger children seeing, in case they should say something by mistake. You go ahead, Rebecca. Make sure the way is clear."

❦

"It is called the underground railroad," Ben said when he came up to bed.

"I know," Bella said.

It was after ten and he thought by now she would be asleep, but she was at her dressing table, brushing her hair. It gleamed, so he thought she must have been doing it for some time. She put down the brush. "Where are they?"

"Liza made up beds for them by the kitchen stove."

"I see." She got up. "Sit. I'll help you take off your shoes."

Ben sat on the side of the bed. Bella knelt in front of him and began loosening the laces of the shoes he'd been wearing since six o'clock that morning. "Oh . . . that feels good."

She smiled. "Here, give me the other foot. Benjamin, I have been thinking about—"

"I know what you've been thinking about. And I admit it's dangerous, but I cannot turn onto the street a woman with a musket ball in her thigh. Or permit someone with no idea what they're doing to dig it out with a knife that ten minutes before she used to chop cabbage." Because of germs, which he already believed were transferred from one thing to another thing, carrying disease with them. Though he wouldn't admit that to Dr. Turner.

Bella reached up under the legs of his trousers and loosened his garters so she could roll down his hose. "Please stop talking and listen to me. I am not thinking about that. Tell me again the names of the men who will be the trustees of this Jews' Hospital."

He was astonished that she would want to talk about that when two runaway slaves were sleeping in their kitchen, but she had taken off his stockings and begun massaging his feet. "That's wonderful," he said, and so she wouldn't stop, recited the names of the proposed board.

"All Sephardim," she said, when this second telling confirmed what she thought she remembered. "All from the ones who came first, members of Congregation Shearith Israel. Not even one of us."

She meant not one German Jew. "I know."

"And do you think it's right?"

"Of course I don't think it's right. But the business with the Ashkenazim and the Sephardim, that's an old story. And it's maybe why the Chrystie Street rabbi isn't wrong."

"Maybe. But right now I am not thinking about Temple Emanu-El and my grandfather, may his name be for a blessing, and the reform. I am thinking about how people always look for someone they can be better than. And about Mr. Tappan."

"Tappan the silk merchant? What has he got to do with this? Oh, you mean because always he was so strong for abolition."

"Exactly." She helped him out of his trousers and extended her massage up to his knees. "Do you remember after the fire, after he'd rebuilt and got his business going again, how then the bad money times came and his business collapsed?"

"I remember."

"You remember what people said?"

"Not everyone," he corrected. "Just one man."

"One man said it first, but plenty of others joined in. 'Mr. Tappan has failed,' they said. 'All you nigras come and help him.' They didn't mean anyone should help him. They were gloating. Because they're afraid of abolition they were enjoying his failure."

"That's an ugly idea."

"I agree. But buying and selling people is worse. The men who oppose abolition, who say that without slaves the South will collapse and everyone in New York will lose enormous amounts of money, they said also that it had to be that *Hashem* did not approve of the New Evangelists like Mr. Tappan and their ideas about reforming society, about giving women the vote and having for everyone free schools. If *Hashem* approved, they said, Mr. Tappan would have been protected from failing."

"They don't say *Hashem*, they say Go—"

"Don't! I can't hear that, Benjamin. Not in my house where my children are sleeping. I am not so sure about all this reform."

"All right, I'm sorry. But something else I think you are sure of. What are you trying to tell me, my lovely Bella?" He put out his hand and touched her hair. When it hung free like this, it reached her shoulders and formed a beautiful black cloud.

"That I don't think we should be worried about the anti-every-kind-of-reform people. They are small-minded and petty, and they put their purse above everything else. If we have to be on a side, Benjy, let it be the side of Mr. Tappan, not those who are against him. Otherwise we are simply like the old men of Shearith Israel. We resist others because they are not exactly like ourselves."

"Not all of them."

"Benjy, please."

She usually called him Benjy only when they were most intimate, here in the bed. Her hands on his legs felt wonderful and she looked beautiful, but he was so tired he could barely move. "Darling Bella, I don't think I can—"

"I know about the Fugitive Slave Act. I know what President Fillmore said. '*Hashem* knows that I detest slavery, but the constitution protects it.' And don't tell me he didn't say *Hashem*. I know that too."

"I wasn't going to say . . . Bella, how do you know so much about politics?"

"I can read, Benjamin. Do you think with all the papers that come in and out of this house I never look at one? But we are discussing those two people downstairs. And"—her head came up in defiance—"many more just like them. We must help them get to Canada. I know if we are caught, it means six months in prison, and a thousand-dollar fine. And that probably no one will ever want you again for their doctor. I don't care. Right, Benjy, is right. So we will tell them that from now on we are a regular stop on their underground railway. The train comes to Hudson Square."

❦

It amazed Carolina how much she loved going up to the turret of the house on Sunshine Hill. At first it had almost made her dizzy; now she adored it.

The vastness of the view was intoxicating, even on a cold January day like this one. She could train Nicholas's telescope on the harbor and watch for any ships that might be flying the Devrey flag, particularly the clippers. Hard to miss them with their great drifts of sail.

Sometimes, however, the view close up was the most interesting of all.

A small carriage had stopped at the foot of the hill. The double gates to their driveway were always locked, and a substantial bell hung beside the gate for visitors to ring to attract attention, but in all the years they had lived here the bell had been rung exactly three times. On each occasion it was someone coming from the town to summon Nick to a patient's bedside. Today Nick was in his office on Crosby Street and easily reached there, and Carolina recognized the person who had gotten out of the carriage.

She practically flew down the stairs, out the door, and down the precipitous path that led to the road. The clanging of the bell still echoed when Carolina flung open the gate. "Mrs. Klein? Has something happened? Is Nicholas all right?"

"Oh dear, I didn't mean to alarm you. He is fine. Please forgive me, Mrs. Devrey. I should have realized you would immediately assume . . . Dr. Turner is fine. I didn't come with bad news. I give you my word."

Carolina took a second or two to catch her breath. "Then why? I'm sorry. I am being extremely rude." She unlatched the second gate and began pushing them both apart.

Bella had come in a small, half-closed carriage known as a doctor's buggy, designed to be driven without a coachman. She was swathed in furs, but her face was bright red from wind.

"You must be exhausted as well as frozen," Carolina said. "Come, drive inside the gates and I'll close them. Then I'll get in, if I may, and we can ride up the hill together."

"Thank you, that was delicious and very welcome." Bella put down her cup of chocolate, now empty, and dabbed at her lips with the fine linen napkin Carolina Devrey had provided. It was, Bella noted, monogrammed with an R for Randolf, which she knew had been Carolina's maiden name. A nice finesse of the irregular situation.

"I should be giving you brandy after that difficult journey," Carolina said. "In fact, I think I shall." There was a tray with a decanter and glasses on a nearby table; she got up and poured a drink for her guest and one for herself. Bella did not immediately take the bulbous snifter out of her hostess's hands. "Take it," Carolina said with a smile. "You have driven yourself five miles up Manhattan in bitter cold and come to call on a woman who, as you know for a fact, is living in sin. Surely you're not going to balk at a few sips of cognac. Nothing will warm you more quickly."

Bella allowed herself a smile. "Perhaps you're right."

"I am."

"Very well. Your good health."

"And yours."

The first sip went down like liquid fire, but Bella found herself immediately wanting another. "I am not an expert on the subject, but I think this is a very fine cognac."

"The best," Carolina said without modesty. "My ships bring it directly from France."

"Yes. Well, that's what I came to talk about. Your ships."

Since it was not some sort of emergency involving the shared enterprise of their menfolk, Carolina waited.

Bella took another sip of cognac. This time it was comforting warmth only. Nothing like fire. "The underground railway." She blurted it out because she could think of no subtle way to introduce the topic. "That's what I've come to discuss."

"Indeed."

"I don't know how you feel, Mrs. Devrey, but . . ." Bella blushed.

"Please, call me Carolina. It is easier for both of us that way. And I think the underground railway a brave and very necessary thing to combat a wicked, wicked injustice. But I have five children, Mrs. Klein—"

"Bella. If you are Carolina, I am Bella."

"Very well. I have five children, Bella."

"I have seven."

"Yes, but I already live outside the norms of society. My children can be made to bear a great deal of suffering because of choices not theirs but those of their parents."

"Whose children can not?" Bella asked. "And you are very wealthy. That will help to protect them."

Carolina's eyes opened wide. Most men would not make such an unvarnished statement about the uses of money. Coming from a woman it was breathtaking. "A thousand-dollar fine is a considerable penalty."

"Six months in prison would be far worse. I am much more afraid of that. I have nightmares about it. Who would look after my babies? My Rachel, my youngest, is still nursing." She had expelled a beaker of milk before she left the house earlier today so that the baby could be fed from a bottle. Six months in prison, however, was something else entirely.

"You have nightmares, but you are actively involved in the underground railway and you wish me to become involved as well. Either because of my isolated house or my shipping connections."

"Both," Bella said. "You have such advantages to offer, and I have heard my husband say that Dr. Turner shares our views on the issue of slavery, so I was sure you must as well. So many blandishments were too much temptation to resist."

"How could you be sure I would have the same opinion as Nicholas Turner on this matter?" Carolina sat back and waited for an answer. It was the measure of the thing as far as she was concerned. To become involved in something so dangerous she had to know this woman's true mettle.

"Because slavery is about buying and selling human beings, but people do not admit that. They talk about how the Negroes need to be protected and how well they are looked after, when what they mean is that they want to own other human beings so they will be richer. I do not believe that Dr. Turner could love a woman who would condone such a thing. I do not think he would risk his entire professional reputation to be with a woman who did not think as he did on a matter of such profound moral importance."

"I take it you refer to an opinion the woman had formed on her own, not simply adopted because it was that of her hus—of the man she loved."

"Of course formed on her own. We are not china dolls, Carolina. We do not have smiles someone else has painted on our faces and arms and legs that move according to how someone else bends them. But if that is not true of you and I with our white skins, why should it be true of a woman with a black skin? Why is she a . . . a commodity to be exchanged for money?"

"In a sense," Carolina said very quietly, "all women are that."

"Not I," Bella said firmly. "And I think not you either."

"Exactly," Carolina said. "Now tell me what I can do to help."

Chapter Thirty-two

"**WHY YOU NOT** go back to Manhattanville place?" Ah Chee demanded. "Why? Always after Christmas festival you go back. Why not this time?"

"Too much education," Mei Lin said. "Head is not big enough to stuff more in."

Ah Chee made a disbelieving noise and turned back to the soup she was making, meanwhile watching the girl tie on her bonnet. "Where you go in black-white women clothes?"

Her school clothes were all Mei Lin had that looked appropriate on the streets of New York. She had carefully unpicked the emblems that marked her as a student at the Convent of the Sacred Heart. "I'm going to church," she said. "It's Sunday and it is a sin not to attend Holy Mass on a Sunday. I will return in one this-place hour. Do not unlock the door, Ah Chee. Do not allow any person to come in."

"How you think this old woman let bad peoples in this house? How? All this time I keep them out, how you think I let them in now?"

"Do not open the door." Mei Lin leaned forward to kiss Ah Chee's wrinkled cheek, but Ah Chee pulled herself away.

"They light joss sticks in this church place," Ah Chee said. "From outside I smell them."

"No joss sticks. None. Not true. Not."

"Yes true. Stand outside when you are little girl. Smell joss sticks."

Ah Chee had smelled the incense, Mei Lin realized. *It is a symbol,* mes enfants, *the rising smoke is a sign of our prayers rising to God.* Just like a joss stick. The thought had never before occurred to her, but Mei Lin turned and left the kitchen without telling Ah Chee she was right.

There was no incense at the early Mass at St. Mary's on Grand Street. A good thing. Services that involved such things as censers and choirs, which were anyway reserved for major holy days, might take as much as two hours, and she had no time to attend a High Mass.

When your father dies, the richer among the civilized men intend to play Ya Pei for the tai-tai. The winner of the game will take her as his concubine. It was her job to protect her mother night and day. But neither could she miss going to church on Sunday.

There was a tall clock in the window of one of the shops on Market Street. Mei Lin had looked as it when she left and did so again on her way home. She had been gone an hour and fifteen minutes. Too long. She would check on Baba before she went upstairs. He had been breathing with great difficulty the night before and wasn't even aware enough to insist she not come into his room. Taste Bad said it wouldn't be long now. He said she shouldn't worry, however, that her *baba* was not in pain.

She came round the corner to Cherry Street and saw too many men. Never mind that they were all civilized. Normally the area would be deserted at this hour on a Sunday morning, but there were at least a dozen men standing in front of numbers thirty-seven and thirty-nine. Mei Lin scanned their faces urgently, looking for Lee Big Belly. Mr. Chambers said it was probably Big Belly who would organize the game of *Ya Pei* that would determine Mamee's fate, but he wasn't there. *Hail Mary, full of grace . . .* She broke into a run.

"In here, *mei-mei*." It was Taste Bad, calling her little sister and motioning her to the door of number thirty-nine. "In here."

He was summoning her inside her *baba*'s tiny room, where normally she was not permitted to go.

❦

Mei Lin's first thought was that her father was dead. His face looked like bones without flesh, only a taut covering of the thinnest possible skin. She wanted to cry but instead she remembered her duty and began to pray. "I confess to Almighty God, and to the Blessed Virgin Mary, and to all the angels and saints that I have sinned—"

Samuel opened his eyes. "Good. Good. I told Taste Bad to bring you."

"Baba, you must pray for the salvation of your—"

He waved away her words. "Hush. Give me . . . under the bed."

"I don't understand, Baba. What do you want me to get you from under the bed?" As she spoke Mei Lin was reaching below the low-slung bedstead; she half expected to discover the opium pipe. It would not surprise her if in these final moments he still craved the poison that had killed him. Instead she felt something large, and of considerable weight. She drew out a canvas satchel. "Is this what you want, Baba? It's heavy. Where shall I . . ."

"For you," Samuel said. "Your legacy. Some day it will be worth . . ."

Samuel stopped speaking.

"Baba . . ." And again, with greater urgency, "Baba!"

Taste Bad had been hovering in the doorway, now he came near and put his hand on her shoulder. "All finished, *mei-mei*. Come away."

Mei Lin resisted long enough to recite the Confiteor again, right through to the end, begging the holy virgin and all the angels and saints to pray for his soul, then when it seemed she could do no more she whispered "Amen" and stood up. Taste Bad was already gone, so she reached down and hefted the heavy satchel Baba had called her legacy, and let herself out of the wretched little room.

❦

Upstairs two strange men stood either side of Mei Lin's front door. "*Guen, ni guen,*" she told them. Go away. She tried to use the tone that said I expect to be obeyed, but she wasn't sure she succeeded. "*Guen.*" The words came between hard, hot breaths because she was trying not to cry. If Big Belly had already come for her mother, and posted this guard, she would need to be very strong to resist him. She must not waste her energy on tears. "*Guen.*"

The men took no offense. They bowed and one said, "Permit me to open the door, honored lady." When he did so she saw that her mother was quite safe and already wearing white, the color of mourning.

"How did you know?" Mei Lin asked.

In reply Mei-hua wailed. She would wail loudly and often until her lord was in the ground. That was her duty as his supreme first lady. Big noises kept the soul of the deceased from becoming confused and wandering off. It would not lose itself and become a ghost as long as it could be kept hovering nearby until the body was buried.

Ah Chee also wailed.

It fell to Kurt Chambers, standing a respectful distance from her mother, to answer Mei Lin. "The *yi,* Hor Taste Bad, came and told her. She was not, of course, surprised."

He had spoken in English. Mei Lin answered him in the same language. "But how did you know? How did you get here?"

"Because Taste-Bad notified me when he was sure that death would come in a matter of minutes. As he was instructed to do. And since I had already been told the end would be soon, I was nearby."

"How dare Taste Bad tell you before he told my mother."

"Be grateful," Chambers said sharply. "I came at once and brought what was needed."

He nodded to the door and Mei Lin knew he meant the guard on the landing and the men on the street. Without Mr. Chambers her mother might already have been spirited away by Lee Big Belly.

"I apologize," she said, finally catching her breath and feeling the panic recede. "I am grateful. Truly. You are very kind."

The English words came too fast for Ah Chee to understand them, but she needed no explanation of the meaning. The lord was dead. The strange *yang gwei zih* was now the lord. The little bud would belong to him. Already she belonged to him, though Ah Chee knew her privates were still closed-up-little-girl-tender. Very strange lord. Looked like a *yang gwei zih*, with yellow hair and square face and square body, square hands even, but acted like a civilized person. Soon as he came into the house, immediately went and bowed to Fu Xing and lit a joss stick; then bowed to tai-tai. Very all-time strange for a foreign devil, but never mind. She interrupted her ritual wailing just long enough to instruct the little bud, who had less understanding of these things than the strange *yang gwei zih*. "Go. Change. Put on proper clothes to honor father."

"I have nothing white. I never—"

"Yes have. Yes have," Ah Chee said. "Lord Kurt bring. Go change."

Lord Kurt, Mei Lin noted. Baba had always been Lord Samuel. But Baba was dead and Mamee must be protected. There was nothing she could do alone, not against a crowd of men such as those on the street who were all loyal to Mr. Chambers. Those she thought would be her allies, Taste Bad and Fat Cheeks and Leper Face and the rest, had already given their allegiance to Mr. Chambers. Apparently even Ah Chee had done so.

Mei Lin walked toward her bedroom conscious that she was still carrying the canvas satchel Baba had given her, and that no one had asked her about it. Mamee and Ah Chee were too busy with their obligatory wailing. And Mr. Chambers chose not to say anything, though she was quite sure he noticed. She went into the bedroom and ignored the white *cheongsam* and matching *lung pao* that had been laid out on the bed. At least long enough to put Baba's mysterious legacy at the very back of the cupboard that contained her ordinary clothes. Only then did she untie her bonnet and prepare to transform herself into a dutiful Chinese daughter.

The death rites pleased Mei-hua. That is what they were meant to do. When Mei Lin objected that her father had not been Chinese, Chambers reminded her that neither was he in any formal sense a Christian. "I do not believe he has had any affiliation with a church here in New York."

That was true, he had not. And surely her mother, who Mei Lin realized was now alone in a way more profound than ever before, deserved as much comfort as could be offered. So Mei Lin wailed with the others and at the appropriate times did the deep bows called kowtows, kneeling and touching her forehead to the ground. She had learned the rite as a small child; it was appropriate when one or other of the gods was being honored at a major festival. But she had refused to perform it after she was sent to the Convent of the Sacred Heart.

Now she must do so for Mamee's sake. When Baba's funeral was over, Mei Lin decided, she would go to confession. Right now the matter of the actual burial was her major concern. Baba lay in their parlor in a sealed coffin covered with a white cloth and many, many white flowers, and a constant stream of Chinese men came to pay their respects—almost none known to them and many, Mei Lin believed, coming repeatedly to make it seem as if the number of visitors was greater than it actually was, thus giving great satisfaction to Mei-hua. After a day of this Mei Lin broached the question. "Please, Mr. Chambers, can you inquire as to where we will be allowed to lay my father to rest? I do not wish him to be in the potter's field, and he was certainly not a Catholic, but even the Protestant churches will not allow us to—"

"Do not trouble yourself. It is all arranged."

"But where—"

"It is arranged. The procession will be tomorrow. I am glad to tell you that the signs are auspicious for a speedy burial."

What signs? She did not ask the question aloud because she knew the answer. *Feng shui* probably, and the *I-ching*, and all the pagan magic done by men like Taste Bad. Not so terrible for them, she had long ago convinced herself. They knew no better, but she did. Mei Lin turned away and made the sign of the cross, then resumed her wailing.

The next morning four strong men carried the coffin downstairs and put it in a hearse covered in white flowers. It had as well streamers and banners on which were written the Chinese symbols for peace and happiness and eternal rest. Even the horses pulling the hearse were white. "Your mother will ride behind in that small carriage," Mr. Chambers said, as the men secured the coffin in place for the journey. "It is traditional to walk, but she cannot do that considering the distance. Ah Chee can ride with her. You will walk behind the hearse. That is appropriate and you are young and strong."

Mei Lin wanted to ask him again where they were going, but the mourners were taking their places. There were at least thirty men, which in a community so small was a huge number and showed enormous respect. They fell into place behind the hearse and behind Mei-hua's buggy. Four of them carried brass gongs and began at once to beat them, this being the most precarious time for the soul of the deceased and therefore requiring the most noise. Those without gongs wailed. Mei Lin spotted some men she knew among the many she did not, and realized that the strangers joining them, like those who called all day yesterday and last night, had to have been summoned by Mr. Chambers. He had made other provisions as well. Lined up either side of the cortege were six policemen, a dozen in all. They wore their blue uniforms, and their copper badges gleamed in the low-slanting January sun. Even their lead-tipped billies were in full view. There would be no trouble, however strange and foreign the procession might appear.

"Keep one hand on the hearse at all times," Mr. Chambers said. "That is expected of a child of the deceased."

Mei Lin put aside any thought of questioning him about where they were going or how far. It was simply easier to do as she was told. She started to take her place, shivering a bit because of the cold and because she wore only a quilted white satin *lung p'ao* over a long white silk skirt.

"Wait," Mr. Chambers said, and snapped his fingers. A man came bringing a long cloak made of white fox and put it over her shoulders. Another man brought a square of white cloth, and this was draped over her head. "Now we will go," Mr. Chambers said, and went to join the mourners, taking a respectful position at the rear.

They progressed slowly north for nearly three hours, along streets that frequently seemed to have been cleared in anticipation of their loud and extraordinary passage. Sometimes, on a particularly crowded block, they had to wait, but soon a way was arranged through the traffic and the procession went on. Gradually the city was left behind. By the time they had reached the Croton Reservoir at Forty-second Street and Fifth Avenue there were no more passers-by to gawk at the spectacle or cover their ears against the noise. Then, some way further on, Mei Lin saw a pair of houses standing by themselves, side by side, separated only by a strip of grass and trees. She knew at once they were the ones Mr. Chambers had mentioned that night in Delmonico's when he told her his plans. *One for first tai-tai. One for us after we are married.*

The houses looked like country mansions, more like those she had seen surrounding the village of Manhattanville than like anything in New York City. They were identical, each three stories tall with a mansard roof and a chimney at each corner and a covered porch in front. Made of wood, which she would later learn had been chosen because in this location it offered better *feng shui* than either brick or brownstone.

Both houses had a large walled garden behind. In the one that was to be Mei-hua's a grave had been dug for the coffin of Samuel Devrey.

"Nick, I've had a letter from the Mother Superior of the Madams of the Sacred Heart in Manhattanville. Linda Di did not return to school after the Christmas holiday." It was no surprise that the nun would write to Carolina; for eight years she had been sending the checks that paid the girl's tuition. She sent them first from the house on Fourteenth Street. When later they moved to Sunshine Hill, the letters simply omitted a return address. In recent years the checks had been sent from the Canal Street offices of Devrey Shipping. That was where the nun had written, explaining the situation and returning Mrs. Devrey's latest check. Zac, who in this winter of 1852 had left Princeton in favor of lodging in the town and working full time for Devrey's, had brought the letter to his mother.

Nick was immediately concerned, though he tried not to show it. "Perhaps she simply had enough of school. The girl's sixteen, after all."

"She wasn't to be graduated for two years more."

"Children do not always do what their parents intend they should do," Nick said. They had both thought Zachary should finish his education at Princeton before taking his place in the business empire Carolina had built for him. He had, after all, three years left before reaching his majority and coming into his inheritance. But Zac had insisted he was not cut out for the academic life. *Let me go to work at Devrey's. I want to start on the docks. Learn everything from the ground up.* Carolina had made him promise he would spend only one day a week in the rough and tumble of the waterfront and work the rest of the time in the office, but neither she nor Nick had thought it wise to insist Zac stay at Princeton.

Linda Di was, however, an entirely different case. "I am not easy in my mind about this, my love."

"Be easy," Nick said, kissing her forehead. "I will go to Cherry Street tomorrow and see what I can learn."

He was gone most of the next day and returned long after the dinner hour, carrying a huge bunch of white lilies, which he presented to her with a flourish. "For my bride to be."

"Nick, what are you saying? And they're gorgeous, but where did you get lilies in February?"

"It seems a gentleman on Staten Island has been raising them in a glasshouse and bringing them into the city to sell. A promotional effort connected with a scheme to build a Crystal Palace in New York next year. Like the one in London."

Carolina took the flowers, burying her face in them and inhaling the intoxicating scent. "Lilies in the dead of winter. Whatever next? Nick, what did you mean by bride to be?"

"You've pollen on your nose," he said, using his handkerchief to wipe away the offending yellow-orange dust. "I mean that we can marry, my dearest love. Samuel Devrey died last month."

"Nick, are you sure?"

"Absolutely. I had it from at least five different people on Cherry Street. Mind you, these days there aren't a lot of people you can speak sense to down there. The neighborhood has become astonishingly unsafe and unsavory. I think you must sell the houses at once, my dear. Or perhaps simply let them go."

It was not Carolina's way to allow any asset simply to go, as Nick put it, but that was another problem for another day. "What about the girl?" she asked.

"I'm told she hasn't been seen since Sam died."

"But she can't just have disappeared."

"To all intents and purposes she has. Forget about it, my love. Will you marry me?"

"Of course I will marry you. But I won't be put off by a not-so-romantic proposal, Nick, not even one accompanied by these gorgeous lilies. You know more than you're telling me."

"Very well. They're all gone. The woman Mei-hua and the servant Ah Chee, and the girl. There was an enormous Chinese funeral procession with a hearse and drums and what-all. And that's the last anyone saw of them on Cherry Street."

"And? Come, Nick. I know you too well. There is an and. Tell me."

"There's a white man involved, a Mr. Kurt Chambers. He serves with me on the board of St. Vincent's Hospital. It seems that Mr. Chambers has business interests in the area, and he is said to have arranged everything to do with Samuel's funeral."

Carolina took a few moments to think through all the implications. "Are you saying this Mr. Kurt Chambers may have simply spirited the girl away with her mother and their servant? Nick, that's dreadful."

"It may be, but then again it may not. I shall have to make further inquiries, my love. But you are not to trouble your head about it. Frankly, given what that neighborhood has become, there's an element of genuine danger in all this and I don't fancy your being involved. In fact, I must insist that you are not."

Earlier that day, while he was in the city, she had led two runaway slaves out of the Sunshine Hill root cellar and down the cliff to a hidden and makeshift dock, where a small rowboat waited to ferry them to a rendezvous with a Devrey ship bound for Halifax. They were to be smuggled aboard, then passed off as servants to a family active in the cause of abolition who were legitimately bound for Canada and with whom Bella Klein had made the arrangement some weeks earlier. The whole endeavor was facilitated by perhaps the most radical preacher in all the northeast, the Reverend Henry Beecher of the Presbyterian Plymouth Church in Brooklyn, whose antislavery sermons were notorious in rabidly antiabolition New York. "Nothing dangerous," Carolina agreed. "Of course not. But you must speak with this Mr. Kurt Chambers, Nick. Promise me you will."

He did promise, not mentioning that he'd already sent a note round to Manon, asking her to arrange a meeting between himself and Chambers as a matter of personal and urgent business.

Nothing in Mei Lin's life had prepared her to live in such a house as the one on what was officially designated the northwest corner of Fifth Avenue and Forty-eighth Street, though the streets were still largely woods and grass grew between the patchy cobbles of the avenue.

In the house in which Mei-hua, Mei Lin, and Ah Chee were installed there was something Mr. Chambers called a bathroom. It had tiled walls and a large tub that was permanently in place and could be filled from its own spigots, one for hot and one for cold water. And while Mei-hua insisted on using the same chair she had always used, with a large bucket below that was emptied by Ah Chee, the house had a privy attached to the rear. One could reach it without ever having to go outside, and unpleasant odors were carried away by a tall pipe that ran to the top of the roof. Additional wonders were a cast-iron cookstove in the kitchen, gas lighting in every room, and heat that came to all three floors from a big, coal-fed boiler in the cellar.

When, after the interment in the garden, they first entered the house, they had found everything from their rooms on Cherry Street already put in place. Mei Lin supposed carters must have collected the things after the funeral procession left, and taken a quicker and quieter route uptown. There was other furniture in the house as well, a necessity since the new living quarters were at least ten times more spacious than the old, but everything looked much like the furniture that had come from Canton with her mother. Whether Mr. Chambers had it all sent from China, perhaps on one of Mrs. Devrey's clippers, or had it made here, she did not know. Either was possible. Mr. Kurt Chambers was a man, Mei Lin was convinced, who could make anything happen simply by snapping his fingers.

After the burial the mourners who had followed the hearse were invited inside, and everyone ate a huge banquet. The food was the sort Ah Chee prepared for major festivals, but more of it and some even more delicious, though of course neither Mei Lin nor Mei-hua said so to Ah Chee. "Poor quality," Mei-hua whispered loyally. "But very kind lord to do all this. Very kind." She looked pointedly at her daughter, who she suspected was going to give trouble of some possibly catastrophic sort as soon as the fuss of the funeral was ended. "Very kind lord deserves utmost respect and obedience."

"Very rich lord," Ah Chee said. She had been calculating the expenditure of money from the moment when the Lord Kurt arrived with the news of the old lord's death, bringing the white clothes the old lord's widow and his daughter would require. But canny shopper that she was and as clever as she had become in the matter of judging the coins and bills of this place, Ah Chee had long since lost track of how many strings of copper cash would have been required to make everything occur as it had. "Very rich," she said, as she drank the soup that ended the funeral banquet. "Very, very rich," and left it at that.

Eventually, when everyone had gone except for two civilized men who were busy cleaning up, Mei Lin went to find Mr. Chambers and thank him. "I am very grateful. We all are. My mother and Ah Chee as well."

Mei-hua was sitting nearby, and though she could not understand the English words she understood what was happening. She murmured that her daughter should kowtow. "Show proper respect. Proper. Very kind lord do all this."

Mei Lin could not bring herself to kowtow to Mr. Chambers. She had been performing the kneeling bows for two days now. Some in front of her father's coffin, others in front of the replicas of all the Chinese gods. She had even lit countless joss sticks and banged gongs and wailed as custom demanded. But to perform the ritual of a deeply reverential obeisance before Kurt Chambers was, she knew, to give him something of herself she was not at all ready to offer and might never be. "Thank you," she said again. "I mean it most sincerely."

Chambers, who had in fact spent upwards of thirty thousand dollars on the funeral (nine thousand alone in bribes to the police to insure that the procession would be allowed to march unmolested from Cherry Street to here) and considerably more on the property and pair of houses, waited a moment, giving her time to offer him the profound respect her mother had correctly identified as appropriate. When after a few seconds it was clear she would not, he smiled and nodded his head. "You are most welcome, Miss Di. Now I will leave you all to get some rest. You must be very tired."

"You mean us to live here, don't you?" Mei Lin blurted. "My mother and Ah Chee and me, here in this house."

"Of course. It has been prepared for you for some time. I told you so a month ago when we were at Delmonico's."

She felt her cheeks coloring, but she didn't care. She really was exhausted, and her tiredness was like a drug; combined with the plum wine she had drunk, it loosened her tongue. "Are you to be in the house next door?"

"I live there, yes."

"And you intend that I . . . You mean for me and you . . . You said . . ."

"You will be my wife. Yes. But not for three months. That is when the official mourning period you owe your father will have passed. Then we will find an auspicious day and everything will be arranged."

"But I don't want to marry you. I don't want to live here. I don't even know where there is a Catholic church. I want—"

"Enough." He spoke softly and in English but in the same tone that demanded strict obedience which he had used at the restaurant. "Tell me please where you can go instead? Where can your mother go? Will she be safe anywhere else in this city? Anywhere she is not under my protection?"

Mei Lin shook her head.

"You are correct. She will not be. Neither will you. What can you do to take care of yourself, let alone your mother and the old servant? What has your convent education prepared you for except to be a rich man's wife, and who besides me is interested in a half-Chinese mongrel?" When he had finished speaking he turned away, ignoring the tears running down Mei Lin's cheeks and not waiting to see if she intended to make a reply. He went instead to bow to Mei-hua and wish her good night, then he left.

The next day he appeared again for just long enough to tell them there was a carriage and a driver at their disposal whenever they wished to leave the house to shop or do anything else, including attend church on Sunday, and to point out the stables in the rear that the two houses shared. "The driver is a *yang gwei zih*," he said, "but he can be trusted."

"By whom?" Mei Lin asked.

"By all of us."

"You are not afraid I will run away?" Mei Lin asked.

"Run to where, Miss Di? The Madams of the Sacred Heart perhaps? I have no doubt they would take you back, and that Mrs. Devrey would continue to pay the cost of your tuition—"

"How do you know about that? How do you know everything? Are you some kind of evil wizard?"

"Stop. You are needlessly exciting yourself, and you will disturb your mother's harmony if you continue to speak to me in that tone of voice. As I was saying, I expect you could return to Manhattanville, but where would your mother go?"

Mei Lin looked around, observing the comfortable and appropriate surroundings in which Mamee and Ah Chee were now housed.

"Yes," Mr. Chambers said softly. "Exactly. I can see you are considering the available alternatives. Very wise."

"You mean," she said, "that my mother and Ah Chee can stay here only if I do."

"Entirely correct. Of course, you can go downtown and find Lee Big Belly and ask him to take your mother. I'm sure he would agree. And that he would also allow Ah Chee to come with her. She could cook for all of them. Big Belly and the others who would be using your mother."

Mei Lin stared at the floor and made no reply.

"Nothing in this world is free, my dear," Kurt Chambers said. "Nothing. It is a lesson you may as well learn now as later."

Chapter Thirty-three

"IT IS GOOD of you to meet me, Mr. Chambers."

"But I am delighted to do so, Dr. Turner. I rearranged my schedule as soon as I heard from Sister Manon. A man of your distinguished reputation . . . No, not merely delighted, I am honored."

Chambers turned and snapped his fingers in the direction of one of the waiters scurrying back and forth in the packed Rotunda Bar of the Astor House Hotel. They were seated at one of the bar's few tables. Clouds of pipe and cigar smoke nearly obscured the flickering gaslight, but the waiter approached at once. Chambers pointed to their glasses. They were drinking straight rye whiskey, both having bypassed the fancy mixtures called cocktails that were so much in fashion. Despite the crowd in the place, all of whom seemed to be shouting for service in that way New Yorkers had of wanting everything done ten minutes earlier, fresh drinks appeared at their table within moments after Chambers had given the order. "Do you come here often?" Nick asked.

"No more often than I go to other venues, Dr. Turner. I am a man of business. In New York City that requires one to visit many places."

"Including Cherry Street?"

Chambers sat back and took a cigar case from the inside pocket of his frock coat, offering it first to his guest. Nick shook his head. Chambers spent the next few moments rolling the cigar near his ear, then cutting the tip, finally lighting it with a wad of paper he held to the gas jet on the wall beside them. "Convenient sort of seat," he said smiling. "If one wishes to light a cigar."

Nick nodded.

"Cherry Street," Chambers said, exhaling a long trail of smoke. "Why do you ask?"

"Perhaps, being a relative newcomer to our city, you didn't know. Samuel Devrey was my cousin. I understand you made all the arrangements for his funeral."

"Ah, yes, I may be a newcomer, but even I have heard stories of the once legendary family feud between the Devreys and the Turners. So perhaps you didn't know how ill your cousin was or that his death was imminent."

Nick knew he'd lose if he tried playing word games with Kurt Chambers; the man was slicker than he would ever be. "In fact I examined my cousin shortly before Christmas. I did know how ill Samuel was, and I was not surprised to hear of his death. My inquiry has more to do with the living than the dead, Mr. Chambers. The household my cousin maintained on Cherry Street was certainly irregular. Nonetheless, I am concerned about a Chinese lady called Mei-hua, and her daughter who is known as Miss Linda Di."

"I understand, Dr. Turner. But I can assure you both women are quite well and in comfortable circumstances. As you say, I did make all the funeral arrangements, then I helped the ladies about whom you inquire, along with their old servant, move to a new home. Since you visited so recently, I'm sure you'll have seen how their former neighborhood has deteriorated. Cherry Street is no longer suitable for respectable people. I'm sure you agree."

"I do. But frankly, Mr. Chambers, it's your involvement that puzzles me. What has any of this to do with you?"

Chambers exhaled another stream of pungent blue-gray cigar smoke and smiled. "I should have explained earlier, Dr. Turner. I am, I think, being overly discreet. Miss Di is my fiancée. We are to be married in the spring."

Kurt Chambers became who he was because in 1810 a man named Cheng Yu walked out of Kwangchow, the bustling city the foreign traders called Canton, taking with him the clothes on his back and a pack containing seven taels of silver, the red silk robe that had belonged to his grandfather, and a few other things only slightly less precious.

He walked for five years.

Northwards the length of China. Across Mongolia into Russia. Through central Europe into the German-speaking lands along the Rhine, eventually into France, and finally, on the only leg of the journey he could not make on foot, into England. He was helped on his way by courage and cleverness and the fact that he had picked up a smattering of many foreign tongues from the traders of Kwangchow.

The most important events of his odyssey occurred at the beginning and towards the end.

Before he crossed the border of his home province of Kuangtung, Cheng Yu acquired a strong young peasant girl. She cost only a few coins because her feet had never been bound. For him that was her appeal; the swaying walk of a women with golden lilies would be of no use to him. This one could keep up and carry his pack, as well as provide him relief during the night. Her name was Kai-kai and she was fourteen when she became Woman Cheng.

Fifty-six months later, while they were waiting for a man with whom Cheng Yu had arranged a rendezvous in the Black Forest of Bavaria, they encountered a blizzard that forced them to take shelter in an empty woodsman's hut.

The blizzard got worse, and the man Cheng Yu expected did not arrive. Kai-kai, pregnant for the third time, went into labor and gave birth to a dead girl-child, also for the third time. They had food for only one more day.

Cheng Yu considered these disasters and did not know whether to go on, perhaps leaving Kai-kai behind, or remain where he was. Such a dilemma could be solved in only one way. Among the treasures in his pack was a leather-bound book wrapped in flowered silk and three hexagonal coins. He would find his answer in the system of divining known as *I-ching*. He had long since run out of joss sticks, but he kowtowed profoundly and fixed his mind on higher things, ignoring the quiet tears of Kai-kai huddled in a corner.

Cheng Yu threw the coins in the approved manner and was led to two trigrams. Together they formed the message the gods were sending him on this occasion. *Waiting on the outskirts you should be patient. Strangers arrive. If you treat them with respect, all will be well.*

It seemed a particularly clear message. Cheng Yu went outside to look again for the man who had promised to come. He found a woman who had obviously been a long time wandering in the storm and had staggered off the path and collapsed in exhaustion. When Yu stumbled over her she was near death. He knelt beside her and disarranged her many layers of woolen shawls to see if he could feel her heartbeat. There was an infant nestled in her clothing, a newborn. "*Er heisst* Kurt," the woman whispered before she died.

"The child's name is Kurt," Yu told his wife when he returned to the hut carrying the baby. "He is starving. Give him suck." Past experience had taught him that by now her breasts would be full, though her child had been born dead some hours before.

Kai-kai's broad, flat face expressed both fear and wonder. Her arms ached for a child, but this was a thing of which she had never heard. "Can a barbarian infant drink the milk of a civilized woman?"

"We shall see. In any case, we must try." Yu did not care much about the child. He was thinking of the *I-ching*. *Strangers arrive. If you treat them with respect all will be well.* The most respect they could show this small stranger was to keep him alive.

Kai-kai put Kurt to her breast. He drank her milk and he thrived.

A few hours later, while Kai-kai and Kurt slept, the man for whom Yu waited arrived. He was a Turk and he led a mule loaded with a chest. Here at last was the quarry Yu had so long pursued, the end of the quest that had driven him across Asia and much of Europe. The Turk was bringing him the first of a promised steady supply of sticky black balls of *ya-p'ien*. It came direct from the source and had not passed through the hands of the British or the Americans. As such it would cost considerably less than any *ya-p'ien* available in the Middle Kingdom. A cheap and steady source of such a treasure would make him a very rich man. He would found a dynasty and be an ancestor.

Things did not work out exactly as Cheng Yu had intended. While he lived he never did return to China, though he maintained his connections to the supply of opium from Turkey, selling it first in the ports of Genoa and Marseille and eventually in London, where he established himself and Kai-kai and the then four-year-old Kurt in a set of rooms in Soho in the heart of the West End.

There were many customers for *ya-p'ien* in London, and Cheng Yu cultivated the better sort, white men who had picked up the habit while in the various colonies of the Empire. It was such a one who in return for a reduced price for his opium helped get Kurt into an admittedly third-class school, but one good enough to give the boy the superficial polish of an English gentleman along with other skills useful for making his way in the West. No lessons the boy learned, however, were more important than those taught by Yu and Kai-kai. Together they made the only child they had, the one miraculously sent to them by the gods, truly a man of the ancient kingdom midway between heaven and earth which looked down on the lesser lands below.

By the time he was grown, Kurt Chambers—the surname he used in the white world—was truly, and without any chinks in what he thought of as his armor, a yellow man in a white man's skin.

Kurt was twenty-four when Kai-kai died. Cheng Yu, recognizing the now pressing need for a female in their household, arranged for a young girl to be sent from Kwangchow. Since he was old and his jade stalk no longer worked as once it had, he decided that the girl should be of tender years and that she would belong to his son.

The one who arrived was indeed young, just fourteen, and a virgin, and quite pretty, with acceptable golden lilies. Unfortunately she was apparently barren, since she never bore Kurt any children. A few years later, when he discovered she had become addicted to opium, he had her killed. For a time he decided to put the idea of a wife out of his mind. There were plenty of whores available to meet his needs, and it was more important that he concentrate on expanding his father's business. He did this so well that *ya-p'ien* became only one part of a vast trade in the things men wanted but society told them they could not or should not have. Yu, who was by then a very old man, watched all this with satisfaction until in 1846 he also died.

Kurt arranged for a temporary burial and two years later had the corpse disinterred and sent his father's now dry and free-of-flesh bones back to Kwangchow. He had no more profound duty, and there was no greater honor he could pay to the man who had, in the most real sense, given him life.

News of the California gold strike reached London soon after that obligation had been fulfilled. It occurred to Kurt that the discovery and resulting chaos might provide him with many opportunities for profit. He entertained the idea of moving at once to San Francisco (there were rumblings of legal difficulties with some of his London enterprises) but the *I-ching* counseled him to wait and he obeyed. Then, a short time later, concentrating on the question of whether he should go instead to New York, he again threw the coins that determined the trigrams. *Favorable result. The two worlds meet and all is well.*

Within a year of arriving in New York, having used the substantial wealth he brought with him as seed money for earning more and to establish himself as a highly respected gentleman of means, he heard from one of the Chinese sailors who had been drawn into his circle of the extraordinary Mei-hua and her half-white daughter. *The two worlds meet and all is well.*

Chambers kept close tabs on the Cherry Street household for the next eighteen months, making it his business to learn everything about it that could be known. By the autumn of 1851 he had decided that the time was right and that he would make himself known to the women after the Christmas holidays. Perhaps in First month, February, during the festival celebrating the arrival of the year of the Wood Rooster. But before that, in Good month, November, he happened on Mei Lin in the lobby of St. Vincent's Hospital and impulsively spoke to her.

That night when he consulted the *I-ching* he was told that precipitate action brings trouble. He resolved to do nothing until the signs were more auspicious. But once more, in front of Tiffany's jewelry store of all places, the gods put the girl and her mother and the old servant in his path. He could only think that he had misinterpreted the trigrams, because it was impossible for him to follow the counsel of prudence and turn away. The *tai-tai* and her daughter required protection from an increasingly hostile crowd, and he had no choice but to act. After all, it was purely fortuitous that he was on the scene. He was there to meet Lilac Langton, alias Countess Romanov (whose use of chloroform was swiftly making her the most successful abortionist in the city) and offer her full immunity from prosecution by either the scourge of abortion, George W. Dixon, or the police. In return she would give him thirty percent of her profits. It was a scheme which she had found acceptable and which benefited them both. That Lilac Langton had turned out to know something about the *tai-tai*'s past he'd discovered nowhere else was a bonus, something he could see only as validation of the choices he had made. Which prompted him to speak as he had to Mei Lin that night in Delmonico's.

Soon after that event Samuel Devrey died, and despite the fact that the *I-ching* continued to counsel delay, Kurt decided he must bring Mei Lin and her mother entirely under his influence. If he did not, he might lose the girl to the care of Carolina Devrey and her lover. He had by then learned that the pair felt a certain sense of responsibility for the *tai-tai*'s daughter. He even knew why and that Mrs. Devrey was very rich. Sufficient money made things possible that were otherwise unthinkable. His two-worlds-meeting woman, the perfect solution to his now pressing need to create a dynasty of his own so that his bones too would some day be honored by a son, preferably many sons, would be his only if he acted decisively and with boldness.

Surely he must be misinterpreting the *I-ching* trigrams that continued to caution against action.

When Dr. Turner requested a meeting, it seemed to Chambers to be the ideal test. He consulted the *I-ching* and was told: *The fool does not see, but the wise man crosses the river with open eyes.*

"If you have any doubts about Miss Di's well-being, Dr. Turner, I think you must speak with her yourself. She is, of course, in mourning for her father, but I'm sure she would receive you for tea. Would you permit me to arrange such a visit?"

"She is living on Forty-eighth Street, Carolina. I am to have tea with her next week."

And after an hour spent in Mei Lin's company he reported, "She seems entirely in accord with the idea. They are to be married as soon as her mourning ends."

"Mourning for Samuel," Carolina said, a hint of bitterness still evident. "Well, I suppose everyone should have someone to mourn them." Celinda Devrey had been dead for some years by then. The children Carolina had borne Samuel had not been informed of his death in time to participate in his funeral. There was no question that Zac would have refused, and at fifteen Ceci was too young to make such a decision. Carolina would have refused for her. "Did you see the others? The old servant, and the . . . the girl's mother?"

"Mei-hua and Ah Chee, yes, I saw them."

"And they approve of this marriage?"

"Apparently so. Certainly it seems she will want for nothing. The house is quite splendid."

"And are they to live there after they are married? Linda and this Mr. Chambers."

"Next door, in a matching house, the inside of which I did not see. No other neighbors. It's quite a rural part of the city, a few blocks north of even the reservoir. But Linda didn't seem to object to the isolation."

"No question but that the land's a good investment," Carolina said brusquely. "The city is sprawling so. We'll likely have neighbors as well."

"Up here?" Nick asked, laughing. "On Seventy-first Street? I don't think so. Not in our lifetimes at least."

She smiled and didn't argue. "Very well. We've done what was required. At least you have. Thank you, my dearest."

"There's nothing to thank me for. Actually, I quite like the child. I mustn't call her that, must I, now she's to be married. She can be an appealing young lady. Very serious and reserved, none of Ceci's sparkle, but not without charm."

"She's had a very different life, and . . . Nick, she's only sixteen, a year older than Ceci. Can you imagine Ceci getting married?"

"No, I cannot. And I do not wish to. There is, however, another wedding on my mind."

Carolina smiled. "And on mine. I've found someone to officiate, dearest. Here at Sunshine Hill, as we hoped."

"That's splendid. I was going to speak to a patient, a judge, but if you've a better idea I'm all for it."

"A minister." Suddenly a stack of magazines on a nearby table required straightening and Carolina began attending to them. "You may have heard of him. The Reverend Henry Beecher."

"Heard of him! Carolina, there is no one in the city of New York who has not heard of him. I rather doubt anyone in the entire nation would claim not to know his name. Here, leave that and look at me," he said, taking both her hands in his and making her turn to face him. "You're joking, aren't you?"

"I am not. Reverend Beecher said he would be delighted to come and marry us. In May, as we planned. I've been thinking it should be towards the end of the month, darling. The roses will be starting to bloom and we can have—"

"Carolina, how in the name of all that's holy did you come to ask the Reverend Henry Beecher to officiate at our marriage? How do you even know him?"

"Business interests, Nick. I know many people in the city. The opportunity presented itself and I asked him and he agreed."

"And he does not object that this union is to take place here in the home we have shared for eight years? With all our children present, including the three you have borne me out of wedlock?"

Her chin came up in that defiant gesture he loved but sometimes found inordinately exasperating. "He made no such objection to me. Perhaps that's the point, Nicholas. The Reverend Henry Beecher has sufficient fame of his own."

"Sufficient notoriety," he corrected. "Not to mention his sister."

"Mrs. Stowe's book is remarkable, Nick. I know you would agree if you'd simply take the time to read it."

"I don't read made-up stories, Carolina, novels. I've not the time."

"But this one is using fiction to illuminate fact. Truly heartrending fact, I might add. And the word is that Harper's has sold almost a hundred thousand copies after only a couple of months. The entire country is gripped by it. Well, the north at least."

"Excellent. I am delighted for the authoress and her publisher. And since I think slavery detestable, I'm sure *Uncle Tom's Cabin* is worthy as well as profitable. How did we get into this discussion? I thought we were talking about our wedding."

"We are. Mr. Beecher has said he will perform the service here at Sunshine Hill. Are you agreed?"

Nick paused a moment, then took both her hands in his. "My dearest Carolina, if I can make you my wife in the only sense in which you have not been such for eight years, in the eyes of the law, then I do not care if we are to be wed by Attila the Hun. Bring him here and we will make him welcome."

"You will find Reverend Beecher not at all Attila-like, my love. I promise."

❧

Mei Lin found that she could come and go exactly as she chose. She could wander the countryside, even command a coachman to bring a carriage and take her wherever she wished. On Sundays she rode into the town and attended Mass. She was nonetheless a prisoner.

Sometimes Mei-hua accompanied her daughter on drives south into the city proper or further north into the countryside. She was always fascinated by what she saw, observing everything, asking questions about what she continually referred to as the Lord Kurt's kingdom, but she was always most gratified by the return to Forty-eighth Street. They arrived to delicious smells of Ah Chee's food—the old woman would not join them on their outings because, she said, she must cook not just for the three of them but for Lord Kurt and the men who constantly milled about next door—and Mei-hua would take her little mincing steps into the front hall, throw open the parlor doors, and sigh with satisfaction as she made her way across a rug of woven silk to settle into a red-lacquered chair and put her tiny feet on a silk-covered footstool. "Beautiful kingdom, beautiful. And this is nicest house. Fitting for first *tai-tai*."

Her mother, Mei Lin understood, had at last found what she'd expected to find when she set out on her extraordinary journey twenty years before. Even if Mei Lin had a safe place to take her and could somehow have got the money to pay for their keep (sometimes she berated herself for not explaining the entire situation to Dr. Turner when he came to see her) she could never reproduce the status and therefore the happiness Mei-hua had at last achieved. "When you are married and live next door," Mei-hua frequently said, "and I am first *tai-tai*, live here all by myself with just ugly old Ah Chee, promise you don't forget to go for carriage rides with old mother."

"I won't forget." Then Mei Lin would kneel and unwrap Mei-hua's golden lilies and rub the horny, calloused skin with the salves and potions Taste Bad sent for her, and keep her head bent so that her mother would not see her tears.

Walks taken on her own were less painful. They did not so much remind her that she must soon be the wife of a man she felt she barely knew and certainly did not love and who was not a Catholic. As February gave way to March she took to spending a part of most days over by the reservoir. It was a peaceful place: the Colored Orphan Asylum a block away at Forty-third and Fifth Avenue was the only other building in the area, and she would sometimes walk the entire perimeter of the reservoir, noting the smooth, high brick walls and marveling at the skills the construction of such a thing must have required.

She was usually alone on these tours, but sometimes she was aware of a man who seemed to follow her footsteps. She might have been alarmed but that he was obviously more interested in the reservoir than in her. He would stop frequently and step closer, sometimes running his hand along a course of bricks, then writing something in the notebook he always carried. One day she spotted him walking high above the ground along the top of the wall, and she watched, fascinated, knowing that an enormous depth of water waited for a misstep to the right and a deadly plunge to the earth if he stumbled to the left.

She wanted to remain until she saw him safely on the ground again, but it was growing dark and she could not linger. The next afternoon she went back and was disturbed when at first he did not seem to be there. Then she rounded a corner and came face to face with him. "You survived," she blurted. "I am so glad."

"I also." He grinned at her. "But exactly what?"

"I beg your pardon?"

"What did I survive?"

"Yesterday. I saw you walking up there on the rim. It looked to be frightfully dangerous."

"It is not. The walkway is quite broad, though you can't see that from here. I am sorry not to be the daredevil you thought me, only an apprentice civil engineer. But also I am very glad that finally you have spoken. Often I wanted to, but how I could not think." He had already removed his hat, now he bowed. "Fritz Heinz, mistress. I am delighted to make your acquaintance. May I know your name?"

"Linda Di." Mistress was a quaint old-fashioned sort of formality, and to her accent-tuned ear his English had a foreign tinge. "Miss Linda Di," she added.

His grin broadened. "Then you are unmarried, that is what Miss means, no?"

"Yes. I am engaged, however. I shall be married soon." She felt honor bound to say so. Besides, a young lady talking to a strange man in an isolated place like this, whatever the reason . . . Mother Stevenson would be appalled. Saying she was engaged seemed at least to confirm her respectability. Mr. Heinz, however, looked disappointed. "You are not from New York, are you?" she asked.

"*Nein*, I mean no. From Munich in Bavaria. That is where I attended the polytechnic. Mr. Roebling, my employer, he is from Mühlhausen in Prussia. But he is very pleased to take on apprentice engineers who speak German as well as English."

"So Mr. Roebling built this magnificent reservoir?"

"No. Many Irishmen, I am told. Only Mr. Roebling is charged with the upkeep. Right now he builds an aqueduct in high New York. So I am left to—"

"High? Oh, you mean upstate. North of New York City."

He said that was indeed what he meant and that he would be very grateful if whenever she heard him make an error in English she would correct him. "That way soon I will be perfect. That is, if there is enough time before you are married."

"Who giveth this woman to be wed?"

"I do," Zac said, and released his mother's hand, grinning so broadly all the while that it was clear he was quite elated, not just with the fact of the marriage but also his role in it. "With enormous pride and pleasure," he added. "Truly."

That was not in the order of service, but no one minded. Nick and Carolina smiled. So did Mr. Beecher. Josh also smiled, betraying two missing front teeth. At seven he was too young to be a legal witness, though he stood in that position beside his father, looking like a miniature

Nicholas, with hair the same fiery red and the same sort of grin and line of jaw. As for Ben Klein, Nick's official best man, he laughed out loud.

Mr. Beecher cleared his throat. Bella Klein took the sheaf of spring flowers from Carolina's hands.

You won't mind awfully, darling, a woman you've not yet met to be your matron of honor? Carolina said she would not. And at the meeting Nick arranged in the Devrey offices for the sake of privacy and discretion the two women had seemed to him to become friends almost at once. For years Nick had told Ben he was sure that would be the case if the ladies could ever meet, though given the irregularities, he understood it was impossible.

When they got to the part about loving and honoring and obeying, Carolina's voice was strong and true. And when Nick slipped the ring on her finger, she almost could not keep herself from melting there and then into his arms.

There was, however, more in the way of benediction and reminders of obligation, until finally Mr. Beecher said, "I pronounce you man and wife."

Carolina, dressed in cream-colored lace with pink roses in her hair, had not worn a veil. It had become the custom of late for American brides to do themselves up in white wedding gowns, Queen Victoria had surprised everyone in 1840 when she chose white instead of blue, the color of purity, and naturally after that white became *le dernier cri* for brides. *Godey's*, however, advised remarrying widows to wear ecru or perhaps rose-beige and said that the veil, the ultimate symbol of maidenhood, was perhaps best dispensed with. Maidenhood, even by implication, was more than absurd, Carolina thought, with her five children in attendance. Her daughters, wearing matching pink frocks and pink ribbons in their hair (Goldie the blonde beaming with delight at being allowed to dress exactly like her adored big sister Ceci the raven-haired beauty), stood either side of baby Simon, each holding tight to one of his hands lest he fling himself at his mama at some inappropriate moment.

The only absent persons truly dear to Carolina were of course long-dead Papa, and Aunt Lucy, dead three years. All the rest stood beneath the rose arbor that overlooked the river—"like a *chuppa* it is, Benjamin," Bella had whispered, "I did not know that was a custom among Christians"— and broke into spontaneous applause when Nick kissed her with a fierce joy apparent to all old enough to recognize the emotion.

Nothing like Attila the Hun, Carolina had promised, and when Nick and Mr. Beecher stood together drinking champagne in the warm spring sunshine, Nick had to agree. Beecher was in fact quite charming and erudite, even a bit bookish. It was hard to connect him with mock slave auctions that raised thousands for the abolitionist cause and fiery antislavery sermons that packed his Brooklyn church even as they enraged nearly every New York businessman, not to mention the Southerners, who were said to have burned Reverend Beecher in effigy on a dozen occasions. "Thank you for coming, sir. And for performing the ceremony. My wife and I were very gratified when you agreed to do so."

"It is my pleasure, Dr. Turner. Would that all of society's mistakes and wrong turnings could so easily be put right."

"Yes, well, I am nonetheless grateful to you. Carolina and I do agree with your stand, Reverend, even if we have not found it possible to be among those active in your cause."

Beecher took a large swallow of his wine and nodded at the children chasing each other across the grass in some game of their own devising, the girls' ribbons streaming in the breeze and baby Simon toddling after his brothers. "Charming," he pronounced, "absolutely charming."

Three *ke* into the hour of *Zi* on the fifth day of Plum Flower month of this Metal Dragon year. In this *yang gwei zih* place that translated into fifteen minutes before midnight on Friday, May 21, 1852. That was the absolutely sure-thing best-auspicious time, according to all the divination systems Hor Taste Bad had consulted.

Mei-hua had sent for him to help choose the date and the hour of the wedding and was gratified when the Lord Kurt agreed. He, she had learned, relied entirely on the *I-ching*, which was something she knew about only in vague terms. No one on the sampans of Di Short Neck, even among the numbers of special teachers brought to prepare her to come to this place, had been knowledgeable about ancient and honorable very much hard to understand *I-ching*. So very good thing that *I-ching* way and Taste Bad way say the same thing. Very too terrific auspicious.

"I have never heard of such a thing," Mei Lin said. "A wedding in the middle of the night. Why?"

"Because that is right time. Everything say so."

"What everything, Mamee? All this silly business with birds' eggs and coins and—"

"Close mouth. Close. You very stupid girl call things silly when everything done to make things good for you. You think I sell you for three chests of *ya-p'ien* maybe? No sell. No sell. Not like honorable father."

Mei Lin, who did not know the details of what had happened on the deck of her grandfather's pirate junk back in the Middle Kingdom, did, however, know the outlines of the story. Now, hearing Mei-hua speak of it in this tone that betrayed an anguish she never realized her mother felt, she hung her head in shame and apologized. "Truly sorry, Mamee. Truly. If you believe midnight best time, I agree. Agree to everything."

"*Mei wen ti, mei-mei.*" No problem, little sister. Spoken with her hands cupping her daughter's face and thinking of the long and painful journey that those odd but beautiful features represented. Grateful for the child's gift of endurance, which, like her own, had brought them both to this place, which was in Mei-hua's eyes so much better than the one before. She had long since lost and mourned the Lord Samuel she'd once loved. He had disappeared many years before the body of the man who remained behind had been put into the earth. "Safe now," she said. "Fu Qing promise but not so. Not so."

It was the first time Mei Lin had ever heard her mother refer to Baba as Fu Qing, the formal word for father. It was a kind of distancing. In those words she saw a recognition of all that had not been said before and would probably not be said again.

"Fu Qing promise I will be a princess. Not princess. Not. But you, *mei-mei,* will have everything this old *tai-tai* did not have. Everything good. That's why pick most auspicious too good perfect day for the wedding."

Most auspicious as well the great gong that had been carried into Mei-hua's front parlor and that was struck with great force at the precise moment when Mei Lin was to come downstairs wearing her red bridal garments and Phoenix Crown. Ah Chee helped her put on the red pagoda-shaped headdress encrusted with jewels—because of its weight, and because of the curtain of tassels that hung in front of her face—but she did not help when Mai Lin tried to slip into the red shoes that completed the wedding clothes. "No shoes," she insisted. "Not until downstairs. No touch the floor now. This old woman carry you."

"Ah Chee can not carry me. Very silly idea." These days Ah Chee was bent almost double, and frequently had difficulty catching her breath.

"Big mouth little bud understand nothing. Nothing." Ah Chee took the silk slippers in one hand and grabbed at Mei Lin with the other. "Put young hand here. On old shoulder. Good. Good. Now we go. This old woman carrying little bud so everything auspicious good." And with this symbolic carrying of the bride they descended the stairs.

The gong sounded a second time, announcing the moment that the bride should be brought to the home of the groom. Four civilized men—Mei Lin recognized them as among those frequently in the retinue of Mr. Chambers, though she had never learned their names—arrived with a small red throne chair fixed to two poles. Mei Lin took her place in the chair. The men lifted it up and carried it out the door, following another man with a flute and yet another with a drum. They played so loudly Mei Lin almost did not hear the sobs of her mother and Ah Chee, which, she supposed, were more traditional than real.

The litter was carried across the small space between the houses and across the threshold of the one next door. The men put down the chair and pulled aside the curtain. Mei Lin stepped out and Kurt Chambers took her hand.

It was done. That was the essential part of the Chinese wedding ceremony, as Mei Lin knew because it had been explained to her by both her mother and her husband-to-be. She was now Woman Chambers, exactly as he had said she was to be. *Fiat*, as the Sacred Heart nuns who had taught her Latin might have said. Or perhaps not, not until after the bed part, the idea of which terrified her so much she did not want to think about it.

So far everything had happened exactly as she'd been told to expect; the inside of Mr. Chambers' house, however, was an enormous surprise. Because to cross his threshold was to become his wife, Mei Lin had not been allowed to visit the home of her betrothed these past months. She had presumed it would be like the house he'd prepared for Mei-hua. Had Kurt Chambers not told her he was Chinese on the inside? Instead it was entirely Western and modern, and more luxurious than anything she had ever seen. She found the surprise a bit unnerving, but at least he was wearing a red silk robe embroidered with gold dragons.

He led her into a room at the back. It was different from the rest of the house and appeared to have been brought intact from the Middle Kingdom that was for her at once so mysterious and so familiar. The walls were covered in red and gold symbols and the ceiling draped in red silk. There was an altar and tablets representing his ancestors, and, as custom demanded, the newlyweds both kowtowed and lit incense. It's nothing to do with religion, Mei Lin told herself. It's a tradition for showing respect, that's all. That was how she had gotten through the funeral rites for her father without feeling she was damned to eternal hellfire. She would get through this wedding the same way. At least this part of it.

The bed part came next.

Not the open privates part that Mei-hua had discussed with her in detail, most of which anyway Mei Lin already knew or had guessed. This was the ritual bed part, where she would show her ability to sit in harmony. Kurt brought her to a room upstairs where there was a heavy, red-lacquered bedstead and a single matching table, above which hung a scroll depicting the goddess of fertility, Chuan Yin. He left her there after lighting a large candle and telling her he would return when it had burned all the way down. "You must sit on the bed. Yes, like that. I see first *tai-tai* has prepared you well." Mei Lin had crossed her legs beneath her and folded her hands in her lap. "You are not to move until I come back."

She had protested to Mei-hua that she could not maintain such a position for the length of time required, as long as it took for her new husband to go downstairs and eat a banquet meal with all the other men. *What are you, stupid girl? Very stupid? Only hold this position until husband leave the room. Then move around. When you hear him returning you get back in harmony position on bed.*

There were sweet cakes and candies on the table, but Mei Lin knew they were offerings to Chuan Yin and she was not to touch them. Anyway, she was too nervous to eat anything. Knowing about the open privates was not the same as actually having it done to one. *Hurts a lot first time,* Mei-hua had said. *Never mind. Later feels good. First time you bleed a lot. Very important good sign. Scream loud, say how much it hurts, say very too big thing he trying to put in there. Make husband feel like tiger. Then let the blood come on the sheet. Don't try to clean up until later.*

She had wanted to bring her rosary beads with her, but she had not dared. Now, pacing back and forth in the room that contained only the table and the bed and watching the candle burn down and hearing the noises of the banquet below, Mei Lin could only recite Hail Marys in her mind and count the decades of the rosary on her fingers.

In the first light of dawn her husband stood over her and threw back the sheets. He spread her legs with his two hands, then leaned over to inspect the result of his act of possession. "A fair amount of bleeding," he said. "Is it honest?"

"What? I don't understand." Nothing Mei-hua had said prepared Mei Lin for such a question.

"Ah Chee," he said. "Shoving a pig bladder full of blood up inside you would be just her style." With that he thrust his fingers into her and probed. It hurt and Mei Lin yelped. "Good," he said. "There's nothing there."

"I don't . . . Kurt, what is it?" He had told her weeks ago that she must call him by his given name and not Mr. Chambers. "Why would you think—"

"The Bavarian engineer you have spent so much time with up by the reservoir," he said. "I had to be sure he hadn't had you first."

She'd had absolutely no idea he knew anything about Fritz Heinz or their afternoon walks and talks. Those visits had always been so isolated and so innocent. "You had me followed," she whispered. "You spied on me."

"I protected what is mine. You can be sure that I will always do so. There's something else you should know." He took hold of her chin and held it so she had to look directly at him when he spoke. "If it had turned out you were not a virgin, I would have killed you myself. Then I would have had the Bavarian killed as well."

The day after the wedding Mei-hua woke earlier than usual. At least she thought it must be so, since Ah Chee had not yet come with her morning tea. Very much too big excitement yesterday. And now, today, too much on her mind. Too much thinking about what had happened to her Mei Lin the night before. She had lit twenty joss sticks in honor of Chuan Yin: asking that the Lord Kurt be gentle with her little bud, that their bed be a place of happiness and pleasure. Hard to say if that was the best ask. Bed very good for her and Lord Samuel. Didn't prevent his putting her in inferior house, having big ugly yellow hair concubine, swallowing so many clouds his mind went away and his empty body die a too-soon death, so she was a white widow, not a red one as she would have been if he'd been over eighty years and thus entitled to a happiness-red funeral.

Never mind. Pretty soon Ah Chee come and bring her tea. Then they would go peek out the window. Wait for first look-see of their little bud, who was now the supreme first lady *tai-tai* of a powerful lord.

When she calculated that another three or four *ke* had passed and Ah Chee still had not come, Mei-hua, who was already quite sure she knew why, got up and dressed herself. She chose the same happiness-red garments she had worn the day before for the wedding. Ah Chee after all was very old. For sure older than eighty years.

Ah Chee had been given a proper bedroom in this big and fancy house where Mei-hua was now first *tai-tai*. The old woman almost never slept there. She preferred a mattress beside the kitchen stove, much as she'd had for all those years on Cherry Street. That was where Mei-hua found her, lying peacefully with a joss stick clutched in her gnarled old fingers, indicating that she had been about to get up and make an offering to the kitchen god.

Mei-hua closed the old woman's eyes, then she took the incense out of her hand and carried it to the altar of Zao Shen and performed a solemn kowtow and completed the offering Ah Chee had intended. "You make very happy everything for her. Wonderful old woman. Wonderful good to me and my little bud."

Next she threw open the kitchen window so the men who were always around the place would hear her when she began the ritual wailing and come to see what had happened.

They buried Ah Chee two days later in Mei-hua's garden in a grave next to that of the Lord Samuel. "Very much happy funeral for her," Mei-hua told a sobbing Mei Lin. "Red funeral. Lots of everything. She will be pleased. The Lord Kurt tell me after two years we can dig up bones, send them to Middle Kingdom. Ah Chee be buried with her ancestors. Very much too kind lord," she added. "Everything all right, yes? You do everything I tell you in bed part?" She had not thought it appropriate to ask the question until Ah Chee was in the ground.

Mei Lin took a deep breath. Before the wailing began that would keep Ah Chee's soul from becoming lost until her body was buried, she had been thinking that she must find some way to explain to the old woman that this was a very bad place and they were in the clutches of a very bad man who spoke without hesitation of murder. Ah Chee, she was convinced, would understand, though her mother never would. It had also been in her mind to send Ah Chee to meet with Fritz. She would give Ah Chee two notes, one for Dr. Turner and one asking Fritz to deliver the other to the Crosby Street office.

All the plans that had seemed foolproof before the wailing began were impossible after it. How could she take her mother away from this place now that even Ah Chee was gone? How would they manage? She would grit her teeth and bear it, she decided. Maybe, after all, she was making a hasty judgment.

A few months after the funeral, however, Mei Lin knew she would have to try and get them away from Forty-eighth Street. She had overheard her husband discussing shipments of *ya-p'ien,* and she was now convinced that much of his wealth came from things that were illegal. Moreover, when the fourth month after the wedding came and it was apparent she still had not conceived, he had beaten her so badly she did not let her mother see her for two weeks. Even then Mei-hua had looked at her with eyes that seemed to see through Mei Lin's clothes, and she had touched the fading remains of a bruise on her daughter's cheek. "So, so," she whispered. "Not so good. Not the kind of beating I tell you about. On your behind part only, meant to get your lord more excited. Maybe you, too."

Mei Lin shook her head. "Not. Not," she confessed.

They didn't talk more about it, but Mei Lin knew she had to get help. She was still driven once a week to Mass in the town (it suited Kurt to have a wife who was Catholic because it deflected any questions about his own religious beliefs) but the driver waited for her outside and always immediately drove her home. In fact, she was in every way less free these days than she had been before the wedding. In addition to the men who now cooked and cleaned for Mei-hua, there was one, a wall-eyed fellow called Both Way Eyes, who simply sat in the hall of the first *tai-tai*'s house and watched everything that happened.

There were watchers too in the house Mei Lin shared with Kurt Chambers, but she was young and clever. One afternoon, after her husband had gone into the town on business, she managed to slip away and hurry to the reservoir. Fritz Heinz wasn't there. After twenty minutes, he still had not arrived. Then, just when she had made up her mind to go back to the house and wait for another opportunity to come and find her friend, Chambers stepped out of the woods.

That night he beat her so badly she was not able to walk for a week. When she had healed enough to join him for dinner as he commanded, he waited until the end of the excellent meal to tell her what he called his decision. "I expect that in the matter of the Bavarian, beating will not be enough to teach you the kind of obedience I expect. Therefore I am giving you fair warning. If you ever again try to see him, I shall not beat you. I will beat your mother. Then I will have your friend killed."

Book Five

1857

Chapter Thirty-four

IT SEEMED TO Manon there was always more sickness when times were hard. The poor might be poor whatever the condition of business in New York, but in this summer of '57, when financial panic gripped the city, the charitable activities of Manon and her Sisters were in ever greater demand. That was a circumstance for which Manon felt more than ordinary responsibility. Three months before, she had been elected Mother Superior, a role that was added to the one she'd held for over a year, that of administrator of St. Vincent's Hospital.

There was, nonetheless, little she could do to influence the economic situation. A bumper crop of wheat in Europe meant less demand for wheat produced here in America. Farmers in Ohio and Indiana and Illinois and the other outlying states and territories telegraphed to the insurance companies in New York, requesting immediate return of the spare cash they had invested when times were better. While it did sometimes seem that the instant transport of news Mr. Morse's invention provided was as much a curse as a blessing, the problem would be just as real had the demands taken longer to arrive. The need to pay out so much money at one time resulted in dozens of New York insurance companies being forced into bankruptcy.

"But why should insurance companies failing have such a disastrous effect on all the rest?"

Manon had asked the question of a few of the clever men of business who served on St. Vincent's board of trustees. Given all her responsibilities and the fact that shortly before, in '56, St. Vincent's Hospital had moved to larger quarters on Seventh Avenue and Eleventh Street, where their overheads were of necessity much higher, she felt she must understand such things.

"In a word, Sister Manon, unreasoning panic." So said the always polite and pleasant Mr. Chambers, whom she still thought of as the English gentleman, though he'd been in New York half a dozen years. "People become alarmed and rush to the banks and demand specie— gold—rather than paper money. Soon enough the gold runs out and the bank must close its doors. When enough banks do that, there is an uproar. It has, I'm afraid, happened many times before."

Indeed, the panic that had started in New York in August soon spread to London and Paris and even Berlin. "The world," Cousin Nicholas told her, sitting across her desk on a frosty November afternoon, "is going to hell in a handbasket. But it's hard to worry about anywhere else when what we have here at home is so catastrophic."

One thing that did not decline was the cost of food. The thousands who lived from hand to mouth in the best of times were now destitute. Unable to find even the most menial jobs, they could not pay their rent and were summarily evicted and left to starve in the streets. In the face of such disaster, the efforts that had been made to help the poor rise into the working class, even those schemes directed to the youngest and most malleable, looked to be a joke.

The apprentice system, which whatever its abuses gave a boy room and board and taught him a trade, had long since disappeared in the glut of cheap labor provided by endless numbers of immigrants. As a result, fully a third of those now homeless and out of work were children. One scheme, from an organization known as the Children's Aid Society located in a fine building near the Opera House in Astor Place, undertook to ship them west, where, it was said, workers were needed. It was also said—indeed, promised—that they would be lodged in kind Christian homes. "Of some kind," Manon was heard to say the first time someone brought her the society's circular. "But certainly not a Catholic kind."

Small wonder that the Irish and Italians who made up such a large percentage of New York's poor were unwilling to hand over their young to the Children's Aid Society. The Irish were known to instead train up their offspring to be pickpockets, while the Italians schooled theirs to become organ grinders. The street concerts of the latter attracted a few coins but also served as a fine distraction benefiting the former, the pickpockets, who flitted among the crowds of listeners and lightened their purses. Street urchins busy with such endeavors who were caught by the coppers were shipped to a House of Refuge on Randall's Island and set to work making socks—sixty pairs a day was considered a decent output—which were then sold in the shops, undermining the jobs of such textile workers as still had them.

Those who took the longer view, mostly Evangelical reformers, continued to believe education the answer to poverty. These days it was thought that more than the basic three R's should be offered. There was a free academy of higher learning on Twenty-third Street and what was now called Lexington Avenue, and in Astor Place Peter Cooper set up the Cooper Union where night classes were offered in all manner of skills and arts, and uplifting speakers were invited to inform and edify the masses.

Archbishop John Hughes was not to be outdone in this matter of education, nor would he stand by and let fervent New Evangelicals steal his nominally Catholic young. There were now thirty-one free schools associated with as many Catholic parishes, and twelve select schools run by various religious sisters for the education of the more affluent members of the faith. All, it was said, were the imitators but not the equals of the Madams of the Sacred Heart.

"I am certainly no denigrator of education, Cousin Nicholas. We have our own Sisters of Charity working in half a dozen parochial schools. But the sick poor will die of illness and starvation whether or not they can read and write."

"If we can at least educate them to the use of strong soap and water, dearest Manon, perhaps not quite so frequently."

"Germs, Nicholas, germs! I am sick and tired of hearing about germs." She nonetheless followed his advice and had all her Sisters pin white aprons over their black habits when they served on the wards. White, Nick said, was better because at least it showed the dirt and prompted change when too badly soiled. Manon also spent as much of the hospital's budget as she could afford on chlorinated lime and carbolic. The latter was a new weapon Nicholas had added to his arsenal, a disinfecting liquid said to be particularly useful for ridding surfaces of the omnipresent germs. Manon was not, however, satisfied with such apparently theoretical approaches to a disaster of such magnitude. "Can you believe that in the middle of all this they are talking about building a park? A park! I ask you. I want to hear about nourishing food and warm clothing and proper medical care."

"According to its supporters, this Central Park will uplift the poorer classes by giving them views of greenery and pretty vistas and fresh air. God knows, what's up in that part of town now is as ugly and depressing as any landscape can be. It's not even proper wilderness any longer, simply a string of shantytowns. As for the medical care, it's certainly better here at St. Vincent's than most places."

"Not good enough, nonetheless." Manon could not resign herself to the limitations of care New York's private hospitals offered. The proposed Jews' Hospital wasn't yet open, but the Archbishop and the Mother General insisted that, like New York Hospital, St. Vincent's must not admit anyone known to be suffering from contagious or fatal diseases. They must go to Bellevue or die in the street. "I'm told Dr. Chance had more than five thousand admissions last year," she added, her tone subdued by the enormity of that number.

Nicholas nodded. "Yes, that's the figure I've heard as well. And despite the new wing, Bellevue still has only twelve hundred beds." Neither he nor Manon was surprised that though Tobias Grant had been dead for six years, Monty Chance remained Senior Medical Attendant. That the post had served him well could be judged by his fine house near Hudson

Square and his elevated place in New York society. "I hear there's a veritable plague of children blinded by ophthalmia in Bellevue, and God knows how many post-parturient women dying of puerperal fever. Both are infections, Manon. Both must come from germs and are therefore preventable. If only we took proper precautions—"

Manon put her hands over her ears. "As Almighty God is my judge, Nicholas, if I hear any more about these mysterious germs, I shall—"

A quick knock interrupted her words. The door was, in any case, ajar. A Sister of Charity, even one with as much authority as Mother Marie Manon and with her reputation for discretion and good sense, did not speak with a man alone behind a closed door.

"Forgive me, Reverend Mother, there is a lady just arrived who is asking for you by name. I'm afraid she's very badly injured, but she will let no one treat her unless you come."

"Reverend Mother Manon, do you remember me?"

"Of course I do, Mrs. Chambers." Manon laid her hand gently over those of the young woman, and leaned over the narrow bed in the admissions room. Linda Chambers's hands seemed to be the only visible part of her that was unmarked. One eye was swollen shut, the other half closed. Both were surrounded by bruises. Her face was covered with crusted blood and what looked to Manon's experienced eye like old black and blue marks. The Sister who had come to get her had already told her that the patient had a broken arm and that the angle of the other elbow did not appear quite right. "I shall send for your husband immediately," Manon said. "Meanwhile we will—"

"No! No! Please, I beg you, that is exactly what you must not do. Please, I will—"

"Shush, calm yourself. We shall do nothing you do not authorize us to do. I promise. But you must allow us to treat your injuries."

"Yes, but first . . ." Her voice weakened. Manon tried to get her to take a few sips of water, but Mei Lin turned away. "Not yet . . . Please, I believe you know Dr. Turner. I must see him, he's the only one who—"

"Hush, you must conserve your strength. I do know Dr. Turner, and as it happens he's here now." She turned to the young Sister who had summoned her and who still hovered by the door. "Go back to my office, see if Dr. Turner is still there. If he is, bring him at once. Hurry."

The young nun had been taught that Sisters of Charity moved always with dignity and modest grace, eyes cast down, hands folded and tucked beneath the habit's short black cape. The woman in the bed, however, had been beaten to within an inch of her life and this, the nun was sure, was a different sort of occasion from any the old novice mistress might have imagined. She ran down the corridor, black skirts and wooden rosary beads flying in the breeze of her passage.

"Dr. Turner, Reverend Mother says—"

The office was empty. There was a note propped up where it was easily seen. *Getting late. Had to leave. Will call again soon.*

The front door was only steps away. The nun dashed to it and pulled it open. A man was just disappearing around the corner onto Seventh Avenue. She had five brothers, all older than she, who when she was a child took delight in teaching her tricks of the most unladylike kind. Sister put two fingers into her mouth and brought forth a whistle shrill enough to be heard six blocks away. "Dr. Turner!" she called, both hands cupped around her mouth and shouting at the top of her sturdy young lungs, "Come back at once! Reverend Mother says you must!"

"Hello, Mei Lin. I am sorry to find you so, but we'll soon have you well."

"Dr. Turner, my mother . . . Please, you must go and get her. Ah Chee is dead and you are the only other person she knows in the city who is not one of my husband's people. She will come with you. Otherwise . . ." Her voice weakened again. Nick, who already had his stethoscope in hand, started to examine her. Mei Lin struggled to sit up, grabbing the front of his coat as she did so. "My mother. Please. If you do not go, something terrible will happen to her."

The burst of words seemed to sap the last of her strength and she fell back on the bed. Nick and Manon looked at each other. "She begged me not to send for her husband," Manon said softly. "She said that was the last thing I must do."

"You're saying . . ." Nick had difficulty taking in the notion. " You're saying you think Kurt Chambers is the cause of all this? That he's a threat to her mother? It seems impossible. He's a gentleman, respected and . . ."

"Remember Tobias Grant," Manon said. "He seemed entirely respectable as well if you only met him outside Bellevue."

Nick nodded. "I shall go at once. That broken arm must be set, however, and the sooner the better."

"I will see to it." Manon stepped forward and began cutting away the young woman's frock. The very best silk, she noted, and the latest fashion. Once upon a time, in another life, she'd had a keen eye for such things, and even now she was not immune. Mr. Chambers had brought his exotic young wife to a number of the hospital's charity functions, the sort attended by the ever growing Catholic upper class. Indeed, Manon had quite admired how proud he seemed of her, how if they heard the whispers, neither of them let on. *Educated by the Madams, they say. A Catholic, I know, but some sort of mixed blood. Well yes, quite pretty in her way, but still . . .* Mr. Chambers ignored the gossips and paraded his wife on his arm, showing off her beautiful gowns and jewels. Covering what, Manon wondered now. "Go at once, Cousin Nicholas. I suspect there is little time to waste."

"Yes, just one thing. When I get Mei-hua, may I bring her here? I don't know where else—"

"Of course. Now, hurry."

Nick did not question the need for speed. Someone had beaten Mei Lin very badly, and on the evidence of his own eyes, not for the first time. She'd all but said that someone was her husband, Kurt Chambers. And she had indicated he was capable of worse. Since that night in the Rotunda Bar at the Astor, he'd known Chambers to be a man of considerable resources. If indeed he beat his wife and threatened his mother-in-law, those vices were probably not the extent of his propensity for evil. While haste was indeed required, Nick did not go directly to Forty-eighth Street and Fifth Avenue.

He had driven himself into town today, and he clucked the horses into motion, turning them east to the river and the nearest of the many docks belonging to Devrey Shipping. The supervisor knew who he was. When Nick asked for the loan of four of the biggest and burliest of the porters, he wasn't required to say why he wanted them.

"I don't know if we shall run into trouble," he told his makeshift army when his now crowded carriage was once more headed north, "but if we do, I'm sure I can count on you."

The men promised that he could and being Irish, seemed undisturbed by the prospect of a fight. Members of the Dead Rabbits gang, he supposed, or possibly the Plug Uglies. Had they not been immigrants, they would probably have been members of one of the nativist America for-Americans gangs that opposed them, the Bowery Boys or the like. It seemed as if every laborer in the city belonged to one or another. As recently as last Fourth of July the old Twenty-seventh—known as the Seventh Regiment now that the militia had been reorganized—were required to come in and keep the peace. And, Nick recalled, even for trained soldiers it was a close run thing. There was nothing inexpert or artless about the nature of the violence practiced by New York's street warriors. At the moment Nick thought that just as well.

Mei Lin's neighborhood was not quite as rural as it had been. Archbishop Hughes was talking about erecting a new St. Patrick's Cathedral a few blocks uptown on Fifty-first Street, and lately the mansions that had begun to be erected on Fifth Avenue's southern end were edging north. But there were still more trees than people on the side streets, and little traffic anywhere nearby. Almost five in the afternoon now, the late autumn daylight all but gone.

Nick thought there might be a flicker of light behind the curtains of the house where six years previously he'd taken tea with an innocent sixteen-year-old Mei Lin and she'd assured him she was completely content with her betrothal to Kurt Chambers. The house next door, presumably the one she now shared with her husband, was entirely dark.

He stood for a moment, looking around, unsure of what to do next. The porter called Liam, biggest of the lot, with a nose that had obviously been broken more than once and a couple of missing teeth, took charge. "Seems it might be a fair and fine notion for one of us to go round the back, guv'nor and keep an eye out. One more to remain out front here. Two maybe. I take it you're not thinking those next door neighbors will be friendly sorts of folk."

"Not in the least friendly. Possibly very dangerous."

"Sure we're well used to that, guv. Hit first, talk later, and stick together if you mean to stay alive. Just one question, if you don't mind. What is it we're after?"

"Not what, who. We're going to rescue a woman. Chinese, and she can't walk very well. We'll have to carry her."

"You, sir, and the four of us?" Liam asked. "For one little woman?"

"Yes. But she may be guarded."

The Irishman smiled. "That's better then. Makes it more interesting." He pointed to one of the others. "You go around the back. You two stay out here in the front. I'll go with Dr. Turner inside." Then, to Nick, "Anything t'ain't the way you think it should be, guv, just give me some sort o' signal and I'll set up an almighty roar. The rest will be after coming in smart as you like when they hear it."

Nick knew they were as likely to terrify Mei-hua as rescue her. He insisted they make a polite first approach. He knocked, but there was no reply. A bell hung beside the door, but when he reached for it, Liam restrained his hand. "T'ain't the best notion to set up a ruckus, guv. If there's no one after comin' to the door, better we get in quiet like." The Irishman meanwhile had done something to the nearest window, it was wide open before he finished speaking. "I'll go first, shall I?" He didn't wait for an answer but put one leg over the sill and disappeared. Nick went in after him.

There were no lights, but the curtains had not been drawn and the faint gray of dusk still illuminated what Nick recognized as Mei-hua's parlor.

"Holy Mary and all the saints," Liam murmured. "What's this then? One of them opium dens?"

The dock workers of course knew all about the opium dens said to be found in China Village. A good deal more than he did, Nick supposed. "No, nothing like that. Do you see anyone?"

Liam shook his head. "Not a soul. Wait here, I'll explore a bit."

"No, I'm coming with you."

"Fair enough, but if there's any trouble, leave it to me." The Irishman raised his fist, and brass knuckles gleamed in the last rays of daylight. Nick was not surprised. There was said to be a woman called Hell-Cat Maggie who fought with one of the Irish gangs. She'd had her teeth filed to points the better to tear apart their enemies.

On their first pass through the downstairs rooms they found nothing. "I'll be having a look upstairs," Liam said. This time Nick allowed him to go on his own. He could not imagine that Mei-hua would climb those stairs if she could avoid it.

The light Nick had first spied from outside appeared to come from a small room at the other side of the hall where there was a red-draped altar with candles alight and smoking sticks of incense. He went back in there, looked around, and was just leaving again when he heard something. Not a sneeze exactly, but the muffled beginnings of one. Nick leaned down and lifted a corner of the floor-length red altar cloth. Mei-hua was huddled as far back as possible, crouching against the wall and hugging to her a bulging canvas satchel that looked as if it had seen better days.

"Every too bad man leave," Mei-hua told her daughter when she sat beside Mei Lin's bed, holding her hand and reporting the events of earlier in the day. "Every one go. Even Both Way Eyes." Mei-hua had always known that the man her son-in-law claimed was there for first *tai-tai*'s protection was there to spy on her. She had spent many fruitless and frustrating hours trying to think of something that might help her daughter in spite of that. Now, in some way that she could only attribute to the intercession of all those gods whose blessings she had implored for so many years, a miracle seemed to have happened. They were no longer in the houses of the Lord Kurt but here in this place that belonged to very ugly this-place ladies in very ugly black clothes, who, despite their appearance, were obviously prepared to befriend them. At least for the present.

"All go," Mei-hua said again. "Leave me alone. I know they follow you, so I light joss sticks, ask all gods protect you this time, even though they do terrible bad job of it so far." She reached out and touched the bandages on her daughter's arm. They felt hard to the touch and she pulled her hand back in surprise. "Rock bandages? Like rock streets? Why they do this?"

"New thing for broken bones," Mei Lin explained just as Mother Manon had explained to her. "If arm not move, bones heal together faster. Bandages are stiffened with plaster, not rocks."

Mei-hua nodded. "Very ugly black clothes, but smart inside their heads. I am grateful that they do the best thing for my little bud. Tell them I am glad they help her when her Mamee can not." Two large tears formed in Mei-hua's lovely eyes and ran down her cheeks. "Nothing I can do, *mei-mei*. Not before. Not now. Only ask really hard. Burn every joss stick in whole house. Promise everything. Then I hear carriage come. Look out window, see *yang gwei zih*. Take your *baba*'s death gift for you," she pointed to the canvas satchel now sitting beside Mei Lin's bed. "Hide. Didn't see red-hair *yi* until he see me."

Mei Lin waited until her mother regained her composure, then spoke to Manon. "Mr. Chambers and his men left her and came after me. I'd run out and taken the small trap. It was the first time I ever—" She broke off without saying that this time she had not simply borne the beating in silence, but made plans. "I had hitched the trap earlier, so I was able to get away quickly. I intended to go and get some of the other men, the Chinese men who are still our friends, and go back for my mother, but when I realized how badly I was hurt, I couldn't think of anything to do but come here."

"And here you will stay, both of you," Manon said, "at least until you are well. Then we shall see."

"My hus—" Mei Lin broke off. It disgusted her to refer to such a cruel and deceitful man as her husband. "Mr. Chambers won't give up, Reverend Mother. He is very powerful and there are any number of men who do what he says. Not just Chinese men. The police are always on his side."

"Then we must move you," Nick said at once. These days the coppers were divided into two forces, separated by a bitter rivalry reflecting the political and social strata above and below them. The Municipals were loyal to the city's mayor, as usual a Tammany Hall Democrat, while a newer force called Metropolitans were creatures of the recently created, reform-minded Republican party, which had gained control of the state. The two sets of police fought each other as frequently as they fought the criminal gangs. Indeed, the gangs sometimes joined the battle on behalf of one or the other of the forces. Nick was alarmed at the thought of St. Vincent's as a pawn between them. "We must not endanger the Sisters and the hospital, much less the patients."

"Do not trouble yourself, Cousin Nicholas." Manon went to the window and pulled aside the curtain. "We have warriors as well. Come and see."

Nick looked out into the gaslit street. St. Vincent's Catholic Hospital was ringed by men. All wore trousers with the identifying red stripe of the Dead Rabbits. The Irish were protecting their own.

Chapter Thirty-five

"How LONG HAVE you known?" Carolina demanded of her son.

"Years I suppose. I don't really recall. But it's become incredibly more dangerous, Maman."

Her other children called her "Mama." For Zachary she had become "Maman," and he pronounced it in the French manner, with the accent on the second syllable. Princeton's airs and graces had rubbed off on her firstborn. Zac was also wonderfully handsome, with Samuel's height and dark coloring, but there was nothing of unseemly vanity about him. Indeed, Zac had a certain sweetness in his nature that delighted her. There was nothing of Samuel in that, nor of her, if the truth were told.

Carolina had quite looked forward to this shared supper by the library fire, just the two of them, supposedly to talk business. Really an opportunity to be alone with her darling boy. Then, before they'd finished the soup, Zachary had admitted that he knew about her abolitionist activities. "Helping runaway slaves was always risky," she said. "If you've known for so long, why are you finding objections now?"

"Because the Supreme Court has ruled that—"

"That does not convince me, Zachary. I will not believe that a Negro, simply by being such, cannot demand a hearing in a United States court or that slaves in a free state are still slaves. I will not. Never. Never. Never."

"But the court has handed down its decision. Dred Scott was returned to his owner."

"May Almighty God help him. And if he comes my way looking for assistance, you may be sure Mr. Scott will get it."

"Maman, the Negroes are not like us. They must be looked after."

"Zachary, where are you getting these ideas?"

"It doesn't matter where. What matters is that you are putting yourself—and, I might say, Devrey's—at great risk. The South will test the decision, you know. They are already traveling with their slaves into free states. Maybe even New York."

"Princeton was a bad influence," she sighed. "All those young southern gentlemen with their charming manners and honeyed accents . . ." All at once the true reason for this conversation dawned on her. "Mr. Royal Lee," she said. "Your school friend from Virginia who is to visit next month. He wants to bring a slave with him, is that it?"

"He hasn't said, but I wouldn't be surprised. And he isn't really coming to see me. I'm just the excuse. It's Ceci who is the attraction."

"I know," Carolina said. "And so does she. I believe she returns Mr. Lee's affection, Zac."

"They've only met twice, Maman. But he's a fine man, I promise you. Ceci could do a lot worse."

"He's a slaveholder. How can Ceci—"

"Ceci doesn't think about things the way you do, Maman. She likes pretty frocks and music and—"

" . . . is an empty-headed beauty. I know that as well. I blame myself. I should have insisted she be formally schooled."

"It wouldn't have made a difference probably. People are as they are, Maman. And Royal is enchanted with her. He has asked me to ask, and I promised I would. Will you stand in their way?"

Carolina twirled the stem of her wine glass for long seconds before she answered. "Not if it's really what Ceci wants," she said finally. "And he must ask Nicholas as well as me. You tell him that."

"Ah, I hear my name. What are you two saying about me?" Nick leaned over to kiss her cheek and Carolina felt the December cold. "You are chilled, darling. Sit here by the fire and take some wine. I wasn't expecting you until later. Have you eaten?"

"Yes. I dined with the Kleins. Bella sets a glorious table, though I must say that pie looks delicious."

Nick leaned forward to help himself to a taste of the venison pie in the middle of the table. Carolina glanced over the top of his bent head and found her son staring at her. There was something in his eyes . . . Dear God, Bella Klein. Zachary knew about Bella's involvement with the underground railroad as well as her own. She must speak more to him and more frankly. But not now. "We were talking about Ceci," she said, pleased to hear how normal her voice sounded. "She is being wooed, and Zac thinks there is to be a formal request for her hand."

"Really? I'd no idea. Who is her suitor and why haven't I met him?"

"You have, sir." Zachary poured wine for his stepfather. "My friend from Princeton. Royal Lee."

"The Virginian," Nick said. "And has he only just now decided that he's enamored of our Ceci?"

"I believe they have been corresponding," Carolina said.

"And you knew?" There was a trace of disapproval in his tone. "Why did you not tell me?"

"I didn't believe it was serious, Nick. Do you have an objection?" She was half hoping he did, hoping it would be Nick who would send Royal Lee packing and all Ceci's wrath and disappointment would be directed at her stepfather, not her mother. You are a coward, Carolina Randolf Devrey Turner, she told herself. "Of course, if you are opposed, I'm sure Ceci—"

"Ceci is as headstrong as her mother. It will take more than my disapproval to put her off whatever she's decided she wants. And as I recall, Mr. Lee is a perfect gentleman and a man of sufficient means to look after a wife. But he is a Virginian and, unless I misunderstood, the owner of a plantation. His livelihood will keep him in the South."

"We were discussing slaveholding," Zac said, "before you arrived."

Carolina shot him a warning look, but Nick didn't rise to Zac's bait, if bait it was. "I'm not going to argue the slave versus free question in my own library with my own family. There's enough of that outside these walls, God knows. But that is, in fact, precisely my point." He got up, taking his glass of wine and moving closer to the fire. "If Ceci is far away in Virginia, how can we, her family who truly care for her, be sure she is properly looked after, properly treated? Particularly if there's a war, as I fear there well may be."

"Royal's a gentleman, sir. I've known him for some years now and I can promise he's always conducted himself entirely honorably."

"Yes, well, the way a man behaves with other men may not be an indication of how he behaves with women."

Carolina had seen that expression on her husband's face only a few times before. "Nick, what is it? You have something on your mind. Do you want to tell me? Zac, would you excuse us?"

"No, I'd like Zachary to stay. I do have something to say. I'm going to ask a favor of Devrey's, so it concerns him as well as you, my dear. Though in another sense, you most of all." He turned to his stepson. "And I must speak of your natural father, Zac, though it's not a subject that gives any of us pleasure."

Zac's expression darkened. "Has he then reached out from the grave to torment my mother further?"

"Not exactly," Nick said. He turned to Carolina. "This is about Mei-hua, my dearest. And her daughter." Then, to Zac, "Do you know who they are?"

"I do," Zac said. "Most of the story, if not all the details."

Carolina was startled but realized she shouldn't be. Zac was twenty-four, a man, and a man of business at that. He traveled in circles that had always been closed to her and always would be. That he should have heard all or most of the family secrets was hardly a surprise, if for no other reason than that Gordon James was still their attorney. "What about them, Nick?" she asked.

"I need to bring them here."

"Here, to Sunshine Hill?"

"Yes. They are in great peril, my dear. Mei Lin especially, but Mei-hua as well. This is the only place they will be safe, and that only for a short time. I am hoping that a Devrey ship can pick them up and take them down the coast to Pennsylvania. We've arranged safe haven for them there with a community of Manon's Sisters, somewhere near a town called Gettysburg. It seems far enough."

"I don't understand. In peril from whom or what?"

"The woman you're calling Mei Lin is more commonly known as Linda Chambers, isn't she?" Zac asked. And when Nick nodded, "Then my guess is that Kurt Chambers, her husband, is the likely villain of the piece. Am I right, sir?"

"You are."

"But I thought he was a successful man of business," Carolina said. "A great philanthropist." Clearly, her husband and son knew far more about the man than she did.

"That's what he'd like people to think, Maman, but the truth is that Kurt Chambers is behind a good deal of the most criminal activities in the city, and nearly everyone knows it."

"But if that's so, why has he not been arrested?"

"He is far too great a source of profit for the authorities to arrest him," Zac said. "Chambers pays bribes to both sets of police and virtually every politician."

"And how does this affect his wife and his mother-in-law? I can't see why, if they are living with a criminal, any good can come from bringing them here." Carolina was being difficult and she knew it, but to bring Mei-hua and her bastard daughter here, to the sanctuary she and Nick had made for themselves and the children after so many years of suffering . . . It was too much to ask.

"Chambers"—Nick didn't look at her when he spoke—"physically abuses his wife." He heard Carolina's gasp and wondered not for the first time how much she had kept from him about what she had endured at Sam Devrey's hands. "Mei Lin is presently a patient at St. Vincent's Hospital, recovering from a vicious beating, the latest of many, I might add. Mei-hua is with her because Mei Lin believes her husband will take out his anger on her mother. Manon has allowed them to stay, and one of the Irish gangs has been on constant patrol at the hospital ever since. But the Mother General and the archbishop are coming in a few days to pay a ceremonial pre-Christmas visit. Manon will be placed in a most embarrassing position if Dead Rabbits with brass knuckles are encircling the hospital, and the wife of a prominent contributor is being kept there, despite his many requests that she be released to him."

"The Dead Rabbits! And you have been involved in all this, Nick? And I never knew?"

He could not suppress a smile. "It seems for once that I'm the one keeping secrets."

For a moment she thought he knew about the escaped slaves, perhaps even about her long association with Bella Klein and Reverend Beecher, but he was saying something about the clippers, and she did not make the serious error of thinking she had been discovered when she had not.

"If Mei Lin were well enough to travel immediately," Nick was saying, "we'd need only to smuggle them onto one of your ships, but she's not. There was a fracture of one of her ankles that went undetected for some time. I had to break it again and reset it." He saw Carolina wince. "Not as bad as it sounds, thanks to anesthesia, but she can't put any weight on it yet. She needs another few weeks to recover before attempting a journey. There's no place she'd be safer than here. And the Dead Rabbits assure me they will look after us."

Carolina had been pacing; now she sat down again. "The Dead Rabbits at Sunshine Hill. And Mei-hua and her daughter. I'm sorry, I—"

"Maman," Zac spoke very quietly, "she is my half-sister. Just as Goldie is."

Carolina knew she was beaten. "Very well, bring them. Hopefully Zac can quickly arrange the trip down to Pennsylvania."

"Of course I shall. As soon as you tell me they're able to travel, sir. Two of the new steamships will be in service on the coastal runs as from next week."

Carolina had long since agreed with Zac that Devrey's must be prepared for a new age of steam, that not even the glorious clippers would hold it at bay forever. Now there were newer and perhaps more bitter pills to be swallowed. "You must tell your friend Mr. Lee that he will be welcome here as well." Nick started to say something, but she held up her hand. "Ceci cares for him, darling. We will arrange things so that she can always let us know if she has any need, but we cannot wrap her in cotton wool and keep her safe forever. She's twenty-one, and I had begun to wonder if she would be an old maid." Then, to Zac, "Please ask Mr. Lee to understand my sensibilities and bring no slaves into my house. And pray God the two visits will not overlap. Heaven knows what Mr. Royal Lee of Virginia will think if he is to be betrothed to a young lady whose house is surrounded by hardened toughs who call themselves dead rabbits."

"Where are you going, Ceci?"

"Into town, Mama."

"On a Sunday?"

"Yes." Her daughter was preoccupied with gazing into the mirror near the front door and adjusting the bow of her bonnet. "I thought I might attend church."

"What?" Of all the many things Carolina and her unconventional family were not, churchgoers probably topped the list.

"You need not sound so astonished, Mama. Mr. Lee is more religious-minded than I have been in the past. I thought it best to make a start in observance."

"Ceci, I do not for one moment believe this escapade to have anything to do with Mr. Lee. You are simply trying to distract me by substituting one annoyance for another. I know you've been spending a great deal of time in the Little House this past week." The Little House was what they called the cottage built for Aunt Lucy but never occupied; Mei Lin and her mother were now housed there.

"I do visit Mei Lin occasionally," Ceci admitted. "She and her mother are the most exotic of guests, you must admit. And the *tai-tai* is so beautiful and elegant." Then, seeing her mother's expression, "*Tai-tai* is what Mei-hua is properly called. In the Chinese fashion. And after all, Mei Lin is my half-sister. Just like Goldie."

"Clearly you and Zachary have been talking. But I fail to see what any of that has to do with this sudden desire to go into town on a Sunday, much less an onset of religious fervor."

"It's not about religion, Mama. I admit I was fibbing." Ceci turned to her mother and dropped the pretense of nonchalance. "Mei Lin is so brave. Uncle Nick says she drove a carriage downtown by herself in spite of dreadful injuries, and that she ran on a fractured ankle when it must have caused her excruciating pain. I want to be brave as well."

"By doing what?"

"Delivering a note. To a man I shall meet in church. He doesn't know where Mei Lin is, so she's written to tell him."

Carolina paled. "Ceci, that's not brave, it is foolhardy. Surely since you have intruded this far into the business of our guests, you know that Linda's . . . that Mei Lin's husband is involved in criminal activities. If in addition she has a lover—"

"Mama! He's not her lover, and it is wicked to say so. They are friends and have been so since before Mei Lin married. Sometimes they meet to talk. Nothing more. I do not believe for one moment that Mei Lin would be involved in anything sordid or dishonorable or that—"

She broke off. The two women stared at each other.

"Sordid and dishonorable," Carolina said softly. "That is your view of a woman taking a lover. Whatever the circumstances?"

"I'm not talking about you and Uncle Nick, Mama. I never thought that. I still don't. But Mei Lin—"

"People do all sorts of things, Ceci, for all sorts of reasons. And I think it is time there was a great deal more honesty in this house, at least about some of them. Now please give me Mei Lin's note."

"I can't, Mama. I promised to take it to Mr. Heinz. That is—"

"I am astounded that Mei Lin would charge you with such a dangerous errand. I must say I think a good deal less of her now."

Ceci flushed bright red. "I can't permit you to think ill of her, Mama. That's not what Mei Lin asked me to do."

"I'm afraid I don't understand."

"Mei Lin said I was to give the note to one of the Irishmen. I was to explain about how to find Mr. Heinz, and ask one of the Dead Rabbits to perform the errand."

"But you thought it would be exciting to do it yourself."

Ceci, still red with shame, nodded.

"My dear child, it is past time for you to be married. Being a wife will surely screw your head on more firmly. Now give me that note."

Ceci took a folded paper from inside her fur muff. It was not sealed, but Carolina made no attempt to read it. "Thank you. Now tell me, please, how whoever delivers this is to recognize the gentleman for whom it's intended."

"Mei Lin says he's not too tall, and that he has fair hair and blue eyes and a round face. And after the Mass he will be waiting for her in a pew in the rear. That's how they saw each other again a year ago. After years and years. Isn't it romantic? Mr. Heinz happened to be at Mass in a church called St. John the Baptist when Mei Lin was there."

"I am delighted Mr. Heinz is to be found in a Catholic church, my dear. It will make it easier for one of these Irish … these Irish gentlemen to do this errand." Carolina headed to the door and the posted guard of Dead Rabbits.

"She was going to drive into town and deliver a note for Linda—for Mei Lin. To a man I presume to be her lover, whether in actuality or only in their dreams. I do not think, Nick, that Ceci had the least notion of how extremely dangerous it would be. Or how vulnerable she would be once she left this property."

Nick ran a hand through his hair. "You're absolutely right. We must put an end to this situation at once. I wanted another week's rest for my patient, but that's a counsel of perfection. Can you get word to Zac to send a ship upriver tonight?"

"I could, but that's not the wisest course, dearest. We believe Mr. Chambers knows his wife and mother-in-law to be here. Why else would we need protection from a gang of Irish toughs? Once they're gone and Linda and her mother are gone, what is to prevent Mr. Chambers from taking out his anger on you or me or the children?"

"Dear God, you're right, Carolina, I didn't think it through. I'm an idiot and I've put you all in the most appalling danger."

"You are not an idiot, my love. Practical things such as this are not, as they say, your line of country. But they are mine, Nick. And I have an idea."

"Tell me."

"I shall, but you will not find it pleasant to hear. So sit down and promise not to say anything until I've finished."

Nick did as she asked. Carolina sat beside him and took both her hands in his. "Some years ago," she began, "in December of 1851, a few months before we were married, Bella Klein came to see me."

Nick was silent for some time when she finished speaking. It was, Carolina knew, the worst possible reaction. "I never meant to deceive you, darling, I just—"

"I'm sorry, Carolina. That's not true." He had long since withdrawn his hands from hers. Now he got up and began pacing. "You did indeed mean to deceive me. To hear you tell it, you went to great pains to do so."

She caught her breath. He was using a tone of voice she'd never before heard, certainly not directed at her. "Nick, I did what I thought was right. I didn't think—"

"Precisely. You did not think. You are my wife. And you were that when Bella came and the pair of you cooked up this scheme. That we'd not yet had benefit of clergy doesn't come into it, and I know you agree."

"Of course I do."

"You are also the mother of my children and of two others whom I care for just as deeply as if they were my own. Moreover, you are far too intelligent not to have known exactly what you were doing and everything you were putting at risk, for them as well as for you and me. Yet you chose to engage in this behavior behind my back."

"Slavery is an enormous evil, Nick. I know you believe that as much as I do."

"Precisely! Why then did you not think it necessary, indeed desirable, to discuss this matter with me before you plunged headlong into it?"

"I don't know," she said quietly. "At the time it simply seemed best. You are not a practical person, my darling. You have always said so yourself. You're a scientist, a man of ideas. And this is the most practical and down to earth work imaginable."

She wanted to say more. To speak of the amount of coordination of schedules and ruses and journeys involved. To describe the clambering and climbing, the swinging of signal lanterns from her turret above the house or from the shore at the bottom of the cliff. What she wanted most to explain was that having once set out on a course of keeping this business from him, she could not find the courage to tell him later.

"I will tell you the real reason for your subterfuge," he said. "It is all to do with your insistence on the rights of women. I have never seriously opposed you, Carolina. I may not agree entirely with your ideas, but neither do I entirely dismiss them. But to go behind my back in a matter so serious, that can only be because you placed your loyalty to these ideas of women's independence above your loyalty to me."

"China dolls," she whispered.

"What?"

"That's what Bella said the first day she came here. 'We are not china dolls with painted smiles.'"

"I take it then that Bella shares your opinions. I wouldn't have thought so, but apparently I can be deeply mistaken about my own wife, why not Ben's?" Then, the idea having only at that moment occurred to him, "He doesn't know either, I suppose."

She was too miserable to find any way to soften the blow. "Yes, he does. Dr. Klein has been involved from the beginning."

"My God. I've really been Billy's jackass, haven't I? The last to know and the least likely to have an opinion worth considering." He had been standing beside the fire, now he started for the door.

"Nick! Please. You mustn't leave like this. We've never left a quarrel to fester."

"This is not an ordinary quarrel, Carolina. I really don't want to speak further to you just now."

"But you must," she said, some anger of her own rising to stiffen her backbone. "I only told you all this because we have to get the two women you brought here out of the house. And do so in a manner that will not leave our family in a still more dangerous position. I don't imagine you think we can have Irish ruffians with brass knuckles and broken bottles guarding us for the rest of our lives."

Nick stopped at the door to the room. "No, I don't think that."

"Nor do I. What we need to do is send the women off to Pennsylvania and at the same time pull the claws of Kurt Chambers."

He did not for a moment doubt that she was correct. He simply had no notion of how such a thing could be done. "You have a plan, I suppose?"

"Yes, I do. I've been thinking about it for some time, but I need to discuss it with you. So will you come back and sit down and talk to me?"

Nick turned around and sat by the fire with his wife.

Carolina was forty-four years old, past her age of charm she often said, but she had never looked more stunning. She wore a plum-colored velvet frock, the skirt held wide with a hoop, so her waist looked particularly slender. Her matching short tightly-fitted jacket was trimmed with black fox fur, and she carried a black fox muff. Her hat—wide-brimmed to balance the silhouette of her skirt—was the same rich purple color, and the long black ostrich feathers that dipped low on one side framed her still lovely face.

Black ostrich feathers adorned as well the heads of the four black horses that pulled her brougham. The bells on their harnesses jingled softly as they trotted up to the Devrey docks on South Street facing the inner harbor. The waterfront, deserted at this hour, was bathed in icy December moonlight. Carolina's driver, dressed in black livery with plum-colored trim, reined in, then jumped down from his high front perch to help her get out. "Sure and it's all looking fine," he said softly, leaning into the carriage's interior as he opened the door. "Don't be after fretting none."

He gave Carolina his hand as she stepped out, and she caught a glimpse of shiny metal across his knuckles. "Thank you. Wait for me here, please." She pitched her voice at the outline of a man waiting a short distance away in the shadows. "We shan't be long, shall we, Mr. Chambers?"

"No, Mrs. Turner. Not long." Chambers strode forward, touching the brim of his topper.

Carolina waited where she was. Chambers came close enough to peer inside the carriage, which she knew was what he wanted to do. "I am alone except for my driver, Mr. Chambers. Exactly as promised."

"I never doubted your word," he said. "And as you can see, I too am alone." He gestured at the expanse of empty wharves on either side. Behind them, riding at anchor at the dock, was a small steamship, the six A.M. Devrey packet for Providence and Boston, according to the notice board. Deserted at this hour.

"Shall we go inside?" Carolina said. "It's bitter out here." The area was shoveled clean each morning, but there had been snow squalls during the day, and the path between the waterfront and the Devrey warehouse was crusted with frozen snow. Carolina took his arm.

"I'd have thought your offices on Canal Street to be a better venue," he said. "Or perhaps even your home."

"But this is so much more private, Mr. Chambers. That seems best under the circumstances. My husband . . ."

"Ah, yes. Dr. Turner no longer approves of me, you said."

"I do think it best if people stay entirely out of the business of other people's marriages, Mr. Chambers. But as I said, my husband—"

There was a noise behind them, and Chambers stopped walking. He turned around so quickly that Carolina was almost jerked off her feet. She cocked her head so that the wide brim of her hat and its ostrich feathers impeded his vision.

There was nothing to see but the driver of her four-in-hand, still standing beside the brougham. One of the horses pawed the ground, its breath making a visible trail in the cold air.

It was only a few more feet to the door of the warehouse, and they covered it quickly. Carolina could feel the chill of the snowy path through the soles of her leather boots. Her hand did not tremble when she took the key from her muff and unlocked the door. "No gaslights in the warehouses I'm afraid, Mr. Chambers, but there's bound to be a lantern at the ready just here beside the door." She reached up and located one. "Can you light it do you think?"

"Of course. Chambers pulled a small box of matches from his pocket.

There was a window in the warehouse door. Carolina positioned herself to the side of it while Chambers went about the business of lighting the lantern.

Outside, Liam still stood at attention, waiting on his mistress as a good chauffeur should. Another of the horses neighed, a soft, slightly impatient sound. Picked up every bit of tension in the air, horses did. Liam McCarthy learned that driving a cab in Galway City. Would have done the same over here if he'd been allowed, but the Italians had the carriage trade sewn up so tight an Irishman couldn't get a look in, not even with brass knuckles. The waterfront, that's where the Irish ruled. "Steady lads," he murmured. "Won't be long now." Even if he had been overheard, it would simply have sounded as if he was calming the horses.

There was a bright burst of light from inside the warehouse.

"That's your moment of choice, Liam," Mr. Zachary had said. "Once the lantern's been lit, give the signal. If he's in the light looking into the dark, he'll see nothing." Couldn't have known about his mother's hat when he said that; better than a curtain on the window now that she'd stepped in front of it. Real smart lady, Mr. Zachary's mum. Hard as nails as well. In her own way, as much of a fighter as Hell-Cat Maggie, whether or not her teeth were sharpened to points.

Liam reached behind him and tapped his metal-covered knuckles on the metal rim of the carriage wheel.

Three men dropped to the ground from below the body of the brougham and rolled into the shadows of the night.

Inside, Carolina and Chambers stood beside the door of the cavernous warehouse. Chambers lifted the lantern and swung it round. There was nothing to be seen but tall stacks of the many boxes and cartons to be laded in the morning, and piles of the ropes and hooks and barrows and the like it took to do the job. Chambers hung the lantern back on its hook. The pair of them were surrounded by a halo of yellow light. Everywhere else was as black as the inside of a sooty chimney.

"It's hardly much warmer in here than outside," Carolina said. *Liam's men will fan out as soon as the lantern's lit, Maman. They'll deal with the henchmen Chambers is bound to have stationed around the dock. Try and give them a few minutes before you move to the next stage.* "Perhaps," she added, "you were right and we should have gone to the Canal Street office after all."

"Yes, but we're here now."

"Of course, you're entirely correct. But this won't take long, I'm sure. Do you have the money, Mr. Chambers?"

"I do. Thirty-seven thousand dollars in bearer bonds, just as you requested. Though I cannot see—"

"My husband, Mr. Chambers. Surely you know just as everyone else does that Dr. Nicholas Turner is a man of the highest moral principles. Given the disagreement between the pair of you over the matter of Mrs. Chambers, though I did mean what I said about not interfering in other people's marriages, and if it were left to me . . ."

"The deeds to the two houses on Cherry Street, Mrs. Turner. You have my payment." He nodded at the papers she now held in her hand.

"Oh yes, of course." Carolina tucked the bonds into her muff, then reached into her pocket for the thick wad of tightly bound documents held together with the lavender-colored sealing wax she had used since she was a girl. She held them out and Chambers took them.

"You won't mind my checking these." He used his thumbnail to shatter the wax. "As I've paid considerably over the odds, given how depressed the market is just now."

Carolina put her gloved hand to her mouth and coughed as long and as loudly as she could.

Chambers looked up. "Here, you're choking. Let me—"

Light burst upon them from every side. "Ain't nothing you have to do, Mr. Chambers, except hand over them papers and them two nigras over there as well. Going straight back to their owners they are." Fearless Flannagan put out his hand. The two coppers beside him lifted their lanterns higher, revealing two black women huddled together by the door.

"Hand over—Are you insane? Don't you men know where those extra hundreds in your pay packets come from?"

"Never seen a penny extra," Flannagan said. "God's truth. Not me and not them neither. You boyos got that? Not a single penny above our wages, what we're paid fair and square."

He was speaking to Chambers and the two other coppers, but the words were meant for the four reporters who had appeared out of the shadows, each holding a notebook and a pencil. Flannagan didn't take his eyes off Chambers and Carolina, but jerked his head toward the men of the press. "Represent the *Sun,* the *Herald,* and the *Merchant's Journal,* they do. And the *Daily Times.*"

"Just the *Times* now," the reporter from that paper corrected him.

"Call yourself what you like," Flannagan said, and turned to Chambers. "They don't always see sense at the *Times,* but a flagrant pro-abolitionist act like this? It's a matter of private property rights, ain't it? I'm quite sure whoever owns these here slaves will be thankful to you, ma'am," he told Carolina. "Seeing as how you alerted us to what was happening and helped the owners get their property back."

"This is complete rubbish," Chambers said. "I came here to buy a pair of houses on Cherry Street that happen to be contiguous to other property I own in China Village. I have no idea about any of the rest of it. I can assure you that if there has been any breaking of the law, it's by Mrs. Turner here, not me."

"My wife need not stand here and take your abuse after she's been so brave," Nick said, appearing out of the shadows to put a protective arm around Carolina.

"Don't worry none, Dr. Turner." Flannagan was peering at the documents he'd taken from Chambers. "These here ain't any deeds to any houses in China Village or anywhere else. A list of sailings from Boston to Halifax up in Nova Scotia they are, and the names of people the nigras were to contact once they got there. Put the cuffs on 'im, lads. Mr. Chambers is goin' off to see the magistrate in the court o' criminal justice." Then, turning to the two black women, neither of whom had so far said a word, "All right, who do you belong to then? Are you planning to tell or do we have to convince you it's a good idea?" Flannagan waved his billy in the direction of the reporters. "You be sure and tell everyone the coppers in New York does their job. Fearless Flannagan best of all."

"Ain't no need to be beatin' on us," Sofie said. "Me and her, we be coming peaceful like."

It was the part of the scheme that had most worried Nick. "Even if Ben goes right away to claim them and straighten things out, Sofie and Liza will be in the hands of the police for a time. Who knows what might happen?"

"No one," Carolina had admitted. "But they understand the risks and have taken far greater ones over the years, believe me. We whites are only occasional helpers. The Negroes are the ones running the underground railway."

"But this isn't about helping runaway slaves. It's about—"

"Aiding two helpless women. And our family," Carolina said. "They want to help."

"Because you've done so much," Nick had said quietly.

She had not answered then and she said nothing now when Chambers and the two women were loaded into the police wagon and driven away.

The reporters jumped into a waiting hansom and followed quickly behind. The story of the arraignment of Mr. Kurt Chambers, gentleman of means, would be more titillating to their readers than any tale of slaves and the underground railway.

"It's why they'll have to actually send him to Sing Sing for the legal six months, if not longer," Carolina had said when she first explained her scheme to Nick. "Because there is so much talk of police corruption. With the press watching and the whole South saying that the federal law concerning runaway slaves is never actually enforced, the judge will have no choice." She did not mention that she would see to it Zac informed whichever judge it turned out to be that it was in his best interest to give Mr. Chambers as long a sentence as he thought he could get away with. Whatever Chambers might pay, the judge would be told, Devrey's would pay more.

Nick had simply nodded—acquiescence rather than agreement she'd thought—and they had spoken few words since. He did however give her his arm now as they hurried along the icy path toward their carriage.

As soon as the police wagon and the cab carrying the reporters were out of sight Liam had yanked open the brougham's door. He was inside now, pulling up the seat, and Nick rushed to join him.

They had drilled airholes before leaving Sunshine Hill, and Mei-hua and Mei Lin had not gotten into the hiding place until they approached the town. Still they had been crouching in the cramped space under the seat for at least an hour.

"Are you all right?" Nick demanded.

"We are fine," Mei Lin said.

Mei-hua, knowing none of the words, understood the meaning. She smiled and nodded. It was she who, as soon as Mei Lin explained the plan, had insisted they must not come later and more comfortably to the wharf. *Very stupid we take any chance someone from this dog turd lord's people see us get on ship. Find out where ship goes. We hide, make sure no one sees. When dog turd lord get out of dungeon place, he not know where to look for you. Very much better idea.*

"But he'll know where we are," Nick had said, when Carolina passed on Mei-hua's advice. "What's to prevent him from taking revenge on us?"

"According to both Mei Lin and her mother, there is quite a vigorous struggle for control of the activities of China Village. With Mr. Chambers out of the picture for half a year, maybe longer, other elements will have taken over. Either he will decide to go elsewhere or he will fight to regain what he's lost. In either case, he'll be too busy to worry about us. And Liam says he can arrange to have an eye kept on Sunshine Hill for a time whenever Mr. Chambers is released."

It was the best possible plan they could come up with, Carolina had said finally. It had to be good enough.

A light appeared on the deck of the packet tied up at the wharf, and a couple of tars hastily lowered the gangplank. Zachary hurried down it to join them. "Ready to sail," he said. "Mr. Heinz is aboard and waiting for you, Mei Lin."

"We owe you our lives," she said. "I can never adequately thank any of you, but you most of all Mrs. Dev—Excuse me, Mrs. Turner. You had the least reason to want to help me, and still you did. Thank you a thousand times."

Carolina wanted to say that she didn't deserve praise, that she had always done whatever she did for the girl and her mother grudgingly and with bitterness, but she did not. "Good luck," she said. "Oh! I almost forgot." She took the bonds from her muff and handed them to Mei Lin. "Thirty-seven thousand dollars will be paid to the bearer. Mr. Chambers owes you at least that much for pain and suffering, as I believe the lawyers call it. These bonds can be negotiated at any bank. They will see you all on your way to a decent future."

Meanwhile, Liam had dived back into the brougham's roomy interior. He emerged with a pair of valises, and a bulky canvas satchel Nick recognized as the one Mei-hua had insisted on bringing with her when he got her away from Forty-eighth Street.

The pair of crewmen who had lowered the gangplank took the bags and started for the ship. Nick touched his stepson's arm. "A moment, Zac," he said softly.

The two men stepped deeper into the shadows. "The copper, the one they call Fearless Flannagan . . ." Nick felt slightly ill as he spoke the words.

Maman's idea about the judge isn't good enough, sir. I've something more definitive in mind. I shan't tell her, but I thought I'd best tell you.

"He knows exactly what to do," Zac said quietly. "Forget about it, sir. As Maman would say, more my line of country than yours."

"Indeed, Zac, but . . ."

"Forget about it," Zac repeated and cut off any further discussion by moving back toward the women and bowing in Mei-hua's direction. "If I may, *tai-tai?*" He didn't wait for an answer to the question he knew she had not understood, merely picked her up and carried her up the gangplank.

One of the tars waited to perform the same service for Mei Lin—Dr. Turner said she must continue to put as little weight as possible on her repaired ankle—but she motioned him to wait, then turned toward New York. Only the faint glow of the gaslit streets indicated the presence of the densely packed buildings and crowded thoroughfares of the mighty city beyond the harbor, but the song of the city was never silent. She had been born here. Half her soul was of this place, just as half was of another distant place she would doubtless never see. Never mind, never mind, as Ah Chee would have said. There was a third place waiting, a new life. Never mind.

She turned to the waiting tar and nodded; he picked her up and carried her up the gangplank.

Nick stepped to Carolina's side and the pair of them watched until the others had gone below, and a couple of crewmen were pulling up the gangplank. "Are we to wait for Zac?" Nick asked.

"No, he's going with them as far as Philadelphia," Carolina said. "We're thinking of opening a Devrey's office there."

"Ah, I forgot. Philadelphia. Another business opportunity."

"It is that," she agreed. "But for Zac, not for me. I'm retiring from business."

"Of all sorts?"

She looked directly at him. "The sort of business one does for money. I can't promise about the rest."

"I know," Nick said softly. "I don't really expect you to. I was only angry because you didn't trust me enough to tell me."

"I won't make the same mistake again," she promised. "Please say you forgive me. You must, Nick. How can I survive without my true and only love?"

He laid a gloved hand along her cheek, then turned to Liam who while they spoke had busied himself adjusting the bridle of the lead horse. "Will you drive us up to Seventy-first Street, Liam? Mrs. Turner and I are quite ready to go home."

"Sure thing, guv."

Liam hurried to help them into the brougham, but Nick waved him away and handed Carolina up himself. Then he climbed in after her and pulled the door shut on the outside world.

Epilogue

July 4, 1863
The Temporary Field Hospital at Cemetery Ridge,
Gettysburg in Pennsylvania

"TELL THE YANG *gwei zih* to take me home," Mei-hua said.

The driver had been with her for half a dozen years, but he was not Chinese and so would always be a *yang gwei zih*, a foreign devil. "I will tell him, Mamee." Mei Lin leaned forward and kissed her mother's cheek, then opened the door and climbed down. She paused just long enough to tuck Mei-hua's book beneath the short cape of the black habit of Mother Elizabeth Seton's Sisters of Charity. In moments it was safe and hidden. Just like her.

Except that Nicholas Turner, the this-place-red-hair *yi* of her mother's long drama and her own, was watching, and he knew everything.

"Take her home, please," Mei Lin called up to the driver. He clucked softly to the horses and they moved away.

Dr. Turner was alone. Mei Lin went to join him. "I didn't want to trouble you when you were so busy," she said. "Particularly with a stranger present."

"Walt Whitman," Nick explained. "The Brooklyn poet. He comes frequently to visit the army hospitals. But you . . ." He gestured to the habit she wore. "My dear, I had no idea. I thought perhaps you and Mr. Heinz . . ."

Mei Lin laughed. "You thought correctly, Dr. Turner. Fritz and I have been married for four years." She didn't bother to explain that neither the Catholic Church nor the government of Pennsylvania gave any trouble about an earlier marriage conducted at midnight and effected simply by carrying the bride across the groom's threshold. "We have two sons. But Fritz is away at present with the Union Army Corps of Engineers. After this terrible battle, I wanted to do something to help. The Mother Superior of the convent Mother Manon asked to take us in when we first came said I could join them to help find the live bodies among the dead. She's a practical woman, like Mother Manon. She simply put me in a habit the same as the others. Fewer questions to answer that way."

"I see. I'm glad," Nick said, adding, "not that there's anything wrong with being a nun. I was surprised to see your mother here. She is well?"

"Reasonably so," Manon said. "She lives with us and is happy with her grandsons, but still much fixated on the past. These days she frequently does odd things, like following me here to give me something she could just as well have given me at home."

"The passing of years sometimes does that to people," Nick said. "And in your mother's case, given her experiences, it's not surprising."

"I suppose not. Tell me, please, your wife and children . . . there was never any trouble after—"

"Ah," he said, "apparently you never heard. Kurt Chambers was killed the same night you left New York. Seems he tried to escape from custody and one of the coppers shot him." His stomach no longer roiled when he thought about what Zac had arranged, not in the face of all the horror he'd witnessed since.

Mei Lin looked somber for a moment. Nick thought she might be saying a prayer for the repose of Chambers's soul. Then she smiled. "I have the fondest possible memories of you and your wife and Sunshine Hill. I hope everyone is well."

"As far as we can tell," Nick said. "Josh is in the army, we know not where most of the time. Blessedly Simon is yet too young to go. He and Goldie are at home with Carolina. And Ceci . . ." His face darkened.

"I know she married her Mr. Lee and went to live in Virginia," Mei Lin said. "She wrote me. We were planning a visit some day." She shook her head. "Perhaps after all this is over. What news of Zachary?"

"Very busy in Washington just now. Advising Mr. Lincoln on matters of wartime shipping and such." Nick did not add that he too was frequently consulted by the president. Indeed, if he had not been in the nearby capital when the magnitude of this battle began to be apparent, close enough to board one of the wagons bringing medicine and doctors, he would not have been in Gettysburg at all.

One of the nuns brushed by; the sight of her reminded Mei Lin of how much there was to do. "I really must go back to work."

"I as well," Nick said.

"Your achievements here in the field hospitals are already a legend, Dr. Turner."

He snorted. "I want no reputation garnered in this wretched war. My worst nightmare is that one day I will look down at the faces of the dead and dying I'm supposed to treat and see my son or my son-in-law. That I will be the one who has to tell my wife her boy is gone or my stepdaughter she's a widow. This wretched, wretched war."

"We are all, every moment, in the hands of God, Dr. Turner."

"So they tell me, Mei Lin. So they tell me."

Acknowledgments

THE RESOURCES FOR *City of God* were in many cases the same as those I used for the earlier three books about the Turner and Devrey families, *City of Dreams, Shadowbrook,* and *City of Glory.* They are many and varied, but Edwin G. Burrows and Mike Wallace's *Gotham: A History of New York City to 1898* (Oxford University Press, 1999) remains the lodestar of these stories, all except *Shadowbrook* being chiefly set in Manhattan.

For details of the evolution and brief reign of the sailing clippers I relied on *The Clipper Ships* by Addison Beecher Colvin Whipple (Time-Life Books, 1980) and *The History of American Sailing Ships* by Howard I. Chapelle (W. W. Norton, 1935). In the matter of the arrival of the Catholic sisterhoods in the United States in general and in New York City in particular, I was much aided by *Religious Orders of Women in the United States* by Elinor Tong Dehey (W. B. Conkey Co., 1913). I also consulted *History of the New York Times 1851–1921* by Elmer Davis (New York Times, 1921) for information about that paper and its competitors. Both the latter books are long out of print and not in my own library. Without Google's digitalization project it would have been, while not impossible, a matter of much time and trouble to obtain them. As it was, I simply clicked my mouse a few times, then pressed Print. I mention this here in the light of the intense controversy surrounding the larger issue of Google's efforts. At least in the matter of out-of-print and out-of-copyright books, it's hard to imagine something more beneficial to readers and writers.

Ditto Wikipedia, which was enormously useful, particularly for information about Chinese deities and dates. Onward the Internet! Life and books would be impoverished without it.

I am yet again grateful for the kindness of friends and colleagues without whom this book would be less than it is. Some deserve special mention: The super-talented Shymala Dason and her charming husband Joe McMahon reminded me of the wonderful Hopkins poem "Pied Beauty" just as I was trying to get my mind around how to frame the religious issues that so much inform this story. Tom Kirkwood's timely assistance saved me from having egg on my face with regard to the two words of German used herein. Janie Chang once again patiently answered my questions about transliterated Mandarin (but whatever I have mangled in my attempts to render the voices of the Chinese characters in this story is entirely my fault and in no way hers). And once more I have chosen to use Wade-Giles romanization because the Pinyin system had not been invented at the time of the story. Henry Morrison as usual proved himself first reader nonpareil and literary agent without peer. He was, I hope, amused to meet an earlier doppelgänger in these pages. Danny Baror, who sells my foreign and translation rights, continues to make it possible for my stories to reach beyond my nationality and my language—sometimes very far indeed—and I am grateful. Sydny Miner's rare ability to wield the editorial pencil with both sensitivity and intelligence once more earns my deepest appreciation. Thanks too to the many others at Simon & Schuster whose commitment to this series continues to stand it in such good stead, particularly Michelle Rorke, Michael Accordino, Loretta Denner, and Tina Peckham.

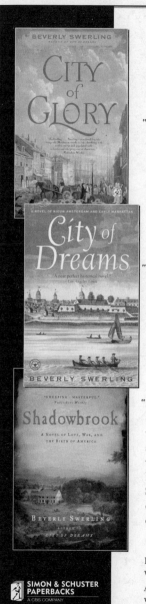

More riveting adventures in Beverly Swerling's acclaimed saga of old New York:

"Clearly, if Swerling had been my history teacher, I would have paid closer attention . . . These private and national escapades play out in a great swirl of plots and counter plots . . . riotously entertaining."

—Ron Charles,
The Washington Post

"A whopping saga . . . teeming with bizarre medicine, slave uprisings, executions, thriving brothels, and occasional cannibalistic Indians—brings forth shocks of recognition . . . A near perfect historical novel."

—*Los Angeles Times*

"Sweeping . . . masterful . . . Swerling tells of two men who straddle the white and the red man's worlds, desperate to preserve the best of each culture, but fearful they will lose everything they love . . . Readers . . . will be captivated by Swerling's intricate plot, colorful characters and convincing descriptions of colonial life."

—*Publishers Weekly*

Learn more about Beverly Swerling and her work at www.BeverlySwerling.com

Available wherever books are sold or at www.simonandschuster.com